THE WORLDWIDE WEBSTERS

MOOREA MYSTERY

THE WORLDWIDE WEBSTERS

MOOREA MYSTERY

M. Scott Hamilton

W3 INSIGHTS PUBLISHING

Cover design and illustrations by **Cecelia Vaye Morriss**

For more information, or to book an interview, contact :

WEB : *HTTP:/WWW.THEWORLDWIDEWEBSTERS.COM*

Paperback ISBN 979-8-9929508-4-7
Ebook ISBN 979-8-9929508-7-8

First Edition: March 2025
Printed in the United States of America

Dedicated to Marilyn "Cookie" Mercurio, who introduced us all to magical Moorea and was with us all the way.

With heartfelt thanks to Sharon for always, always encouraging me to "write your book!"
I finally listened.

Prologue

You're doing what???!!!

November 28, 2005, Monday
Pihaena, Moorea, Society Islands, French Polynesia

Just then, Meg felt a drop of rain plop on her head, and quickly another. In only seconds, it began pouring with a vengeance. The kids, standing in the middle of the beach, looked around for somewhere to hide from the torrents pounding the sand and rocks and their heads.

Screeching like a wild animal, Linc, wearing his swimsuit, ran straight into the water and started splashing around amongst the rocks and coral. Cal ran in to join him while the girls watched in a combination of amazement and irritation. It looked like a replay of their crazy dancing scene at the airport when they'd arrived!

Keely and Tiare pointed to some tall tropical shrubs on the edge of the marae walls and yelled in unison, "Come on, Cal and Linc, let's head to the trees over there, and get out of the rain!"

In response, first Cal ran back from the edge of the water, and then Linc - in a rush to follow him and the others to get under cover - sloshed unsteadily out of the low surf while the rain swirled and pounded the sea and sand around him. A bit disoriented by the downpour, he stumbled and put his foot down in a hole in the sand. Suddenly, they all heard a horrible 'screech!' and Linc came half-running, half-limping toward them, yelling "OWWW, my foot!" as they sheltered under some trees by the edge of the *marae*.

Careful to avoid entering the enclosure of the sacred clearing's ruins, they hid under one of the shorter bushes with some, but still minimal, leaves and branches offering cover. As they huddled in a small circle, trying to avoid the pouring rain, Keely noticed that not too far from them, a number of huge construction vehicles that sat idle, apparently ready to go to work.

"Let me look at your foot," Tiare said to her brother, and while he winced in pain, she pulled it up to see what had happened.

While Linc stumbled a bit to keep his balance, his sister turned his foot to the side, and then she saw the problem. "You stepped on a sea urchin - several spines of one, it looks like - based on all the 'pinholes' I see."

"Oh WOW!" said Cal, and Keely and Meg gasped. A small amount of blood oozed out of several tiny holes in Linc's foot. Tiare calmly wiped it away with a somewhat soggy napkin from inside their bag of *firi firi* doughnuts.

"Ow, it stings!" said Linc, fighting back tears.

"What should we do?" said Keely, now more than a little concerned.

Locking eyes with her brother, Tiare answered. "Well, Linc, you know what to do, just what our uncle told us, right?"

Linc looked at his sister, then down, then at the other kids, and said with much fright and embarrassment in his voice, "Really?"

She nodded and said "You can do it yourself, over there."

Keely, Meg and Cal watched in bewilderment as Linc limped and almost tripped over the marae's short outer walls, then hopped to a small tree near a large, nine-foot by four-foot or so tall, boxy structure - a tower of some sort of large triangular rocks with some wood and thatch, made of palm leaves, mostly covering its top. Luckily, the rain had almost stopped, but the clouds hadn't yet cleared.

Cal stepped quickly, up and over the stones bordering the enclosure - a bit higher than his waist - and ran to join his friend.

"Are you OK, Linc?"

"Yeah, but DON'T come over here!"

"Why not?" Cal asked.

Tiare suddenly said something that shocked them all…

Chapter 1

Musings on 'Mauru'uru'...

Thursday, October 13, 2005 - *about six weeks prior*
Tacoma
5:55 am

Creak, creak, crack...there it was echoing down through the hemlock-beamed ceiling, somewhere above Alex Webster's head. The sounds of a child rising for the day. The flush of a toilet, on/off of water in a sink a few times, faint gurgles from the drain and pipes in the wall, then quiet padding down the hall. This was followed by a couple of prominent stair squeaks, and five seconds later, into the kitchen strode his daughter Keely, yawning her way to the fridge.

"Morning, Sweetie!"

"Gooood moooorning," mouthed the 12 1/4-year-old, rubbing the dust of sleep from her dark brown eyes with the tops of her clenched fists - then reaching for the carton of orange juice inside the fridge.

Half a glass of gulped Florida goodness later, eyes now fully open, Keely asked her dad "How'd you sleep? What's up today?"

His reply was partly unintelligible, or at least in English. "Sleep good. Big presentation wrap-up, but 'aita pea'pea'..."

"DAAAD!" Keely groaned with the familiarity of this ritual - always a bit different and repeated over many days in the past. "All right, at least give me a hint...?"

Alex kissed her on the cheek, rubbed the top of her head of long brown hair, then grinned as he walked to grab his gym bag and two hangers, one holding his business suit, pants, and belt, and the other a blue oxford dress shirt from the dark walnut and brass antique hall tree near the door. Shifting the load - which included his work briefcase as well - to his left hand, he bent down to pick up a light jacket from a side table.

Except he almost forgot his car keys - which Keely grabbed from a bowl on the table and handed him as he neared the front door. Alex turned and whispered just loud enough for her to hear: "Mauru'uru," followed by his usual morning 'kid-missive,' "Be good - and don't get arrested!"

Shifting the keys and his other bags carefully to his other hand, he pulled on his waterproof windbreaker across one arm and shoulder, then set everything down to pull the other arm through. Finally, with everything in hand, he was ready to go. "See you tonight!"

The heavy mahogany front door slammed behind Alex on the way down the porch to the silver SUV waiting outside, already remote-started, warming up and ready to take him to the local YMCA, thanks to his press on the black key fob two minutes before while still inside the house. Modern marvels on a very cool Northwest day indeed!

Keely watched her dad cross the yard, its grass still growing but doing so much more slowly now than a few weeks ago. She chuckled as he opened the door and threw, with at least a little care, the several bags and hangers of all his stuff into the front seat.

The oldest Webster sibling tried to ignore the growing drizzle on the wavy glass panes, now past 101 years of installed life amid steady Pacific Northwest weathering (or more accurately "wettering" given the notoriously rainy conditions for much of the year here). A century of "service" had rendered the view through most of the house's windows a bit uneven, as the original glass panes sagged within their solid fir frames. Alex caught his firstborn's wave goodbye through the window and returned it as he drove away.

Keely pursed her lips, sat down at the large rectangular kitchen table, and flipped up her laptop's screen. She typed her dad's strange words (or what she thought he had said) into the search engine screen. Each time she tried the two phrases she guessed he'd actually uttered, the answers returned from the marvelous 'answer book from the ether' were all over the place. However, one link that came up in her search brought a quizzical look to her almond-tinged face. A few additional mouse-clicks and keystrokes later she jumped up to take a look at the giant map of the world that monopolized one wall of the 50-year-old kitchen.

"Hmmm," Keely mused to no one in particular...as she traced her finger over the Pacific Ocean, down to the south, and then stopping just below the equator....

A couple of minutes later, she glanced up at the large clock on the kitchen wall and realized it was time to get ready for her ride to swim practice and then after that, to school. She stood and traced an invisible arc across the map, then headed upstairs to grab all her gear.

Just then, a key turned in the front door, and in strode Jessica ('Jess') Forrester, 24-year-old part-time caretaker/nanny to Keely, her sister Meg, almost 11, and Callan (but they called him "Cal"), their 'goofy' little brother with a penchant for gadgets that stretched far beyond his 9 1/2+ years of life experience.

"Morning, Keely! - Meg and Cal up yet?"

"Good morning, Jess! Not sure...but they will be soon!" Keely yelled back down the stairs. She banged on their bedroom doors on opposite sides of the big square hall that was the centerpiece of the second-story of their three floor "English Cottage" style house. Experts would say it was really just a typical craftsman from the early 1900's, regardless of relentlessly creative real estate sales descriptions - whether then or now.

"Time to get up!" the "big sis" called to her siblings as she opened and closed the door to her own room. She turned the brass knob to enter the old-fashioned closet, then still in her bare feet, pulled a t-shirt and blouse combo off a hanger on the top rack, piled them atop her favorite jeans and some underwear and socks from her early 1920's walnut dresser, put everything but the socks on, then threw the rest and her shoes for school into the swim bag that sat at the foot of the bed. It already contained her training suit, towel and goggles.

Punching off the old-style push-button light-switch was Keely's last 'morning ritual, get-ready-to-go' step...

Oh, yeah! She suddenly remembered the other two pieces she'd almost forgotten, and grabbed her school backpack from her desk, closed the bedroom door behind her and galloped back down the weathered but still solid century-old oaken staircase as she always did. With a familiar flourish, she whirled her left hand around the corbel at the top of the banister, then rapid-tapped in her bare feet across each stair tread the last flight to the bottom. She breezed through the kitchen with a quick nod to the young woman who stood by the counter - now busy preparing her brother and sister's cereal bowls for breakfast and who, with a graceful pirouette in exactly the right direction, handed Keely her favorite blue hoodie.

"Thanks, Jess," said Keely, then "See you at 5:30!" as she breezed back into the foyer, slipped on the flip-flops she'd tossed under the hall tree (purposefully ignoring its mirror at this hour), and opened the front door just as a light "beep" from her best friend Shannon's mom's car sounded outside.

Time now for practice...then later to solve this puzzle...Keely thought, with a quick glance back to the map on the kitchen wall.

She just barely heard the nanny cry "Have a great day!" before the door slammed shut behind her and she scurried across the wet lawn to the waiting minivan for the short trip to the pool.

Chapter 2

A normal day?

Jess busied herself putting the lunches together for Meg and Cal. She didn't usually do so for Keely, who had lunch money for hers at the middle school. Today was the same as usual for the younger siblings: yogurt, granola, and celery sticks for the tall and lean Meg - who had recently been obsessing about nutrition, though at least some of this interest came from the fact that one of her favorite band's lead singers had a similar predilection for healthier food. It was the more typical turkey and pepper-jack (with wasabi mayonnaise) sandwich on whole wheat bread, carrots, and a small cookie for Cal. Neither of the two youngest Websters were really demanding or finicky kids. Well not that much anyway.

With a quick look at the clock, she called upstairs: "Don't forget to bring down your laundry baskets!" then, "Make sure to pack your books and homework in your bags!" She was hoping, but not fully counting on the fact that they would heed both (or either) of her suggestions.

As the graduate university student from New Zealand folded the kids' lunch bags and swept off the breadboard, she wished she had time to check her laptop for new emails. But she did have her phone handy, and quickly glanced at its small, LED screen for any new voicemails or text messages - a newer form of communication she was just getting used to - but it was still pretty primitive and frankly harder to read compared to emails on her much larger laptop screen.

Jess had a very busy daily schedule, and this job was one of the reasons she could even afford to attend the nearby University of the Cascades, where she spent most week days in between 'kid duties.' Mr. Webster (actually, he insisted on being called "Alex" to everyone she knew except his kids), had been extremely flexible and accommodating to her school and class requirements. Luckily, the fact Keely, Meg, and Cal were in school themselves from before 9 am until 3:30 or later each day meant that, with a little schedule-juggling and car-pooling here and there, the arrangements worked well for all.

Sounds of vigorous activity echoed from the upstairs bathrooms (punctuated by more than one "Hurry UP, Cal!" from Meg to her dawdling younger brother). A few minutes thereafter, both sporting teeth brushed and hair combed - if a bit haphazardly - Jess's last two charges entered the kitchen.

"What's this?" asked Meg. Her shoulder-length light brown hair swished across her face as she pointed to the large white erasable family message board next to the refrigerator. On it, Keely had scrawled a note - or something?...she tried to pronounce it. "Mow ruh ruh?"

"Oh, I think your sister wrote that up there before she left...not sure what it means," replied Jess, smiling and turning her attention to Cal as he sat down next to his sister to eat his cereal. Despite more healthful options for their lunch meals, they both still liked that honey-covered oat stuff that purported to be "nutritional" for breakfast. Their dad finally gave in as he thought it might be a bit better for them than the sugar-packed variety featured in that hugely popular old TV ad - the one with the freckled little boy enthusiastically diving in to a bowlful of cereal after his brothers dare him to do it. Unlike their dad, however, Meg and Cal, and their older sister, for that matter, still drank 1% milk most days and poured it on their cereal liberally too.

"Well...that's dumb," Megan cracked. "Maybe it's '*Mowrooroo*'...like a kangaroo-oo - from the same place as you-oo?" She forgot for a moment that kangaroos were from Australia, not New Zealand.

"Well, maybe you're right, and it should be pronounced "*Mow...roo roo*," Jess surmised, (ignoring Meg's smart-aleck comment) "with emphasis on the second and third syllables." She scrutinized the letters hurriedly scribbled by Meg's sister. "Sounds like something a cat would say, huh? Maybe it's a song? Probably from a musical theater play or a book she's reading at school. You can ask her later. But right now, you two need to finish your breakfast so I can get you to school. I have two classes today and can't be late this morning."

As the nearly 11-year-old gulped down the last of her breakfast and stared at the whiteboard, she frowned, though not in an angry way...Meg was always curious, and she just hated to not know EVERYTHING going on around her. Her perpetual curiosity was the subject of frequent comments and jokes by her family and friends, and her teachers as well. Jess, too, was amazed at the girl's unquenchable thirst for knowledge, but then again, her older sister Keely was sort of the same way, and for that matter, Cal was following right in his sisters' footsteps, a voracious reader since he'd been in kindergarten. Now, though, the youngest Webster mostly focused on pre-teen readers' detective stories and, somewhat more unusually, classical Greek mythology. Meanwhile, Meg's interests for casual reading fell more in the genre of slightly older readers' 'scary' tales. As evidence, the bookcase in her room held - and she had read each twice or more - the entire set of 20 volumes from one particularly famous author in that genre.

In fact, that's one of the reasons Jess really enjoyed this job, beyond the good pay and reasonable hours and nice room she was able to stay in when watching the kids while their dad was away on business trips. The Webster trio were smart, but they were really pretty nice, and well behaved too. Their father was generous (within reason anyway) when it came to encouraging each of them in most pursuits. Whether reading, educational tools, or other opportunities to learn or stretch their understanding a bit, all three children in the Webster family, and their dad as well, regularly added new books, games, computer software, and similar resources - fun ones like geography and map-reading and history-focused video games, for instance, to their household collection.

This family really likes to hang out together! Jess had figured this out soon after starting her nanny position. And it was true - at least most of the time - though there were the occasional conflicts and crises common in nearly any family. In fact, a big part of the Webster kids' growing up included going on periodic trips together, where the emphasis was certainly having fun and relaxing but also exploring new ideas, new places, and the history of the places they went - well beyond typical tourist activities. They traveled a LOT!

Jess popped out of her reverie, picked up her keys and walked towards the front door, looking back toward the kitchen table. "Time to go!" she announced. Meg and Cal dutifully took their bowls and empty glasses to the sink, rinsed them quickly, and grabbed their backpacks. Jess waited for the reddish-brown-blond - and relatively tall for his age - Cal to pass by, then closed and latched the door behind her as the kids crossed the lawn and piled into her compact car for the trip to school.

Chapter 3

Meet Keely!

Thursday, October 13, 2005 - *about 7:30 am*

Keely Anne Webster was one of those people you'd call *driven*. Since minutes after she appeared on the scene following her birth, she was determined to be not just a part of life around her, but to make the *most* of it, all the time. This meant that the term "precocious" was used by many who met her - and many, even strangers, took notice of the "cute" little girl with the round face and quick smile - but it wasn't her physical side that got the most lasting attention. It was her intellect and curiosity, about *everything*.

Keely was born on her parents' first anniversary in mid-July, about 12 years and three months ago. And she had never missed much from the morning she was born - when she grabbed the phone cord with a chubby little hand while her mom and dad relayed the exciting news to Keely's new grandparents on both sides of the family. Since then, walking and talking had come early, learning to read as well, and Keely always made sure hers was an active, adventurous, and exceedingly curious life.

Doted on as is typical for a first-born child (especially by her maternal grandmother for whom she was the first-born grandchild too), the bouncy young human with the shining eyes, winning smile, and relentless energy was always ready for an adventure. And usually, first in line for a challenge, wanting her place at the table with adults from about the age of six. In school, where her parents had been encouraged to enroll her early in first grade when she was still five years old, hers was always one of the earliest hands up when the teacher called for answers to a question or volunteers for a project. Her classmates and teachers had taken little notice of her comparatively younger age ever since.

Keely was a leader. A performer, albeit with a soft and occasionally shy side for sure, maybe sometimes a bit insecure despite all the high marks she had received at school, in musical theater performances, and in nearly every competition she'd ever entered.

Right now, that keen competitor was completing the last of the final set of 5x100 yard freestyle intervals assigned - the last at a slow pace - called a 'warm-down' - for her morning workout, which now amounted to 4,000 yards in total since she'd jumped in the pool at 6:15 am. Fortunately, the pool (located at the high school not far from her house) was indoors and heated of course. Right now, Keely felt quite warm as she accelerated for the last 25 yards, or usually, one length of the pool, to finish up the drill.

She glanced up at her time on the giant clock behind the starting blocks above the deck, then pulled off her goggles and watched her teammates coming in to the finish in the lanes directly to each side. Pulling herself out of the water, she reached out next to grab her plastic and latex hand paddles and blue foam kickboard and carried them to the large closet built-into the wall next to the pool deck. She dutifully deposited them into the appropriate bin for each, then, waving "bye" to her coach, she then headed into the locker room. It was 7:30 am, and her hour-and-fifteen-minute workout for this Monday morning was done.

There was just enough time for a five-minute shower, about the same time to get dressed, then she and Shannon Slater - her friend and fellow member of the Defiance Bay Dolphins swim club junior team - would need to hustle out to the parking lot where Shannon's mom was waiting to drive them to their middle school about a mile away. If they were on time and had no traffic issues, that meant they'd arrive before the school's 8:05 opening bell with ten minutes or more grace to get to their lockers, store their coats and lunches, and head to their first class.

Logistics! Sometimes, Keely was amazed she could keep up the schedule and still manage to get very good grades in school with morning workouts three times per week and evening ones (from 7-8 pm) twice a week on Tuesday and Thursday. Saturdays and Sundays were reserved for any meets held during each week, though they occurred only around once per month on average during the fall and winter - at least until high school. Moving up to that next level of competition, which Keely would be doing in less than a year for 9th grade, would mean morning workouts every day and afternoon practices not just after school but also on Saturdays - plus meets after school on some weekdays - and most weekends were busy too! Oh well, *for now*, Keely mused, as she donned the last item of clothing and picked up her bags, *I think I can handle it all...*

Keely and Shannon opened the outside locker room door, went briefly into the hall and then through the exit to the outside. As they walked around the glass and aluminum-paned pool building to the adjacent parking lot, they saw the familiar blue minivan they'd just been in less than 90 minutes ago - before practice. Mrs. Slater started the engine as they approached.

Keely opened and climbed in the rear door and Shannon jumped in the front, slammed the door, and buckled her seatbelt. Mrs. Slater reversed out and to the right of her parking space onto the quiet street, then began the short five-minute drive to Madison Middle School. Keely ran her fingers through her hair, which was still damp. She hadn't shampooed it today, but did rinse it pretty well during her short shower. Not that unusual, but her hair still smelled distinctly of chlorine or whatever chemicals made up the mélange within the pool where she seemed to spend so much of her life lately. As they came up to the first stoplight, and then proceeded on the green, Keely thought again of her dad's words earlier that morning.

Alex Webster loved giving his kids riddles and clues. It was his way of trying to engage them in games that made education and learning fun. Some of the time, they thought his efforts were "lame" or corny, but Keely had to admit that they had done some fun things together in the past four years, and really even before, when her parents were still married.

As the oldest, she had lots more memories of those good and then not-so-happy days than her younger sister Meg and brother Cal, respectively. She still wondered now and then what it would have been like had her parents not divorced when Keely was only just over eight, Meg six-and-a-half, and Cal a little 5-year-old kindergartener. She knew some of the reasons why her parents were no longer together, but didn't think about it much. What she did know for certain was that living with her dad as a single parent could be challenging sometimes, but he really tried hard to make sure they were well taken care of - especially given his demanding travel schedule. Plus, her mom had a busy life too, though they saw her every other weekend, and some days in between plus holidays and vacations when they split time with each parent. That's why they needed a nanny, because even if they'd had after school care arrangements or stayed (as they did on occasion) with their grandparents on some afternoons or overnight visits, it would have been tough for any parent (or grandparent) to cover all the kids' after-school (or before school, like her swim club) activities when Alex had to travel out of town on business.

One such arrangement was what they'd had in place for the last year with Shannon's mom - she drove the girls to swim practice three mornings a week, then usually grabbed coffee and looked over office paperwork while she waited in her car for the girls to finish their workouts. Mrs. Slater's schedule was flexible and she typically began work as an accountant for a regional real estate company just after dropping the girls off at school. When he was in town, Alex often took care of the evening workout pickups on Tuesday and Thursday, but because his office commute could be unpredictable, more and more lately he had asked Jess to take care of this chore.

Keely smiled to herself and took another bite out of her energy bar. Shannon's mom didn't mind them eating in the car as long as they took any wrappers with them and left no crumbs behind. She gazed out the window as they drew within a couple blocks of her school, thinking about their family's current living situation. It was pretty good, actually. For one thing, she really liked their nanny, Jess - not too bossy, smart and fun to hang out with, and all her friends LOVED Jess's "Kiwi" accent. *Yep*, Keely thought, the fact Jess was from New Zealand was cool too.

"Down Under" - to Australia and New Zealand - was one of the many places Keely and her family hadn't been yet, despite all their other trips together to other destinations. And that was saying something, because they traveled as a family as much as practicable. Since Keely was a little girl, she had been to many states - including Hawaii a few times - western Canada, England, and France. And of course, Disneyland, and even Disney World once - but then that wasn't out of the country, even though Disney's parks seemed like amazing alien lands sometimes! Disneyland Paris was an unplanned treat their dad had sprung on them during their visit to that city, about a year-and-a-half ago. She fondly recalled them taking the Eurostar train from London through the "Chunnel" - right under the English Channel - to the 'City of Light' - and then a couple of days later the shorter trains to and from the Disney Park 40 minutes away. Tastiest memory? The unusually sweet popcorn they'd enjoyed as a staple concession offering of Disneyland Paris - well before kettle corn had started to really catch on in the US!

Keely glanced up as Mrs. Slater slowed down to pull into the long semi-circular drop-off area in front of Madison Middle School. As they inched forward, Keely and Shannon prepared to exit the car with their backpacks. They saw several friends from their eighth-grade classes walking towards the main door. All Madison's students wore blue sweaters or school sweatshirts and khaki pants (no jeans or hats allowed!) as part of their 'official uniform' school attire options. Most had coats on too, but the drizzle had stopped and it was near 60 degrees outside already.

Keely's mind swung back to her guess to her dad's riddle earlier. She wasn't sure, but she thought maybe it had something to do with the South Pacific - at least that was what came up when she searched for *"Mauru'uru"* after her dad's clue. OK, she hadn't spelled it anywhere close to that in the initial search window, but luckily what she typed was enough for the system to guess what she was really seeking. It had brought up a bunch of lines regarding some place in the South Pacific and another reference to a book by a famous author.

I'm gonna find out more during our computers class, Keely thought. As the car stopped in the school driveway, she pulled the latch and hopped out with her stuff, Shannon close behind her. The girls thanked Mrs. Slater for the ride then strode quickly through Madison's main entry door. Keely glanced at her watch and saw it was 7:51. Time for some juice (in her bag) before heading to homeroom. Shannon was in one of the other three eighth grade homerooms, so she said a quick "Bye!" and they split at the next junction of the hallways, Keely to the left with Shannon going right. A quick visit to her locker to store her stuff, a few gulps from the bottle of juice, then Keely dropped it into the garbage can outside her classroom door, and went inside.

Her desk was in the second row, over on the far side near the window. As she set her backpack down and removed her books and notebook, the room slowly began to fill with students. A boy took the seat in front of and just to her right. He turned and smiled at her. Keely smiled back, her face reddening a bit, she realized. It was Kyle Kunz - and Keely had a bit of a crush on him. *But I'll never admit it to anyone else.* Kyle was nice to her, but then, she had to admit, he was pretty nice to everybody. *Oh well*, Keely thought, *there are plenty of fish in the sea, right? Plus, still plenty of time until the holiday dance during the first week of December.*

She pulled out her homework and pencils. Mr. Chen was also Keely's first period teacher, for Algebra 2, after home room, so she wanted to be ready. She had seen him down the hall on her way to class, talking to another teacher as she and Shannon walked in from the car.

Suddenly, the warning bell rang. It was 8:00 - and even though she really looked forward to school, as was the case with most days, Keely couldn't help but yawn. After all, she'd been up for almost three hours already, plus had completed a tough swim workout. She shook off the quick burst of fatigue and ran her hands through her hair, then sat up in her desk, alert and ready to go as with the next bell five minutes later, Mr. Chen announced with WAY too much enthusiasm, "Greetings, everyone! Welcome to another *Marvelous Monday* at Madison!"

Chapter 4

Meet Cal!

Thursday, October 13, 2005 - *five minutes before 9 am*

Callan Scott Webster - from afar - looked like what most observers would probably call a "normal" kid, though what that really meant was questionable in itself. For a nearly-ten-year-old he was taller than average for his age at 4 ft. 11 inches, slim and with brownish blond hair (but with tints of red in it). He actually looked a lot like his older sibling Meg, though not in hair style or color. His mane was combed simply to the left side of his head, not anything special, like many of the boys and even some girls in his fourth-grade class.

What *did* make Cal unusual - he always went by "Cal" in family and friends' circles, unless he was in trouble - was his very strong predilection for slightly offbeat subjects. Most recently, that meant Greek mythology, where he was an expert already. He'd done voracious reading and research in both books and perusing sources online. And then there was his love of hippopotamuses of all kinds, whether in zoos, in books, on TV, or as stuffed or hard plastic replicas - even though hippos definitely aren't the "nicest" of animals in terms of their demeanor in the wild. In fact, Cal had told many people, at least those who'd listen, that the lumbering and very fast semi-aquatic mammals are quite fierce and dangerous to be around, actually.

Cal was definitely a bit obsessive about his latest interests at times, but he was loyal to friends and mostly not a distraction in class. He was a very smart, deep thinker, as his teachers knew. Maybe not the most dedicated student, but not a "slacker," either.

It was no surprise then that, still in deep thought, the youngest of the Webster clan stepped out of Jess's car and scooted out to follow

Meg across the sidewalk, but in doing so, he unknowingly slammed the door.

"Not so hard please!" came the response from Jess in her really cool New Zealander, or "Kiwi" accent.

"Sorry!" Cal headed toward the school's front door only vaguely aware of the light rain falling. He didn't bother to pull up his hood as he concentrated on the book open and cradled in his hands instead. It was a miracle he didn't run into someone on the way, or into a wall, for that matter. His sister and the friends who'd just joined her out front helped in that regard, as they pulled both sides open and half-ran through the double doors to join the cascading flood of rapid-speaking first through fifth graders recently reacquainted for another school day.

Cal looked up just in time and slid in behind them, entering the school's main corridor then heading off to the left and down one of the side hallways to his home room. Mr. Tallman, one of two teachers in charge of the fourth grade here at Armour Elementary, stood half in/outside the door.

Chapter 5

Meet Meg!

Thursday, October 13, 2005 - *about 9:20 am*

Meghan Jane Webster ("*call me Meg!*") was having a pretty good day. The fifth grader had already been honored with a mention during the school's morning announcements for her strong showing as a district finalist in the recent spelling bee. She hadn't won, but came very close, only missing the spelling of "potpourri" by dropping one of the r's in her nervousness.

The funny thing was, *I knew that word!* thought Meg. Her mom often put potpourri in a bowl with hot water to "smell up" the house (in a good way) when Meg was younger, and still did. Prone to occasionally getting ahead of herself due to a consistent lack of patience, Meg had in her excitement committed the misspelling. But, with her usual cheerful spirit, she admitted that she did still have fun competing (as she did in everything - sports, academics, acting, really just about anything). Plus, the girl from Waterside Elementary - nearby - who'd won and was headed to the state finals now - was pretty nice, so *no big deal*.

Now, Meg, with her usual spirit for action, was on to other things. As she walked into class earlier with her friends Jason Boland and Carly Yamashita, they'd heard some gossip: apparently it involved a new teacher rumored to arrive after the holiday break.

As she watched their home-room teacher, Ms. (Leilani) Halamea, jotting a few assignment notes on the board, Meg had her "Trapper Keeper" workbook open to the tab labeled **"Language Arts"** - her first subject of the day. She reviewed last Friday's vocabulary assignment (the topic was transportation), and made sure - though it was nearly always a 'sure' thing with the diligent and very fast-working Meg - that she had completed all the definitions required.

Yep, she noted to herself, *perambulation* was the last word on the list. Done, defined, and used in a sentence: "*The boy and his dog came up to the river and rather than swim, decided to perambulate over the bridge to the other side.*" Meg always liked to be creative with her answers, and it sometimes drove her teachers crazy! *Sheesh,* she thought, *that will probably be the LAST time I ever use that word, ever!*

Ms. Halamea turned around and smiled at the class. In her younger thirties, she had been a teacher at Armour Elementary for almost 10 years. *And now I bet she's going to leave!* Meg was sad - she really liked the Hawaiian-born instructor and had growing trepidation now (that was a word from the prior week's vocabulary assignment) about who might replace her in January.

"Who has heard of the expression 'let the cat out of the bag'?" asked Ms. Halamea.

About five hands out of the 20 in the class went up right away.

"Leticia, tell us what it means."

"It means to tell someone a secret?"

"Yes, it does...and can anyone say where it originated?"

No hands went up this time, until Meg raised hers, somewhat tentatively.

Nodding to her, Ms. Halamea said, "Go for it, Meg, what do you think the answer is?"

Meg began, "In ancient times, people captured cats, and a kid opened up the bag that a mean cat-catcher guy was using to carry them and one jumped out, so everybody knew he was doing it - and they stopped him from doing it anymore!"

Not sure whether to laugh or agree, several of Meg's classmates looked at her, then transferred their gazes to the front of the class, where Ms. Halamea gave a grin and a 'thumbs-up' to her effort.

"Nice try, Meg, gotta give you credit for creativity on that one, but of course, that's no surprise!"

Without commenting on the veracity of Meg's hastily prepared answer, the teacher continued. "This is a perfect segue into our next project assignment. She turned around and pulled down one of the rolled poster sheets on the blackboard behind her. On it was written in bold, black pen "***Colloquialisms***."

Meg glanced at the word, then turned sideways to Jason in the seat to her right and joked, "Now, *that* should have been in the spelling bee!"

The teacher continued. "Our next class project, which each of you will work on individually, is to take a colloquialism, which means, as Webster's dictionary (she held up the hefty red book sitting near the front of her desk) defines it: '*a local or regional dialect expression*' or as **Dictionary.com** says..." she leaned over to read from the screen of her computer, "we first need to define its root word '*Colloquial*', which is an *adjective characteristic of or appropriate to ordinary or familiar conversation rather than formal speech or writing; informal. involving or using conversation.*"

"Next," added Ms. Halamea, indicating a sub-list of points under the word on the whiteboard, "each of you will choose a colloquialism used here in the United States, or in another language or anymore culture, define its accepted meaning, explore its origins, *and* report to the class on whether you think it makes sense in today's world."

The teacher pointed to another list taped up to the side of the main one shown on the board, which was a printed sheet - copies of which the teacher then strode across the room and handed out in groups of five to the occupants of the last desks in each row. With a sample held in front of her as the sheets were passed forward by the students, Ms. Halamea concluded her explanation with one more key instruction as she returned to her desk in front of the class: "You MUST use primary sources for this assignment, meaning nobody gets to just look up their colloquialism in (the increasingly popular new online tools) **Wikipedia** or **Google Search**. You need to use the library, or books you or your family already own, or magazine articles, or newspaper stories, to not just *define* your chosen expression, but you must also find and *cite* three examples where it is used in a literary work, or a news story, or feature article."

The teacher paused..."Finally, (several barely-suppressed groans were heard from the students), you are encouraged to use audio or video to present your project - and you'll get 15 extra points above a maximum of 90 available if you do so...

"Oh, one more thing - this will count 25% toward your grade this term...but I'm sure you all knew that because you'll remember that we discussed the importance of this particular project at the very beginning of the school year." Scanning the students, she observed several knowing glances back and forth among them. Ms. Halamea grinned. "Any questions?"

Glancing first at the sheet, then forward to where her teacher stood, Meg caught her eye. "When is this assignment due, Ms. Halamea?"

"Great question, Meg - if you turn over the page in your hands, you'll see a chart of steps and dates...that's your guide to all the stages and deadlines for this project. It starts today - and your first step is to define your chosen colloquialism by next Friday. You'll then have two weeks to find your sources, which you'll verify and share with me when you return this form. Then, your draft presentations will be due the following Friday...or as the schedule shows: November 18. Final presentations, including any audio or video used as a bonus, need to be turned in for my review by the end of the week after Thanksgiving. We'll then set aside just under an hour each Wednesday and Friday mornings during Language Arts class for the first couple of weeks of December to observe each student's presentations to the class."

Their teacher then delivered the news that was most exciting to Meg and others in the classroom: "We'll be putting all of your presentations on camera and creating a DVD to showcase the best moments of each - as judged by me and a team of other teachers in the 5th and 6th grade, plus Principal Davenport. Then, we'll show that collection to parents at our final Family Holiday Night on December 21, two days before we break for holiday vacation!"

A palpable buzz of excitement ran through the room. Several students whispered to their classmates, some eager to get started, some clearly dreading the assignment. Meg's friend Carly raised her hand and Ms. Halamea invited her to speak: "Yes, Carly?"

"How long do we have to present our *co-llo-quio-lizms*?"

"Another great question, and the answer is - each student will have five minutes to deliver their project presentation." This elicited protests and complaints about the too-short time from several of the pupils, and a few questioning looks from others, but they were silenced by the teacher as she held up her hand to stop the discussion.

"This will not be an easy assignment. It will be a challenge to cover this topic and do it well within five minutes, especially if you use audio or video examples. But I'm confident each of you will do a fantastic job.

"OK. We won't spend any more time on this now, but if you *do* have further questions, look over the assignment tonight and we'll talk about it again tomorrow. Meanwhile, time for our Language Arts homework."

Gesturing to another of Meg's classmates and member of her soccer team, Ana Rodriguez, Ms. Halamea said "OK, first word in our Transportation vocabulary: '*Amphibious*'. Ana - define and use it in a sentence, please..."

Meg was thrilled. She loved assignments like the project that had just been explained by the teacher. But she still had a few questions, and she was surprised that Ms. Halamea hadn't said anything about the rumors swirling through the school. Shifting back to the work at hand, Meg saw that the teacher was thanking Ana for her completion of the first word's vocabulary usage and moving on to the next. Five minutes later, they were down to "perambulate" and Joey Mixon (who Meg didn't like very much, *though I have certainly tried*, she mused), had just been asked to define the final word in the assignment and give an example for the class: "The man perambulated the castle with his horse."

Ms. Halamea twisted her face in a combo of disagreement and reluctant approval. "OK...Joey, I guess that'll work. Good job."

Suddenly, the teacher rose from her desk, put her hands on her waist, and walked to the front of the class. Her cheeks were a bit red, and Meg thought she saw her brush away a tear from underneath one eye. "And now, I have some other big news to share."

Meg and several of the other students stole quick glances at each other, waiting with the rest for the words to come from the teacher. Ms. Halamea pulled down the classroom's western hemisphere map from the rolled collection on the left side of the blackboard.

"I have a very exciting opportunity to work in a school in Honoka'a, near my hometown of Waipio Valley, here (pointing at the map) on the Big Island of Hawaii. They are losing one of their teachers due to his wife having to move to the mainland for her job. I get that, because it's like a move I made 15 years ago when I left Hawaii to come to the University of the Cascades here for college. Now, I've been asked to return and take that teacher's place. It's a great chance to go back home and help the administration and community continue their tradition of excellent academic performance, as an elementary school teacher like I am now. I've decided to accept the job, and my husband and I will be moving back to the Big Island at the end of this year. And…" as real tears welled in her eyes, "I will really miss all of you and everybody here at Armour Elementary…So," she wiped her eyes, then continued, "I'd really be honored if you all made a commitment to me, to do your very, very best on our special project assignment, so I can have a nice memory of our final work together here in class before I head to Hawaii."

Gazing out at the sad and stunned faces in the room, Ms. Halamea brightened up and hastily added, with a smile, "Hey, hey, everybody…we still have more than nine weeks left before winter break and there's lots of work to be done in the meantime. But right now (she quickly checked the clock on the wall), it's time for library." The students stood up and made their way quietly to the door, pencils and notebooks in hand.

"Wow!" Jason said to Meg and Carly, as they walked together out into the hallway, "Lots of news for the first hour of the week…and not sure I like all of it, either!"

"That's for sure! I wonder who will be replacing Ms. Halamea?" said Meg, and Carly nodded her agreement with the question.

"Yeah, I guess we will find out soon, right? Meanwhile, at least we've got an exciting project to think about…do either of you know what you're going to choose as your - what is it called - *colloqueamin*, I mean *colloqueelism* - for the assignment?" asked Jason.

They continued down the hall, and as they neared the door to the library, Meg, who had been in deep thought, replied with her usual determination, "Not yet. But I think this is gonna be a very, very interesting project, for sure!"

Chapter 6

A celebrated assignment

Thursday, October 13, 2005 - *9:20 am*

After being dropped off at school, Cal had hurried to his locker, entered the left/right/left combination, then placed his lunch bag on the top shelf and threw in his coat. He shut the locker door and spun the dial, then darted to his seat, last to arrive in the mostly-full classroom as the big clock on the wall showed *9:01*.

He received a slight glare from Mr. Tallman, though surprisingly no other comments today. *Must be something big going on or he would have called me out for being late,* thought Cal.

Shortly thereafter, following the day's announcements over the school public address system, and review of one of their class assignments Cal's suspicions were confirmed. "As we head into the holiday season, it's time for our special project to close out the year before vacation starts," said Mr. Tallman. "The theme for the project is 'Holiday Celebrations Around the Globe' and each of you gets to choose one country or culture that you'll learn all about and then share what you've found with the class and your parents, guests, and the rest of the school. You'll have until December 5 to finish your projects. However, there are a number of key dates and assignments before then to help you stay on track. First one is to pick your topic."

The teacher gestured at the multi-part chalk and dry-erase board behind him, then turned to face the class. "I've put a few ideas on the board to get you started, but you don't have to choose any of these. Be creative!"

Cal scanned the list of topics. He noted familiar ones like Christmas, Hanukkah, Kwanzaa, and similar winter holidays, but also others he'd never heard of such as *Eid al Maulud, Dragon Boat Festival,* (*that sounds cool,* he thought) *Aurungu, Diwali,* then a couple different spellings of one he had heard of: *Carnival/Carnevale.* There were about 15 more too.

The fourth-grader focused his attention back to the teacher, who continued with more details. "Don't forget, this isn't just about winter holidays either, though winter and summertime are reversed in the bottom part of the world vs. the Northern Hemisphere, where we live. Wide open topic - If you have another culture or country you'd like to explore for their holiday traditions, feel free to do so and let me know...but the deadline to pick your topic is two weeks from today. I'll then verify everyone's project choices by the following Wednesday. Then by the Monday after that, you'll have your next milestone: listing your topic, the sources you'll use to explore it, how you'll find them and keep notes on them, and how (*not whether*) you'll be using any audiovisual methods, such as sound, music, photos, or costumes, to portray your topic to the class."

Finally, the teacher pointed to a "Project Outline" box up on the board with several steps and deadlines for each. "Special treat: you'll also get the chance to display and discuss what you discovered about your chosen holiday topic during our Holiday Parents' night - which (he gestured toward the bottom of the project box) is on a Wednesday evening, the 21st, just before we leave on break that Friday, for vacation in the last week of December."

Mr. Tallman paused, looked around the room and saw a variety of expressions on the faces (and in the body language) of the students. Most were smiling, a few frowned, some appeared to be thinking deeply.

"And a couple more key points," the teacher added, "Again, be creative, think outside of your own country and culture if you like. You don't *have* to do your project on somewhere else than America and our most well-known traditions, though it sure would be great if you helped us all understand more about people and their celebrations in other parts of the world."

The teacher's eyes came to rest on Cal, and he held up his hand for quiet. "Mr. Webster...I'm sure with your imagination, you'll come up with a very creative and informative presentation for the class - and even get it done on time, this time!"

Caught off-guard by the sudden direct attention from his teacher, Cal wasn't sure whether he should blush or smile, but he offered a little of both in response. And raised a quick "thumbs-up" in reply. "For sure, sir!" he stated eagerly.

Several in the class giggled, then Mr. Tallman began at each row to pass out the project details and assignment sheets. As he finished the task at the side of the classroom, he signaled it was time to get back to their 'standard' routine.

"Now, it's time for math. Pull out your homework and turn to page 66 of your books as you see on the board...Amy, please come up and get us started by diagramming the problem and your answer to #3."

While his classmate Amy Watkins stepped up from her seat across from Cal and walked to the board, he was thinking, pondering the possibilities...*Holidays, hmmm...this should be interesting.*

Suddenly, Cal was jolted back to the work at hand. He realized he'd better open his own book, pull out his worksheet, and follow Amy's explanation of their math homework assignment from the previous Thursday. Cal knew he needed to improve his grade in the subject by the end of the term - he was only getting Cs in it right now after their first two tests. His dad had challenged him to do so, if he wanted help buying that new *Greek Gods and Legends* game, and *that*, he thought, was a pretty big motivation to *pay attention and improve all my grades - soon!*

Chapter 7

Moorea on the horizon?

Monday, October 17, 2005 8:35 am

It had been a mostly uneventful drive up to Seattle this particular morning. Not bad for a Monday for sure, and even better that the light rain had stopped before Alex reached the area around Seattle-Tacoma International Airport, aka *"SeaTac,"* where multiple highways converged to often cause traffic problems and delays. As a result, though there had been periodic slowdowns, he had pulled off Interstate 5 and reached his office parking garage about ten minutes earlier than expected for the first business day of the week.

The 6-foot-three-inch tall Tacoman entered the doors of the One Emerald Square office building just before 8:20 am, and made his way via ultra-fast elevator to the 23rd floor. He dropped by the restroom first, then stuck his key in the office door, and walked past the glass-enclosed conference room overlooking Seattle's gray-blue Elliott Bay. Its chairs were unoccupied at this hour, the view slightly obscured by some low clouds, which was a common scene most fall mornings. Alex had completed the weekly phone call with members of his European regional sales team during the drive up. Now, his thoughts were back to North American business, and how his core Seattle staff would support the upcoming Moorea project. He had continued down the hall past several outer offices on either side, then around the corner to the other side of the headquarters of the fast-growing hotel management software company.

LodgeSoft's Global Sales team's headquarters hub was on the south side of the building, and when Alex arrived back at his desk in one of several sort-of understated 'cubicles' (they had shoulder-high walls with clear windows on all sides) it was almost 8:30. He waved 'hello' at a team member, Francis McBain, who was typing and talking through a phone headset at the same time. Francis, a former

New York-area resident, grinned and gave a 'thumbs up' as he sat at a desk in the next row over from Alex's cube.

Seated with his coat off, Alex snapped his laptop into its docking station, moved the mouse a bit to wake it up, and entered his single-sign-on password into the screen. Shifting in his seat, he clicked on one particular internet browser and then a saved website link among the many available options, then typed a few characters on the keyboard. Soon the screen brightened to display one of the most picturesque home pages anybody could ever choose for their online 'brand'. In this case, it was a tremendous, almost-otherworldly photo of a blue-green lagoon ringed by white-tipped ocean waves, which broke against a reef several hundred feet offshore. Above it all, rising majestically to the sky and covered with deep-green foliage, sheer rock faces and with nothing in the way of visible roads to reach its summit, was a huge mountain. Not the type of perpetually snow-capped, glacier-covered mountain like Rainier (actual name *Tahoma*, like Tacoma, the city, but that's another story) which both Seattle and Tacoma claimed as their 'own' local treasures to the world. This peak was tropical and lush and - where you could see them through the thick foliage - covered with rocks.

Gazing away from his two monitors for a moment, off to his left, Alex searched in vain through the typical morning clouds for a glimpse of Mt. Rainier, which he could often (at least when it wasn't raining or cloudy) see through the office window around 75 miles away. *Nope, not today, or not yet anyway*, he thought.

He glanced back at his screen and eyed the front page for a tour company based in French Polynesia. *Hello, Bali Hai*, he said to himself. *Can't wait to meet you!* He scrolled down though a number of options available at the site's main page: *How to get here, What to do, Weather, Prepare for your trip, What to bring, What to expect, What to buy,* and a number of other choices.

Moorea. French Polynesia. Tahiti. But most of all *Mt. Rotui.* This, Alex read from the photo caption, was the famous, majestic, and jagged mountain now displayed on screen. In his initial research the previous Friday, he'd learned that some people claimed it was the peak James Michener had used as inspiration for the mystical "*Bali Hai*" described in the famous 1947 book **Tales of the South Pacific**, based on the author's experiences as a young officer in the

U.S. Navy during World War II. More likely, Alex had found through further research, Michener's mythical Bali Hai was imagined from a peak on an island in what's now the nation of Vanuatu, where the lieutenant and "Special Duty Officer" was stationed for about a year during his military career. Apparently, the later movie version of the book Michener finished writing as the war ended was mostly filmed on the lush island of Kauai, in Hawaii. Indeed, the mountain used in the filmed shots of the jagged peak was actually Kauai's Mt. Makana.

Alex brought his mind back to Moorea: Mt. Rotui was the most prominent sentinel seen in photos guarding the joint harbors of Cook's Bay and Opunohu Bay, on the north side of a verdant isle a few miles off the coast of the island of Tahiti, itself once a battleground staging area for Allied Forces during the war. Now, it was a quieter alternative to the larger and more touristy Tahiti and another famous island in the same chain, Bora Bora.

Michener's book had been the basis for a famous Rodgers and Hammerstein musical that debuted on New York's Broadway three years after the book was published. Then, in 1959 came the movie version of the show. It too opened to wide acclaim, and *South Pacific* was its name also.

Alex had only seen the film once, any years later, and had forgotten most of it, but he did remember Mitzi Gaynor, who played the lead as an army nurse and her famous singing number "*I'm gonna wash that man right out of my hair.*" He couldn't recall much of the plot or action beyond that, though. The thought of the movie *South Pacific* did, however, prompt him to look back fondly on memories of another place: the several beautiful beaches he'd visited on Kauai, known as Hawaii's *Garden Isle* and the oldest of the major Hawaiian Islands. Several of the sound stages for the film were at or near Hanalei Bay on Kauai's stunning North Shore.

Alex hummed a bit of the catchy tune while he clicked through the screens on his computer. *Luckily*, he thought, no one was in immediate range in the office to hear his dissonant attempt at replicating Gaynor's signature song. Indeed, Alex admitted to himself, he was *not even in the same hemisphere, much less the same island chain* in terms of talent or rhythm or pitch compared to those gifted leading actors and singers who'd performed in the film, *for sure!*

Back again to the subject at hand...Moorea. If Alex could work out all the details, this was to be the next destination for what their family and friends - and even Alex and the kids themselves - liked to call the *"Worldwide Websters." Our own 'traveling clan brand,'* Alex mused with a grin. *Could Moorea be the family's next adventure stop?*

Among the larger in size of the islands in the archipelago nation of French Polynesia, Moorea was close to the country's socioeconomic and political center, just ten miles across the water from its largest and most populous island by far - Tahiti. In fact, many people referred to the whole country as "Tahiti," but it was just one of around 120+ islands (including smaller islets, or atolls) in the Society Islands group, which were themselves only one part of French Polynesia, a nation which stretched for more than 2,000 kilometers, or 1,200 miles, from end to end.

Why Moorea, and why was Alex looking at it now? Well, a chance mention between two friends had now led to a business opportunity - which Alex had heard about as of just the previous Friday. The CEO of LodgeSoft, Roger Thomson, knew the head of a hotel company, Montcalm Resorts, that had just purchased a property on the island. It didn't hurt that the new General Manager at the Moorea resort was the CEO's cousin as well, so these exceptional connections had made the chance to capture the hotel's software business by LodgeSoft even stronger than it might have been.

LodgeSoft had done lots of work for the Montcalm chain in the past. Now, Alex's company was being contracted for a complete overhaul of the computer systems at their acquired Moorea hotel. The trick was, they needed to get the project started and on track before handing it off to their local contractors and the resort staff themselves for ongoing operations. And this had to happen before the end of the year, preferably by December - for financial reasons and also because soon thereafter it would be too busy to undertake amid an expected holiday increase in guest bookings at the resort.

When told before the weekend about the urgent software install request, Alex had asked Roger, his boss, if - given the short notice and the fact holidays and school vacations conflicted with the desired project time line - there would be any issues if he brought his kids along on the trip? Thomson hadn't hesitated, replying "Not a problem!" However, he didn't need to point out to Alex that in fairness to others in the company who wouldn't have such an opportunity, Alex, as its Global Sales Head, would still need to cover the cost of airfare for his kids to fly over to French Polynesia on his own. That said, Alex had gained agreement from the Montcalm's GM that the Websters' lodging and breakfast and a few other meals would be provided at no charge by the resort as a special perk given the urgency and time of year of the project.

Since the previous Friday, things had already begun to move fast. The only major questions left to figure out were transport and other preparatory details. *Of course, those aren't exactly small questions at all*, Alex thought. However, if everything worked out, he and the kids would leave together for this tropical destination in a few weeks. *But it's not as simple as just traveling across the country*, Alex reminded himself.

He clicked the screen back to his online calendar for the exact dates of the upcoming project engagement and, with the Montcalm chain's website open to the location of the Moorea resort, he started to enter details in a second window - LodgeSoft's travel agent's internet 'booking' screen - for potential flights. *Great way to start a Monday*, Alex thought, smiling, as he pulled up the menu and entered his sign-in details and trip info. He left that browser window open while it searched and opened another general travel website in a new window to put in the details for each of his kids, their ages, etc., and then accessed a couple more specific airline websites as well - to do some cross-checking. *"Mr. Research"*- a nickname he was proud to acknowledge - was at it again!

Indeed, given his penchant for exhaustive detail and fact-checking, that's what some Alex's friends and colleagues joked his name should have been from birth. One big part of any trip was always the preparation and Alex - though not a certified travel agent nor had he ever been paid for or charged for his work in the trip-planning arena - certainly was as creative and determined in exploring and arranging options for flights, lodging, and interesting activities as probably any travel agent on earth. He often helped friends and colleagues with compiling their own travel plans to destinations all over the world.

Now, with the fast-evolving internet at his fingertips, and an exciting new adventure to be mapped out, his work had already begun. One positive point: all the Webster children had valid passports, having ordered them more than a year previous for a trip to London and Paris that included a side-trip to Euro Disney too, a surprisingly nice interlude in an otherwise history and sightseeing-focused adventure.)

What a trip that was! He recalled that the kids drove him a bit crazy after eight days 'on the road' in several hotels and he'd become irritated with them the morning before the family's last night in Paris. In fact, while taking a walk through the streets of the 'City of Light' that day to do some shopping and clear his head, he had come to the realization that he likely drove them crazy too!

Fortunately, all *had* worked out for the best to finish up their European vacation. At the end of that windy, rain-spattered April day, Alex stopped in a small grocery store near their hotel and bought some snacks, baguettes, meat, cheese, and crackers, plus a split of wine for himself and bottles of local fruit sodas for the kids. They ended up having a blast together, a "Parisian indoor picnic" on their last night. It was a great family memory, and also an epiphany for him at the time that he'd never forgotten: *The huge value in life of patience, calm, and what it means to be a family, no matter what, and after all.*

While his fingers tapped over the keyboard in front of him and he shifted his gaze back and forth between the two screens and multiple browser windows, Alex's excitement began to build, as it always did when he was planning a trip. *Soon, the real fun begins*, he thought. He focused his attention toward the website and services of *Montcalm Resort Moorea*, where the Worldwide Websters just might place a special new twist on the Thanksgiving holidays!

Chapter 8

Logistics, logistics...and more logistics

Monday, October 17 8:55 am

Now about 15 minutes into his multi-site exploration of all things Moorea, Alex clicked over to his online calendar again. *No meetings until 11*, he confirmed with an audible "Whew!" of relief. Alex enjoyed travel planning and learning about places and their history so much that he sometimes got carried away with his research. *But remember*, he thought, *you have a job and you have to **do** it to be able to afford the time and money for all this traveling and exploring new places abroad - and especially if you want to bring the kids along!*

By this time, most of his Sales and Service team staff were actively engaged in various duties. One, Cynthia Nguyen, looked up and smiled when he walked by a few moments later. "Morning, Alex!"

"Hi Cyn! How was TJ's soccer tournament this weekend?"

"LOOOONG...five games in 2 1/2 days, and 2 1/2 hours each way driving! But they won four out of the five, and TJ (Cynthia's 10-year-old son, Taron Jesse - a talented midfielder for his age) scored four goals and added two assists for the weekend, so he was certainly happy. At least the other parents, kids, and I had some fun going out to meals while we were there. Also, the weather was surprisingly clear, so we got some fantastic views of Mt. Hood, Mt. St. Helens, and of course Mt. Rainier and the Cascades down there. Not to mention while driving between Vancouver and here, in both directions."

"Cool, glad you all had fun, and tell TJ *great job* for me!" Alex answered, continuing his walk to the office kitchen. Once there, he grabbed a fresh cup from the shared coffee machine and returned to his desk. He sat down, spun his chair frontwards, moved the mouse to 'wake up' his screen, and signed back in to his work computer. A quick check of his emails, then Alex was back to the travel sites he'd surveyed earlier.

Key dates: He had to start work on the *Montcalm Moorea* project on Monday, November 28, though ideally, he and his

LodgeSoft team would have lots of prep work completed even before the Websters arrived on the island. Alex had already (on the previous Friday) checked out a summary list of the local hotel's current software applications and future requirements, and also had reviewed the resort's *needs survey*, which would help define the project's scope and work to be done.

Besides the native-English speaking General Manager, the Moorea property had an excellent local team on site. Better yet, the IT Director from the Montcalm's headquarters seemed - as Alex's colleagues had confirmed - well-prepared for the project. The hotel's staffers would definitely be ready to go by Alex's arrival, along with Alex and his remote Seattle team. After about a week of work on the island, all should be on track for the resort's implementation. Then, *fingers crossed*, they'd conduct tests and a final 'hand-off' of next steps for the project by Friday a week after Thanksgiving, before the Webster clan's return to the U.S.

Alex paged through his travel search screen. It looked like individual airfares might vary a lot, depending on what exact days the family picked to fly - though none were nonstop. *Yep*, he thought, *we'll surely have at least one layover in each direction.*

First, they had to fly from Seattle-Tacoma International Airport (code name *SEA*) to Los Angeles. The best flights to get the family from "Sea-Tac" to Los Angeles International Airport (*LAX*) in plenty of time to catch the next, much longer yet also direct flight to Papeete, Tahiti's airport (*PPT*), would be sometime after noon. Unfortunately, flights at that time of year were some of the more expensive ones from Seattle-Tacoma to LA. *Of course, it's the holidays*, Alex reminded himself.

Clicking another link on his browser, Alex confirmed that based on their available days, work schedule, and budget, their main flights to and from Papeete would likely be on Tahiti Air, with a capacity of nearly 300 passengers in three classes of service on its giant Airbus A340 planes. Sometimes, Alex's company policies allowed him to travel in Business class for work, if the flight exceeded six hours in length. He had also been lucky enough to get 'bumped up' to First class on occasion. But not this time...he needed to consider the significant extra costs of transporting the whole family sitting together, so Economy/Coach seating it would have to be for the whole clan for the Worldwide Websters' trip to Tahiti!

Alex pondered some of the other logistical realities of this trip. Flights on different airlines for the domestic and international portions of this Polynesian adventure meant they might need to push and pull a caravan of bags (he kept trying to get the kids to pack light on prior trips, but it was always a battle) around the huge airport, but LAX was actually pretty organized and fairly easy to navigate. Unless something really went awry with the first leg of their trip, they'd have plenty of time at LAX to transfer bags, have dinner, and check in before their nine-hour flight to Papeete. Hopefully, on that long flight they'd all be able to sleep a bit - not always a likely proposition with kids who tended to stay occupied with reading and movie watching and playing video games (Cal, especially, and sometimes all at once) on the airplane. *But one could hope, right?*

Alex surveyed the prices for each day surrounding their outbound journey, and saw an opening: SEA to LAX then LAX to Papeete (PPT) on Thursday, November 24, Thanksgiving Day. This particular date had an excellent price for the whole itinerary - not just to the French Polynesian capital, but down to LAX and back to SeaTac on either end of the trip - if they picked the Saturday evening a week after their departure to fly back to the US from Tahiti.

The selected return flight from Papeete on Tahiti Air left late in the day on the Saturday a week following Thanksgiving in the U.S. Actually, as Alex had checked, it departed just before 9 pm local time, almost two hours earlier – local time - than their flight from LAX to PPT was scheduled to leave on the outbound portion of their trip. A slightly faster flight was part of the good news for their return journey from the French Polynesian capital. This, Alex guessed, was due to the jet stream tailwind pushing their plane as it headed eastward to North America. Combined with the time difference (Pacific time zone was two hours ahead of the island nation's time), they would be arriving back into the States early the following Sunday morning. With the Thanksgiving holiday rush having been completed earlier that week, there were more flight options available at lower prices to get them home to SeaTac from Los Angeles throughout that day.

Now the real complexity came into play. Doing a 'split' airline ticket purchase like this for several people at once was not an insurmountable task for those who know how to focus their attention and complete keystrokes carefully (and calmly) between systems. *It's easiest if you can have two screens open at your computer at the same time,* Alex reminded himself.

He first made sure - by clicking through the Tahiti Air website - that there were enough open seats for all of them in close proximity on the larger aircraft to and from Papeete on their preferred days of travel (it had a 2-4-2 seating configuration in Economy class, unlike Alex's preferred Boeing 747 airliner for such long flights, but *oh well,* he thought). He then quickly entered the passenger details for Keely, Meg and Cal - almost forgetting to put in their full names as he was so used to calling them by their nicknames.

Alex realized he had everything he needed to make the reservations, except each child's passport numbers. But he could add those details later, and like most airlines, once he was done inputting all the traveler info, even though this was a special discount and 'nonrefundable' fare on each of two different airlines' tickets, he also had a 24-hour window during which changes or full refund cancellations could be made to the flight details.

He repeated the seat and fare confirmation process for their SEA-LAX flights. *Bingo!* Plugging in and double-checking - twice - the seating arrangements to verify they could all sit at least in the same row of the planes together on four separate flights took some time. This was true largely because Alex had to jump back and forth between his business travel site and the two airline sites where he entered the info for the Webster children.

Finally, after he'd entered his credit card details (from memory) into the airline reservation forms - twice - he was set to push the last button for "*Purchase*" on each. Alex scanned back through the flight details, hesitating just a moment, and thought: *Anything to mess this up? Potential roadblocks to leaving?*

Not being able to find strong reasons not to, and knowing he still had one full day to iron out any issues or challenges without losing the right to a refund, Alex clicked the on-screen buttons with his mouse...and their trip to Moorea was officially ON! As anyone who has ever used online systems - or made any other important decision that required a financially-significant action to be taken – knows, the MOMENT after he did click that "*Purchase*" button, he flashed on two questions he'd forgotten to ask himself before doing so: 1) *What about Jessica, the kids' nanny...Do I pay her while we're gone? And...2) Can the kids all be absent from school for a week? They already had Thursday and Friday of Thanksgiving week off, but not the following week after the holiday. Hmmm...*

Alex took a deep breath and slowly exhaled. *Nothing to get upset about now*, he told himself. *Just take the questions one by one and figure out the answers so I can (hopefully) make the big trip announcement tonight and surprise the kids!* He was very confident he could get the details he needed to finalize their arrangements - but again, things don't always turn out exactly as we hope - or expect.

Alex's mind flashed, just for a moment, back to his marriage and past family travels...*Nope, no time to go THERE right now*, he told himself.

With the flight plans taken care of (for the present, at least) Alex moved on to the other questions. *What about their rooms at the resort?* One thing about hotels in Moorea, he had noticed through his quick initial research, is they aren't that big - meaning they don't have nearly as many rooms or facilities in general as was common in hotels or resorts in more heavily-visited tourist areas.

The focus of the experience in French Polynesia was on the setting, and not so much the sleeping rooms - among some of the lushest landscapes and inviting seascapes anywhere in the world. Breathtaking beaches, vast coral reefs, jagged mountains, tropical flowers of every kind nearly everywhere. Tahitian culture mixed with strong French influence on food and business customs. The *Montcalm Resort Moorea* was no exception. *It looks beautiful*, Alex thought.

*We should just need one room and could share one bathroom, but...*Alex stopped and shifted his thoughts. Not to money, not about traveling, and not about work or schedules either. He thought of his kids. Keely, Meg, and Cal had gone with him on a bunch of cool adventures together. They didn't *always* get along, sure, but in the end, all had appreciated the trips and what they had learned and experienced individually, and as a family, from each adventure.

It was much more fun, even when you're busy, to be traveling with someone you can share the experience with, explore the area and enjoy it together. A warm rush of gratitude for his good fortune to be father to his kids flowed from his head and heart down through his toes.

Alex smiled to himself, perked up, and clicked another couple of options on screen, then paused suddenly. He pulled up an email message, glanced at it, then picked up the phone on his desk and dialed his contact at the hotel in Moorea. Though it was still early in the day there, luckily, Montcalm staff had already arrived as a large group was checking out and leaving at 7 am, Tahiti time (that's what the local time zone was called.)

To his amazement, his plan worked: a few minutes into the phone call, everything was arranged, surprisingly easily. Alex was now one last step away from turning his attention - for the next few hours at least - to other important details directly related to his job. *He did after all have to sell some software to pay for all this family travel around the world!* So, he got busy and returned his energies to doing just that. But first, he texted a message to Jessica, who, as a very organized and tech-savvy Millennial surely had him stored as a 'favorite' contact in her phone.

Hi Jess! Can you call me as soon as you have a break from class? Thanks, Alex!

Chapter 9

Filling in the holes

Monday, October 17 10:55 am

Alex saw the call come in from Jessica's cell number, but couldn't answer the pop-up notification on his own phone because he was already on hold for the principal at Keely's school. He let Jessica's call go to voicemail, because he had to make sure he reached Mr. Sarlevich ASAP. He didn't know him very well, as they'd just met briefly during the orientation in late summer then again in passing during the student-staff-family "Welcome Back" barbecue dinner event the first week of school. Now, Alex needed to have a brief conversation with the Madison principal about the Websters' travel plans. His goal? To gain agreement for Keely to complete some sort of special makeup assignments during the trip - given her absence during the week after Thanksgiving.

Middle school was a lot more serious about academics than when he'd gone to junior high, Alex thought, *and that's a good thing!* Uniforms were just the start of those differences. Madison was the first school in the district (though others had followed their lead) to require kids to wear specified clothing options each day rather than the motley assortment running from high preteen fashion to t-shirts and torn jeans. School administrators also questioned kids missing days for reasons other than sickness, but the huge saving grace for Keely was that she was such an outstanding student. Alex had been fairly studious in junior high (and elementary school) himself, but that was 30 years ago, and he had not quite performed to the level of excellence of his two daughters, for sure.

He was a bit nervous about this call, though optimistic too, following his previous conversation with another principal, the one at Meg and Cal's school, Mrs. Davenport, had been cordial. She had given her approval for the two youngest Websters to go on the family trip, though she did ask Alex to 'clear' their absences with their respective teachers, outreach he had already initiated via email.

One of them, Meg's teacher Ms. Halamea, had already sent her enthusiastic approval ("Sounds awesome, wish I could go!"), yet he still awaited Cal's teacher Mr. Tallman's response. Alex was hopeful that he could wrap up things today with Mr. Tallman as well as the Madison principal on a plan for make-up work by the kids during the time away. He had already gotten preliminary approval via a quick email exchange with Keely's home room and first period teacher, Mr. Chen, but to "cover all the bases" and include her other teachers for the rest of the multi-period school schedule, he had to get approval from Mr. Sarlevich first.

Suddenly, the music stopped and Principal Sarlevich was on the phone: "Hi, this is Mark Sarlevich," came the deep, friendly voice. Alex quickly introduced himself as well, though he'd already done the same to the school secretary a few minutes before.

"Oh, sure, Keely's dad, right?" the principal answered.

"Yes, and I'm calling to follow up on a conversation I had with her homeroom teacher, Mr. Chen, earlier this morning," Alex began.

"I hope nothing's wrong?" Mr. Sarlevich said, but Alex quickly explained otherwise.

"Oh no, to the contrary, I have a special opportunity with my job that just sprang up to do some work in a very interesting place. It is a short-term assignment in the country of French Polynesia. The good news is, it involves only about nine days away from home and some of it would take place during the Thanksgiving week holidays. I really would like to bring my kids along on this trip, but we won't be back to Tacoma until the following weekend. I am prepared - and I'm sure Keely is as well - to make sure she gets all required work done, special assignments as well as regular ones, during our time away. Is that possible?"

The principal hesitated for a moment before replying, then first asked, "Have you cleared the absence with Keely's other teachers?"

"Not yet," Alex said, "But I'd like to do so next if you approve."

"Hmmm...Keely's an outstanding student. How about if I send out a quick message to all of her teachers letting her know your plans, and that you've advised Mr. Chen and me of your commitment (and Keely's) to get appropriate make-up homework completed during her week-long absence? That will make it easier for you, and I'm fairly sure your plan will be OK with them. But she does have to do the work they assign her, Mr. Webster, or her teachers will surely mark her down for the absences and missed assignments."

"Oh, I am 100% confident she will!" said Alex, knowing his daughter's dedication to schoolwork, while away on vacation trips or even when home sick from school - which was very few times - in the past. "And thanks so much Mr. Sarlevich. Really appreciate your consideration of this request. It means a lot, and on that note, would you please ask the teachers not to mention our plans to Keely just yet? We've only just arranged the details over the weekend and into today - I haven't yet had a chance to tell Keely or her sister and brother about the trip yet, and I want to surprise them with the news tonight if I can."

"Absolutely, Mr. Webster, we'll keep it on the down-low for now. And I envy you all getting to explore such an interesting place! I'll look forward to seeing some cool photos and stories from Keely when you return!"

"You got it!" Alex replied, before pressing the "*End*" button on his phone. *Nice, reasonable guy*, he thought about the principal and his sensible manner. *We're lucky to have him at Madison.*

Just then, he saw an email notification pop up on his computer screen. It was a reply to his message re: Cal missing school, sent earlier to Mr. Tallman. He quickly clicked on the link with the teacher's response.

"*Hi Mr. Webster. Thanks for your email and for your courtesy in reaching out to advise of your family's travel plans. I'm fine with Cal missing a few days of school, but he will have to complete all of his homework that's assigned before Thanksgiving and I'll have a couple assignments to give him for the week after as well. Most important, we have a special project starting this week that is due for completion just before our winter holiday break. Cal can tell you all about it - and I suspect your trip might just give him some ideas to help him with it too. Can't wait to hear all about it when you and the family return, but meanwhile, please make sure Cal remembers to bring his assignments with him - he sometimes forgets, as I think you are aware! But he's really a great kid and a good student. I like having him in my class. Best regards, Bob Tallman.*

Alex grinned to himself, as it was clear Cal's teacher already 'knew' his son well, didn't he? In the short month and a half since school began, he'd already observed some of Cal's "quirks" first hand. But the key point about Cal was: he was kind and considerate - even if a bit 'out there' or unusual in his interests and behaviors compared to other students his age.

Alex heaved an audible sigh of relief, glad that the kids' "passes" from school for the trip to Moorea were all but finalized. Now he had one more key trip planning task to complete - but it would have to wait until after his next work meeting, which was starting in four minutes. He put his headset on for the phone call to come, and the "making money" part of his work week had begun.

Chapter 10

And one more makes 5 WWWs!

Monday, October 17 11:55 am

Just about the same time Jess finished her sandwich and fruit, took a last sip of her coffee, pulled together her notes and textbook, and put her phone in her backpack to get ready to head to her next class, Alex played back the voicemail she'd sent him earlier. He resolved to try her number one more time before going to grab lunch downstairs. He pushed the green "Start" icon on his phone to complete the call and heard it ring a couple of times. Alex was about to give up and reluctantly leave another message when Jess answered on the fourth ring.

"Hello, Alex!" she said, actually a bit out of breath after fumbling in her bag to find and answer her phone. She stopped walking, midway up the small hill that led to her next class on the far side of campus from the cafe.

"Hi Jess, so glad we connected! How's school going today?"

"Fine, just was studying and taking an early lunch break. I'm heading to my next class now, is everything all right? I saw your message earlier...I'm going to be picking up Meg and Cal this afternoon at the normal time, and Keely gets home after her band practice around 5:30...any changes I should know about?"

Alex realized the kids' nanny was likely a bit nervous about the reason for his earlier outreach, and he felt a little embarrassed. "Hey, Jess, I'm sorry if my message this morning had you concerned. I didn't mean to do that at all...it's just, there's lots going on at work right now and I was short of time when I called you. Then, when you called me back after my text, I was on another phone call and I couldn't talk to you. But it's all good - and I'm hoping that it will be even better...."

"That IS a relief! Thanks for the explanation."

Alex continued: "So here's the thing. I have a business trip coming up right around Thanksgiving, and I'll be gone for about nine days afterwards. I've worked out a whole bunch of details already and I'm going to ask the kids to come along on this trip. It's to a very interesting place - Moorea, near Tahiti, in French Polynesia - and I think they'd really enjoy it, plus learn a lot. I haven't told them my plans yet, but I have worked it out (for the most part) with their teachers, principals, etc. You know, make-up assignments, homework, all that stuff. We'll be gone starting Thanksgiving Day, a little more than six weeks from now, until the Sunday morning a week and a half later."

"Oh," Jess answered, stopped now at the top of the small hill near the entrance to the hall where her next class would be starting in 10 minutes. "So, I guess you won't need me during that time, right?" She felt a quick pang of loneliness, and a bit of envy of the family's destination - there were no classes that whole week after Thanksgiving at UOC - and she wasn't sure what she was going to do. And it was surely going to be a lot colder and rainier here than Tahiti! *Guess I'll sit around and watch lots of movies? And study...ugh!* she thought, feeling just a bit sorry for herself...

"Actually," Alex said, "that's why I wanted to talk to you...we are staying at the resort where I'll be working on a software installation, for most of the days we're there, but not all. How would you like to join us on the trip, Jess? You can help make sure Keely, Meg, and Cal stay active and out of trouble during the days while I work. Unless you have school or other commitments, which I would totally understand if you did, of course...or maybe you've got your own travel plans for Thanksgiving? We haven't even talked about the schedule for the holidays this year yet, so please forgive me if I'm assuming too much!"

Jess was about to answer when Alex added a few more details. "Oh, and I was able to make some special arrangements with the hotel to stay in their family bungalow while we're there. It's got two main bedrooms and two bathrooms plus a small attached bedroom on one side. You'd have your own room and bed, though you'd still have to share a bathroom with the girls. Cal and I will stay in the other bedroom, also with its own bath. We'll have a small fridge and ceiling fans in each main bedroom - but no air conditioning, but it looks like there are doors to the outside from each too. Oh, and we won't be over the water as you may have seen in the travel magazines, but we will be right near it, and it's going to be warm water and beautiful beaches. We're talking temps in the 70's and 80's this time of year. This resort is nice, on a small bay, and it has just received some needed renovations. The management of a French firm, Montcalm Hotels, purchased and is renovating the property, part of which involves an installation of new software from my company." Alex paused, realizing he'd probably been talking too much. Not hearing a reply on the other end of the call, he continued. "I'm sorry to go into such detail...so do you need to think about it, or maybe you can't make it, Jess? And that would be fine too, just - "

"Are you kidding? That would be AWESOME, Alex!" Jess was thrilled. *What a fantastic way to spend the Thanksgiving holiday!*

"That's GREAT, Jess!" answered Alex, both relieved and excited that the New Zealander was able to join them on this adventure to the South Seas. "So glad you'll be able to be there with us. I'll have more details to share tonight - oh, and I've found really good airfare for the kids and I've got a bunch of spare miles in my frequent flyer account which will mostly cover your airfare at no cost, except for some taxes, which I'll take care of, no big deal, as well as the meals and of course hotel expenses other than breakfast and dinner - those are included as part of our room with my work contract. You'll just need your own spending money for souvenirs and stuff. Not sure what there is to buy over there yet...but I guess we'll find out, right? Anyway, our lodging and main meals are taken care of by my customer, the resort company. Of course, you'll be paid your normal salary and have plenty of time off too while we're in Moorea."

Alex remembered the key point he had to make. "So, that's about it for now, but I need to ask one big favor, OK?"

"Sure, Alex, what is it?" Jess asked.

"Don't tell the kids yet...I want to surprise them tonight at dinner."

"No problem, I'll zip my lip until you make the announcement...it should be a very fun dinner conversation for sure!"

Ending the call, Alex looked at the screen in front of him in his office. *And that...is that!* he thought to himself, very pleased that their trip plans were already happily springing into motion after such a short period of time to prepare. *Now we just have to figure out together what we're all going to do while we're in Moorea (or just me, when I'm not working, at least) and what to bring along on the trip...hmmm. We'll need to put together a worksheet and checklist to cover all the plans, logistics, questions...*

Chapter 11

Big pizza, bigger plans

Monday, October 17 3:45 pm

With the travel details mostly taken care of, tonight he'd be ready to announce the surprise trip.

Alex was excited, and he continued to muse on possible activities and other details. He wasn't too worried about what they would do once on Moorea. He had read up a little on the activities around the island, but no matter what, he realized, they'd enjoy the warm, calm waters, sandy beaches, and snorkeling through the colorful reefs. Of course, he would be working for much of the time there - certainly during the weekdays. Still, there would be plenty of opportunities on the first weekend and during the evenings for other activities like hiking or otherwise exploring the island's eight mountain peaks, shopping in the local stores (they'd all love doing that), and seeing what they could in drives around various local sites. But the water was going to be the key to most of their adventures, for sure. At least that's what he surmised from the online guides and brochures. They probably wouldn't have time for shark feeding or anything like that. Surfing or body-surfing maybe? Probably...Meg had learned how to surf in Hawaii, and she and Cal enjoyed Boogie-boarding. Keely of course was a super-strong swimmer, a little more confident than her younger sister and brother in ocean waters, but they were all proficient at most things aquatic in nature.

When you traveled like the Websters...it was a process. The family always had fun, but it followed an organized plan, almost always. Part of that plan would be to put together a *Trip Page* using a simple but wide-ranging summary of its details (Alex jokingly called it the *"W4"* - or *Worldwide Websters Way*), with an overview of major dates and details, including flight, hotel and ground transport info, and a comprehensive cost & contacts spreadsheet. It was something Alex had become fond of doing after wrestling with all the various details surrounding the family's first "complex" trip to the UK and France 18 months ago. He had the template stored in his home computer and he'd use it again for this trip. It was very helpful for not just their own preparation but also to communicate their plans to all who needed to know, *most of all, himself!* he thought with a chuckle. But first, he needed to wrap up his workday and get his job duties done.

Alex had nearly completed the call reports for his two customer meetings earlier that morning and afternoon, but before he got back to them, he took a look at his upcoming calendar for Tuesday and the rest of the week. *No proposals to do right now*, Alex thought, but he did have some follow-up required for one of his client calls, and that might lead to a proposal, likely next week. He decided to set that task aside for now, but while he finished up the call reports for the day, he thought about dinner plans.

A good first step would be pizza and salad for the meal. Alex texted Jess to let her know that he'd pick up two pies on the way home from their favorite place - *South Sound Pizza* (they called it *SSP*), and asked her to put together a salad, which she fixed quite often for the kids anyway. An hour and 15 minutes later, it was time to head home.

Freeway traffic being fairly light (again, like that morning) for a Monday, Alex stopped off right before reaching home to pick up the pizza he'd ordered before leaving Seattle, and only missed the restaurant's "ready" time by five minutes. That was a minor miracle given the growing and often unpredictable traffic congestion between Seattle and downtown Tacoma. He pulled up in front of the Webster house just after 6:30 pm.

When Alex walked in the door, his heavy work backpack in one hand, and the pizza boxes in the other, the two younger kids were watching television or doing their homework (he couldn't tell at first glance which was the priority), and Keely must have been upstairs in her room. Jess waved from the dining room, where she was completing her own college homework, as Alex walked by.

"Yum...pizza!" said Cal as he and Meg came into the kitchen, hovering around the table in the center while their dad set down the boxes and opened each up for easier access. Jess walked into the room and pulled five plates out of the cabinet. She then placed a large prepared salad bowl next to the pizzas and opened two bottles of salad dressing. Napkins were next, and soon they were all scarfing down slices of either pesto, mushroom, and peppers (Jess was mostly a vegetarian but ate eggs, dairy, and seafood so called herself a "pescatarian"), or pepperoni, sausage, olive, and onion. All thin crust.

Keely came bounding down the stairs. "Hi Dad!" She breezed up behind Jess - who had selected a slice and some salad for her plate. Keely added a serving of each to hers then turned around and opened the fridge to get a can of sparkling water. "Anybody else want seltzer?"

"Sure, I'll have one," replied Cal.

"Me too," Meg added.

Jess nodded and smiled. "I'll have one also, thanks, Keel."

Alex reached into the fridge for a bottle of beer. In this case it was a dark, hop-heavy IPA brewed in nearby Gig Harbor. Popping the top with a bottle opener from the drawer, he faced the kids and Jess, all now sitting around the kitchen table. "Time for an announcement!" he cried.

Everyone stopped talking, not sure what to make of Alex's remark or loud voice. He looked serious at first and began on a stoic note as well. "I found out some news last Friday, about my job. Today I learned a bit more, and I thought I should come home and tell you all about it. You deserve to know."

"What's the news dad?" said Keely, frowning a bit and glancing at the others. "What's going on, did you lose your job or something?"

"Haha, just kidding you guys!" Alex answered, receiving a bunch of relieved expressions in return.

He pointed at the whiteboard on the wall, where his clue was still scribbled in the corner from earlier that day. "Actually, Keely there isn't a problem - except I need to travel over the Thanksgiving holiday."

The three children's faces now showed a combination of dismay and disbelief. Meg jumped in first with, "What??"

Cal shook his head and said, "Wow, that's too bad!"

Keely chimed in, "Oh, that's a bummer!"

Alex smiled inside at the long faces and completed the second part of his sentence with "And...the best part of *this* trip is that you are ALL coming along, and we're going somewhere lush, warm and beautiful!"

"I knew it!" exclaimed Keely, "I figured out your clues from this morning, it's somewhere in the South Pacific Ocean, right?"

"Great guess, Keel, but a little too general. Here's where we're going." He pointed to the side of a small series of dots on their huge world map on the wall.

Alex's finger was aimed at a spot in the Pacific almost directly below Hawaii, but instead of being near the Tropic of Cancer, it was south of the equator, just a little above the Tropic of Capricorn. The kids and Jess crowded around and Alex urged them to get closer to read the name "*Tahiti*" on the map, noting as he slid his finger a smidge to the left to indicate an unmarked island just to its west.

"*That's* where we're going. *Moorea*. We leave Thanksgiving Day, and we'll be gone for nine days!"

"That's AWESOME Dad!" Cal exclaimed.

Both Meg and Jess beamed. Keely looked a bit concerned, and Alex was curious. "What's wrong, Keel?"

Keely stole a glance at Jess. "I'll just miss Jess while we're gone, and it's Thanksgiving and stuff. Where will she go while we're gone?"

Jess stepped forward. "Thanks, Keel, I really appreciate your support, and even better, I know exactly where I'll be at Thanksgiving... (her voice rising) - I'LL BE WITH YOU GUYS. I'M COMING TOO!"

The kids were stunned. They looked at their dad, all at once. He grinned like the famous Cheshire Cat.

"YAY!!!" they yelled in almost perfect harmony.

All three kids hugged Jess, and excited questions followed nonstop.

"When do we leave?"

"How long will it take to get there?"

"What about school?"

Alex waved both his hands to stem the tide of eager inquiries for a moment.

"All great questions and in order...as I said, we leave on Thanksgiving Day, from SeaTac airport, in the early afternoon. We will take two flights each way, one direct to Los Angeles, about 2 1/2 hours, then another of nine hours or so to Papeete, Tahiti."

"Taheeeeteee." Meg said drawing out the musical sound of the word.

Her father continued. "After that we'll take a van to a ferry and then that ferry will jet us across to the island of Moorea. We'll then be picked up and delivered to our hotel nearby. It's called Montcalm Resort, and it's right on a lagoon off the ocean. Here's some pictures of Moorea and the hotel."

Alex pulled out a file from his backpack next to the table, and showed printed copies of some of the web pages he'd accessed earlier. He handed them around to the others. They took turns looking at the pictures and details, with lots of "oohs,", "aaahs," and "wows." Clearly, this was going to be a popular trip.

"But what about school, Dad?" asked Keely.

"Yeah, Dad, I've got a special project to do," added Meg.

"So do I!" said Cal.

"Whoa, whoa, I told you I'd answer your questions, and that's already a bunch!" Alex said. "I've spoken with your teachers, principals, etc. You are all excused from school the week after Thanksgiving - but you MUST complete all your assigned work and yes, I know at least one of you (two? All three?)," he said, looking at the raised hands, "have special projects as well, and maybe you can do some work on them during our trip?"

Meg looked at Keely. They were both starting to get ideas on just how this trip might play into their school project plans, but neither knew of the other's specific assignments.

Alex turned to Cal. "From my conversation with Mr. Tallman, it sounds like our trip could help with your special project, Cal. Tell me about it."

Cal proceeded to share the details of his assignment, then Meg and Keely did the same for theirs.

Alex, Jess, and the kids were all excited. Especially the kids. Not only would they be going on a super-fun trip to the tropics, but they'd be able to keep up on their schoolwork and possibly tie it all in with their special projects too. *Maybe*, thought Cal, *this will help me bring up my grades for this term?*

Alex looked at his watch. It was already heading towards eight o' clock. He was tired after a long, albeit exciting day, and the beer and pizza combined with his general exhaustion to weigh on his eyelids.

"Hey guys, I know you have lots more questions. For now, just remember this: we're all going, there are a few more details to arrange and discuss, but we'll start planning the trip, figuring out what to bring, all that stuff, soon. Meanwhile, time now for bed - or for finishing up your homework and then bedtime. And don't forget to talk with your teachers tomorrow about your plans. They already know the basics, but over the next couple of weeks you'll need to make sure you work out all the requirements for your assignments while we're gone."

Alex turned to Jessica: "Jess, so excited that you'll be joining us, it'll be a blast." As she smiled and the kids nodded their agreement, he rose from the table and rinsed his plate and glass in the sink, then put them into the dishwasher. "Good night, everybody!" he said.

Meg and Cal and Jess all said "Goodnight!" together to Alex as he started upstairs. Keely grinned and replied "*Mauru'uru*, Dad!"

Alex turned around halfway up to the landing, in mock surprise, then answered, "*Aita pea pea*, Keel!" That left his oldest daughter giggling, while the other three looked quizzically at each other, then back at Keely.

"Don't worry, I'll explain tomorrow." She grabbed her notebook to go upstairs and finish her homework.

Alex undressed in his room, opening up his laptop before he climbed into bed. Checking his office mail one last time, he saw there was a confirmation of the details that he'd discussed with the hotel staff in Moorea. Plans were all set for the five of them to stay in the family bungalow. The manager there had also shared a list of some key things to remember to bring on the trip, as well as a few specific details about the French Polynesian currency, exchange rates, and the Tahiti-Moorea ferry's updated schedule for November and December sailings. He'd also included a list of amenities and classes available at the resort. And they had bicycles for rent!

Once a competitive swimmer and water polo player, Alex was an avid cyclist too now, and he'd completely forgotten, with all the focus on the kids and his work duties, to ask about bicycle availability at the Montcalm. They also had kayaks and body boards for rent there and at various places around the island. Plus, as is common in many tropical destinations, there were numerous tours available by water or land (or both), including snorkeling and SCUBA trips, sailing and sunset cruises, and hiking and jeep excursions to many of the higher, more rugged parts of the island. Even opportunities to go swimming with sharks!

There would be no shortage of things to do over (or down) there, Alex thought, *but we'll need to watch our budget.* Alex's head started nodding off in front of the screen, despite his exciting new discoveries. He closed the laptop and set it on his bedside table, switching off the light. Not too long thereafter, Jess left for her apartment, and the younger members of the Webster household also settled down for the night, though it was a very excited and happy house indeed!

Chapter 12

Groundwork on the home front

October 25, about one month before the trip

The last week of October in the Webster household was even busier than usual for the already active family. And not just because of the exciting trip looming on the horizon. Alex had lots of team meetings, sales calls, and proposals to work on for other clients, even as he continued to fine-tune arrangements for the LodgeSoft implementation at the Montcalm resort in Moorea. Despite the demands of the important business project, he tried to set aside time each day to focus on addressing the myriad details of the family trip that would be a big part of it around the Thanksgiving holiday.

While their dad stayed on top of his job responsibilities, Keely, Meg, Cal, and Jess were fully involved in classes, fall sports, and other activities. With Halloween coming up, there were parties planned this week at school, and Keely had one to attend at a friend's house on Saturday too. Of course, she still had swim practice every day of the week except Sunday, and even had competed in a two-day meet the prior weekend in Seattle. But no further events were planned from now until January, so the coast was clear as far as swimming was concerned, and she'd promised her coach that she'd swim (and possibly hike) every day while the family was away in Moorea to make up for practices missed during her absence. School preparations were not a problem for Keely...she'd already discussed her assignments and make-up work with her teachers, even though the trip was still almost a month away. *Organized and driven, as always!*

After Alex had announced the trip details the prior week, each of the Worldwide Websters (+1, Jess) had started to think about what their adventure in French Polynesia might be like, and how they were going to get ready to go in late November. Keely had pointed out the following morning at breakfast that, obviously, the people of the area spoke French, which she was studying at school, and also the native

Tahitian language was still very prominent in the culture, as expected. She shared with Jess, Meg, and Cal the riddles that her dad had puzzled her with the morning before the big announcement, noting that once she figured out (after he explained it) that the language he used was Tahitian, she had searched online to 'decode' his words.

Aita pea pea meant "*No Problem*" or "*Not to worry*," which was a phrase that was used with similar intent in lots of places, and evidently it was also very common in Tahiti, Moorea, and throughout the Society Islands and all of the country of French Polynesia. This phrase was often the answer to someone saying "*Mauru'uru*," in Tahitian, or translated to English, "*Thank you*."

Keely had just started to dig into the language to find more key words and phrases to help get ready for the trip. Now in her second year of French at school, she was hoping for a real chance to try out her language skills with native speakers after a very weak effort to do so during their trip to Paris a year and a half earlier. That she'd have such an opportunity to practice '*français*' with fluent speakers pleased her French teacher, Mr. Borgan, very much, or "*beaucoup*." In fact, he had given her a challenge - to research and write a short paper on an issue surrounding the culture of Moorea or French Polynesia and share it with the class - as part of her make-up work for missing school during the trip.

As for Meg, she was thrilled when she heard about the languages they'd be hearing (and hopefully speaking) on their adventure. She checked out a book at the school library to explore a few other cultural details of Moorea, Tahiti, and the area around that part of the world in those first few days after her dad's 'big reveal.' *It all fit perfectly with her special project assignment!* She was eager to research a few colloquialisms of the Tahitian language and culture to share as part of her presentation, and Ms. Halamea had been very enthusiastic about her final choice.

Aita pea pea seemed to have a fairly complex history and meaning, as the fifth grader had noted in her submission on the topic as the initial part of the assignment. She had just started working on the presentation portion, which was due in about 2 1/2 weeks. The audio-visual part of it - and of course Meg would be going for the extra credit offered, as she always did - would need to be completed while she was on the trip, coming up in less than a month. That meant she had to have a video camera, but no problem there, she could borrow her dad's camcorder. For what exactly, she didn't yet know, but she'd figure it out once they were there.

Cal had been super excited about the trip right from the start. He thought it was great to be going on what he saw as a fantastic voyage to a warm, tropical paradise. He'd explored various websites with photos, videos, and facts on Moorea and French Polynesia. He wasn't called *The Oracle* by his family for no reason - partly in jest, but quite deservedly actually. Cal was really smart about facts and trivia related to lots of topics, especially for a kid who wouldn't see his 10th birthday for five more months!

In fact, he was already advising the family on key things to remember - and not forget to observe - when they flew to the country in the middle of the South Pacific and explored around the islands of Moorea and Tahiti. "They have whales there, Dad, humpbacks, just like Hawaii! But they tend to be there only until early November, then they go back to Antarctica, so we might miss most of them during our trip."

To his older sister as they shopped at a store one Saturday: "Did you know, Keely, that the average high temperature during the month of November in Moorea is 83 degrees F, and the low around 72?" To Meg and Jess around the breakfast table one morning, a few days later: "We better be prepared...the rainy season normally starts around the time we get there, but it pretty much rains a lot in Moorea anyway. Oh well, it supposedly clears up quickly and is sunny and hot and humid most of the time. We better bring good rain jackets...and sunscreen, and bug spray!"

Cal's school project was also relevant, it turned out, to the family's trip plans. The fourth grader had figured it would be fun to study up on local Tahitian traditions and find a holiday he could feature in his special presentation. Right now, sitting at the kitchen table doing his homework, he was still leaning toward how they celebrated Christmas, even though that choice seemed kinda boring, but he still needed to look some details up on other holidays there. He had to hurry, because Mr. Tallman's deadline to choose a topic had actually been the prior day. Cal shuddered as he recalled how the teacher had reminded them all in class right before the final bell - giving them one last, extra day to get their topics turned in *or face a one-grade reduction!*

Yikes! Cal thought. He jumped to the family's computer and typed "*Moorea holidays,*" into the search engine. *Well, that didn't work very well...*he groaned to himself. The screen filled with links to vacation trip packages and other details. "*Holidays*" meant "*Vacations*" in Moorea, I guess, he thought. *That's interesting!*

Just then, Jess - sitting in the adjacent dining room - said somewhat loudly, "What's wrong, Cal? Need help on your homework?"

"No, I just couldn't find what I was looking for at first. I'll try something else. No problem, Jess!" He didn't want Jess to know he was late with his assignment and tell his dad. *Then he'd be in real trouble.*

This time, Cal typed "*Holiday traditions in French Polynesia*", hoping for a better result. His eyes were drawn to the link onscreen for "*French Polynesia Holidays and Festivals*" and he clicked on it eagerly. Scanning the list, he saw a few vaguely familiar names for holidays as on the board at school, like "*Carnival*" and some sort of sports festival. But what really captured his attention was this: "*Heiva i Tahiti.*"

Its description said it was the biggest of all Tahitian festivals. It began on June 29, with French Polynesia's *Autonomy* celebrations, and extended until July 14, "*when French territories celebrate Bastille Day.*"Papeete's waterfront *To'ata Square* was apparently the center of the action. Cal kept reading: "*People from across French Polynesia's five archipelagos take part in Heiva i Tahiti's countless sporting competitions, beauty pageants, parades, and food tastings.*"

Wow, Cal marveled to himself, *a two-week long party! He read further: "*There are also competitions in stone weight lifting, palm tree climbing, and coconut cracking. Colorfully dressed Tahitian dance troupes perform to traditional music on To'ata Square's open amphitheater and stage as vendors sell their handicrafts nearby.*"

This tradition seemed to be more Tahitian than Moorean, but it did say people came from all the nearby islands to join the competitions and events. Cal had already figured out what "archipelago" meant when he first had looked up Moorea in the encyclopedia at school. French Polynesia included more than 100 islands, of which the Society Islands, including Moorea and Tahiti, were just one part.

"*Heiva i Tahiti* it is!" Cal exclaimed, with huge relief. He quickly grabbed his notebook and wrote down the key details. *He couldn't forget to turn in his topic choice to Mr. Tallman tomorrow morning!*

Chapter 13

Halloween prep and a view of The Bounty

October 29, 6:30 pm

Jess, Keely, and Meg stood with Cal at their kitchen table. All wore t-shirts they didn't care about, torn, tattered, and Meg's covered with old paint. Their hands were mostly coated with goo. Why? Because they had finally gotten around to carving the pumpkins their dad had purchased more than a week ago for Halloween. Next to the pumpkins was a large bowl that was getting filled up with seeds as the 'excavation' of each continued. Luckily, they had newspapers on the table where they deposited most of the stringy guts from the orange squashes.

It was a messy business indeed, but Halloween night was coming up in two days and they had kicked off their Friday late afternoon with the necessary pumpkin-carving chore. Since she had a party to go to on Saturday at 7 pm, and had swim practice earlier on that same day, Keely planned to stay home tonight and watch a movie with her brother and sister and dad and go to bed at a decent hour. Normally, she'd set up a sleepover at a friend's or have one or two over to her house, at least on weekends when she didn't have to compete in a swim meet.

As their dad was finishing up an important work report, Jess had stayed a few extra hours for the evening, with plans to head home to her apartment later as she had to study all weekend for upcoming mid-term exams. She reached over and turned on the oven to get it ready to roast the seeds. Meanwhile, each of the kids was fully involved clearing out their chosen squash, so it looked like it would still be a while before she could add the spices on top and get them roasting into the treats they all enjoyed.

Keely was near the bottom of her pumpkin and scooping out the last of its innards. One final big spoonful of strings and pulp, a few seeds pulled off and dropped into the bowl, and she took a pen from the table and sketched a scary face across the surface. Next, she picked up one of the special knives from the carving set they'd been using for a few years now. It was getting kind of beat up and bent (*mostly 'cause of Cal*, she thought to herself.) Cal wasn't the most careful kid in the world when it came to things like pumpkin carving, or for that matter, other things too. *But he was certainly fun to have around - most of the time* - she reflected while rolling her eyes.

She glanced at her little brother's pumpkin, which was tall and skinny. *I have NO idea what he's going to do with that one*, she thought, with some serious doubt that it would turn out looking like anything but something out of a horror movie (and an unintentional one, at that!)

Meg, meanwhile, was also finishing up the scraping and pulling part of the task and had already sketched a very unusual face on her pumpkin. She too, like her sister, went right to work with the small, thin knives and files from the kit. *It'll be a masterpiece!* she thought. And based on her oft-proven artistic talents, it probably would.

Jess eyed Cal warily. He watched as his sisters carefully cut into and around the traced 'faces' on their pumpkins. When he reached across the table to pick up one of the knives, Jess came to his side.

"Hey Cal, how about I help you out a little with the cutting part?"

"OK," he replied, a bit relieved because he wasn't really confident about how well he could use that knife on the slippery surface. He decided to draw what ended up being a 'crazy' face on his pumpkin, and hair with multiple streaks of black marker down the sides. Then he added glasses. Jess looked for a moment at his 'creation', took a deep breath and started the process of cutting it out, while the girls busily carved through theirs.

15 minutes later, Cal's masterpiece was complete. And, they all agreed (especially Cal) it was actually kinda cool, even out of this world cool! Cal explained, quite seriously, to Jess and the others that it might be unworldly looking, but some of the statues and masks they would soon see on their trip to Moorea were even more so!

"Of course you said that," Keely replied wryly.

Meg added, "Sheesh, nerd!"

Cal was irritated. "Well, they ARE!" he protested.

Jess quickly put her arm around his shoulders, commenting reassuringly, "Absolutely, Cal! And I can't wait to see some of those things when we get there. Don't they have a museum that we can visit?"

"Yes, but there are also tours that we can probably take from our hotel up into the mountains, where there's a viewpoint, called a 'Bellva...belva..Belvedeer'. And near that are some ancient burial sites and stuff."

"Sounds really interesting," said Jess with a smile.

Cal beamed with pride at the recognition and respect given his exhaustive knowledge and research completed thus far.

"OK!" Jess announced, surveying their little garden of orange statues, er pumpkin heads while grabbing a small bag from across the table. "Look at these awesome jack-o-lanterns! Let's get these candles in them and put them outside - or should we wait until Halloween night?"

Keely and Meg both nodded at the latter suggestion.

"Probably wait on the candles, just so they don't get all burned up before the trick or treaters come. But we can put them outside now anyway," Keely said.

"And then light the candles on Sunday," Meg added.

"I agree," said Cal.

So that was that. They carefully reached in, with Jess assisting, and placed small, squat votives inside each carved masterpiece. Pumpkins done, each of the kids picked up their creations and carried them carefully outside, each set on the stairs or railing of the Websters' front porch. Jess cleaned up the kitchen table, folding up and throwing away the newspaper in the process.

"Yuck!" she exclaimed as some of the leftover goop dropped on her pants. Then she spread the separated seeds out on a couple of large sheet pans, sprinkled some garlic, pepper and a bit of salt on top, and loaded them into the oven. With the pumpkin seeds roasting, Jess opened the fridge and removed a 2-liter bottle of soda. The Webster children generally didn't drink soda pop too often, but Friday night was special. Reaching into the freezer, Jess removed a half gallon carton of French vanilla ice cream and pulled a special scoop out of the large middle drawer next to the sink.

"Who wants root beer floats?!" she exclaimed.

"Me!" said all three Websters with gusto, then a fainter fourth voice came from the den, where their dad was apparently finishing up his project.

"Me too!" Alex answered.

Two minutes later, Alex walked into the kitchen, grinning. "Smells good in here! Thanks, Jess for staying to help," as he sniffed the pleasant aroma of the roasting pumpkin seeds coming from the oven. Glancing at the ice cream carton, Alex exclaimed, "Vanilla! What if I told you guys that vanilla is one of the main crops grown on Moorea?"

"Really?!" said Keely. Meg, Jess, and Cal were all very surprised too.

"Yes, in fact, while we're on the island, I thought it might be fun to go to a vanilla farm and try some right from the source while we're there, and maybe bring some home to share with our friends as a souvenir of our trip."

"Sounds like a great idea," Jess agreed as she spooned out the ice cream into five individual glasses, then poured root beer from the bottle into each, stopping just before it foamed over their rims.

Each person took one float-filled glass and headed into the living room, where the TV was on. Alex said "How about we watch an old movie?" and the three Webster children all groaned at once.

"Daaaaad..." Meg said, "Do we have to?"

"Can't we watch something new, and exciting, like "The Brothers Grimm?" said Keely.

"No way, creepy!" said Meg.

Cal voiced his choice: "Harry Potter and the Goblet of Fire!"

"You already saw that in the theater," Keely reminded him.

Their dad jumped back in to the conversation. "What if we watched a movie that was filmed in Moorea? Or at least, near it?"

"Sure, but if it's lousy, we get the right to switch, OK Dad?" Keely replied.

"Agreed." Alex pulled a DVD off the shelf above the large 36" TV. He slid it into the player, while Jess picked up the case.

"*The Bounty*?" she asked, looking at Alex.

"Yep, I rented it, and it's based on a true story - maybe dramatized a bit of course - that took place right in Tahiti and all around the islands there."

"Maybe I'll stay for just a bit to check it out with you guys," Jess replied.

Five minutes later, the oven beeped that the pumpkin seeds were ready, and after parsing the crispy, fragrant snacks out into a few small bowls, and with root beer floats in hand, the Worldwide Websters (+1) all sat down to watch the fifth version of the movie based on the true story of Lieutenant William Bligh, his first mate Fletcher Christian, and the sailors of the *HMS Bounty*. As they watched it - or at least part of it, including its interesting costumes, scenery, and especially the dancing and drama that unfolded after the British navy ship landed in Tahiti. They also got a nice view from the film's local shots and sets of the type of landscape they'd see again, in less than a month.

Jess said her whispered goodbyes for the weekend to return to her apartment midway through the movie, with the rest of the family except Keely already passed out in front of the TV. (Meg and Cal from fatigue and boredom, Alex as he quite often did after his long commute, then long day at work, then the EXTRA-long commute home from Seattle which was unfortunately typical for most traffic-clogged Friday afternoons.)

Two days later, as they were about to prepare for activities on Halloween night, Keely, who had finished watching the film on her own while everyone else slept through it on Friday, asked her dad a question.

"You know, it must have been a huge shock, for both the Tahitians and the British sailors, to be almost "crashed" together like that with so little real understanding between them or their really different cultures. Why did the sailors think they could act so out of control, and lots of them pretty disrespectfully to the Tahitian people who welcomed them? They were really rude, especially around the women and girls of Tahiti who were so friendly to them when they arrived. They would never have done that stuff they did in their own country, back home, would they?"

Alex who had read the plot summary and comments about the movie, and thought he remembered an earlier version (with Marlon Brando, he recalled) couldn't speak to what had occurred onscreen in the newer version - mostly because he had been asleep during much of it. He just shook his head. At first, he thought he'd try to answer his eldest daughter with something really 'pithy' or 'smart', but then he just sighed.

"That's a really good question, Keely. It was a strange situation - I mean how the sailors and Tahitians came together after the long voyage from Britain to the islands. It's like their curiosity about their cultural and economic differences clashed with their usual behaviors. Even though the men on the Bounty weren't the first European sailors to make contact and trade with the Tahitian people, the meetings between them didn't turn out well at all over the next few centuries for the people of Tahiti, and probably for those living on Moorea too. There were some successful trade connections, and marriages too, that came from outside explorers 'discovering' places and cultures like in Tahiti and other islands in Polynesia. But in the opinion of many, maybe even most of its people, those 'connections' didn't end up being viewed, or lived for that matter, as very positive or enriching over the longer term. So, some good, and some real bad, except for maybe a few of the Tahitian people, within a very few years after the Bounty came and went, and as they portrayed its visit in the movie. That's probably still the case, but I'm not really certain. I guess when we go, we'll find out, if we ask, what the local people's viewpoints are about what modern life means when compared to how much simpler, less complicated it was before the arrival of all these outsiders from Europe and elsewhere. But who really knows?"

Standing next to his sister, Cal, who had missed at least the last half of the movie, had his own questions regarding the growing conflict (in the mostly true story, and as depicted on screen) between Captain (actually, Lieutenant) Bligh and his first mate, Fletcher Christian.

"That must have been really confusing for Christian, Bligh's buddy before he signed up to join him as First Mate on the ship for the voyage to find the breadfruit trees, which served as Bligh's excuse to find faster ways to sail around the world, which turned out to be really dangerous to his crew. By the time Mr. Christian had settled into the easy life in Tahiti with his new wife - the daughter of the Tahitian king - he didn't want to return to England, and neither did a bunch of the other sailors."

"Yep, that's right, Cal. Christian must have felt that he had a new home now, and even though he'd agreed to sail both to and from

England as part of his contract, he didn't want to leave it. And he didn't like the way Captain Bligh was treating the other men either."

Alex looked into his son's eyes, always aware that history's lessons - and realities - could be painful for kids, and for that matter, many adults, to understand. "Christian had to make a tough choice. In the end, he forced his friend and commanding officer out to sea on a little boat with almost nothing, and very likely assumed he was going to die, while he and his fellow mutineers from the crew took over command of the Bounty."

"Gosh!" Cal exclaimed.

"Yep," Alex agreed. "And that's not even the whole story, though the whole tale is a sad one, for sure."

Chapter 14

A holiday to (really) remember

November 24, 2005
Thursday, Thanksgiving Day

For Keely, the best part of this particular Thanksgiving Day, 2005, was the anticipation. But the fact that each of the members of the Webster household could sleep in an hour or two for the first weekday in quite a while came in a reasonably close second, for sure. Plus - the brunch sandwiches their dad had prepared - with either bacon or sausage, on English muffins with egg and cheese, or a veggie alternative for Jess - made for the perfect pre-travel meal. Pretty easy to fix, very easy to clean up afterward (they all helped) and then it was time to load their bags in the car and run through their individual "to do/to bring/don't forget" needs and their dad's crazy "W4" list of just about every detail and logistical point about the trip one more time.

And...it wasn't raining. The sun was actually peeking out from under the clouds on this late fall morning in Tacoma, but it was quite chilly, expected to hit only the low 40's for a high temperature later that day. However, they were going to LA, where it would be about 20 degrees warmer even though they'd scarcely be going outside the airport terminal anyway. Then they'd jet off a few hours later to Tahiti and ultimately make their way by ferry to Moorea, around one whole day from now. French Polynesia, where the temp (in Fahrenheit, at least) would probably be 20 degrees warmer than that! *Lots of time and miles to go before we feel that sunshine*, thought the 12-year-old.

Alex had made sure to check them all in for their flight to LA earlier that morning, using his laptop computer. But he'd have to do so again manually with Tahiti Air once in Los Angeles as that company didn't yet allow this function to be done online, and they had no electronic "code sharing" or baggage handling exchange with the Webster's US airline either. Paper tickets were required. And they'd have to do that "slog through LAX" that Keely remembered having to endure on a prior trip to Hawaii through Southern California's largest airport, when the four of them schlepped all their bags from terminal to terminal after landing there following their journey from SeaTac.

But they should have plenty of time, Alex had reassured Keely, Meg, Cal, and then Jess, who had arrived a few minutes earlier from her apartment. She was all geared up for the tropics, and also to watch the Webster kids for much of the time while their dad worked on the software project in Moorea.

For now, all Keely cared about was that their first flight departed on time. And so far, there were no weather or other delays anticipated, according to the airline's website, which she had checked 20 minutes ago.

Speaking of their bags, they were all packed with clothes and snacks and equipment, individually weighed to ensure they were less than the no-fee limit of 50 lbs. each. Each of the Webster party passengers had made the cutoff by a wide margin, except Alex, with all but his bag coming in under 45 pounds per the family's digital bathroom scale, now placed in the middle of the living room. Alex's large suitcase was the heaviest at 49 lbs., as it was kind of a catch-all for the family's extra stuff, and included some optional clothing for his business and (potential) bicycling attire. Of course, as had been the rule since late 2001, nobody had liquids in their second bag carry-ons - instead including them in the larger suitcases they planned to check at the airport.

Alex was especially pleased that almost ten-year old Cal hadn't filled his suitcase with books that would have disproportionately weighed it down. Jess had helped ensure discipline among the kids by monitoring each's packing progress, especially Cal's, the day prior. She was forced to suggest, several times, that Cal leave out a few things he'd included. In the end, his bag came out fine, well under the weight limit. Of the two Webster girls, Keely's was the heftiest, right at 44 lbs.

These luggage weight restrictions also addressed a potentially unforeseen downside. Even though all their transport plans were fairly set in stone, Alex loved to say that a "Plan B" was always a good idea when traveling. For example, if for some reason they needed to take a flight between Tahiti and Moorea instead of a ferry, as they planned, there was a limit of 44 lbs. for inter-island transport via air. Even though it wouldn't apply to them except for extraordinary circumstances, *it never hurts to consider and prepare for all possibilities,* the veteran of many business and family voyages emphasized to traveling friends and family. He could always figure out a way to split up his own extra four pounds among the rest of the family's bags, but only if absolutely necessary.

As the time drew near for them to load the bags and themselves in the car for the drive from their home in North Tacoma's Old Town neighborhood to SeaTac airport, where they had set up an advance reservation at a decent discount valet parking lot, Bob and Mary Jo Webster walked in the front door. Alex's parents, the children's grandma and grandpa, were in their late sixties and had come to see the family off on their Polynesian adventure. They were also going to check in on the house periodically during the Websters' absence and feed Meg's goldfish, "Moe" while they were there.

Mary Jo walked into the living room where Jess sat with Cal and Keely. "Hi Jess! Hi, you two! Are you all ready to go?"

"Hi Grandma! Hi Grandpa!" the two Websters answered while Jess smiled and also returned the older woman's greeting.

Keely continued, "Yes, I guess we are ready as we'll ever be!" She smiled, then rolled her eyes with a touch of sarcasm. Trips were always a 'major production' at the Webster house, but they had each gotten pretty good at the drills and discipline involved in getting ready and getting out the door.

Cal added his response to his sister's. "Yep - Moorea here we come!" as he took one game cartridge out of his portable system and inserted another.

Jess saw this and had a suggestion. "Cal, why don't you put that back in its pouch, and in your bag now..." and as he'd been reminded twice not to forget it, he quickly did so.

Meg came downstairs from her room and greeted her grandparents with a cheery smile and a hug. "Happy Thanksgiving, Grandma and Grandpa!"

Alex stood up from the family computer he'd just powered down in the other room, after checking weather and personal email messages one last time. He walked in to greet both his parents with warm embraces, and a paper printout, which he handed to his dad.

"You guys all set, son? Anything we can do to help?"

"Nope," replied Alex, "We've got everything handled. But here's a copy of our contact info and itinerary."

"Aaah, the famous 'W4' trip planner!" his dad chuckled.

Alex grinned. "Of course! We Websters must have a plan to follow for every trip! (he smiled mischievously as he pointed at the packed printout). And as it shows, we'll still be reachable via email during the trip, and I'll try to call a couple of times from the hotel office during my workdays."

He continued, "Don't forget to pick up the newspapers and mail while we're gone, please."

"We know...don't worry about anything," answered his mom. She leaned into Keely, giving her a big hug, then did the same to Cal and Meg and Jess. Bob was next...he and Mary Jo loved their grandchildren dearly. They were able to see them fairly often, but they had busy lives too, even though both were semi-retired.

Alex's dad had formerly worked as an Industrial Engineer for more than 40 years. Mary Jo - a part-time teacher and homemaker for the first part of her life while raising Alex and his brother and three sisters - was now actively involved with her husband in running the specialty yacht fittings business they operated from their home, about 15 miles away. Since they had moved to that house located on a cove of South Puget Sound two years prior, visits to their son and grandkids in Old Tacoma weren't quite as common as they used to be.

Mary Jo and Bob next turned their attention to Jessica. They had really grown to appreciate how well Jess had risen to the challenge of helping take care of Keely, Meg, and Cal over the past couple of years, especially given their busy dad's work life - and her own demanding post-graduate college schedule.

"So excited you are going along, Jess," Mary Jo said.

Bob grinned and added, "Of course she is, what would they do without her? Alex, you better give her a raise!"

"Hey, wait a minute!" Alex pretended to protest to his dad, a few inches shorter and a few inches wider than his son, with graying dark brown hair and mostly bald head. "I already told Jess that it was absolutely cool for her to hang out on the beach every day...as long as she took the kids with her, and what more would a college kid (*OK, grad student*) want?!" He turned to Jess, grinning, then said, "But seriously, Jess and I have agreed on a schedule that provides her ample time off, the whole time we're on the trip. So, she will have a chance to explore or hang out on her own, and that's important because she'll have a bit longer, fuller days watching the kids than usual, while I work in the hotel office with the software implementation team there and in our Seattle HQ."

Jess nodded. "Yeah, all I really want first, though, after all the pre-trip preparation we've been doing for the past six weeks, is to relax and hopefully sleep for some of the 11 hours we'll have today and tonight on two plane rides. Though I'm not sure I can do it while sitting near these two "Type A" girls and their brilliant little brother!"

"Hey!" Cal said, "I'm sitting next to dad on one of the flights!" Alex clapped him on the back, as that was true. Though the five of them were in the same rows of each airplane, their seating arrangements varied somewhat from one flight to the next, both to LA/Papeete and back through California and for their return to Seattle-Tacoma.

"Well, let's get going, everybody!" Alex announced as he kissed his mom's cheek and hugged her, and then his father. The kids exchanged embraces with their grandparents as they trooped out, lugging their backpacks, and Jess followed. Alex stowed each of the larger suitcases in the rear of the car, then turned around as he opened the driver's door. "*Nānā*! Goodbye!" he called, using translating from Tahitian to English.

Keely glanced at her dad, hearing the term's different meaning - as it was coincidentally the same spelling and similar pronunciation - of what they had fondly called their grandmother on their mother's side. Their "Nana," Mary Lynn Mercato had played a major, loving and supportive role in their early lives, yet had died five years prior, not too long before her parents' divorce. Keely, Meg, Cal, and Alex - and of course their mom - still missed her very much.

The oldest Webster sibling smiled to herself, recalling the conversation she and her brother and sister had enjoyed the previous night with their mom, who had called to wish *"Bon Voyage"* to the children from her home a couple of towns away. The three of them had also spent the previous two weekends at her house, to balance out not being able to 'share' time between her and their dad as was their usual custom around the Thanksgiving holiday. She had given each of the kids a going-away present - a nicely-bound small journal to write down their thoughts and any interesting notes while on the trip.

With a sigh, Keely followed her brother and sister into the middle seat of the family's SUV. Jess opened the passenger side after stuffing her backpack in the rear of the vehicle, and Alex slid into the driver's seat and closed the door. As they backed out of the driveway and looked toward their house, Alex honked the horn and they all returned the waves from the children's grandparents. Pulling onto the street, Alex announced, "The adventure continues...Worldwide Websters hit the road to Tahiti!"

"Watch out Moorea!" Meg chimed in. And they were off to the airport to begin a very long day of traveling - with a few surprises yet to come...

Chapter 15

The planes, the planes!

Thanksgiving Day Afternoon 1:00 pm
Seattle Tacoma International Airport

"Finally!" Meg exclaimed, as they all climbed into the shuttle bus from the parking lot to the airport for their first flight of the day. They were fortunate, as more of the traffic on the freeway was headed south rather than north as the Websters traveled in that direction toward SeaTac. Luckily, there had been no wrecks or car problems along the way, but it was a holiday, so the trip had been a bit slower than usual. However, that wasn't a big concern because her dad had planned their schedule to get to the parking lot and onward to the airport in plenty of time.

Now it was 1:00 pm, about two hours before their flight to Los Angeles. Even for Alex that was quite a bit of cushion, as during his business trips he rarely arrived at the airport so early. But because he was traveling with all the kids - and even with Jess along to help - given the nature of their next international flight and all their bags, he wasn't going to second-guess his original decision to take no chances and arrive early.

As they exited the shuttle bus at the terminal, Meg watched her dad give the driver seven dollars as a tip for her assistance with their bags, and the five members of the Webster "family" trooped in to the airline check-in counter.

Alex reached in his bag to find their tickets and passports for the representative, and Meg mused on the complexity of travel procedures. She knew that at this point, passports weren't truly necessary for their domestic US flights, but each had to show some sort of ID to check in their bags, clear the security lines, and board the plane, so passports were the perfect choice, especially since they would definitely need them to fly internationally and to enter French Polynesia, much less fly back to the USA in 9 1/2 days. Meg had possessed a passport for more than a year now, but this was only the second trip where she'd ever needed it since going to London and Paris with her dad, sister, and brother in early 2003.

Soon, after their bags were checked and Alex placed all their boarding passes and the matching bag claim tags in his travel folder, they arrived at the security screening station closest to their gate. To keep everybody organized, they'd all agreed that Keely and Meg would place their carry-ons on the bag conveyor first, with Cal to follow. Jess's job was to make sure each had pulled out their iPods and game devices before doing so, and also that nobody - especially Cal - forgot to do so, or dropped anything important out of their pockets, or neglected to take off their shoes and put them in the conveyor bins. After that, she and their dad were just hoping each of the traveling party made it 'unscathed' through the X-ray machine.

After Alex had gone through, Jess followed with the girls. She made sure they had all their belongings and their shoes, and then put on her own, while Alex kept a close eye on Cal's backpack and helped him with his sneakers (about which Cal said very clearly "I can do it myself, Dad!")

Such an "old hand" at travel! Alex thought. He muttered under his breath "I wonder where he gets that confidence?!" He watched as, after a momentary delay while the operator moved his backpack loaded with lots of electronic gear forward, then back, then examined it closely on their screen, and then finally buzzed it forward again, it was free of the X-ray scanner. Alex grabbed his shoes and his belt off the conveyor and began to slip them on.

Meanwhile, his backpack moved to the end of the moving track, and before he could reach over to grab it himself, Jess had whisked it off and into his hands. "Thanks, Jess!"

"Happy to help, Mr. W! But now you owe me a free movie on the flight!" she joked. Alex frowned in mock-concern, then broke into a wide smile. As a group, they glanced around and down at their backpacks, zipped them up, with a quick check back towards the conveyor belt just in case they'd forgotten anything.

Cal looked up at the flight screen on the wall in front of them, quickly located their departure details, and proudly confirmed to all that their gate was still the same. Then he strode out in front of the group, backpack bouncing up his small frame. "This way, guys!" the nine-year-old called out, beckoning them to follow as they headed out to their departure gate, still with only a bit less than two hours before their flight to LAX.

That pre-flight time, it turned out, went very fast, and after each of them had visited the restroom in turns, and they had found a couple power outlets to charge their electronic gadgets with one last top-up near their seats in the boarding area, it was time to get on the plane. Alex led the five Websters (including Jess) up to the gate agent, and handed over their boarding passes to be inspected and validated.

"Welcome aboard, Websters! And Ms. Forrester," the friendly airline agent exclaimed, looking somewhat quizzically at Jess, then Alex.

"Thanks!" Alex replied. He explained to the agent, "She's their nanny," even though he realized he probably didn't need to. But being Alex, he did so anyway.

They trooped down the Jetway and entered the plane. As his dad usually did, Cal was about to check the manufacturing details of the plane, on a small metal plate just inside its doorway, when Meg turned back to him and beat him to the punch. "Boeing, Renton, WA, 737, October, 1998, Dad!"

Again, Alex thought, "*Like father, like daughter!*" He marveled at Meg and her siblings' intelligence and energy, just as he did almost every day. *I really do have great kids!* Then he followed their nanny and the 'Websterkins' down the aisle to their seats for the relatively short flight straight down the coast to Los Angeles International.

Chapter 16

Relief and recharge

12:35 am PST, Friday/Thursday, November 25/24
Day after Thanksgiving, 10:35 pm in Tahiti, the day of.

Somewhere over the Pacific...

Jess sipped her sparkling water as the huge jetliner cruised at 40,000 feet above the ocean. *Wow!* She continued to marvel that things had turned out fine after the earlier crisis at LAX airport. She was so relieved that it had been resolved, just in time - and had no idea what she would have done in a similar situation. And the kids?

Keely, Meg, and Cal had been loudly thankful about how things worked out, although with all the traveling they had done, they were somewhat accustomed to the occasional glitches that could occur with even the most uncomplicated itineraries to domestic locales, much less international destinations. Thus, at this point, they were already well into their "flight routines." These consisted of focusing on books, music, games, and movies, most supplied right at their seats from their own bags or via the seat back screens and earphones provided by the airline to each passenger. But Jess could see that they, like her, were starting to wind down, quickly. Her own head started to nod and she knew she'd be asleep in her seat very soon.

Keely and Meg had already watched a movie together for the first part of the flight. The plane took off right on time, its departure not impacted by the Webster clan's boarding. Now, they were 1 1/2 hours in and about to have the option of eating their first of two meals being served on the nine-hour flight. It was actually common to have two meals plus two or more snack service "runs" on international flights of such a long duration as theirs to Papeete. It kind of depended on the airline - especially in recent years with the rise of cheap, no-frills carriers flying between major tourist destinations, some of which did not offer such passenger perks except for an extra charge. However,

Tahiti Air was the leading carrier on routes to their island nation's home and thus maintained a generally high level of service on all flights, and in all cabins/classes. At least that's what Keely had explained to the others after she looked up info on their trip - once they heard where they were going on this holiday.

Jess turned her thoughts back to Alex. *That poor man! Just getting on the plane in Los Angeles looked like it had drained ten years of his life!* Once he had followed the kids and Jess back toward their seats and helped them stow their bags under the seats, he'd put his backpack (minus his laptop, headphones, notepad and a couple of pens) above in the overhead bin. That chore completed, with Meg and Keely to his right on one side of the plane, and Jess and Cal to his left filling the middle section of their seven-seat row, #38, Alex slumped into his seat and let out a huge sigh of relief. He glanced over at Jess, and gave a weak grin. He didn't want to get his computer screen cleaning cloth wet, so asked her if she had any tissue available? She handed him a Kleenex, then thought better and passed him another, both of which Alex used to soak up the remaining sweat dripping from his face and neck.

"Thanks!" he'd said to Jess, then "Whew! That was a little closer than I'd like, especially for an international flight. I feel very lucky right now. Wow!" He shook his head in wonder.

Jess sympathized with her employer. "Actually, I'm amazed you were able to figure out what happened, Alex. Not sure I would have!"

"Yep, you are so right about that, Jess. I was lucky. So lucky. Now, I'm going to decompress for a while, maybe eight hours...!" Alex answered wearily, then closed his eyes, leaned back into his seat, and stretched his legs all the way under the one in front of him.

When the flight attendant came by, Jess noticed Alex ordered a beer and ate a bag of snacks that was given to him with it. Next time she looked over toward his seat, he was OUT, no more meals for him tonight! It had been a long day with absolutely maximum stress for the last part of it, she knew. Clearly, Alex needed a physical and mental break, and with everybody safe and seated while they flew their way to Tahiti, Jess was glad he was able to drop into dreamland (for a while at least) in peace.

Chapter 17

Just a plain old plane trip?

About 6 1/2 hours earlier: 6:05 pm Pacific time
November 24, Thanksgiving Day
Los Angeles International Airport

Their flight down to LAX was uneventful. Alex had started his usual process of 'dotting I's and crossing T's" related to their trip details soon after take-off by doing a quick inventory of all of his personal and work materials. He'd opened and sorted through his backpack, looked at his sheaf of notes, and reviewed a number of paper and electronic files on the upcoming software implementation, looking for anything missing, just in case.

With all business items in order, paperwork and drives where he'd placed them, and all of the logistical details confirmed for his first meetings with the Montcalm Moorea team on Friday morning after their arrival, Alex shifted his attention to personal matters.

As he reviewed the checklist on his laptop screen, he briefly stopped to make eye contact with Cal. He winked, and got a quick grin in response, though the boy returned his focus to his video game a second later. As for Keely and Meg, they were each engrossed in reading, and writing, respectively. Next to them sat Jess, book and sparkling water on her tray table.

Another passenger occupied the window seat on Alex and Cal's side of the plane. She was a friendly woman from Olympia, Washington who had remarked upon arriving at the aisle "What a nice family! Where are you all going on this Thanksgiving Day?"

Cal had told her proudly, "We're going to Moorea!"

"More what?" she answered, and the 9 1/2-year-old sitting next to her in the middle seat proceeded to tell the woman all about French Polynesia, how far away it was, what languages they spoke there, and was starting to get into the history of the country and other details when his dad nudged him, and smiled at the woman.

"Hey Bud, you said you wanted to play Nintendo games nonstop on the plane, which one are you going to play first?"

"Oh Yeah!"

As Cal reached into his bag, pulled out his Nintendo, and flipped it on, their aisle mate smiled back at Alex, then pulled out her own book to read. She had told them as she sat down at boarding time that she was on her way to meet her own grandkids in an LA suburb for a "late" Thanksgiving meal (around 7:30 pm) and an exciting weekend at Disneyland the next couple of days, so she surely understood the concept of excited children!

Following a couple drink and snack service runs up and down the aisle by the flight attendants, the sky was already getting dark outside the plane, but the view was still spectacular, first with the mountainous landscape of western Washington and central Oregon. Alex never tired of gazing at the chain of Cascade Mountain peaks: Mt. Rainier, Mt. St. Helens, Mt. Adams, and just over the Oregon border beyond the Columbia River, Mt. Hood. Soon, after a series of other snow-crested summits, the pilot announced that Crater Lake was below them on the left side of the aircraft. Alex had never actually been to this particular national park, which was surprising as he had visited the nearby cities of Medford and Ashland several times on business. But he'd never made the trip up and around the magnificent remainder of the park surrounding Crater Lake, itself the product of long-ago eruption of Mt. Mazama. *Bucket list*, Alex reminded himself.

Now past the Oregon-California border, after a few more minutes of flying he could just make out Mt. Shasta below, to finish up the peaks of the Cascade Range. Then, he noticed the gradual moderating of the topography as they passed into Southern California. *We're chasing daylight*, Alex thought, as the plane headed south and darkness fell during the last 45 minutes of their flight path from Seattle-Tacoma. Soon, the pilot announced their "gradual descent" into LAX.

Meg and her sister put their gear away, stowed their backpacks under their feet in front, and watched as the plane almost seemed to "coast" directly above the houses and then office buildings near the airport. They touched down just after 5:35 pm, about five minutes late, but took a surprisingly short taxi to their gate given the sprawling size of the LA airport, so they actually arrived there almost on schedule.

Keely frowned as people in nearly every aisle jumped up, but as usual they then had to wait about ten minutes for everyone to leave in the rows ahead. Next, following their well-established flight debarkation routines, each of the Webster contingent stood when those directly in front of them began to leave. Alex and Jess reached up to help the kids with their backpacks, checking around their seats, and then they all exited the plane together. Alex brought up the rear. Nodding to the flight attendants and captain at the cabin door, with a chorus of "Thanks!" to the crew, they headed up the Jetway for the next leg of the trip. Alex checked his watch. *5:53. Plenty of time. Next stop (after bathroom) Bag Claim.*

Refreshed and ready for the rest of their journey after visiting the restrooms and waiting another 15 minutes to pick up their bags at the LAX claim carousel, the Webster clan headed outside with Meg, like a Pied Piper, leading her fellow family travelers toward the street. Pointing up at a sign, she said *"Bradley International Terminal. That's Us!"* and started down the brightly lit sidewalk in the direction of the arrow, pulling her main roller bag, with her backpack strapped securely through its rear panel over the larger bag's telescoped handle.

Following her, Keely and Alex looked at each other and rolled their eyes in unison, "Here we go agaiiiiiin," said Keely. Cal and Jess brought up the rear as they began the trek from Terminal 6, where they had arrived, around to the International gates where they'd check in next for Tahiti Air.

The relentless and repetitive "scrunching and clunking" sound of their rolling suitcases followed the Northwest travelers along the wide sidewalk while cars, taxis, and buses sped by on the adjacent roadway. Keely looked back and around to her brother and nanny, and she watched a shuttle bus drive by her to her left. "Hey, Dad...how come we didn't take that shuttle?"

"Because we need the exercise!" yelled Alex, "And we have plenty of time for our connection, easier than loading and unloading bags." It was tough to hear or be heard over the combined noise of the rolling bags and constant traffic alongside.

It took a total of about twelve minutes for them to complete the distance, and this time Cal led their 'group turn' into the cross-border flight terminal. Alex sighed with relief that all was working so well, so far, on this trip. The rest of the Webster contingent swooshed and clattered in to the large hall around the youngest member of the clan.

With everyone back together, Alex steered his bags in the direction of Tahiti Air as indicated by the directory screen on the far wall. As they drew up to the waiting line, about four passengers were in front of them, but that quickly dropped to two. Each of the Websters and Jess placed their bags on the scale at the counter as Alex pulled the travel pouch containing all their key info out of his bag. He removed the tickets and passports for each person, so they'd be ready to hand to the agent. He glanced at his watch. *6:25. Flight at 10:55.* Then looking at his ticket, he saw the actual boarding time was blank. *No prob, the agent will tell us when and where to board,* Alex assured himself.

When he'd finished presenting all their ID and ticket details, the agent handed Alex the five tickets and passports together, along with a full set of baggage claim tags, then looked at the assembled Websters with their backpacks and told them where to go. "Please use Security Gate number 1, around there (pointing) to the left. Your flight #45 to Papeete will begin boarding at 9:40 at Gate 22. *Nānā,* and enjoy Tahiti!"

"Thank you!" they replied mostly together, though Keely went for the 'local' language of the airline, saying *"Mauru'uru"* - bringing a smile from the agent. Alex raised his eyebrows at the long timeline for boarding, but at second thought wasn't really that surprised at the one hour-plus window for such a long international flight with so many seats.

Now, the group made their way, lighter again with only their backpacks, the three minutes or so it took them to reach the Security gate entrance. The line was a bit longer here than at SeaTac, but there were more agents on duty so it moved very quickly. Within only ten additional minutes, the family was in front of the TSA agent, Alex once again presenting all of their documents one by one for inspection. The agent verified each, handed them back to Alex, and the group duplicated the drill they had completed earlier at SeaTac, as they lined up with their carry-ons in front of the conveyor belt and

X-Ray machine, their last luggage checks to go before embarking to Papeete.

For the second time on this already long day, Alex, feeling a little tired and hungry like the others, pulled his computer from his backpack, took off his shoes, removed his belt, and stuffed his own passport and tickets into his shirt pocket, temporarily. He dropped everyone else's travel documents inside his special pouch, and put it into his pack, which he then zipped shut. Everything in its place, Alex then proceeded through the X-ray without a 'beep' after the others. He picked up his bag, computer, and shoes off the belt, then followed the others to the transition area where they could put shoes back on, repack their bags, etc.

Sitting down, Alex realized his hiking boots might be pretty uncomfortable on the long flight to Tahiti, and his feet were already hot and tired from all the trekking around SeaTac and then LAX airports. Luckily, he'd packed his flip flops in a pocket in his backpack at the last minute - that he might have forgotten them for a trip to the tropics was beyond his comprehension!

Reaching into his backpack, Alex pulled the sandals out and quickly removed his socks and stuffed them into his boots along with his documents which had just fallen out of his shirt pocket as he leaned over. He partially folded each boot and squeezed the bulky footwear into his front backpack pocket. *Backpack's a little thicker than I want, but really glad to put on my sandals instead of those boots for a much cooler 9+ hour flight!* Alex thought.

Because of his footwear change, Alex was the last one of the Webster traveling party to get 'situated' for the final march to their departure gate. Everyone looked at him as if to ask "What next?" without actually using their mouths. Alex glanced up at the monitor for gate updates, something he had learned from experience to do frequently. *Never assume that changes weren't possible, even last-minute, especially with international flights.* The screen still reported the Tahiti Air LAX-PPT flight was leaving from Gate 22.

Back together as a group, the Webster party followed the left arrow toward Gates 20-30, and as they made their way, with their backpacks hunching them down just a bit, Keely announced, "I'm HUNGRY!"

Meg added "So am I," and the others nodded as well.

"Me too!" said Alex. He glanced at his watch: *still only 6:55.* They had plenty of time 'til boarding and their gate was right down the hall.

Meg spied a family pizza restaurant and bar down the left side of the terminal, on the way to their gate.

"Let's go *there!*" the second sibling cried, and the others agreed enthusiastically.

After a short wait, they were ushered to a table. As they received menus from the host, Alex wondered if perhaps it being Thanksgiving was what accounted for the surprisingly small number of diners?

"Pizza for Thanksgiving! Cool!" Cal exclaimed, eliciting chuckles from the others.

It was a very satisfying meal for the weary travelers, and they took their time eating pizza and salad and chatting excitedly about their upcoming adventure in the tropics. Still, when Alex paid their restaurant bill it was only 8:15 pm. Creaking to their feet, the tired yet well-fed and watered group returned out into the concourse and resumed their trek to Gate 22. After a few minutes they passed another Flight Information board. Keely glanced at it and scrolled across it with her eyes to the "P's" to "Papeete." Next to the airline and flight number, it read *"Gate Change - Now Gate 6."* And then at the far-right column, it read *"Ppt Chk 8:55."*

"DAAD!" Keely yelled to her father, walking about ten feet in front of her. "Our flight's gate has changed. We have to go back this way,", she said pointing in the opposite direction.

Alex returned to where Keely was standing, glanced up and confirmed what she had noticed. He summarized the situation in his head: *It is still only 8:25 pm. It's only a five-minute walk. We'll just need to sit down in the immediate gate area, then do this passport check thing, then we can hang out, read, hit the restrooms one more time before we have to board, probably after 10 pm since we're not in the front or all the way back of the plane. No problem.*

A few minutes later - after reversing their direction in the terminal - they had plopped down into a row of seats adjacent to Gate #6, with these ones conveniently sporting electrical outlets every other chair, something still not all that common in most airport waiting lounges in the early 2000's.

Keely and Meg decided to go to the restrooms, and Jess walked with Cal to join them. Once they came back, it was still only 8:45 and no Tahiti Air agents were at their gate area yet. However, Alex noticed that there was a line forming in front of the desk as passengers began to do what they always did on flights - queue up even if told not to.

Everyone in the Webster traveling party became engrossed in their books, games, and magazines for the next several minutes. Hearing noises from the direction of the gate, Alex looked up and saw two airline representatives had arrived, and shortly after they started earlier than previously expected to check passports and tickets. An announcement came across the local area public address system: "For those of you flying to Papeete on Tahiti Air flight 45, please bring your boarding passes and passports up to the counter so we can check them prior to departure."

Keely and her sister and brother probably knew more than most kids about this process. It was actually quite common when flying internationally to have seemingly strange things occur, such as gates changing once or even twice in a three-hour waiting-to-board period, extra ID checks or security lines established, random searches of carry-on bags, etc. They were veterans of such drills!

Meg knew what her dad, sitting next to her, was likely thinking. He was waiting for the line to get shorter as he relaxed with the other members of the Webster traveling crew.

Indeed, Meg was spot-on...Alex had found a plug two seats away, plugged in his laptop, just to give it a little extra charge for the trip, and looked at his watch. *9:05.* He checked his email messages. *Nothing critical, and it's Thanksgiving anyway*, he thought. He noticed a voicemail icon on his personal cell phone. Pushing the VM button, Alex listened to the message:

"*Ia Orana*, Alex! This is David Thomson at the Montcalm Moorea. Bernie and I and our team here are excited to see you and of course your family too! Just a reminder to confirm that we will send one of our staff and a driver to pick you up at the Vai'are ferry dock tomorrow at 8:00 a.m. Bon Voyage!"

Alex chuckled. *With all this trekking around airports, I wonder if we'll be able to even walk at all by the time we reach Moorea. They may need to come onboard and wheel us and our bags off the boat - especially me!*

He glanced again at the lengthy passport check queue, and decided there was still ample time. He walked over to the closest newsstand/candy/souvenir shop, ignoring the Duty-Free section as he'd already determined there wasn't anything he wanted to bring into French Polynesia to eat, drink, or use while there, and otherwise everything but a few unique items would cost less in the U.S., even with tax added, anyway. He had found through previous travels that it was often - though not always - a toss-up between cost and convenience with Duty-Free transactions.

After briefly perusing the latest books and magazines along the store's wall, Alex saw his favorite candy bar and decided to splurge for one, then opted to buy candy for all the others too, taking educated guesses on what they would like. The cost was of course ridiculously high - *but it was the airport and a special occasion, and a holiday too, right?*

It was now 9:20. Leaving the shop with the candy bars in a paper bag, and his wallet more than $25 lighter, Alex walked back to where the Websters were sitting. Meg caught his eye. "They just said, if you haven't already to please immediately present your passport and tickets Dad," she said, anxiously.

"I know," Alex replied, "I'm going up now to take care of it. Meanwhile, SURPRISE!" He handed Meg the bag. "Pass them around, but save one for me. Last American chocolate for ten days!"

It was now 9:23 and the passport check line was down to about five people now. He grabbed his backpack and moved behind them. A few moments later, an announcement rang out: "*Ia ora oe i teie po*, Good Evening and Welcome/*Maeva* to Tahiti Airlines Flight 45…" The male voice continued with a pre-boarding announcement, noting that general boarding would start in a few minutes by class and row.

Alex was just starting to feel his usual heightened sense of awareness as the time to board an airline flight grew closer. But, the passport line, though quite short now, seemed to move slower than ever. Finally, he reached the front and it was his turn. He pulled everyone's passports and tickets from the pouch in his backpack and handed them to the gate agent. She examined each, checking her computer concurrently.

Alex glanced over at the boarding line starting to form at the gate. There had been no announcement to do so, at least for most of the passengers. Irritation and just a bit of weariness colored his thoughts. *Of course, they're lining up when they're not supposed to, just clogging everything up, trying to game the system, hog the front of the line. Hoping they can sneak onboard early. Why? This direct flight includes free luggage in the price of every ticket, so no need to lug and store your bags onboard. Why else would one want to board a flight so far before takeoff? Do they really enjoy using airplane restrooms or something!?* Then, *boy, am I tired!*

Alex's thoughts were interrupted when he realized the agent was speaking to him: "Mr. Callan, pardon me - Webster?"

He looked up. "Umm, yes, I'm Mr. Webster, Alex actually."

The agent frowned. "Mr. Webster, I see you have a reservation and we are trying to check you in, along with the rest of your party, but *your* passport is not here."

"Of course it is," Alex said and leaned forward, spreading the documents across the desk...*1, 2, 3, 4.* He counted only four passports. "Do you have my boarding pass, though?" he asked?

"No, I'm sorry, *it's* not here either," she answered, "but I do have the passports and boarding passes for the rest of your party."

Alex, feeling his temperature rising, said, "Is it possible it's stuck in with another ticket, or fell on the floor perhaps?"

The agent stepped back, bent down to check under the counter, and again spread the Webster kids' and Jess's passports and boarding passes across the counter in front of her. "Not here, I'm sorry. Perhaps they are in your pocket, or your bag?" she said, indicating his backpack.

"Let me check again," Alex said. He jammed his hand into his travel pouch, flipped through the papers, and quickly scanned all the items with his eyes, and with his fingers: *Itinerary, Hotel details, NO passport or boarding pass for me. What the HE...!*

Alex looked up, and noticed that three more people now stood behind him in the service line, waiting to speak to the agent. Meanwhile, the other gate agent announced that First Class was just about to board. Coach/Economy class would be next in about five minutes, he surmised. It was 9:38. The plane wasn't taking off for more than another hour. He urged himself to keep calm, and was sure there'd be plenty of time, still, *if I could just find my ID and boarding pass!*

"One moment," he said to the agent, who was waiting patiently for his response. He motioned those standing behind him forward, then walked back to where the Webster kids and Jess stood in a semicircle with their backpacks, wondering what was going on.

Jess saw the worry on Alex's face. "I can't find my passport or my ticket, you know, my boarding pass. It's not in my bag either."

"Is it in your pocket?" Jess asked.

"No, I checked there too, and anyway, I never put my ticket in my pocket anymore when I travel, I always put documents like that in a manila envelope - all in one place - so I don't lose them. See?"

He pulled out the travel pouch. Realizing the others' passports and passes were still at the counter, he returned there quickly. As he arrived back in front of the now empty service line, an announcement rang out. They were just about to board the economy section of the plane from the back to the front, just to his right. About 50 passengers were lined up on the other side of the movable stanchions and rope barriers, as usual. "Rows 51-58, please have your passports and verified boarding passes ready to board the plane."

Alex looked into the gate agent's eyes and lowered his voice. "OK. I can't seem to find my passport or boarding pass. What can I do?"

"Well, the other members of your party have all their documents here, they are fine. Unfortunately...hold on a moment," she turned and spoke to the male agent on duty next to her, while another airline representative continued to check tickets of boarding passengers. The agent shook his head, and the woman helping Alex turned back.

"I'm afraid that I could replace your boarding pass, if you had ID, because of course we have your reservation in our computers, but you'd still need to have your passport checked and, in your possession, to board the plane, Mr. Webster."

Alex paused for a moment, then, his voice rising, answered, "I do have my driver's license...but...." He stopped - knowing that domestic version of ID literally 'wouldn't fly' in this international travel situation. He was wracking his brain. *Where were his documents?*

He started rifling through his backpack, now with both hands, pulling all of its zippers to the bottom. Nothing, at least nothing like the needed papers, was in any of the pockets. *Think, Alex!*

He addressed the agent again, now with his face getting hot, and he was starting to sweat. "OK, I'm going to try one more time to figure out where my travel documents are. Meanwhile, I'll take my children's and their nanny's documents to them so they can board the plane." He reached for the passports and boarding passes.

"I'm sorry, Mr. Webster, but we can't allow minors under 12 to fly without a parent or guardian. We might be able to allow one..." She checked her screen and looked over at Keely. "Ms. Forrester and your oldest daughter, could fly, but the other two, unfortunately, cannot."

Alex stared at the airline agent. *Oh my God!* He thought. *This is now a full-fledged nightmare. Of course they can't let the kids fly, or at least the two younger ones unless...*

"Can I sign something to let them board, if I certify Ms. Forrester is their nanny and can fly with them and be in charge when they arrive in Papeete, until I can join them there?"

The agent replied, very sympathetically. "You could, sir, but the problem is, those forms you describe need to be turned in at least three hours ahead of the flight time."

Alex closed his eyes and tried, very hard, to keep his cool. *This isn't about bureaucracy - it's about ME*, he realized. He pulled together the boarding pass and passport documents for the rest of the group and walked back to Jess. He explained the situation.

"Where did you last use them or show them - or remember seeing them?" Jess asked.

Alex stopped and thought, very intently, of one strong possibility. "Not the restaurant...or...had to be Security...maybe? I'll run there now. Go ahead and be ready to get in line. It's fourteen after 10 o'clock now. I've got maybe 20 or 25 minutes to find my travel documents and get back here before they close the flight to boarding. Bye!"

Alex hustled down and around the corner of the concourse, and then broke into a trot in the direction of the restaurant where they'd eaten their pizza dinner. As he drew closer, he groaned. It was closed!

He walked up to see if anyone was still there, but the sliding doors were locked, with no lights visible inside.

What now?

A very cold sweat formed on his brow, and another trail of perspiration trickled down from his neck to his back. His shirt, under his jacket, was getting soaked. Alex searched deep inside his brain for where to look next. It didn't help to look at his watch - which showed that time to find his missing documents was running out.

The security station. *Could they be there, somehow?*

Alex struggled to keep calm, and started running in the direction of the TSA security gates, his backpack feeling much lighter than before as it bounced on his back with every step. His flip flops were definitely not the most efficient running gear, but his stride was buoyed by the nervous adrenalin surging through his body. Unfortunately, his thoughts were another matter entirely - increasingly weighed down by his sinking heart. All that kept running through his mind was the prospect of possibly having to miss the flight - which would screw up all their plans, *and then what?*

As he rounded the corner near the TSA lanes, Alex zeroed in on the particular machine and conveyor where their bags had been scanned after arriving from SeaTac, which of course had been several hours earlier. He hurried up to the TSA officer standing next to the end of the belt. "Excuse me, did you get a report of a lost passport and boarding pass?"

"What's the name, sir?" the officer curtly inquired.

"Alex Webster," the now sweat-drenched traveler answered, as he tried to remain calm, yet alert, aware that every moment was critical now.

"Let me check," the officer replied.

Alex watched, agonizing while the TSA staffer opened a large drawer behind the station, rifled through its contents, then lifted a tray to view some papers underneath. He then walked quickly over to the next security line and spoke to the officer there. That officer turned around, then asked the other officer on duty there a question. Both shook their heads when they looked back at the man Alex had addressed. He was apparently the supervisor on duty, and strode back to Alex. "I'm sorry, sir. No passports or boarding passes have been found or turned in to us here during this shift."

Alex glanced quickly around him. He felt like his heart had sunk through the concrete floor of the gleaming terminal. *Not so shiny now*, he thought. He couldn't believe this had happened. With all of his experience flying, with the checklist, *with the procedures he always used! I must have dropped the documents somewhere. But where? How?*

In a low, slow voice, he thanked the officer for checking, turned around and started to trot back toward the restroom where he'd stopped earlier, or maybe it was the shop where I bought the candy, or...*But I didn't take the pouch out at either of those places, or did I?* Now Alex wasn't sure of anything. His brain, he decided, *was totally fried.*

Right as he was about to reach the corner and head toward the restroom, which was nearer their flight's gate, the officer he had initially spoken to called loudly from behind him. "Did you check your shoes?"

Alex stopped in his tracks, and wheeled around. "What?"

"Your shoes, maybe your ID fell into your shoes? It happens more often than you think. You'd be surprised, sir."

Alex gritted his teeth, and answered. "The passport is pretty wide, I'm sure I'd feel it in my...." He stopped speaking abruptly, then looked down at his flip flops. Then his entire body went cold.

He quickly set down and unzipped the large outer compartment of his backpack, grabbed the socks stuffed into both of his half-folded boots, and pulled them out in one motion. He peered into the left, then the right one.

There. They. Are. Boarding pass and passport. He flashed back: remembering it now. *He had put the documents, all nicely arranged with the boarding pass nestled in between the pages of his passport, in one of his boots for just a second while retrieving the rest of his stuff from the security line, while he watched the kids and Jess get their gear together. He had - in a rush - forgotten he'd left his travel documents in the boot, even as he put everyone else's in the travel pouch. Where they belonged.*

Alex raised his head and turned towards the officer. Clearly, he realized what Alex had just discovered in his bag.

"Found it, huh?" he said to Alex.

"Yes sir, and THANK YOU, SIR!" Alex replied loudly, and with a huge grin. "In my shoes, indeed! Happy Thanksgiving!" And then, backpack bouncing on his shoulders, he RAN around the corner, documents crammed in between his fingers and palm, holding them just tight enough not to squish and crumple them, but close to that point, for sure.

As he neared the Gate 6 area, previously filled with hundreds of passengers and airline staff, only a small huddle of people remained near the gate. It was the three other Websters and Jess, actively searching for Alex, realizing their time to board was just about up.

"WAIT!" Alex yelled, abandoning any sense of decorum or embarrassment. He ran closer, his documents held high in his hand, sweat pouring down his face. "I'm here!"

The agent was at the door to the gate, about to lock and close off access to the plane. He stopped and turned around, hearing the commotion, and saw Alex, puffing, his backpack swinging back and forth around his body as he ran to the front of the now-vacant line's empty ropes and chrome stands. The rest of the Webster party followed right behind.

"Here's my ticket and passport, can you please check it?" Alex begged the agent.

"Sir, we're about to close the door. It's less than ten minutes until the flight departs. We..."

Alex cut him off with a desperate smile. He knew it was time to beg. "Please, I'm going to Moorea on important business, and my family here is joining me. It's a holiday for them, us...It's Thanksgiving. Can you PLEASE let us board?"

"Did you say Moorea? I'm from Moorea," the agent said. "Where are you staying there?"

"Montcalm Moorea Resort," Keely piped up, smiling widely.

The agent smiled back. "I know where that is. *'E,* Yes! Let me see your documents."

He took Alex's passport and boarding pass from his outreached, sweaty hand, typed something into his computer screen, and stamped the pass, slipping it back between the passport's pages.

"And the documents for the others in your party please?"

Jess quickly handed him the combined passes and passports for the Webster kids and herself. The agent flipped through each - and then uttered the most relief-inducing words Alex had ever heard.

"You may board now, and thank you for flying Tahiti Air. *Haere Tatou!* That means *'Let's go'* in Tahitian," he said, grinning widely.

Meg looked up at the agent. "*Mauru'uru,* sir!"

As they filed through the door into the Jetway they heard those now familiar words, "*Aita pea pea*" from the agent behind them, then in English: *You're welcome. No problem!*

Chapter 18

Maeva e Tahiti!

4:25 am Tahiti Time, November 25, Friday
High above the Pacific

Keely yawned and stretched her legs, then pulled up the window shade by her seat. Only a small glow was yet visible on the horizon. *Glad I got some sleep, not sure how much though*, she thought. Meanwhile, the entire cabin had just gone from darkness to bright artificial daylight, a bit of a shock for all the slumbering passengers. Just prior to that, Keely had seen a few 'glows' from individual lights around the seats from her viewpoint in the aircraft. Clearly, most people were either sleeping like she had been a few minutes ago, or just waking up - and probably very thirsty like she was.

The oldest of the Webster kids thought back to the early part of the flight. She and Meg were just beginning to watch their second movie together when she started nodding off, and when Keely glanced over at her sister, she saw Meg's eyes were already closed. So, Keely had reached over and pushed the button on Meg's screen to turn it off, then did the same to her own. After their very, very long Thanksgiving Day, even starting later than usual at 8:30 am, she was absolutely wiped out and sleep had come quickly. Just as her mind fogged over, she wondered if the constant eating they'd done all day was part of the cause: *I guess it helped that we all stuffed another meal in our mouths - and that the food was actually good!* - though their "dinner" had been served by the Tahiti Air cabin crew after 12:30 am!

So, now it was "magically" just about four hours later, though her watch still read 6:25. She'd really slept longer than she thought, as she accounted in her head for the two-hour time difference between their home Pacific time and what it was now. In something like another 90 minutes, they'd be landing in Papeete. And actually, she was a little hungry. Her back was kind of sore too.

Keely glanced over at her dad, across the aisle from Meg, who was stretching her back and arms straight upward.

Alex, in his aisle seat had tried not to, but his head kept nodding into 'traffic' while he slept and he was constantly getting bumped by people and carts passing by all during the previous night. Now, he was leaned over toward Cal's shoulder on his left, his inflatable pillow scrunched up against him and across his own arm rest. Meg looked over, then back to meet her older sister's eyes, and the two exchanged hearty giggles, though they tried valiantly to suppress them in the still mostly quiet cabin. Their father was snoring!

Poor Dad, that situation at the airport was MASSIVELY stressful for him, and *it gave us some serious worries, too,* thought Keely.

Meg leaned across the aisle and gently nudged her dad to try to stop his snoring, and Alex stirred and opened his eyes. Then he lifted and shook his head, looked at Meg and groaned, then smiled, sort of. He tried to say "Good morning!" but struggled to free his lips, now partly stuck together. *The joys of flying red-eyes,* Alex thought. *My mouth feels like wet cardboard that dried.*

He reached down in the small food bag below his seat for the Contigo water bottle he'd filled at the airport and glanced over at Jess and Cal next to him. Both were awake, though Cal looked much like Alex was feeling - a bit groggy - with his Nintendo headphones dangled loosely around his neck and wrappers from snacks he'd eaten on his seat and the floor. He was bending down to pick some of them up just as Alex had looked over, and after doing so, crushed them all together in a clump on his tray table.

The flight attendants were now heading methodically in their direction from the front of the plane to the back, bringing coffee, drinks, and then breakfast. But their refreshment carts were still fifteen or so rows away, so Alex figured they had just enough time for a bathroom break before landing.

He whispered in his son's ear. "Hey sport! Want to join me on a trip to the restroom?"

"YEAH, I gotta go!"

So, while it looked like his daughters pondered doing the same, but weren't quite ready yet, Alex unbuckled his seat belt and stepped forward out into the aisle to let Cal by, and he followed his son back to the closest bank of restrooms about ten rows toward the rear of the plane. Another passenger exited one toilet as they drew closer. "Perfect timing!" Alex said to Cal, who then opened the door.

Cal was an "old hand" at airplane lavatories, as all the Websters were, seasoned travelers and pretty good planners when it came to timing restroom trips during flights. Soon, Alex switched places with him when Cal finished up and opened the door.

A few moments later, as Alex slid the door lock to open it and stepped out, he was a bit startled to see Meg was standing right in front of him, looking a bit impatient - and maybe a bit desperate from drinking more than one soda with dinner, then sitting and sleeping without visiting the restroom for several hours. As Meg entered, and he saw Keely behind her around the corner, Alex figured his oldest daughter was also pretty eager to make use of the plane's tiny toilets.

Alex and Cal returned to their seats, his father gently directing Cal's waist with one hand, and using the overhead bins to steady himself with the other every couple of rows. He had learned this trick from watching flight attendants...it was a good way to keep balance and not knock into people sitting on the aisles (like he was), despite any pitching or swaying of the plane, which was certainly not that unusual during long over-water flights like these.

Reaching their seats, Alex glanced ahead and saw the cabin crew was now about seven rows in front of them and busily unpacking hot dishes and handing breakfast trays to those passengers who were a) awake and b) wanted breakfast despite looking (and probably feeling) just like the Websters. Almost everyone was drowsy and bleary-eyed after the very long flight across the Pacific.

Jess stood up just as Cal returned to his seat, and asked the woman next to her if she could get out to go to the restroom herself. As she did so, Jess said "Thanks!" and hastened back on the other aisle to join the girls at the restroom before the flight attendants reached their row. Somehow, she was able to get there and back only a couple of minutes after Keely and Meg had returned to their seats.

Jess's more of a pro at traveling than I thought! Alex mused. Clearly, she had been a real "find" as a professional caregiver, and also a really cool and caring friend to the family too. *She's almost a full-fledged, seasoned "member" of the Worldwide Websters traveling circus!* he thought to himself.

The breakfast meals that came soon thereafter were actually very tasty. A small-sized cheese and thinly-sliced sausage omelet came with, of course, a croissant and butter. The compact tray also included French yogurt, jam, a nice, fresh fruit cup, milk, and, Alex chuckled to himself - *gotta love the French, or Tahitians, or maybe a combination?* - a chocolate-flavored yet light, sweet biscuit to finish the meal off. Of course, both Alex and Jess enjoyed the coffee too, Alex already leaning out five minutes later to get his second cup of *cafe au lait*, with whole milk poured straight from a pitcher the flight attendant carried along with the coffee pot as she offered refills to anyone interested.

Just as Alex took a long sip of his coffee, the intercom crackled with the crew chief's announcement that they would soon be landing in Papeete. So, they undertook the usual drill of stowing and locking their tray tables and getting all their bags situated. Luckily for the Webster traveling party, just then the flight attendants swept by, and Alex thanked them a bit sheepishly for the huge quantity of wrappers, cups, etc. the five family members (and Jess) had generated, and which they now handed over to be placed in the garbage sacks for disposal.

Soon, as everyone pulled up their window shades in the now fully-lit cabin, the rising sun shone even more brightly through the airplane. They banked to the left and started moving steadily lower in altitude. Alex leaned over to join his daughters in gazing out through scattered, puffy clouds at the azure seas, with white-capped waves breaking over the unspoiled Pacific Ocean below. Across the aisle, Cal was stretching to see, and Jess craned her neck for a look as well. Suddenly, the plane banked even more steeply for their final approach, and they caught fleeting glimpses of palm trees and the bluest water Alex had ever seen, along with sandy beaches dotted by deep green, tropical foliage. As they neared ground, they passed over buildings that appeared increasingly close together, and in greater and greater quantity than just a few moments earlier.

They landed very smoothly given the size of the huge plane, with a tap, then a couple of bumps, and soon they dramatically decreased speed and turned onto a taxiway leading toward their gate. Meg tried to listen closely as the head flight attendant made announcements in both French (and Tahitian) and then finally English. She heard the beginning of each 'speech', catching "*Bienvenue/Maeva*" then a bunch of words she couldn't quite understand, then "Welcome to Tahiti and Papeete, our nation's capital" in her English translation.

As they taxied towards the terminal it was pretty clear they weren't in L.A. or Seattle! It was so green, so lush, with towering, swaying palms and bright flowers on both sides of the airport, *you'd almost not think you were in a major city*, Alex thought. And of course, *Faa'a*, where the airport was located and as it was named, was a suburb of Papeete - itself a fairly small-sized city for a national capital - so it wasn't much more than a big town that happened to have an international airport in its midst.

Their plane was about ten minutes early, Alex estimated. It slowed for a few moments to let another massive aircraft proceed to its own gate, then made its way steadily toward the terminal with a smooth turn and then an abrupt stop. Shortly thereafter, the passengers heard the engines power down.

The lights blinked off and back on, signifying the connection of airport power to the plane, followed by another announcement from the crew about making sure to not leave any belongings behind, and to be careful walking down the stairs and then onward to the terminal. Keely was surprised - they would be exiting "old style", down fairly steep portable steps and then led across the tarmac to another set of stairs up and into the terminal building!

The Websters and Jess watched as the "great migration" began, out of the aircraft that had brought them more than 4,000 miles across the Pacific Ocean and below the Equator from Los Angeles. It ended up taking about 15 minutes before their row of passengers more towards the rear of the massive aircraft got its opportunity to exit, but as Meg had noticed on similar long flights in the past, being on the right side of the plane's cabin seemed to be advantageous, with departing passengers moving very quickly up the aisles across from the exit side, once they'd actually gotten the chance to move at all.

Soon the Webster party had grabbed all their stuff (everyone double-checking to make sure they - especially Cal - hadn't forgotten any items in seat back pockets) and moved in a line quite rapidly down the aisle, or as fast as anyone could go after flying nine hours while carrying a full backpack.

As they neared the front of the plane, they turned left to exit through the middle 'supply' corridor onto the stairway via the open cabin door, making sure to thank the assembled flight attendants and other crew as they passed. Then they each grasped the railing with one hand while descending the wide metal stairs into the already warm and somewhat steamy air, even at this early hour. Amid the pungent odor of airplane fuel, Cal swayed a bit under the weight of his backpack, then detected a more pleasant, slightly fragrant aroma in the breeze.

"We're definitely in the tropics, eh guys?" said the youngest of the Websters. The three of them and Jess - and definitely Alex - all looked a bit bedraggled, if still excited, as they reached the bottom of the stairs. But they kept in step with the line of passengers ahead of them, marching with backpacks now over one shoulder for a short while across the tarmac and then through the big doors and into the terminal. As they came to the top of a long flight of stairs into the building, they all were perspiring already, and soon they followed Alex and Jess to the restrooms for pit stops before heading to Baggage Claim.

Cal emerged from the men's bathroom to join his family (which like the women's room, to everyone's surprise, was air conditioned, unlike the terminal itself), and exclaimed "Do you hear that?!"

And they did all hear what sounded like some sort of drum line and music combo, *like from a luau or something*, thought Meg, as she walked alone down the corridor between the restrooms and an adjacent cafe (which was closed given the early hour). Glancing to one side she saw some large framed art prints on the wall. Moving a bit closer, she noticed they featured women, dressed in what she thought looked like historical clothing - probably from the area. The portraits, painted in bright colors, were quite old, or at least they seemed like it to her. Something about one of the prints, with three women depicted in the original painting, made her look again, and she didn't quite understand the reason for her fascination...but then she laughed to herself, thinking, *Girl, you are REALLY tired, better stop spacing out!*

Meanwhile, Alex had spied - across the concourse from the restrooms - a bank ATM, with a sign above it reading in French "Billetterie." He quickly pulled out his debit card to withdraw a small amount of local currency, roughly $200 US dollars' worth of French Pacific Francs (designated CFP or XPF) at about a ten-to-a dollar exchange value. While the Websters stood by with all their cabin baggage and Alex completed his CFP2000 financial transaction, Keely began to (try to) translate in her mind some of the wording on the airport notices and posters on the walls around them, though it wasn't really that hard because most had English versions of their messages somewhere, even if in smaller print.

Five minutes later, as they proceeded through the terminal together, the music they'd heard upon arrival grew louder. And what they encountered just after that forced them all to wake up for real, and quickly. *What a way to start a vacation!* Jess thought, probably the same reaction as most of the other bleary-eyed passengers joining them for the morning in this island nation.

That's because as they rounded a final corner, the relative calmness of the terminal was fully replaced by a raucous scene, punctuated by a rapid drumbeat from a band of fancifully attired male Tahitians performing a song of welcome for the visitors. All this amid a steadily growing heat in the open-air hall, and it wasn't yet 6:30 am!

Alex grinned at the performance, but he was focused most on just taking care of their next steps at this point. He was ready to go grab their bags and find their transportation to the Moorea ferry terminal. Instead, he stopped in his tracks, along with Jess and the Webster girls, when suddenly, and for some unknown reason, Cal, and a boy from another family that Alex vaguely recognized from their plane from L.A., started dancing wildly up and down and from side to side, thrusting arms, legs, and heads to and fro. Alex and Jess glanced at each other to confirm their thoughts on this 'other' show to accompany the drummers. They both burst into laughter at the impromptu performance by Cal and his new dancing partner!

In a moment more passengers, including several other parents, siblings, and perfect strangers, all initially shocked by the outburst and cacophony, stopped to watch the spectacle. They began to clap in unison, roughly in tune with the band's pulsating drums. Everybody was soon smiling and/or laughing at the instant rejuvenation via the Polynesian rhythm provided by a couple of cute kids who just a few minutes earlier had been difficult to rouse from sleep and had to be half-dragged up the terminal stairs. Now, it seemed it was a whole new day of energy and anticipation - here in an inviting tropical paradise, albeit inside a crowded airport terminal.

Alex marveled at the craziness, just drinking in the festive spirit of their warm welcome to French Polynesia. Meanwhile, his daughters looked half amused and half embarrassed by Cal's antics, though they were leaning more towards the former than the latter, he thought. The other boy's sister, however, was standing off to the side, hiding her face in her hands.

Gotta give him credit, that kid, thought Keely of her brother. *He's not afraid of how he looks, he just responds to the moment and goes for it!*

Meg was actually moving to the beat where she stood too, not nearly as demonstrably as Cal, but 'feeling the rhythm' herself.

Anyone witnessing the joint performance really couldn't help joining in, at least a bit. The rapid high and low taps and thumps on the various drums were both insistent and friendly. *It's like they're saying "Welcome to your adventure!"* Jess mused.

After a few minutes of standing and watching the enthusiastic, percussive greeting and spontaneous dance routines of the young visitors, Alex felt his momentary sense of awakening starting to melt under the warmth and humidity of the terminal.

Back to business! He motioned to Cal and the others to follow. They still had to clear Immigration and Customs, *and then* they had a ferry to catch.

Chapter 19

Bienvenue (Websters), or is that Maeva?

6:25 am Tahiti Time, November 25, Friday
Faa'a Airport, Tahiti

Walking past the band, continuing to play as loudly as ever while the remaining passengers from the Los Angeles flight followed behind them, the Websters entered the line for what turned out to be a surprisingly quick and easy journey through Immigration- just presenting the forms Alex and Jess had jointly filled out for themselves and the children, and a few questions about the purpose of their visit. Alex guessed it might have been easier and faster than typically the case at some airports because there weren't too many flights arriving - along with theirs from LAX - at this early hour.

Soon, they exited through a door to Baggage Claim, then walked onward to the revolving carousel assigned to their flight. Meg accompanied her dad toward the huge line of moving bags, where they and the others were able to spy and remove their five pieces of luggage by the second full turn of the baggage belt. As experienced travelers, they all felt not losing any bags from a flight was lucky, and a pretty good result - both for the airline, and for the Websters. Counting bags and matching them up with each family member, Alex readied himself and the rest of the crew from Tacoma to go through the next phase of entering French Polynesia, the Customs line.

Passengers were queued in two designated lines at this point, but like the Immigration line, the one for non-citizens and visitors, which included the Websters and others who didn't fit the Tahitian or French designation, moved surprisingly quickly. Alex presented all their travel papers to the uniformed agent at once and answered the typical questions about items they were 'declaring' for duty ("Nothing, thanks," answered Alex and Keely piped up *"Non, Merci,"* which drew a smile from the official.) He handed back Alex's sheaf of documents, and waved them all through. Finally, the Websters, pulling bags and lugging backpacks that seemed extra heavy at the moment, exited the baggage claim facility through two surprisingly small doors to the main terminal outside.

As they emerged from the Customs area, Alex scanned the crowded scene, then said, "Follow me," and led the Websters across the sidewalk to the waiting shuttle driver, standing in front of a van parked along the street. He waved a big, hand-printed sign that read "*Moorea Ferry, Webster*" and something else on its reverse.

After handing off their luggage to the driver at the rear, Meg, Cal and Keely headed straight to the large seat that stretched across the back of the vehicle to sit down. Jess followed, and sat on one side of the center-facing seats just in front of them.

Alex spoke with the driver who had now finished loading their bags and was consulting his clipboard, then he made his way back to sit down next to Jess. A moment later, the three other members of the family and the boy who had been dancing with Cal a few minutes earlier boarded the bus. Mom, dad, daughter, and son mounted the steps after handing off their own heavy bags to the driver for stowage. Jess thought the parents looked to be in their early 40's, the boy around Cal's age, and their daughter probably around ten or eleven or so, in between Keely and Meg.

"Hi there!" Alex greeted them from the rear as their four fellow travelers from L.A. claimed facing seats on the van's other side.

"Bonjour! Good morning! Are you going to the Moorea Ferry too?" the woman asked, in slightly accented English...but Alex couldn't ascertain its foreign source.

"Yes, on the 'foot ferry, the *Moorea Express*," he replied.

"Oh, we will be taking a car on the *Aremiti*."

Meg had noticed that the woman's complexion was fairly light, yet she bore a resemblance to some of the Tahitians they had observed on the plane, in the terminal, and at the customs gates, as well as in the intro movies she and Keely had watched on one of the flight's video channels.

"Are you coming to visit like us, or are you from here?" Meg asked the young girl, seated across from her as the van began to roll down the road toward the airport exit.

Instead of responding, the girl turned her head and looked down, ignoring Meg's question.

"Actually," answered her father, "my wife and I met here about 15 years ago when I was visiting on vacation with friends. We well, you know, Polynesia, paradise and all that..." He looked at his wife and they both smiled. "We fell in love...and the rest," sweeping his arm to indicate his son and daughter, then returning to face Meg, Alex, and the others, "is history, as they say!"

"I'm Victor Martinez," by the way, the man continued, extending his hand to Alex, "and this is my wife Rai - it's actually Raiana - and this is our daughter Tiarenui..."

The girl abruptly interrupted him and said "It's Tiare!" with a bit of an edge to her voice.

"And our son Lincoln - 'Linc' for short," Victor went on. "We were creative with their names, as I'm Mexican-American third generation and Rai is originally from here, or Moorea, that is. The kids' names are a 'combo' of their backgrounds. We now live in Denver."

"Great to meet you all," Alex replied. "I'm Alex Webster and these are my three...Keely, Meg, and Cal - short for Callan, and Meg is short for Meghan. This is their nanny Jessica, who's joining us on this trip too. It's actually a combination business and vacation trip for all of us – at least for some of the time! We're here from Tacoma, Washington and staying at the Montcalm Resort on Moorea."

Raiana nodded in recognition. "Oh yes, I've heard from my family about the work they're doing there. In fact, my brother is the superintendent for the construction company that is just finishing up its renovations. My uncle and aunt used to manage the hotel that it's replacing as representatives of our family, before it was purchased by Montcalm, plus the property next door as well - that's where we are staying while we're here. Our family hated to give up the resort that has now become the Montcalm, but we just couldn't compete with the big hotel chains coming in, and we liked their approach most of all the bidders for our property. They did offer us a very fair price too...Anyway, I hear they're doing a nice job and the updates and additions are in excellent taste, and authentic to Tahitian traditions."

"I'm really glad to hear you say that," Alex said, "because I like to think that my company is part of improving the travel industry and the guest experience, and not tearing it down, even if sometimes that happens literally...Because in this case we've been contracted by the parent company of the Montcalm Moorea to update software and systems to, you know, make it easier to run the property efficiently and better serve their guests."

"We're trying to get some things figured out while we're here too," Vic said, glancing over at his wife. Alex waited, but he didn't say any more.

Vic changed the subject to their immediate transport plans. "Like Rai said, we are picking up her sister's car and driving it across on the other ferry. She had to travel over to Tahiti for an errand in town and left it for us to use for a few days, then she'll ride back on your ferry and we'll pick her up with the car on the other side."

"Hey Dad...we're almost there!" said Cal, drawing everyone's attention to the side window. The van was arriving at the ferry dock, where they could see a large sign, bearing the name "*Moorea Express"* in front of a large loading area. Another sign near it pointed to the landing berth and boarding for the *Aremiti,* a few hundred yards beyond to their left.

The van driver pulled into the passenger drop-off lane on the side of the parking lot and they began to disembark. As Alex followed the other Websters out, he turned to Raiana and Victor and said, "Well, hope you have a great trip, maybe we'll run into you on Moorea!"

They both smiled and nodded, Victor chuckling, "I bet we will, it's a pretty small island!"

"Bye!" the boy said to Cal as the Websters left the van.

Cal returned the well wishes, adding, "See you on the island?"

"Sure!" answered Linc's mother in response, flashing a quick smile and wave to Meg.

Catching her eye, Meg gave a start and almost dropped her bag. *What the heck?* She thought. *No way...how?*

Keely followed her sister's gaze, and saw her rapid change of expression. "Wow, you must REALLY be tired, you're spacing out!"

"No kidding! I think I am, because for some reason I could SWEAR I have seen that woman before!"

"And where would that have been? Actually, could have been on the plane, plus we saw them in the airport...come on, sis. Forget about it! Let's go get changed for the ferry ride!"

In a moment, the Websters were reunited outside with their luggage. They all thanked the driver and though tips weren't required or expected by local custom, Alex handed the man a CFP1000 note – about ten dollars - for his help with the bags. With a smile, the driver got back in to move the van a short distance to the next ferry landing. That's where the Martinez family would also unload and apparently pick up their car for the trip to the island on the other side. Cal waved and Linc waved back.

His sister Tiare looked the other way.

Chapter 20

Morning sail to Moorea

7:15 am Tahiti Time, November 25, Friday
Papeete Ferry Port

Keely was really glad she'd done some last-minute research on the ferry ride details while on the plane from LA. The 'welcome' videos onboard were helpful, and the in-flight magazine had included a detailed travel guide for their destination. All of this supplemented the info she'd already put together online, from the encyclopedia, and from books at the Tacoma library before they left on the trip, plus what her dad had relayed to them from his conversations with contacts at the Montcalm resort.

As they waited with their baggage for the arrival of the fast passenger-only catamaran, Keely looked to the side of the terminal building and saw a small cafe and inside waiting area. There she also saw a sign indicating "*toilettes*" next to the Tahitian spelling "*fare iti.*"

She turned to her father. "Hey Dad, we've got 15 minutes before we board the ferry. Can we change clothes and hit the restroom again?"

Everybody agreed this was a good idea, as they were not only getting hotter in the rising Tahiti sun, but really starting to sweat and feeling a bit confined in their jeans, long-sleeved shirts, and shoes. Except for Alex, still in his flip flops from his ill-fated (but ultimately convenient, he could at least admit now) change of footwear at the LA airport. Keely thought that it was kind of awesome that they had left LAX just over ten hours previously - and suddenly it was time to dress down and get really comfortable for their new, temporary "home" here in the tropics.

As the Webster clan reached the building and entered through the glass doors, they all felt a bit cooler, even though it wasn't air conditioned. Still, it was a relief from the hot sun, Keely thought, as she spied the arrows for the restrooms pointing towards the back of the spacious room.

Alex proposed a plan: "Let's split up here...Jess, how about you and the girls take your bags with you to the ladies' room and Cal and I will go to the men's. There are supposed to be dressing areas in there as well, or at least room to change. Don't forget your hats! We'll meet back out here in seven minutes, so don't take too long!"

Jess, Keely, and Meg found the women's restroom to be quite large, and it had several benches with little partitions between plus big mirrors with plugs on the wall above three separate sinks. Toilet stalls, with partitions stretched floor to ceiling, lined one side.

After taking care of business, they washed up and wiped off their faces, then moved their bags over to the changing areas. Each of them opened their larger suitcases and found shorts, t-shirts, and hats and quickly exchanged them for the clothes they had worn on the plane - Keely grinning knowingly at Meg as she used the "special" plastic bag their dad had given each of them for such purposes (he was crazy about splitting things into separate bags - to "stay organized" - as he put it - on trips.) In the process, the two girls switched out their underclothes for swim suits. "We want to be ready to jump in the water RIGHT when we get to our hotel!" said Keely and Meg nodded her approval. Jess did the same.

Meanwhile, Alex and Cal were making similar decisions in the men's room, both changing to lighter shirts and hats to top off shorts and flip-flops. Alex took Cal's 'plane clothes' and stuffed them in one of the plastic bags he'd brought for laundry and other essentials, like lotions and sunscreen, adding his own as well after carefully checking both his and his son's pants pockets for anything important left behind. He decided to take a couple minutes to brush his teeth and encouraged Cal to do the same, handing him the small tube of toothpaste and a fresh toothbrush still in the cellophane wrapper from the zippered heavy cloth travel kit - shared with his son - that he'd brought in his checked suitcase.

Refreshed, the male members of the Webster party stepped back into the waiting room and the girls emerged momentarily as well. Glancing at his watch, Alex saw they had less than ten minutes 'til the Moorea Express would arrive, and he noticed across the parking lot that some of the people were now lined up at the boarding platform.

His eyes glimpsed a small souvenir/food shop, and he walked quickly to it, using one of his 5000 CFP notes to buy a package of

French breath mints and what appeared to be a decent quality tourist travel map, with Moorea on one side and Tahiti on the reverse. The small selection of sunscreen available was super expensive, around 1800 CFP so he passed on it - they would need to find "reef-safe" stuff on Moorea anyway - and this wasn't it. Alex cursed himself for forgetting to buy it in the U.S. before they left on the trip. *Have to find it locally!* On the spur of the moment, before he left the counter, he bought five candy bars and five small bottles of water, taking a quick sip from his own and slipping it next to the candy bars in the top of his suitcase to keep them cool, all inside a plastic bag containing one of the bottles of regular sunscreen (SPF 40) they HAD brought along, some SPF 30 lip balm, and a bottle of aloe vera lotion for after-sun moisturizing and sunburn relief. The kids often teased him about the separate, small bags he used during traveling, but it sure made finding and storing things easier 'on the road'!

Alex quickly applied some of the sunscreen to his face, neck and arms, and added a bit more to his legs and toes. Cal was next, getting the same treatment. When he offered the sunscreen to the girls, Jess said "Thanks, but we've already put it on while we changed."

"Great...now is everybody ready for round three of our South Pacific adventure?" Alex asked.

"Onward, Captain Webster!" said Meg, with a mock salute to her father. They all followed him outside where the Moorea Express catamaran - bigger than any boat of this type any of them had ever seen before - had just arrived into the dock. They joined the growing line of people in the brightening sun near the boarding ramp as a small number of passengers streamed off after completing the crossing from the island across the channel.

Alex noticed the girls had taken off their hats, and he gently suggested they put them on and keep them on, as they'd need the protection as the sun rose further in the sky, even though it was still really early in the morning. He didn't normally worry as much about things like that in places that were further away from the equator such as Washington State and even Northern California, but this place was hot and the angle of the sun meant quick burning, especially to light complexions like theirs! Alex cinched the neck cord – which he rarely used - on his own wide-brimmed hat a bit tighter to keep it from blowing off during the upcoming crossing.

Reaching into the top of his backpack, Alex pulled out the manila travel folder, remembering with a brief shudder the near-disaster of the flight over. At this point, having cleared customs into Papeete with their passports and immigration forms all approved for the week, he only needed the five paper vouchers he'd arranged to be mailed to him ahead of time. Each covered round-trip passage on the Moorea Express, and he thought they were pretty inexpensive tickets at only about $14 US dollars each. For a 30-minute trip, both ways, it seemed to be a real bargain compared to all the other trips the family had taken elsewhere, especially on the water. Soon, the line switched direction and the Websters joined those trooping onboard.

Keely and Meg took the lead once they'd been checked in by the agent onto the ferry. It was around 136 feet long, as they had read, and there were several staircases on both the starboard and port (right and left) sides, both fore (front) and aft (rear) of the ship. The two Webster girls, with some difficulty but buoyed by their excitement, carried their backpacks up the steep stairs to the second deck, while their dad yelled "I'll meet you up there!" and checked all of their suitcases in with the attendant at the room provided for their luggage during the crossing. He then followed Jess and Cal up the stairs to join his daughters, who had commandeered a prominent perch and saved five seats near the bow of the ship's sundeck. On the way to the upper seating area, Alex noticed a nicely-equipped (and empty) cafe, and also enjoyed, just for a few seconds, its air conditioning, before stepping through the glass doors to the deck and the stairway beyond.

As the ferry finished up its boarding, there was a small whistle, then they began backing out of the berth. When the ship reached the middle of the small harbor, the captain transferred to forward power and slowly brought the bow of the ship around to face the sea beyond and they cruised slowly out beyond the breakwater area. Once they cleared the harbor, their speed increased steadily until they were moving very fast.

An announcement came over the public address system. Alex couldn't discern its exact meaning, though the French portion was roughly translated by Keely. He did catch the word "cafe" and with a glance over his shoulder and down on the deck below, he saw that it was now open - or would be soon - judging by the handful of people who had lined up in front of it. He heard "*Ia Orana*" and "*Maeva*" and at the end "*Maururu*", but the rest went waaaay over his fairly tired and uncomprehending head. *Better start studying the language a little more*, Alex thought.

In a few moments, the initial welcome they'd heard was followed by "*Le Café est maintenant ouvert. Veuillez nous rejoindre sur le pont supérieur où nous avons une variété de rafraîchissements disponibles à l'achat.*"

Figuring they had probably 25 minutes more to go on the ten mile trip across the Moorea Channel (called "Te Tai Mo'orea" in Tahitian, according to Alex's map) to Moorea's Vai'are ferry landing, Alex walked down to join the queue at the cafe counter and reached in the glass case near it for five very cold cans of fruit juice, longingly eyeing the beer cans sitting on another rack in the refrigerator but quickly reminding himself that a) he would have to do some work after they arrived, and b) it was not even 8 o'clock in the morning yet, even if this did feel a LOT like a vacation right now! Paying for the purchases with a 2000 CFP note, he got a little change back. *Building my supply of local small bills and coins already!* Alex thought. Tucking the cans into his backpack's top pocket, he walked back through the doors to the deck, beckoning Cal on the way and handing his son several of the coins, which he eagerly examined before putting them into his own pocket.

Rejoining the girls, Alex shifted his feet a bit to keep his balance as the boat bounced lightly over the waves, mild at this time of day as was the wind - the island of Moorea directly in their view in the distance as they skimmed rapidly across the channel. He handed out the drinks to Jess and the girls, opening his and Cal's thereafter.

"Cheers!" he said.

Cal corrected him, substituting the Tahitian word for the salute, which he had just learned from watching a group of young travelers toasting their own trip together. "Menu-ee-Ya!" he exclaimed with a flourish, (which Alex found out later was actually spelled "*Manuia*") and they all clinked their cans together in toast.

"Yay!" Meg said, "we made it to Tahiti!"

"And we're almost to Moorea!" added Keely.

Jess beamed at them all and thought to herself, *So cool to be a part of this family*.

As if reading her mind, Alex raised his can of fruit juice in her honor. "Jess, just want to say thanks so much for joining us on this trip."

"Yeah!" chimed in Cal.

The girls raised their juice containers, then did so again in a (somewhat) coordinated salute to accompany Meg's final toast.

"To the Worldwide Websters, all five of us!"

Several prominent mountain peaks loomed larger and larger in front of the ship's bow as the ferry drew closer to Moorea. A few smaller boats, some with sails, some under power, passed around the Moorea Express and in the distance.

"OK, Cal...what mountains are we looking at now?" asked Jess, and the boy quickly consulted the little booklet of key facts he had printed out prior to their trip.

"Let's see...I think that's *Mt. Tohiea-or Tohieva?* right in front of us, the tallest at just over 1200 meters high, or almost 4,000 feet. *Mt. Rotui* is the one that sits on the other side of the island between the two bays, then there's *Mouaputa, Tearai, Tautaupae,* and *Mouapu*...well anyway, those are the top six tallest ones."

Alex was proud of his son for trying to pronounce each, though he guessed the true names might be pronounced a bit differently in Tahitian than Cal had stated. "We're staying right in between the two bays you mentioned," Alex explained, "but like you said, to get to the Montcalm, we have to take the highway around that point there to *Te'avaro* on our right, or to the north, and then continue in a westerly direction after we pass the airport and the town of *Temae* over to the north side of the island. He looked toward where the ferry was heading, and could now see an expanse of beach and vegetation punctuated by some low buildings and a few roads to and from what was clearly the *Vai'are* ferry landing.

Just then, an announcement came across the ship's speakers. Like with their debarkation, Alex heard a few words he recognized (after the Tahitian) in French: *"Attention les passagers, nous arriverons sous peu à Moorea. Veuillez revenir pour récupérer vos bagages et être prêt à débarquer. Merci!"*

Time to get ready to departure leave the ferry, they all understood *that* much.

Walking down the staircase, the Webster contingent dropped their empty juice cans in the recycling bin provided and joined the group lining up near the exit/entrance where they had boarded the boat in Papeete. Alex pointed out their five large bags to the luggage attendant and he wheeled them out to them. Soon, the boat had docked aside the pier and passengers began to disembark.

Saying "*Maururu!*" to the crew, the Websters strode together, dragging their bags across the loading ramp onto shore. "*Moorea*" said the sign on the row of low buildings opposite them, and off to their right was a parking lot full of various vehicles, rental cars and scooters. In addition to the unassuming ferry terminal, there was a small restaurant, a food truck-looking thing, and a long vehicle that looked like an old bus.

"I think that's what they call '*Le Truck*'" Alex whispered to his son, "It's like their bus service, goes all around the island."

Cal replied "Are we going on it?"

"No, we have a van from the hotel picking us up," answered his dad.

They noticed a few people selling souvenirs, including one woman with a table of jewelry and a small rack holding several bright sarongs (a sign said "pareu/pareo") in various colors and tie-dye patterns, which the girls immediately walked towards and began to admire. Alex turned his attention towards a group of people standing in a line near the parking lot holding signs. One, a tall woman with long dark brown hair held up a sign reading "*Resort Montcalm Moorea*" and bearing its logo, while underneath was printed "*Utuafare Webster*."

The Webster entourage walked over to her and she greeted them with a smile. "*Iorana, Manava e Moorea*," then "You are Mister Webster?" in stilted English.

"Yes, umm, *Oui*," Alex replied, thinking French might work better as a means of communication. Pointing to all of them, he wiped his brow, gave up and reverted to English. "We are the Webster party."

Next, the woman introduced herself, just as he saw her name tag. Extending her hand, she said to Alex, also nodding to the others: "I am Ravanui Temauri, Assistant Manager at the Montcalm Moorea Resort. So happy you to meet!"

Chapter 21

Montcalm - meet the Websters!

8:10 am Tahiti Time, November 25, Friday

Once they had pulled away from the parking lot, Ms. Temauri turned around from her front passenger seat in the large transport van and reiterated warmly that she was glad they had come. "Is this your first...umm.... trip Tahiti?"

Alex answered for them. "Yes, none of us have been to French Polynesia before. Other warm places, but not here!"

The hotel representative smiled widely. "Welcome to our island, my home. Soon, we will be at Montcalm Moorea."

For the next 15 minutes, the Webster party marveled at the lush, yet primitive landscape, the tall palm trees and, of course, the towering mountains. Yes, there were more heavily populated sections, especially by the airport. Yet, they still occasionally caught whiffs of sea air, and passing by a grove of trees in full flower, a sweet, pleasant scent from their blossoms. It was green just about everywhere, until the road wound back toward the ocean and that deep, cerulean blue water came into view. Boats bobbed lazily in the lagoon as they made their way in a northwesterly direction, counterclockwise via what they'd all seen on the map was the only round-the-island road. They passed small strip shopping centers (tiny, by US standards) and a few offices and similar-looking buildings, and then began to change direction again, following the road down the side of a long inlet to its head.

Cal proudly pointed out they were circling *Cook's Bay*, according to his map. Their escort, Ms. Temauri nodded her agreement with a smile. They observed no small number of chickens and a few dogs too along the sides of the roadway. Not many people, though.

They continued around the other side of the bay, then followed one last bend in the road around the shore and reached an understated, yet very nicely carved wood and iron gateway sign, reading "*Montcalm Resort Moorea.*" Keely giggled as she glanced at her sister, her look of excitement saying what she was thinking. *Let the fun begin! We are here!*

Once the van stopped, Alex stepped out last to join his family standing and waiting as a bellman unloaded their luggage.

"Please follow me," Ms. Temauri said, leading the way into the beautifully landscaped, yet fairly compact lobby, which was framed by rings of live flowers and large plants of several different varieties.

As they walked toward the front desk, their Tahitian escort moved her arms widely around and said "*Maeva!* Welcome to our resort!" After speaking quietly to the attendant, she then walked around the edge of the carved wood desk and into the back room. In a moment, Ms. Temauri re-emerged with a tall, middle-aged man who spoke with what Jess immediately placed as a Scottish accent.

"Thanks, Rava. Hello, Mr. Webster and family! Welcome to the Montcalm Moorea." He extended his hand to Alex. "I am David Thomson, General Manager here. My team and I are eager to work with you on the software installation. It's great that we have that family connection to your company through my cousin Roger, and," he turned to face Jess and the children, "we're even more thrilled that you brought your own family to visit with us."

"Great to meet you, Mr. Thomson. We -"

Thomson grinned and waved his hand to the side. "Please call me David, all of you."

Alex grinned. "Same goes for me, David. Alex is fine!"

David smiled at Jess and the kids: "I'd wager that you would all love to see the beach, right?"

"YEAH!" replied all three of the Websters in unison, and Jess's face lit up as well.

He turned to the girls. "Are you ready to enjoy a swim?"

"We've already got our suits on!" answered Keely.

"Well, then, that's perfect, I'll walk you down to the beach now. But if you, Cal, need to put your swimming trunks on, don't worry, there is a small changing room there, ample towels, a small shower, and even a little beach cafe and bar along the way. Do you have sunscreen?"

'Um yes, but it's not the reef-safe kind," answered Jess.

"No worries at all." Thomson walked to his office and came back shortly with a small tube. "This is a special non-harming sunscreen," reading its label to them, "containing no oxybenzone or octinoxate or other ingredients harmful to sea life, and it's concocted right here on Moorea, by one of our local businesses, in fact. It's excellent and provides good sun protection, and doesn't have ingredients to bleach our coral or poison the fish. We're trying to protect our sea life and reef, as they still represent some of the most beautiful, unspoiled marine habitat in the world. There has been some major damage in the past, so it's not an easy task."

"Thanks so much, Mr. Thom-I mean David. That's really helpful and I'm glad we have the 'good stuff' to use in the sun - and water - here," Alex said.

Keely opened the bottle and sniffed it: "That smells wonderful!"

"Yes, there's a small amount of oil from our local species of gardenia, the *Tiare,* as part of its ingredients, many of which are imported. But it works!" said the friendly Scotsman.

Alex turned to the others. "Hey guys, do a quick check and make sure that nothing in your backpacks will melt, then take them down with you to the beach, or just leave them here and the bell staff will take them to our room. Either way. I've got to get some things set up here for our software project, but it shouldn't take me too long. When I'm done, I'll be joining you down there. Don't forget to wear lots of that sunscreen and your hats when you're not in the water! See you soon!"

And with that, Thomson handed Alex off to Ms. Temauri, then strode off with Jess and the Webster kids walking alongside him down a path to the lagoon.

"Please call me Rava," the hotel employee said, and Alex replied "And you can call me Alex," as she led him through double glass doors to the office, a large room in the rear of the building. There Alex saw three desks which held a couple of personal computers and monitors, a printer, and a large central drive station. *All looks in pretty good order so far*, he thought to himself.

Alex had told his family he was already very optimistic that this installation would run more quickly and smoothly than many he'd been involved with in the past. That's because he had not only found a solid contact to work with locally at the hotel, but also had been collaborating with a helpful and knowledgeable representative from the hotel management company's information technology (IT) department. That made for a strong start in any situation, but the extra pre-testing they'd already been able to do meant they were possibly two days ahead of a typical schedule for a software install, which usually took a full week from start to finish. If he could complete a couple more steps today, and collaborate with his team in Seattle to ensure the results turned out well on the tests, Alex projected the project could be done before the following Thursday, or at least by Thursday morning.

And that, hopefully, meant *lots of time to hang out with the family and see the island*, he thought.

Alex was removing his USB "thumb" drives and unpacking other equipment from his bag when in walked Bernard Tetuanui, his main contact during all the project's preliminary long-distance discussions. Bernard, or "Bernie" as he preferred to be called, was part Tahitian, part French and was an expert on the hotel and the local history and happenings. He was the one who had helped ensure all the logistical details were set for the visit by Alex and the kids and Jess.

"Alex!" Tetuanui said, rushing in to shake his hand.

"Bernie!" Alex returned the greeting. "So glad to finally meet you in person. Thanks so much for all you've done for me to make this a great trip - and for my family too. Really appreciate it."

"*Aita pea pea*, Alex. No problem! You are part of our family now, our *utuafare. Maeva e Moorea!*" Now let's get you started so we can get you back to your family for the long weekend!"

And they sat down at the table across from each other to do just that.

A couple of hours later, with way more progress made even than Alex had initially hoped for (much due to coordination between Bernie and Alex's team back at LodgeSoft in Seattle), they were ready to take an early break on the project for the weekend. *They must have something like 'Aloha Friday' (get off early) here in Moorea,"* thought Alex. *At least I hope so. I'm ready to hit that water for a swim!"*

Chapter 22

A 'calm' and pleasant plunge

11:55 am Moorea Time, November 25, Friday

Using the magnetic key card programmed for their room - one of two assigned, the other had been given to Jess by David while she was with the kids at the beach - Alex entered their shared rooms, called the "Family Bungalow" by the Montcalm in its brochure. As he looked around the tastefully designed and surprisingly spacious main room, he was impressed by the quality and decor, from the Tahitian patchwork bedspreads bearing prominent images of tiare, bougainvillea, hibiscus, and other flowers, to the walls with photos and etchings of various elements of Polynesian life, including more flora, fauna, beach and lifestyle scenes.

Whales here, breadfruit trees there, a print of an ancient painting of a Tahitian celebration - with dancers and a royal court, it appeared - and two turtles swimming undersea in a placid lagoon in a framed painting mounted across the room. The medium-sized refrigerator was a nice touch, and opening it he felt that even more, as it contained several bottles of fruit juice and water. The sign above it said - as he was able to eventually guess - that they would be replenished daily at no charge. "Bonus!" Alex exclaimed with a grin.

Looking further, he saw that there was a bank of two outlets right within the queen sized (and very solid) wood bed frame, with sort of a ledge built into the headboard, and on one side of the long desk with two chairs was a small coffee maker, coffee, and creamer packets, plus two large size bottles of what Alex surmised was local spring water. On the other side of the room was a dark wood dresser with two large and three small drawers on each side. A small CD player/speaker combo sat on top. But, he noticed, no TV in the room. No phone, and no internet service either. *No loss there!* Alex thought wryly. He imagined the kids would have plenty to do without these modern 'conveniences' and, he mused *hopefully they'll be so tired when they return to the room that they'll fall right asleep each night*, as he envisioned a very active nine days ahead for all of them.

Walking into the main bathroom, Alex admired its simple design, with a tub and shower and toilet, elegantly appointed with coral-colored tile and cream accents over a deep brown-colored tile floor. There were several towels of varying sizes in a thatched basket on top of the dual-sink tiled vanity. He examined the basket more closely; it appeared to be made of bamboo and pandanus leaves, like some of the plants he'd seen being tended and trimmed on the resort's grounds. Cal had called them "giant houseplants" when they arrived. *He's right about that!* thought Alex. *This is the lushest landscaping I have ever seen - just like an indoor/outdoor tropical garden!*

Taking a quick look into the girls' bedroom, he saw their bags sitting in the corner, next to a double bed, flanked by two side tables and a cushioned chair of what looked to be native wood in the corner. He walked through the smaller bathroom adjoining it, with shower, sink, and toilet, and opened the connecting door to another small room. He was pleased to see it contained a single bed with several quilted pillows, as well as a small table and chair and a screened window. *Should work well for Jess*, he thought.

Alex sighed with approval and a bit of relief as he returned to the main room where he and Cal would sleep. With two hours of solid, productive work in the books, and more progress towards getting the implementation going than he had expected in his best estimates, it was almost Friday afternoon - time to change clothes and relax. He was finally ready to really *experience* Moorea!

He pressed the 'power' button on the CD player, then 'play', and a peaceful Polynesian tune began to fill the room. Unzipping his suitcase, Alex pulled out several separate bags which held his clothes and transferred them to one side of the drawers in the dresser. He stripped off his travel/work clothes and underclothes and switched into his swim suit (board shorts) and a light t-shirt. Just as he was about to open a bottle of water for a sip, he heard a key being inserted in the door, and seconds later, in walked the four remaining members of the Worldwide Websters (+1, Jess), looking a bit 'pinker' (slightly sunburned) and with wetter hair than when he'd last seen them.

"Hi Dad!" came the stereo greeting from his daughters, followed by others from Cal and Jess as they all took off their flip flops, dropped them by the entrance outside on the mat provided, then re-entered and sat down on the chairs in the room and on the main room's bed.

"So, tell me, how's the beach look?" Alex asked, looking around the room.

Keely was first to respond. "Oh, Dad, it's amazing, the sand is really grainy and HOT, but the water is so nice, it's almost like bathwater. We found a nice tree to set our stuff under - David -the manager - suggested a special place on the beach he really likes. We all went for a swim and Cal even came out for a while with Meg and me."

"Anyway, we saw soooo many fish!" added Meg.

"Yeah!" Cal chipped in, "And there are sea urchins all over the rocks. We decided we need our water shoes on, at least on some parts of the shallow water, because everybody warned us to watch out for them."

Jess turned to Alex, adding to Cal's comment. "Definitely lots of sea urchins in the water, not many jellyfish, but mostly they're clinging to the rocks, or in holes, so if you're careful, you won't have to worry much. It's gorgeous water, around 80 degrees - or 27 Celsius or warmer, I think - and very clean and safe to swim around and see all the marine life. The coral's definitely damaged, but still in relatively good shape, especially compared to some places I've visited in the Caribbean and Mexico."

"Sounds awesome to me!" Alex replied, then added, "But why are you guys back here? I would have thought I'd find you lounging on towels and in sunglasses when I came down to the beach!"

"We wanted to drop off our backpacks...don't really need them down by the water," Meg explained. The others nodded.

"Also, we are getting a bit hungry and wanted to see what you were doing for lunch," Keely chimed in.

"I've had a small bite a while ago over at the office," said Alex, "but I think we should definitely get you all some lunch down by the beach. How about we head down there now so I can experience more of this *Moorea magic* while you guys enjoy some of the local food and drinks?"

"Sounds like a plan to me!" said Cal.

Jess and the kids took a quick first look into the other rooms and marveled at how nice and "Polynesian" everything was...depositing their bags and other stuff on the floor and beds.

"How do you like your room, Jess?" Alex asked.

"Beautiful, just like the rest of this place, Alex, thanks!"

"Great, hopefully it will work out well with you sharing the bathroom with the girls and Cal and I sharing the other one. Everybody can hang out in this room too whenever you want to. We can keep some snacks and drinks in our fridge and I can ask for another one for your room, Jess."

"I'm sure that will be fine, Alex. No need for another fridge."

The girls and Jess took turns visiting their restroom while Cal used the other, and then they were all ready to head back down to the beach. Alex brought his book to read and his backpack containing several water bottles and a few snacks. When they arrived first at the small restaurant/beach bar along the way, they grabbed a menu and ordered lunch for Jess and the kids.

Keely and Jess chose Mahi Mahi fish sandwiches and tropical tea, and Meg and Cal got chicken sandwiches with the same drinks. Each meal came with chips and salad, but no French fries. Cal said he thought that was kind of strange, given they were in *French* Polynesia!

With the ordering done, Alex showed his room key and was told they would be brought their food on the beach when it was ready. He quickly remembered to add a beer to their tab, and the bartender poured him a tall draft of *Hinano* - a lager produced locally in Tahiti. While he was waiting for the cup to be topped up, he surveyed the bar menu and setup: Only two draft beer taps in total. Both handles read "Hinano," and he made a mental note to try the other variety of the two brews next time.

They thanked the bartender, and with Alex leading the way, and the others carrying the tropical soft drinks ordered by Jess, Keely, Meg, and Cal, they turned toward the beach, accessed down a pleasant paved path through a small grove of palms and other tall plants. It then wound to its end past an adjacent restroom/shower building.

As the somewhat rugged but sand-covered beach came fully into view, Alex gasped. "Wow, that is incredibly beautiful! Nice breeze too....and look at the color of the water!" There were only a few people on the beach at this time, and Alex figured some must be eating lunch as it was now getting towards 1 pm local time.

Meg exclaimed, "See, that's our tree! That's where we set up our towels and bags earlier." She pointed to a corner of the beach to their left with a nice ring of sand in front of it and easy access to the water beyond. They showed their room key to pick up several fresh towels from the hut at the edge of the beach trail and made their way to *"Webster Island"* as Keely called it.

Pulling off his t-shirt, Alex applied some of the local sunscreen they'd received earlier from David Thomson. He smeared it liberally across his face, neck, shoulders, stomach, upper back, arms, and finally his legs and feet. Gesturing to Keely he asked, "Can you help me with the lower back?" and she squeezed some lotion out and rubbed it thoroughly into the skin above his waist.

Alex realized he was a bit hungry now, as despite his earlier snack it was about three hours past his usual noon-Pacific lunchtime. But he was even more eager now to do one of the things he loved most - swim in the ocean. He secured his sunglasses in his backpack, pulled out and put on his swim goggles, and reminded himself to seek out rental snorkel gear for those who wanted to use it later in the week.

"Keely...want to join me for a short swim workout? Meg, Cal, Jess, you can come along too!"

Keely looked up and nodded, then finished her drink and removed her t-shirt before retrieving her goggles from her bag. This was a good chance to start the daily swim practice she had promised her coach...as during their earlier time at the beach, they had just waded around a bit and frolicked in the light waves, getting acquainted with the beach and water.

Meg, Cal, and Jess answered, "No thanks," saying they preferred to lounge and read on their towels in the semi-shade near the shore. Everybody was a bit tired from all their travels over the past thirty hours-plus. It would be easy to sleep tonight!

Alex and Keely, who had now joined him a few feet, or maybe a couple of meters, into the lagoon from the edge of the sand, waded in to the crystal-clear water, each adjusting their goggles. They then spit in and wiped a bit of saliva around the insides and rims of the plastic lenses. The lagoon was quite shallow near shore, and they both sunk into the sand to almost ankle-height as they continued to wade out until there was room to actually stretch out and swim.

Keely yelled "Here I go!" and launched herself forward into the momentarily chilling water, then immediately started to swim the crawl stroke away from her father, out across the shallow rocks towards the reef line visible several hundred yards distant heading northward. Meanwhile, Alex, following his standard practice at most ocean beaches, took a few moments to prepare himself and move beyond the shallows before he gathered the courage to plunge his own head under the water. But once he did, he noticed with relief that it was warm...chilling his body only for a few breaths as the lagoon temperature wasn't too much below his own.

As Alex followed Keely out a couple of hundred strokes from shore, a whole new world opened below them. They swam steadily, only bobbing up and down a bit in the light surf through the pristine, clear water over the sandy, rock and coral-strewn bottom that grew further away as they progressed steadily out towards the reef. During a brief stop to adjust their goggles, Keely and Alex gauged the strength and direction of currents in the lagoon as they treaded water and looked back to shore, around 500 feet, or 150-60 yards/meters +/- away by this time.

They could clearly see where the rest of the family was sitting on their towels by "their tree" at the top of the beach, and both waved, receiving waves back from Jess, Meg, and Cal in turn. As he scissor-kicked slowly to keep his chest and shoulders above water, Alex let his body feel for any prominent or dangerous currents - using the tree landmark on shore to mark his movement one way or the other from side to side along the beach.

"Not much of any rip tide here today," he said quietly to Keely, who nodded, then turned and began to swim out another 100 strokes, her dad following a few yards behind and marveling at the fish of many species swimming below and around them.

Soon, the two strong swimmers came to an outcrop of rocks where the volume of sea life increased substantially. Keely recognized Yellow Tang, Sunfish, those long silver spear-like fish she couldn't remember the names of, and tons more. Black Moors, Trigger fish like the Humu's (actually called "humuhumunukunukuapua'a") in Hawaii, but with slightly different colors. She even saw an eel, and grabbed her dad's arm and gestured toward where it stuck its big, menacing head from a rock probably ten feet below them, though its presence was magnified a bit in the clear water because of the goggles. *That spit method really does make it easier to see,* Alex thought as he followed his daughter's gaze.

They both stopped a few dozen strokes later to 'go vertical' in the calm lagoon, and Alex began to egg-beater kick again, this time lifting his arms out of the water while he executed a couple of four-point turns for both exercise and to again check if there was any strong current to be concerned with. Repeating his previous drill, he watched his relative position each time for any drift or rip that might be dangerous to even well-accomplished expert swimmers like Keely and himself. *Still good!*

As he shifted his gaze back to shore, he could now clearly see the jagged mountains of Moorea towering above the beach and framing its background. Far below, he could also see a few of the hotel's buildings and other structures along the road behind it.

Turning once more to face the reef, Alex pointed out to Keely as they floated how the ocean waves broke against the protective barrier in continuously changing patterns...some twisting, some crashing against the rocks and coral and occasionally sneaking through to eventually break very lightly onshore. "But none of them are very big...this is a pretty safe beach overall," he noted to his daughter.

Keely restarted her swim out towards the reef, continuing to count her strokes and distance for her daily swim workout. Alex returned his eyes to the beach, still slowly churning the water with his legs to stay upright. Then he followed a tradition he'd started many years before during one of the Websters' first trips to Hawaii. To Maui, actually. He said a prayer to thank God for bringing them to this beautiful, peaceful place and for a safe and thoughtful experience for the family.

After a few more moments of reflection, Alex flipped back on his stomach and swam another 100 strokes out behind Keely, catching up to her as they drew within about 50 yards of the breaking waves. It was then that he saw the turtle, suddenly looming into his field of vision, probably eight feet below him. It glided through the lightly churning waters being filtered towards the beach by the coral reef and waves beyond.

"Hey Keely!" Alex called to his daughter. But she was still swimming out toward the reef line. Turning back in the direction he had been looking, Alex greeted his fellow swimmer, *Hi there!* He actually said the words inside his head while his eyes remained riveted on the graceful animal. The turtle (*it looked like a green sea turtle*, Alex thought) continued swimming by, lightly moving its legs/fins to propel it across the rock and coral covered bottom, among the sea anemones and other abundant undersea plant life, including some fish larger than those he'd seen closer to the beach.

Keely was starting to feel the surf and current a bit more now, and she decided to surface and stop for a bit. She turned back toward the beach and waved at her dad, who was now about 50 feet away. He flipped up his goggles, and saw that Keely was looking back at him. They had now been in the water about 25 minutes, Alex guessed, and he confirmed this with a glance at his waterproof sport watch. *1:30. I'm hungry. Time to go back in for now. We'll have many more opportunities to enjoy this lagoon and this island in the coming days.*

He rinsed and re-coated his goggles, then noticed Keely had already turned back and was swimming in his direction. He adjusted the straps around the lenses and placed the goggles firmly back around his eyes again and began the swim back to shore, laughing to himself as Keely caught up to him in a burst of speed. *This is absolutely, freakin' beautiful,* Alex thought as they made their way beachward with strong, steady strokes. *I'm so lucky, and so happy to be here with the kids...and Jess too,* Alex mused. Keely, meanwhile, was pondering the same thing. *One thing about swimming,* she thought. *There's always lots of time for thinking!*

They passed over a familiar group of rocks, bearing closely attached and projecting coral and plants. Just as she recognized they had crossed over this lush outcrop on the way out, suddenly Keely saw something that made her freeze. Her dad clearly saw it too, at exactly the same moment. Stopping instantly in front of his daughter, he looked down and to the side of his field of view and there it was: *a shark!*

Alex's adrenaline was pumping, and Keely's blood had gone cold. However, Alex's shock quickly wore off when he realized it was just an eight foot long (or so) Black Tipped Reef Shark. He'd seen these before in *Anaehoomalu Bay* on the Big Island of Hawaii. They generally didn't bother human beings and were fairly common sights to swimmers and snorkelers near the reefs on many ocean beaches, especially during more quiet parts of the day, in his experience.

He turned back to Keely, right behind him and now also treading water, and told her not to worry, and why he wasn't concerned.

Both of them now sufficiently calmed down, they watched the shark swim lazily below and away from where they sat vertically in the water, focusing their eyes downward, with their legs partially tucked beneath their bodies. Once the shark was several feet past them, they swam back toward the shore with new vigor, and definitely more rapidly than they had on the way out. Soon, they both had counted more than 250 strokes and their knees and elbows began to brush the rough sand.

Alex stood up, let the water run off his body, then, followed by Keely, staggered a bit out of the sand and low surf to make their way to their family tree 'headquarters'. Stripping off their goggles, the two swept their hair back and out of their eyes. Keely was suddenly very conscious of the heat on the beach - and maybe in her body, as well, likely from increased blood (or adrenaline) flow caused by what they had just seen out in the lagoon!

Alex and Keely exchanged knowing looks. "Let's not worry the others, OK?" Alex said to his daughter in a low voice, to which she nodded as they strode to the Webster's tree vantage point. There, they saw several trays of food arrayed among the towels, with everyone else already heartily eating their sandwiches.

"Hi guys, how's lunch?"

Meg gave a thumbs-up and Cal replied "Great!"

Jess concurred, using a now-familiar Tahitian word: "*Maita'i!*"

That sounds just about right, right now, Alex thought, but wondered about the slightly different pronunciation - "May-Tay" - as he walked up and asked Jess, "Are you talking about the drink - or is that just really good tasting food!?"

Jess laughed. "Maybe both - but it's definitely the perfect term for this sandwich. REALLY tasty and fresh...I learned the word to describe it from the Tahitian server when he delivered our food!"

Alex chuckled and spread his towel out a few feet away, but still in the sand, being extra careful to not kick the sand onto its surface.

He reached into his backpack (*Ouch, it was hot! Good thing I left everything that could melt in the room!*) He pulled out his sunglasses and almost sat down, then decided it would probably be a good idea to rinse off first.

"Hey Keely, where's the shower?" he asked his daughter, who sat on her towel, digging heartily into her sandwich.

"Right back towards the bar, and then off to the left side in a little building there. They have restrooms and a small changing area too. The shower is outside between the entrances to the male and female restrooms."

"Maururu!" Alex answered, finally feeling like he was starting to 'get' the local lingo down. He smiled and began the short walk toward the shower building, then stopped after a few steps. He turned around and asked, "Anybody need anything else?"

"No thanks, Dad," came two replies, but then Meg said "Hey, Dad, can you take our trays back up to the bar area with our empty plates and stuff? Wait, never mind, I'll come with you, I gotta "go" anyway."

"Me too!" Cal exclaimed.

With that, the trio of Websters made their way up the path to the restaurant and shower/restroom buildings. Keely remained on her towel to finish her sandwich. A few minutes later, still sipping on her drink, she plucked a paperback book out of the top of her bag, while Jess did the same.

"This is the Liiiiiiiife!" Keely said, with a very happy sigh,

Jess echoed her comment. "I'll say!"

The two were lodged against their mostly empty backpacks, propped up against the tree and reading their books with hats and sunglasses on to shield against the super bright sun when they both looked up and saw someone approaching from down the beach to their right. It was the boy from the airport bus, the one Cal had joined in an impromptu dance when the Webster troop had first walked through the Papeete terminal early that morning.

"Hello!" he said as he walked up to Jess and Keely.

"Hi there...it's Lincoln, right?" said Jess.

"Yep. That's me! Sorry, I can't remember your names though..." Lincoln looked down. "But you can call me Linc, OK?"

"No problem, Linc," then winking at Jess, Keely said "*Aita pea

pea" to use the Tahitian equivalent. "I'm Keely, that's Jess, and," she gestured toward the path to the restroom building up the beach, "Meg, my sister and Cal, my brother are with my dad using the restrooms and showers over there."

Linc crinkled up his nose. "I still don't understand Tahitian very well, but my mom has been trying to teach me words for a while now...and ever since we started planning our trip back here, she's really doing it even more. We just met one of my aunts, her husband my uncle, and a bunch of cousins from here on Moorea over at our hotel. It's just around the corner of the beach over there," he said, pointing to the far-right side of the beach beyond the section that fronted the Montcalm. "But..." he looked around him, "This is a nicer beach than the one where we are staying." Linc finished his sentence with a bit of a frown.

"Is there something wrong with your hotel?" Keely asked him.

"Not really, but my mom says they're ruining it by building on top of a special place or something. She called it a 'mer-eye' - I think."

"Oh...you mean a *marae*?" Turning to Jess, Keely explained. "A marae is what they call ancient ceremonial sites built by Mooreans long ago. Supposedly there are several here on the island. I didn't know exactly where, but I guess that must be one right over there!"

She and Jess stood up and looked across the sand about 300 yards away to what did look to be a flat area with no trees, just inland from the beach and ringed with many dark rocks in sort of a wall configuration, roughly equal with four sides each about three feet tall. It was probably quite large in size when you looked more closely at it.

"I see it now," said Keely.

Jess nodded. "Oh yeah, I do too!"

Linc continued... "I'm sure it will be fine, but there is going to be lots of construction soon I guess, starting this next Monday, so I hope it isn't too loud. But I also don't want to upset the ancient people's place either, you know? Well, anyway, that's what my mom and my dad say about it. My mom was born here, so was everyone in her family. They go back hundreds and hundreds of years on this island."

Jess and Keely looked at Linc thoughtfully and nodded their heads - both also a bit more curious now than before. "I remember your mom saying she was from Moorea," said Jess. "Maybe we can talk to her more about her family's history while we are here."

"Oh sure," Linc replied. "We'll be on the island for a couple of weeks. Mom says she has to take care of some business here before we go home.... something to do with her family business— "

Abruptly, the boy cut off his speech when he glimpsed his sister, who Jess and Keely saw at the same time he did. She strode quickly up the beach and called loudly and curtly to him from several yards away. "Linc! I had no idea where you went! Next time, you *have* to *tell* me before you go wandering around!"

As the young girl arrived near the Websters' shaded spot, Keely tried to remember her name. *It was Tahitian, ummm, Ti...?*

The girl frowned and said, "Sorry if this little brat was bugging you!"

"Oh no, not at all!" replied Jess. "He just stopped by to say 'hi' and we were talking a bit about the work being done by your hotel. Linc was telling us there's going to be lots of construction soon."

"Oh, yeah...my mom thinks it's a big deal and so do most of her family here. Some sort of scandal. I don't know, it's all kinda boring to me..."

Finally remembering the details around their introduction, Keely asked, "Isn't your name Tiare?"

"Yeah, and thanks for not saying the whole thing, as if you even could, it's so loonnnng!" the girl replied.

Jess noticed Tiare's striking features, guessing that a mix of Tahitian and Mexican heritage might contribute to her appearance. "I think that's a beautiful name, it's after the flower, right?"

"Yeah, my mom is all sentimental about that stuff. I actually have a couple other names too. She really thinks keeping the Tahitian names and traditions is important."

"My middle name is "Teva!" Linc piped up proudly. "It means 'inf...a...nit'"

"That's *infinite*, dummy," said his sister with an embarrassed look.

Jess ignored Tiare's rudeness and smiled at her brother. "I think that's a really cool middle name, Linc and you've got a great first name too!"

Linc beamed, then remembered why he had come over in the first place when he'd seen them by the tree: "Where is your son, it's Cal, right?"

Jess laughed and exchanged glances with Keely. "Oh, yes, Cal, well, he's not my son, I'm actually his nanny, Jess. I'm the caregiver for Cal and Keely here and their sister Meg. Or, if I'd watched them when they were younger - you'd probably call me their babysitter. Except they are all getting so old they don't need care from me that much anymore. Mostly, I keep them out of trouble!" she laughed.

Keely replied, "Yeah, but she's also a really good transporter and cook too. Not that great at video games though!" They both giggled.

Tiare, clearly not really interested in having a friendly chat, rolled her eyes again, and grabbed her brother's arm to drag him back down the beach. He pulled away from her, glowering angrily.

Jess wanted to leave the conversation on a happy note and said, "Hey, Cal's just up by the restrooms with his dad and sister, if you can wait a bit, he should be right back, Teva," calling the boy from Denver by his middle, Tahitian name.

"No!" Tiare said, before her brother could answer. Then she turned to face Jess and Keely. "We have to go back; we have a family event coming up later this afternoon and we're already late getting back to our hotel. My mom will be mad if we don't go right now."

Jess forced a smile. "OK, well bye Linc/er Teva, bye Tiare, hope we can see you again...Linc, I'll tell Cal you came by, maybe we'll get you guys together to spend some time at the beach in the next few days while we're here. I'll try to reach your mom to arrange it, OK?"

As he was being half-dragged by his sister, Linc looked back and smiled, then quickly pulled his arm away from her, and turned around to follow Tiare of his own accord. Keely watched as they trudged back down the deep sandy beach to their hotel.

"Wow, is she ever mean to him, huh?" Keely said.

Jess shook her head, sadly. She thought for a second and replied, "Yeah, and I wonder why she's got so much attitude. Something's going on with that family for sure, but we might never know. Anyway, no matter what, I'm going to ask your dad if we can set up a play date between Cal and Linc, and we'll invite Tiare too."

"I doubt SHE will want to come over here again," Keely said with a frown.

Jess looked at her and then back at the two young Martinez family members just disappearing from view down the beach. "You never know until you try."

Chapter 23

Dinner and 'drop-off'

4:45 pm Moorea Time, November 25, Friday

The Webster clan was back at their bungalow now. They had returned from the beach more than an hour prior, each of them becoming more and more worn out by the minute. Abundant sunshine - even sitting in the shade like they had for most of their time at the beach - was fun but tiring. Plus, the swimming, humidity, jet lag, not to mention all of the excitement combined with the few hours of sleep they'd been able to catch during their flights and various transportation legs to finally get to Moorea and then the resort - it all meant that full-body exhaustion was coming on fast.

None of them was immune, and Alex knew that they'd probably be in bed very soon after their dinner that evening. *Which was coming up in another 30 minutes*, he thought, as he checked his watch. It was now almost 5 pm, *which was 7 pm in the Pacific time zone* from where they had traveled yesterday, Alex reminded himself.

He leaned into the girls' room and also craned his neck to make eye contact with Jess in hers. "Let's get ready for dinner soon. I think we could all use an early evening tonight."

"Yeah, and more water for sure!" Meg said as she drank from one of the bottles provided in the refrigerator.

No doubt that all the heat and humidity here can really take a toll, Alex thought and agreed with her comment. "That's right, Meg," he said. "We all need to be careful to stay hydrated - and coated in sunscreen - especially for the first couple of days here and when we're in the sun or near the water. For now, though, just pick out something comfortable to wear to dinner - you don't need anything fancy - but no swim suits, please. We'll head over to the main restaurant in about...15 minutes."

He closed the door to the girls' room and rummaged through his side of the dresser shared with Cal for a pair of light-colored slacks.

Alex also picked an "Aloha" shirt - one of several he had purchased during trips to Hawaii - from inside the small wardrobe tucked in the corner of the room. *Good to hang at least a few things up,* he thought, and he'd also put some of Cal's shirts on hangers too. If he hadn't, he thought with a bit of a smirk, *no doubt they'd be all balled up in one drawer for our entire next week on the island!*

Keely had previously rinsed her face with cool water and applied some aloe vera after-sun lotion to her (*amazingly,* she thought) just barely sunburned, but still very dry skin. She had heard her dad reminding Cal to do the same. She glanced in the mirror and noticed the fatigue in her face.

A few minutes later, Alex knocked again on the girls' room door. "Ready for dinner?"

In a moment, out came three somewhat rosy-cheeked but relatively unburnt young people into the main room.

"Great job keeping yourself protected from the sun!" Alex said.

"Yeah," Jess replied, "that sunscreen David, the GM, gave us really works!"

"But we'll likely run out in a couple of days at this rate," Keely said, adding a note of caution.

"Good point," Alex agreed. "We'll have to ask David where we can buy more. I'll see if he's around tonight, it's still a little early, maybe he hasn't gone home yet...anyway, let's go! I'm hungry, though I'm angling toward a very short dinner - swimming and sunning and traveling all over the Western hemisphere before that has really wiped me out!"

Everyone agreed, and after Alex closed the main door behind them, they trooped down the path - all with a lot less energy than when they'd arrived, but still with healthy appetites from all the activity and excitement of the first day of their adventure. That day was almost behind them - and now on to the restaurant for their first real Moorean meal.

Chapter 24

Early up to a spectacular sunrise

5:55 am Moorea Time, November 26, Saturday

Jess felt like she had just dropped off to sleep for a moment when suddenly, an ear-piercing sound broke through the darkness around her in the small room. Jumping quickly from her bed, she pulled back the understated Tahitian-floral print window covering and glanced around. She couldn't see much. It was just a little bit lighter outside. But she certainly could hear it - *it sounded like somebody was dying! Except...oh yeah!* She suddenly remembered.

Just then, Keely and Meg opened her door and Keely, with a look of fright mixed with consternation said, "What the heck was that?!"

"Something I'd almost forgotten existed here...and many islands like it, or not even necessarily islands, pretty much anywhere..." answered Jess. She frowned, then rubbed her eyes and yawned.

"Oh Yeah!" exclaimed Meg, "Roosters!" And it was true, their first night's sleep on the island had come to an end with the pre-dawn calls of several of the ubiquitous fowl kept by the locals on the premises of their homes to breed with their female chickens. Or maybe just wild. Even near resort hotels.

Note to self, Jess thought: *Earplugs.*

Glancing at her watch, which she had set before they left Los Angeles and the US to match local time, Jess noticed it was just about 6:00 am. *Not TOO early,* she thought, *but wow, am I tired.* Realizing that in their own time zone it was after eight o'clock already, Jess started shaking the cobwebs away inside her head and remembered two things: *1) I am on vacation (well mostly, I still have a kid-care job to do for much of the time),* and *2) We are on an island in the South Pacific!* She figured a quick stroll down to the beach would be fun...*but what about Alex and Cal?*

She walked over and carefully listened at the connecting door from the girl's room to the main one in the bungalow, and couldn't hear much, so figured the male members of the Webster clan were sleeping quietly (well mostly quietly, as Alex was emitting a snore every few breaths), *but it IS a relatively QUIET snoring,* she thought with a grin.

Jess turned from the door and motioned to the two sisters as she whispered, *"Do you want to join me for a sunrise stroll to the beach?"*

"Sure!" Keely whispered back, continuing in a low voice, "I have to swim every day anyway...remember I promised my coach."

Meg - not quite as enthusiastically and still sleepy - answered, *"OK..."*

The three of them quickly donned their shorts and t-shirts - Keely with her swim suit underneath - grabbed towels for the beach, then put on their flip-flops sitting at the bungalow entrance and quietly opened the outer door from Jess's connecting room. As they exited and rounded the corner to meet the short path to the lagoon, they saw the brightening light from the rising sun. It highlighted in pink and gold the lush surroundings and deep aquamarine-colored waters in the distance. Serenaded by several lilting calls from tropical birds, one which Jess recognized as that of a mourning dove, they padded to the beach. The tide was lower than it had been the day prior, but looked like it was starting to come in.

As they walked the path, Jess couldn't help exclaiming, *"This really IS gorgeous, isn't it!"* The sisters nodded. Reaching the beach, all three kicked off their sandals and stepped into the warm surf.

At this hour, it was a typical sunrise temperature of about 78 degrees F/25.5 Celsius, and they luxuriated in the experience and the stillness - with not another soul except them on the beach - *well except for the fish and birds, that is,* thought Keely.

As the girls admired the view, they heard a sort of rustling sound up the path from where they stood in the lightly lapping waves and slowly emerging light that shined from the east, or to the right of where they were standing. They couldn't see any land across the sea from their vantage point, though the island of Tahiti was near - just on the opposite side of the island, around the corner to the southeast of Moorea and across the "Canal de Moorea," or Moorea Channel.

They all turned to look back toward the resort, and saw the source of the noise. It was Cal, followed by Alex, who emerged from the path just then. "We heard you leave the bungalow and thought a morning beach walk was a great idea!" said Alex.

"Yeah" said Cal, "And with all those roosters, it's a lot more peaceful down here anyway!"

Alex grinned wryly, then looked at Jess, and they both voiced, simultaneously, her earlier self-advice - "Earplugs!"

Carrying his flip-flops in his hand, Alex waded a bit into the nearly non-existent surf, drinking in the spectacular, almost otherworldly views, then turned to the others and said, "Let's walk down the beach a ways...I haven't done much exploring yet, have you guys?"

"Nope, not yet," said Keely. The five of them strode together through the thick sand, down past the marae site Keely and Jess had been introduced to by Linc the prior afternoon. She pointed it out to her dad, who walked up across the sand near it and began to examine the ruins more closely, his children looking on, a bit hesitant to join him.

"Interesting...I'll have to ask Bernie about this," said Alex as he inspected the carefully arranged, and obviously quite ancient rock-rimmed enclosure. Meanwhile, Cal continued down the beach, and the others increased their walking speed to catch up to him. Alex, being the history buff he was, reluctantly left his exploration of the marae to rejoin them a few moments later.

Continuing eastward, they rounded the corner of the beach and saw, set back from the shore in a clearing under some palm trees, a large collection of construction materials and heavy equipment. Behind it all sprawled an older looking hotel of what appeared to be traditional Polynesian-themed design. Lights shone from only a few of its buildings, with no noise at all coming from the property at this still-early hour.

Alex lowered his voice as they continued walking. "I had heard a little about this place from my contacts at our hotel. Evidently, there's some controversy with the project and its renovation (or demolition), maybe in ignorance or, you know, disrespect of the area's historical significance - something to do with those ruins back there, but I'm not sure."

"That's what we heard yesterday from Linc and Tiare," Jess replied. "You know, those kids we saw at the airport and ferry landing. They're staying at this hotel but said that construction was starting in a couple of days - so it is probably going to get loud soon."

Alex frowned and shook his head.

"That's right. We heard from them that the marae back there is part of the reason why it's a controversy," said Keely.

"Hmmm," said Alex, "you all definitely know more than I do about this...Well, for now, let's head back to the Montcalm, I'm getting hungry. Don't know about you guys, but it's way past our usual breakfast time back home, and no next-day or day-after-next turkey leftovers in the fridge for us this year!"

Meg laughed with the rest of the Webster "clan" as they turned to walk back down the still calm, unpopulated beach towards their resort. She'd almost forgotten that it was two days after Thanksgiving - after all of the hubbub of flying out from SeaTac and then to LA on the holiday, and then a day of mostly recovering and sitting by the beach. Still, it was just the beginning of their adventure in this hot and mystical land called Moorea.

As her dad and the others returned toward their hotel, the still cool sand soft under their feet, Meg got a strange thought. *Something weird is going on...I can feel it.* She stifled an involuntary shiver in her body as they passed back by the ancient stone walls of the marae. She stopped for just a second to look at it again, and then quickened her steps to catch her family members, who now approached the beach path back to the main resort buildings.

"I'm so hungry I could eat a...whale!" Meg exclaimed, refocusing her attention from her mind to her stomach. The others laughed as they neared the Montcalm and the walk through the shrubs and trees up to the restaurant for their first sit-down breakfast on the island. It was now sunny and warming steadily, approaching 27 Celsius - or around 80 degrees Fahrenheit - already, though there was still a bit of a cool breeze in the air.

Keely turned away and headed over towards 'their' tree on the beach. "I have to swim first, but I'll just do laps back and forth in the shallow part here. Meg, will you stay and watch me?"

"Sure, but I warn you, I'm so hungry, I might just jump in and eat some fish right out of the lagoon!"

The others laughed, and Alex made a suggestion. "We'll see you back at the room in thirty minutes, OK? You can take a shower down here by the beach if you want, or take one and change into your dry shorts and shirt back in the room. We'll shower there."

"Sure, see ya everyone!" Keely replied as she pulled her goggles out of her pocket, threw off her shirt and shorts, and jumped into the lagoon in the swim suit that she'd worn underneath.

As Jess, Alex, and Cal continued up the path, Cal thought *I wonder what fun stuff we'll be doing today?* He looked at Jess.

She smiled back. "Hey, kiddo, I get to sit by you at breakfast, right?"

Cal grinned, and answered, "Definitely! But if they serve whale, I'm going to say 'no way!'"

Alex glanced back and chuckled at his son's comment. His watch showed it was just after 7 am on this Saturday, and he felt a growing sense of adventure - along with a bit of intrigue or something else he couldn't quite place. *I think it's going to be a very interesting first full day for the Worldwide Websters on Moorea, for sure!*

Chapter 25

Breakfast beyond belief!

7:45 am Moorea Time, November 26, Saturday

What a spread! Though he had done tons of research for this trip (*in a fairly short period of time too,* Alex thought, giving himself a 'virtual' pat on the back for his accelerated planning efforts), he hadn't drilled down much into the details regarding the meals included in their lodging arrangements while he worked on the software implementation. Alex realized that it might have been important to do so if any of the Websters had serious allergy issues or were vegans or anything like that. As it turned out, nobody in their traveling 'family' had any real food concerns, though Jess was a semi-vegetarian, and he recognized it would be a challenge to get Cal to eat some of the more unusual seafood and other dishes they might encounter during the trip. B*ut that was a problem they could handle, no problem...er...aita pea pea!* He smiled to himself.

But this breakfast - which they all continued to enjoy after Keely had finished her swim and hurriedly returned to the room to don dry clothes - really was amazing. Guests at the resort could choose from a true 'bounty' of choices: At three medium-sized buffet tables, there was a nicely-displayed selection of fruit, and breads both fresh (baguettes and rolls) and sweet, like pastries and croissants. There was even a fish dish and another with slices of imported ham. And of course, several types of sliced cheese. *The French influence on the cuisine here is pretty clear,* Alex concluded.

They'd found seats at a large table just outside of the enclosed portion of the resort's restaurant, overlooking the pool. Then, as one, the Websters pushed back their rattan chairs, stood up and trooped over to the buffet. First, there were large bowls and plates with many kinds of local fruit (or mostly local, Jess surmised), including mango, papaya, pineapple, guava, and even bananas and watermelon, some not as familiar to her from other travels to tropical locales. At the end of the table was a dish of coconut pieces and a carafe of coconut milk too, which - based on their drinks yesterday on the beach and last night's dinner too - they were all discovering was an ingredient that seemed to be in just about every dish served on the island.

"Check out this huge grapefruit!" said Keely, who being a major fruit fan in general, was clearly loving the variety of the breakfast spread.

"Don't you mean '*pamplemousse*'?" countered Meg, pointing at the small sign and ribbing her "French student" sister a bit.

"Hah!" said Keely, as she picked up one of the large, green/yellow round fruits, conveniently sliced in half already, and spooned several sections of onto her plate.

Meanwhile, Alex and Jess examined the offerings on the last table. They saw what appeared to be both fresh fish fillets and something else - a 'combo' dish with chunks of fish swimming in coconut milk, amid bits of coconut and citrus pieces, maybe lime?

Jess suddenly remembered. "Aah!...that's *poisson cru*," just then glimpsing a little card off to the side of the dish that confirmed her guess.

"That's the most famous dish in French Polynesia, with fish, lime, coconut, and other spices. Can't wait to try it!" Alex nodded his agreement. He put a small selection on his plate, then doubled back to the bread and fruit tables to balance out his choices and, well, because he loved bread and *who does bread and pastries better than the French, right?*

Back at the table, they all toasted to their first breakfast on the island, with glasses of the "pamplemousse juice" (which Cal decided he'd dub "PowerMoose Juice"), and then said "Cheers!" a second time, "To Saturday!" which Meg insisted upon. Keely, the budding French student, vaguely remembered 'Santé' or something like that, but decided it was cool to just go with the English version of the toasting prompt for now. For this occasion, probably due to their hunger, or fatigue, or both, they all forgot to use the local term *"manuia!"* as they had on the ferry ride over to the island.

After downing some of the slightly sweeter-than-expected grapefruit juice, Alex also took some long, much needed sips from the very tasty French coffee they'd poured from a small heated pot their server had set in the middle of the table.

"This pamplemousse is amAZING!" said Keely, chewing on a spoonful of its wedges. "So sweet!"

"And the mangos are killer too!" said Meg.

The rest of them plowed steadily through their fruits and bread, Cal putting slices of ham and cheese together on a croissant to make a sweet and savory sandwich. Of course, there was plenty of butter available to add to the rolls and slices on their plates.

"I'm ready to give this poisson cru a try," said Jess.

Alex added, "Me too!"

They both took bites with their spoons, then exchanged looks of joint appreciation before voicing their approval of the popular dish's smooth mix of fresh, mildly spicy flavors to the others.

"Even for breakfast?" Keely asked, and her dad nodded enthusiastically.

Soon, as a table of now "very-full-visitors," the recently-arrived US travelers started to talk about plans for a weekend of sight-seeing and other adventures.

"OK, we've got two full days to explore together before I have to get back to work on Monday morning," Alex said. "How about we start out with a tour of some of the 'highs and lows' of the island…meaning we venture up to some of the mountain overlooks and around some of these amazing peaks, and also explore at sea level and check out as many of the beaches as we can along the way?"

"YEAH, that's what I'm talking about!" answered Meg.

"Great idea, especially since we don't have a car," Jess added. "Once we see what's around, if we want to go back later in the week while you're working, we'll know the best places. Plus," she added, looking at the three Webster children, "if it's close enough and an easy bike ride, maybe we can visit a beach or store on our own while your dad is working at the office."

Keely suggested they plan to eat lunch along the way on their first excursion and then maybe watch the sunset together, with a 'picnic dinner' they could bring from somewhere nearby to a beach.

"Sounds great to me!" Cal exclaimed, and Alex and the others nodded their approval as well.

"I'm sure we'll have lots of stops to eat and explore along the way." He glanced at his watch. "It's almost 9 now. Let's get our stuff together and make sure we each have suits, towels, sunglasses, sunscreen, and that beach blanket from the room with us. I'll check over at the activities desk and make sure we can catch a tour - they told me last night there wouldn't likely be a problem given they're sort of in the off-season now, but I just want to firm up details and pay for our tickets. See you all back at the rooms in a few."

As her dad walked away to take care of their tour arrangements, Keely said, "I'm eager to hear more about the marae and what they really mean."

"And I want to see that place from the movie South Pacific, you know, 'Bali Hai', or at least the place people say was why the author wrote about it," Meg added.

Jess, Keely and Cal agreed, the latter pointing out, "I bet Dad will love that too!"

Chapter 26

Around the Island Tour - Part 1: Magic mount, faded fun & a curious culinary combo

10:00 am Moorea Time, November 26, Saturday

The small, bright yellow and green van from *Le Truck Tours* (air conditioned!) stopped by their hotel just over an hour later. Jean-Paul was their driver and guide, a tall and very friendly mid-30-something who proudly told the group (all the Webster clan plus two other couples without kids) that he was a locally-born "Tahitian/French Moorean." As if to prove it, he proudly displayed several large and smaller tattoos, each its own elaborate design, on his arms and back, which he obliged everyone to see by lifting up his shirt and turning around in a circle. Jess stifled a quick cough and then saw that two other women (and one man) had the same reaction, and she looked down with a slight grin.

"You all know the '*tatau*' eh? Well, you may call it "tattoo", or body art, and you may have seen it before, or even have some yourselves. But you can only get the original tatau here - in French Polynesia - where it all began!"

"Wow, Dad, I didn't know that!" cried Meg.

"Me neither!" said Cal.

Alex grinned. He knew, but had decided not to mention it...*don't want anyone in this family to get any ideas - at least not with the oldest of the kids being twelve years old!*

As the Webster group grabbed seats together near the back of the 12-seat vehicle, he spread out a brochure containing a map with arrows and info points printed in various locations to show everyone the projected route of the day's tour.

Now back in the driver's seat, Jean-Paul continued his introduction. "*Ia orana! Bonjour,* and *Allô,* everyone...Any French speakers here?"

Keely tentatively raised her hand, answering, "*petit peu*," and then translating in English: "*A little bit*, I'm studying it in school."

Alex couldn't help but think of "*Pepé Le Pew*," the cartoon skunk, but held it to himself in the interest of keeping the conversation going with their driver, a*nd also so he didn't completely embarrass his daughters with his geeky sense of humor (at least not right now!)*

Jean-Paul smiled at Keely, and did a quick survey of the other passengers. "Really, no one else *parles français*? Very surprising. OK, well, let's make this the *Le Truck Tahitian and English tour* today, eh? All of you are Americans?"

"No." said a woman in the first group, "We're Canadians...but we also speak a little French," and the other couple answered, "Yes, Americans."

So, Jess thought, it was indeed going to be a bit easier to learn and understand - hopefully, and she decided not to broadcast her Kiwi roots as the key issue was speaking English - *but I accept the challenge to recall some of my own French from school*. There would certainly be lots of opportunities to do so, as they passed around, through, and over the sites they'd be seeing all over the island today.

After pulling out of the Montcalm's short entrance driveway, the van continued just a bit above the very slow island speed limit of 40 kilometers per hour/24 miles per hour on the small road along the shore, meandering near the coastline. They passed by a few small homes, resorts, restaurants, and shops, including a kayak and boat rental shop as they began to travel inland, in a counterclockwise direction from the resort along what Jean-Paul announced was Opunohu Bay. Only about three minutes later, the road turned back, heading north toward the lagoon/ocean side of the large inlet. Soon they took a left-turn and Cal was trying to read the sign at the corner when their driver/guide called out "First stop, *Magic Mountain!*"

As they headed up a fairly steep hill, traversing many winding turns, they each made sure (from experience) to look outside. Keely - who tended to be a little motion-sensitive - stifled just a bit of rising car-sickness. Luckily, a short time later, they pulled into a small parking lot.

"Here we are!" Jean-Paul announced, explaining as he turned around to face the passengers that they had just traveled much of the way to their mountain viewpoint, but there was some moderately steep terrain still in front of them. "Can you all walk and climb a bit?"

Everyone, nodded their heads or answered, "Yes."

Thus, their first real trek of the trip began with Jean-Paul leading the way. The tour participants trudged steadily upward, Keely and Meg right behind Jean-Paul. Jess followed them, with Alex at the rear of the group with his son, occasionally stopping to support Cal around the waist or arm to keep him on the walking path. The views of the other mountains, the sea, and of course the trees and plants all around them improved as they completed the 20-minute ascent to the lookout point. Then they mounted the last small hill and realized they'd arrived, everyone sweating and breathing loudly in the building heat and humidity. Several in the group, including Alex, emitted audible sighs.

What they saw from where they stood literally took their breaths away: a sweeping view of this part of the island, including the small village, roads, mountains, and sea below. "Spectacular!" choked Alex.

As he took it all in, the lanky American handed a plastic water bottle from his backpack to Cal, then took a drink from his own new Contigo he'd filled at the restaurant. Jess, Keely, and Meg were also quenching their thirst. Alex decided it was a good time to capture the views with camcorder and camera. Holding both, he turned his head and the devices to get both landscape video and candid family photos, including one cheesy but cute pose from Keely and Meg in front of the cliff to the sea. Nobody was saying much as they finished their water break and their breathing began to return to normal.

Jess and Cal walked to the guardrail and Jess pointed in a circle with her arm. "You can see almost all the way around the island here, except for those mountains blocking part of it - but I'm not complaining!" The others marveled with her at the lush green landscape and blue - almost turquoise - waters in their field of view.

They now began to realize just why Michener and countless others had written so fervently and frequently of Moorea's beauty - *it IS pretty darn awe-inspiring,* Keely thought.

Cal pointed towards the ocean. "Check out the lagoon, you can see the reef really well, it looks like it circles all around the island...see the waves breaking outside of it?"

Meg marveled at the sight - a few paddle-boarders, swimmers, and snorkelers looked like little ants in the distance. She also saw a couple of sailboats, one just exiting the bay below them to their right.

"See that bay, where we were just a while ago in the van?" Alex asked them, following Meg's gaze. "Anything look familiar to you?"

The Webster clan turned their heads almost in unison, Keely staring intently. Suddenly, she blurted out "Is that from the movie?"

"You got it, Keel...several key scenes from the 1984 version of The Bounty were filmed right down there in Opunohu Bay...though the vantage point's a bit different from up here, of course. It was a 'stand in' for old Tahiti, from the 1780's, to make it look more historically authentic. Apparently, there was still less development and signs of civilization here in Moorea vs. Tahiti at the time, even in the 1980s."

Jess said, "Can you imagine what all of this looked like back when Captain Bligh, and Captain Cook and all those European explorers before them, first saw this bay in the 1700's?"

As Alex took some video of the scenery, and framed all in the tour group enjoying the view, Jean-Paul walked over to them.

"That's right! You already know a lot about this island! But don't forget Pedro Fernandes de Queirós, the Portuguese explorer credited as the first European to sight our island in the year 1606. Later came England's Samuel Wallis - and of course Louis Antoine de Bougainville," he said, noting with special emphasis the French explorer who circumnavigated the globe in the 1760's.

"Anyway, Bougainville also arrived here before Captain Cook. Cook was one of Bligh's earlier commanding officers, including when he last came here to Tahiti in the late 1770's."

"Capitan Bougainville's got interesting connections to all of you!" he continued, winking at the assembled group of Canadians and Americans. "From battles during America's Revolutionary War, and not just the attractive plants you may have seen - Bougainvillea."

"Oh wow!" said Alex, as he recalled the name of these shrubs in various colors, which he knew from business trips grew profusely along Southern California's freeways. Not so much in the cooler climes of Western Washington state, however.

Observing that the entire van-load of tour guests were standing together, Jean-Paul had an idea: "Would you like me to take a photo of you all, to kick off our adventure?"

The group agreed and lined up to get a remembrance of this first stop at the "magical" Moorea viewpoint. Then the Websters and the other four adventurers and their tour guide walked to the other side of the overlook.

Jean-Paul began to explain further: "What you were saying a few moments ago about the filming of the latest version of *The Bounty* was quite accurate, Mr. Webster. When I was young, in the early 1970's, there was very little development on this side of the island, just a few modern homes of any size - and almost none of these resorts existed. In fact, the only resorts were quite small and certainly not very luxurious at all, even if one of them - the **Hotel Bali Hai** - was built around ten years before I was born as the first over-water bungalow resort in the world. And that was built by Americans who'd settled here. But my people, the Tahitian side of the family anyway, had been here on the island at that point for nearly 1,000 years already."

"We learned some things from the movie and other research before we came...but we don't really know too much more than that," said Keely. "So, you were born here, Jean-Paul?"

"Oui/Yes, I was. My father was a policeman who was also born here. His mother had come to Moorea from France in the late 1940s. Her father was part of the government, and she eventually married my grandfather, a native Tahitian. My mother, unlike my father, is a full-blooded Tahitian. So, I am a small part French and a big part Tahitian, though because I was born here, I really consider myself "Moorean." Oh, and my brother Bernie works at the hotel where you are staying. Maybe you've met him, Mr....umm...Webster?"

"Bernie Tetuanui?"

"Yes, that is my last name too!"

"Of course...oh, that's great! Bernie's been a huge help to the software project we're doing for the Montcalm. Very sharp guy - he referred me to you and this tour! Alex grinned at Jean-Paul. "Now, I know why!" and they both laughed as their guide winked in response.

Cal was just dying to ask a question... "Sure is a beautiful place, Jean-Paul. Do you like living here?" he said, looking up at the 6' 4" (193 cm) tall tour guide with shoulder-length dark brown hair and brown eyes. "And why do you call it 'Tay-shun?' - I thought it was "Ta-HEE-shun!" the young American continued.

"Ha-ha, young one, that is how we locals pronounce our nationality, and language. Hmmm...do I like it here? Yes, most of the time...though sometimes I long for more space, and maybe more adventure, and sometimes..." Jean-Paul looked off into the distance for a moment, "Sometimes, I wish the world was simpler like Moorea was during the days of my ancestors."

Alex stowed his video camera in its bag, looked at their guide, and ventured a comment. "Well, if it helps at all, I'd say many of us have similar feelings of ambivalence regarding where we live, where we are from, and what it's like now vs. in the past. And definitely regret for the damage we've done to it through "civilization." But...we don't have quite such a lush and peaceful and absolutely gorgeous view to command our attention every day as you do."

"Oh, it wasn't always peaceful, I assure you of that!" said Jean-Paul, with another wink and a wry grin. "But more on that later in our trip today...is everybody ready to walk back down the hill to go to our next stop on the tour?"

The visitors, including the two couples and all the Websters began the slightly quicker hike back downhill, where about ten minutes later they all again climbed into the van. Soon they were driving out of the parking area, down that steep incline they'd come up an hour earlier, and on towards the lagoon and west side of the island they had glimpsed from the Magic Mountain viewpoint.

As the ocean and reef loomed up ahead and to their right, Jean-Paul shared details for the second leg of their trip. "Why don't we stop at one of our small food takeaway shops? If you like, you can get lunch there and bring it with us to our next destination, one of our best beaches, or *plages*, called Tiahura, where we will spend about 30 minutes exploring before we continue around the island."

"Yay! I'm hungry!" answered Cal. Several other passengers laughed in agreement with the famished boy. A food stop clearly was welcome!

Five minutes later, they were parked in front of a small building that looked much like a mini-mobile home by the side of the road. A sign on it read *Snack Tiahura*. A lone woman was working there, as an electric fan whirred back and forth just inside her sliding window. A big sign on the wall showed photos and names of several dishes and sandwiches in French, what looked like Tahitian, and even a few words for dishes they recognized in English. There were also a handful of fruit and salad offerings, and bottled drinks of various flavors.

As they all lined up to decipher the menu - with matching pictures of most items - on the wall of the "Snack" wagon, Meg exclaimed, "Hey, they have Chicken Chow Mein on a French roll! Or at least it looks like it. Is that crazy or what!?"

"Wow!" Jess said "What a strange combination." Then she grinned when each of the Websters said - all five nearly at the same time - "That's what I want!"

Jean-Paul nodded his head vigorously. "Delicious. I bet you will love them!"

Jess decided she'd stick with the veggie version of the unusual entree and saw that a half-roll size was also an option, which she chose, as she still felt a bit full from their sumptuous breakfast.

After they all ordered, Alex paid for their food and they grabbed some napkins and spoons to include in the bags with their cans of fruit punch - plus one box with a mini-sized but still substantial cake featured on the menu under "dessert" that Alex had insisted on buying and having split six ways. Bags and box in hand, they headed back to the van to join the others. Only a minute or two later, they pulled up next to Tiahura Beach for their lunch break.

The beach looked spectacular as advertised, and as they all exited the vehicle again, they gazed in wonder, and maybe envy, toward a nearby resort they had just passed. What made this area especially interesting and alluring at first glance were a couple of smaller palm and vegetation-covered islets that stood within easy view offshore.

"There's a full-blown restaurant out there, can you believe it?" said Alex to Jess, as he had just glanced at the map and brochure before stepping out of the van.

"Wow," she replied, gazing across the lagoon at the palm tree-lined islet.

"It is a *motu*," explained Jean-Paul, as he walked alongside, "and the one with the restaurant is called *Motu Tiahura*, like the beach."

"Do people have to swim there to get their dinner?" said Cal, eliciting a peal of laughter from their guide, and his whole family.

Jean-Paul grinned. "Well, you could, but it's a lot easier to take the shuttle boat! And, you can stay there most of the day with a reservation at the restaurant. The snorkeling is really good around the motu."

"We should go out there, Dad!" said Keely.

Meg added "Yeah, how cool would that be?!" Cal nodded and Jess glanced at Alex.

"Sure!" Alex said. "Let's figure out a day to do it while we're here, but right now, let's eat our lunch! I'm hungry!"

They all spread out on their blankets, kicking off their sandals to take a few moments and eat their unusual sandwiches.

"This is super-good!" said Meg. As she and the others bit into their own French roll/chow mein mixtures, they agreed the tangy, spicy insides 'worked' really well with the bread surrounding it to make a tasty meal.

"Who would have thought?" Jess said. "Chinese food and a baguette combined in one for lunch on a beach on an island in the sunny South Pacific!"

"No kidding!" Keely laughed, as they all chomped away in between frequent sips of fruit punch or soda.

As he finished up his half-sandwich (chicken chow mein roll, split with Cal) Alex pulled out the cake box - inside of which was this really creamy sort of traditional flour-based cake with mango filling. He doled out pieces on a plate with a small fork, offering additional forks for each family member, then, gazing out across the beach toward the motu and restaurant, followed up his earlier comments on visiting the islet and its restaurant later in their trip.

"I like Jean-Paul's suggestion. Let's see if we can work out a good day for both lunch out there and a couple more hours on the beach, snorkeling, and swimming...maybe towards the end of this next week before we go home?"

"Go home!?" Cal cried, with an exaggerated frown, and his sisters mock-frowned as well.

Jess laughed as she stashed her finished sandwich in its bag. "Hey guys, we still have a whole week to explore Moorea, and with these chow mein sandwiches, you gotta admit we're off to a great start!"

She arose from the blanket, moved downwind a bit to brush a few crumbs off and started walking down the beach, with the kids close behind. Alex stopped a moment to take a sweeping view of the stunning setting with his eyes alone. Then he did the same with his video camera, adding a couple photos of the beach and the kids with his other device.

Alex pondered for a bit on how they'd gotten here, of the general good humor of the kids, (thus far, at least!) of how lucky they were to be able to travel together as a family, *even if they didn't always get along,* he reminded himself ruefully. They'd had a bit of a multi-sided argument before getting on the bus, the stress and strain of the long days of travel prior bringing sharp words between Meg and Cal and a complaint from Keely about not being able to find her sunglasses. He'd overreacted to that one the most, telling her to "shut up", which he immediately regretted.

Sometimes, Alex cringed with guilt, *I really suck as a dad...but that's the reality of any family,* he forced himself to admit. *We're not perfect...but we can learn from our mistakes, and we must.* Even so, the father of three reminded himself, it was so cool to even be in a position to do so, much less actually *doing* it, like traveling together on this trip. As usual, Alex then thought also of the hard parts - the divorce from his children's mother and the many times in the past, even sometimes recently, when he wasn't sure he could "pull off" being a single dad, with custody of the kids, working full time, often flying or driving for days on business trips, and trying not to miss their sports and arts practices, games and performances. *Divorce truly sucks, too, for everyone involved,* he thought.

Alex remembered feeling a tremendous sense of almost constant embarrassment and shame for what he and his wife were putting their kids through at the time of the separation a few years back - though certainly he wished and hoped even then for happier times. Ultimately came a legal decision, an especially unusual one for the time - in that (he) the father was granted sole custody as the primary parent. However, the work of being a good dad and caregiver to his children - with so much critically important help coming from his parents/their grandparents, other family members and a few close friends, as well as their mother - with whom he'd mended fences eventually - had really just begun. Not one of them was yet a teenager, after all. *I still have THAT to look forward to,* he mused with a grin.

"DAAAAAD!" Alex was jolted out of his reverie, and turned to see Cal, Meg, and Keely waving at him from near the shore of the lagoon.

They'd found some tidepools and were pointing at something. He took a deep breath, exhaled, and jogged across the beach to join them.

Cal was carefully poking a small stick around a massive starfish, with vivid purple and red colors.

"Look, Dad!" Meg shouted, "It has 18 legs, and boy does it look scary!"

"Yeah, check out those spines all over it. Not something you want to step on or pick up and take home!" said Keely.

"Well, let's leave it alone," Alex said, and he pulled his camera up and framed a picture of the sea creature, then one with it and the kids in the background. Then they all stood up to resume their walk down along the beach. Keely glanced back at the scary-looking starfish and shuddered.

As they headed west and looked back across the sand, they saw a pier and a large collection of buildings stretching up from the trees at the far edge of the beach. They looked like essentially nicely constructed, albeit well-worn, thatch roof huts. Alex noticed the landscaping was overgrown around them, and that the huts appeared to be closed, or abandoned. He doubted anybody was living or staying there.

"I wonder what that place was, or is?" asked Jess.

Alex answered quickly. "I saw it on the map. That, I believe, is the former *Fou de Joie*, or *Wild Joy* resort, aka *Fun Club Moorea*. It was part of a huge global network of resort style, often all-inclusive hotels, you may have heard of them elsewhere in typical travel destinations. The company decided to close this one on Moorea a couple of years ago. looks like they haven't torn it down yet, but from the looks of it, they clearly haven't done anything to reopen it or fix it up either."

That was the nature of resort properties in many places, Alex knew from his travels, and from his particular work experience as well. Even very popular resorts, perhaps like Moorea's Fun Club outpost right here, sometimes closed. The reasons tended to be many and varied, but what Alex had heard mentioned at their hotel's office yesterday when getting background on the island - the "lay of the land" - from the GM of the Montcalm, was that part of the reason why this particular property hadn't been yet renovated or transformed was that multiple members of one Tahitian/Moorean family owned the land upon which it was built. Apparently, the last time they had tried to negotiate a new lease, the European-based operators of Fun Club abruptly decided - and in doing so shocked their local competitors and resort staff - that the price to stay open was just too high. So, they simply closed the resort with very little notice and walked away from the property, leaving everything behind. Now, it remained shuttered, with an uncertain future.

"Check out their beach and the various buildings, it must have been a cool place to stay, with pools, full landscaping, all of it looks like it was really nice - at one time, anyway," said Keely, her eyes peering through the grounds of the abandoned hotel.

"I wonder if it's haunted!?" said Meg.

That got a quick response from Cal, who grabbed his dad's shirt. "I like where we are staying, Dad!" Then he walked briskly in the opposite direction, toward where the van was parked, which elicited knowing smiles from the others.

"So do I!" Meg agreed and she turned to follow her brother.

Jess watched as Cal and Meg walked toward the parking area and saw that Jean-Paul was standing with the others from their tour, waving at them. "Well, I guess we should *all* head back to the van," she said, and the remaining three of them made haste to rejoin the rest of the tour group.

Once they'd all taken their seats inside, Jean-Paul (who graciously accepted Alex's offer of the last piece of cake from lunch) started up the van, pulled out onto the road, and headed further south, still traveling counter-clockwise on Moorea's sole round-island route. As they drove along the two-lane road, they passed the fading sign and no longer 'grand' entrance to the *Fun Club* resort grounds. *Too bad*, Alex thought. It looked like it had been a beautiful and probably fun place to stay - as its name claimed - at one time, anyway.

He raised his voice a bit to their driver up front, pointing at the tropical-themed strip mall on their left. "How are all these stores doing, Jean-Paul...now that Fun Club is no longer open?"

The guide shook his head and said "Not so good...it has been very hard for the shop owners...some are my friends. But most are trying to stay open, even though the old resort property is in pieces. Some of the owners of the Fun Club land have actually removed and transported whole buildings and huts from there and placed them on property they own elsewhere on the island! It is all very sad," he frowned, "especially for the former Fun Club employees...who lost their jobs there. Not good for them, and not good for Moorea, at all."

Chapter 27

Around the Island tour - Part 2: Art, sacrifice & a starfish mystery solved

12:15 pm Moorea Time, November 26, Saturday

"What's our next destination, Jean-Paul?" Keely asked from her seat in the back of the van.

The driver answered as he kept his eyes on the road ahead. "We'll visit our first ancient site, a place my ancestors built and maintained for religious or ceremonial purposes. We call them *marae*."

Meg piped up, "We have a marae near us too!" She explained to the driver what they had visited that morning. Keely mentioned their encounter the previous day when the two children they had met on the ferry shuttle told them about the ancient ruins in between their two hotel properties.

"Oh yes, of course," said Jean-Paul. "That is a very interesting marae you describe, because it is near where one of our most famous local families - related to mine in fact - once lived. They had many houses all together in - how do you say...a *com-pound*?"

"Yes, that's what it would be called in English," Jess said.

"How far do your family ties here go back?" Alex asked.

"Several hundred years," replied their guide, "and I hope for many more forward into the future as well."

They continued on their pleasant journey, with some local Tahitian music playing on the van's speakers to set the mood. As they made their way down the road, they passed by a number of small farms, beach cottages, and drove in and out of an incredibly lush canopy of trees, flowers, ferns, and glimpsed a few streams that carried the rainfall down from the soaring mountains. Not much in the way of hills by the shoreline, however.

Keely marveled at the constantly changing views, offering an assortment of jagged green peaks of different heights that loomed into and out of their vision from the van as breaks in the vegetation offered the tour group glimpses from their left side windows. There were a variety of sea and landscape views to their right, or westward, as they proceeded in a southerly direction on the far side of the island.

She was intrigued by the varying angles and colors of the ever-present sea, easy to see most of the time since like in America, it was French custom to drive on that side of the road. Their route did meander a bit, sometimes closer or further away from the shore. Soon, they felt the van slow, and to Keely's surprise, they pulled up in front of a large outpost of some sort, surrounded by palms and many other local plants.

Jess was surprised too, and a little bit skeptical. *Uh oh*, she thought, *tourist trap...*

Jean-Paul called out to the van passengers as they turned into the parking lot. "Welcome to the *Ti'i Village*...where we'll see our first marae of the day, up-close. This is also where artisans of many kinds share their skills with visitors like you, and they have dinner and dancing shows some evenings. These are called *Tama'ara'a*. But right now, it's a quiet time here and you are welcome to roam around a bit, see the houses we call *fare*, and watch the experts work. Some are teaching classes or demonstrating their crafts, so go see their exhibits, and I'm sure they can answer any questions you have. Also, you may wish to visit the *toilette*. In 15 minutes, we will join together for a brief talk hosted by one of the guides, and you will learn more about the marae here and other historical sites in Moorea."

As the Websters and other tour participants spread out around the Ti'i Village grounds, Alex smiled wryly at the well-worn, faux-primitive buildings. Yet, the facilities inside were very clean and tidy, with the hosts and workers around the site smiling and chatting with visitors from various groups who had stopped by to see the place. The artisans here were clearly trying their best to share their culture and history, despite modern society's almost inexorable destruction of it. *This seems like a nice, friendly operation*, Alex, a veteran of many interesting (and a few not-so-interesting) tourism experiences, thought to himself.

The *Tama'ara'a* stage setting looked sort of familiar. One of the most interesting things Alex - together with the kids in most cases -

had discovered after attending many luaus and other Polynesian-themed dinner shows and theatrical performances on several islands in Hawaii - and even at Disney World in Florida - was that they were usually fun and well worth the time and money spent. And the food was almost always tasty and authentic. That came as a surprise to some used to unappetizing buffets at other group events.

Many of these activities looked and felt very touristy, especially at first, but they tended to please most guests/tourists who actually gave them a chance. It just required them to suspend their cynicism and tolerate a little glitz on top of the local food and exciting music and dancing. Alex had originally been, like many visitors, cynical about such gatherings, but he, and the kids too, had really come around after initial and subsequent experiences. Conversations with Hawaiian friends had confirmed what they'd experienced in terms of authenticity - these *kamaaina* (locals) said that the food served at typical tourist luaus tended to be very similar in quality and variety to what they had enjoyed at luaus with their own *ohana* (families) and friends over the years.

Would Moorea be different? Alex noticed a substantial seating area and stage over to one side of the large site, just behind the gift shop. Meg was there, with Jess, and the two of them beckoned to the rest of the Webster party to join them. With Cal and Keely by his side, Alex walked over toward a towering pyramid-shaped rock structure, where a small crowd of two dozen or so people had gathered. This must be the *marae*, he thought.

As they made their way to the marae, they passed a small circle of artists in the compound's center section, overseeing and instructing tourist "students" sitting on blankets, working with what looked like palm fronds, painstakingly weaving them into baskets and other pieces.

Next to the blankets was a small table, where a man displayed several handmade postcards and packages. Keely pointed to them and told her dad she'd like to purchase a set to send home to her mom, grandparents, and a few school friends. Alex agreed, and she picked out a very reasonably-priced ten-card pack of various designs. They were quite attractive and colorful, mostly showcasing local flowers but also several landscapes of popular local viewpoints and beach scenes.

As they moved closer toward the growing crowd next to the marae, another exhibit featured women sewing squares of fabric into a patchwork quilt. Then, at the next booth they passed, a woman kneeled over a large piece of tapa cloth, dipping into several small half-coconut buckets full of various dye colors with her fingers and sticks and feathers of various lengths and widths to apply a multicolored floral design to the cloth, which looked to be about the size of a pareo like those they'd seen worn by many local residents. Finally, in the last enclosed area near the marae, a man was carefully crafting some large pieces of wood into a what was apparently to become a table, albeit with no electric-powered tools in evidence. There were also bowls, drums, and other examples of his handiwork displayed on the wall of the artist's booth. He glanced up and smiled at the Websters as they walked by.

The history talk their driver had mentioned was starting just as they arrived at the rock structure. "Maeva, Mesdames et Messieurs! Bienvenue and Welcome to Ti'i Village. My name is Pierre. As I understand most of you speak English, I will try to do so as much as I can as well. Please be, you know, *être patient*, or, bear with me, or as we say in Tahitian, *'A faaoroma'i e o vau!*"

This tri-lingual apology in advance brought chuckles from the audience, as the presenter continued. "What you see here is a replica of an ancient ceremonial site, or temple, built by early Tahitians, called *marae,* whether speaking of one or many. There were similar temples near this site, but this one is not original. In fact, it is much smaller than most. However, there are many surviving examples of these marae around the island. Have any of you seen them?"

One of several hands that shot up was Meg's, and the speaker addressed the American girl, standing directly in front of him. "Ah, *jeunesse* (young woman), you have seen a marae?"

"Yes," said Meg, her cheeks reddening from slight embarrassment (if not from the heat). "Near where we are staying - in between the Montcalm and..." Unfortunately, she couldn't remember the name of the other hotel next door just then.

But the presenter/expert clearly *did* know, and to her great relief, he helped Meg finish her answer.

"Oh yes, at Pihaena. That is a very significant marae. It was erected, archaeologists believe, by the *Maohi* - what ancient

Mooreans were called, by those who settled that area and coastal villages nearby. It may have been built to celebrate a victory over warriors from another island, and has remained an important place for more than 700 years now."

"What were the temples used for?" one visitor with a German accent asked in English. Turning to her, Pierre answered. "As I said, for celebrations, to honor our gods, and...occasionally for animal sacrifices, and" - he gazed around the assembled visitors - "sometimes for human ones."

"YIKES!" Cal exclaimed. He looked at his dad with a mixture of horror and excitement. The rest of the crowd nodded, or grimaced, as some had evidently heard of this practice or seen it on TV or in the movies, or read about it before their visits.

"Yes, there were some human sacrifices as part of Moorean rituals, in fact, that was the case in many parts of Polynesia, far beyond this island. Usually, animals would be sacrificed at certain special times of the year or during weddings or other religious ceremonies. Some of the humans killed would be captured warriors or others from rival tribes. They were sacrificed at marae by order of district chiefs to win the favor of the gods for the local people. But over time, these rituals became less common."

"When did the practice of sacrificing people end, Pierre?" Jess piped up, as he nodded at her raised hand.

"We don't know for certain," the speaker said, "though it was not known to still be done when European explorers like Bougainville, Cook, and others visited in the 1700s. But not too long before that, enemies and others were still sometimes tortured and burned in sacrificial ceremonies."

Several in the audience shuddered and shook their heads. Keely leaned in and whispered to Jess, "Doesn't seem quite so peaceful here anymore, huh!"

Jess whispered back. "Good thing nobody has a lit torch around here!"

Keely giggled, then she saw her dad touch his finger to his lips. She re-framed her face into a serious expression while Jess glanced the other way. Pierre continued his explanation.

"Sacrifices were often made to the war-god *Oro* or other gods ancient Mooreans worshiped, to thank them for victories won, or to seek their support before military campaigns had begun. They were places of much *mana* - what you might call spiritual power. Archaeologists believe there were somewhere between six and forty thousand people living on this island from the 900's until Europeans arrived, split into many separate chiefdoms. They didn't always get along, nor did they always welcome off-island visitors - but not all of the reasons they gathered at marae were associated with death and war. Harvests and royal births were also commemorated and celebrated here. Big feasts would accompany such occasions, but the ones we have here at Ti'i Village now are always happy ones!"

Pierre smiled, and several in the audience apparently knew about the dinner/dancing programs, because they laughed and exchanged knowing glances, or pointed to the stage and covered seating on the other side of the compound.

"But while there were many restrictions to common people, the ruling chiefs and their families - the elite of the community - ate well and lived well. Others in the community had to work very hard to supply the food needs of a village, to fish the waters, to hunt, or farm. It was not easy to be a 'normal' Maohi citizen."

"How big were these marae, Pierre?" Alex asked.

The presenter nodded to the American visitor's question. "Some marae were very large, estimated to be nearly 350 square meters or more, some were more than 10 meters tall, though others were smaller. Many had flowers and trees and other decorations placed around their borders. All played very important parts in village and community life...and death. You see, they were also where meetings were held, important decisions were made, and in some cases, burials were conducted."

Cal whispered to his father, "How big is 350 square meters?" Alex started trying to do a quick calculation in his head, but Keely beat him to the answer.

"That's almost 3,800 square feet," she whispered to her dad and younger siblings. Jess leaned in to listen as well.

Alex replied in a hushed voice, "That is um, around three fourths the size of a pro basketball court, which is almost 100 by 50 feet, roughly."

As the speaker was turned to a corner of the marae, explaining details of its construction, the Webster sisters considered the information they'd just heard: "Great, we are staying right next to a haunted temple!" Meg said to her sister quietly.

Keely shivered, as Meg continued, her eyes now wide. "We gotta go back there and explore...at night!"

"Are you crazy?" Keely retorted, as she shot an incredulous look at the almost-11-year-old. "No way are you getting me over there at night, maybe not even during the day!"

Their presenter, Pierre turned back to finish his talk and answer a couple more audience questions. "*Merci pour votre attention*," then, in English, "Thank you for your attention," he concluded.

Keely replied, "*Je vous en prie*," which garnered a surprised look from her father.

"Hey, I said you're welcome!" Keely told her dad with a grin.

Cal glanced at Pierre and repeated the 'thank you' in Tahitian. "Mau'ru'uru!"

The history expert smiled at the boy, and turned back for a moment before continuing his walk toward the office across the way, "Mau'ru'uru roà...thank *you* very much, ari'i nui!"

Cal walked up to Pierre, Alex close behind, and asked, "Excuse me, what does that last part mean?"

"It means, 'great chief!'"

"That's awesome!" exclaimed Cal, shaking his hand. "Same to you, sir!"

As the Webster contingent returned to the van in the Ti'i Village parking lot, Alex sidled up to Jean-Paul and thanked him for the visit to the exhibit and talk. He pulled out his camera and brought up the saved image of Cal touching the unusual starfish on the beach earlier.

"Do you know the name of this starfish, Jean-Paul?"

"First, you can call me "JP," the tall guide beamed, as he peered at the photo on the tiny screen. "And yes, that is unfortunately a bad, bad animal - it is called the Crown-of-Thorns starfish and is very damaging to our coral reefs here in French Polynesia - and all over the Pacific, I guess. It actually eats the coral, so we would love to have these starfish die back, or just go away as they do naturally from time to time, because we want to protect our coral for now and the future."

"Does anyone know why these harmful starfish have grown more plentiful here?" Alex asked.

JP shrugged, answering, "They have some theories, maybe rising water temperatures, changing currents, but along with people touching the coral, and chemical irritants like suntan lotion and runoff from fields and roads, it's just one of many natural and man-made threats to our coral reefs. You can see the reefs, all the animals that live there, the fish that swim in and around and eat the plants and smaller animals off the reefs, plus how they protect the shore from most large waves. We cannot afford for such a resource to be destroyed."

"Thanks for letting me know, JP. We'd heard of reef-safe sunscreen but we need to remember also not to touch the coral. I'll share that info with my family members - and friends and business associates back home too. It's important that more people are aware of just how delicate that world out in the ocean really is - no matter how much we all like snorkeling, swimming, surfing, and boating. Hey, speaking of that, do you know where we can get some more of your locally-made reef-safe sunscreen?"

JP nodded. "Sure, they sell it at the pharmacy and the activities shop back across from the beach near the old Fun Club. But we will also drive by several other shops where you can buy it today before we finish the tour - I'll make sure to let everyone in the van know to get some when we take our next break for shopping."

Chapter 28

Around the Island tour Part 3: Shopping, marae, & scenes from a movie

2:05 pm Moorea Time, November 26, Saturday

"Speaking of shopping," Alex asked JP, as they walked together, back to the van, "Where is the best place for souvenirs, you know, high-quality local ones that we can bring home with us, the kind that would be fun, yet memorable and not too expensive?"

JP pondered this for a bit before answering the American. "Many of the stores that are run by local people, artisans, have nice carvings, and of course "*Moorea Black Pearl*" jewelry - as it is sometimes called - is one of the things this area is famous for, even if most of the pearls are not actually grown on Moorea but elsewhere in the Society Islands. However, there are some talented jewelry designers here who make beautiful - how do you say it - pieces - earrings, necklaces, bracelets, pendants of various types from pearls and other naturally produced materials. Also, you may know that our Moorean vanilla is exceptionally high quality...but honestly, one of the very best items you can purchase other than handmade artwork, woodwork, and quilts, like some that you can see them working on here at the Village, is at roadside stands and small shops. Pareu, or pareo, sometimes called *pareos* for several in English, as you see on the women and some of the men here, are very nice, always different and unusual - if made here on the island and not imported or mass-produced, make sure you confirm this - and they are great for both women and men, boys and girls, believe it or not. Also, they don't cost too much. Those are some of the things I would take home as gifts for my *feti'i* - my family - or you to your parents ("*na metua*") or friends, which we call "*hoa*" in the Tahitian language."

"*Mauruuru*, JP, and please call me Alex!" the software sales manager replied, as everyone else piled in the van behind them.

"*Aitapeapea*, Alex!" answered the tall Tahitian.

As he got seated and started up the van for the rest of their island-circling adventure, JP turned his head back towards the passengers. "Now, we will be driving to a town for a little shopping time, and maybe ice cream, *E? oui*?" He caught the eyes of the very warm, perspiring passengers, as several wiped their brows, necks, or faces with small towels and handkerchiefs. "Good idea?" he asked, for confirmation from the crowd.

"*Oui!* Yes, for sure!" said Keely and Meg, in unison. The other travelers, perfectly happy to have these two spunky American girls speak for them, grinned and echoed their agreement. And they were on their way.

Alex glanced at his watch: it was just past 2 o'clock, and while the time seemed to have flown by, he marveled at how much they had already seen and learned about Moorea, its history and culture. *I get the feeling that still more is in store for us*, he thought.

Jess sat chatting with Cal. Meg and Keely were pointing at places on the map, trying to read the words in French and Tahitian. Taking advantage of the open seat beside him, Alex opened his camera case, turned on the viewfinder for the video camera, and checked the shots and videos he'd taken that day - making sure battery power was still sufficient in both of his devices. Luckily, he'd remembered to bring (and charge) extra batteries. He'd need lots of 'ready power' just to get images of so many intriguing sights and sounds on this magical island - and it was still only the first real day of exploring it!

The rest of their trip around Moorea went by quickly. The van passed a couple more small marae, and lots of small guesthouses, or *fare*, which JP told them they were called, as well as a surf lodge ("Next time") Alex nudged Cal, as they passed in front of the establishment's sign. They continued around the southern tip of the island through a couple of villages bearing small signs, "*Haapiti*" first, then a bit later, "*Vaianae.*"

Meg noticed that the reef continued almost all the way around the island as they drove, only occasionally broken by a small opening, where boats (and surfers) ventured in or out.

"I bet there are sharks there too!" she said, when Jean-Paul pointed one such break in the reef.

"Oui/Yes, we do have sharks here, but very few attacks," their driver asserted. "Some places actually have been doing 'shark-feeding' recently as a tourist attraction of sorts, but we are trying to discourage it...it upsets the natural balance that we have had here for thousands of years, and by luring too many sharks close to shore, it can cause dangerous, ummmm 'side effects' just like when motorboats get too close to our migrating humpback whales. The reef and all of our waters are very fragile, we must keep them the way they are...but I fear sometimes we are losing that battle."

They had just passed another small village near mile marker 15 on the side of the road, and soon they rounded Moorea's southern tip. Now heading northward on the road, after a few more minutes they entered what looked to Jess like a fairly large town - its sign said *Afareaitu.*

It was 2:30 now, and they all exited after JP parked the van in a lot that fronted a cluster of small shops. JP pulled Alex aside and noted, quietly, that one of the better jewelry shops was located in a building on the right side of the lot. Then, loud enough for the others to hear he pointed and announced, "The small pharmacy over there carries a locally-made reef-safe sunscreen - I highly recommend you buy some now if you don't already have it and plan to go swimming. The coral will thank you, and so will I!"

As the group was about to split up, JP added, "Let's meet for ice cream, my treat, in 15 minutes, OK? Right there." He pointed toward the small ice cream and grocery store at the corner of the small shopping center.

By the appointed time, with some quick shopping done, the Websters had filled a couple of bags with sparkling water made with fruit juice from a company based in Tahiti, boxes and tins of excellent French hard and soft cheese and crackers, several pieces of fruit, including local mango, papaya, limes, and even a bunch of the small 'apple' bananas. They'd also purchased a few candy bars from Australia, plus a six-pack of the only local beer, Hinano for Alex (and Jess) to share later during their trip.

The grocery bags holding their purchases were the heavy-duty, nice souvenir fabric types that could be carried over their shoulders. One had a picture of the island on it, while the other bore the script *"Moorea, Polynesie francaise"* in large print on one side. When he'd seen the fresh baguettes while in the market, Alex realized that if purchased now, they wouldn't still be fresh when they really wanted to eat them - probably tomorrow - so he had decided to wait for another day and occasion to indulge his (and his kids') 'bread dragon' - as none of them could resist professionally-baked fresh bread. Which reminded him of pizza - and he made a mental note to make sure they all tried some of the local-style pies he'd heard of in the resort office on Friday morning. *That*, he thought, *would be perfect for one dinner some night* during their next week on Moorea.

But now, it was all about the ice cream. And after he deposited their shopping bags under the seat in front of his place in the still cool van, Alex joined JP and the others to sample the local treats.

"Wow, this is AWESOME ice cream!" said Meg - and her sister, brother, nanny and dad all nodded their heads vigorously, eating their ice cream in small paper cups, with little wooden spoons. The travelers in the group had selected a variety of guava, coconut, pineapple, and nut-filled combos. And of course, Cal insisted on chocolate for his second scoop. One very enjoyable surprise was their first taste of vanilla - as JP had said, grown right on the island and one of Moorea's delicacies. Each one of them had been encouraged to try one scoop of a local vanilla variety, and the creamy, butterfat-rich confection combinations were - like their location - out of this world. They all nodded their enthusiastic approval as they licked up the luscious treats.

Not too surprisingly, it didn't take long for everyone traveling in the van to finish their ice cream given the very hot temperature, not too far now below 90 F/30 C and super-humid. This meant that their scoops began melting almost immediately. Second reason? The fact the stuff was SOOOO good! They all thanked JP, and now re-energized despite the heat, piled back in to finish the tour. And what a finish it turned out to be!

It was just before 3:30 pm when they drove past the ferry dock, then the airport and onward through the main population center and hotels. They noticed the sign for Temae Beach, then continued beyond it and shortly thereafter, gesturing to his right, JP called out, "We just passed by one of our best beaches and our largest freshwater lake, Lake Temae, and you probably know as you all either came here by boat or plane, but I forgot to mention *that* (he pointed past the beach to the side of the van) is the island of Tahiti over there that we've been driving across from for a while now. If you had binoculars, you might be able to see the town of Faa'a past these hotels' buildings and overwater bungalows and across the channel. Temae and Maharepa – on this side of the island - are some of our best beaches, by the way...you should come back to visit them at least once during your stay on Moorea."

They continued westward now, traveling again down and around Cook's Bay, and Alex pointed out the Montcalm as they passed by its entrance, then all the way down one side of Opunohu Bay. Less than ten minutes from the Montcalm they came to a turnoff, well-marked and clearly a popular route judging by the several cars coming down the hill as they ascended the two-lane winding road. Their last stops were immediately ahead, JP said. First, a prominent marae they had heard about, and then, shortly thereafter, the *Belvedere* - which he called "One of the most famous places in the South Pacific."

The van's passengers gazed around through the van's windows while JP drove slowly up the hill, taking in the sheer lushness of the deep green-hued, primitive multi-volcanic peak landscape before them - especially as it contrasted to the reef-ringed azure waters of the lagoon behind them. In a few moments, they pulled into a small parking lot.

"OK everyone, let's stop here...welcome to *Marae Titiroa* - one of the most celebrated on Moorea," said JP. As they clambered out once again, he led the group toward a large clearing, rimmed by short stone walls and with several trees growing in its center. Alex noticed the phenomenal views from this spot, and took a quick photo. Seeing him do so, Jess and the kids turned to look as well.

"Wow!" said Keely. The view was spectacular near the top of the twisting road, with jungle, sea and jagged mountains all around.

JP explained the significance of the area to the group. "This was and is a very important ceremonial and religious site for our Moorean people. Chiefs, priests, and other elite in society would have meetings, services and other - events - here, in ancient times. It's only part of a larger complex. You can see more sections of it through the trees up there," he explained, pointing past the small compound where they stood, respectfully, outside of its stone boundaries.

"Before the European explorers - and western religions - arrived, this was a major center of tremendous importance, much more impressive than now, with wooden structures, platforms, dances, gatherings. At night there would be feasts and fires."

A Canadian guest raised their hand. "Any human sacrifices here?"

JP turned toward her, then answered. "We don't know that for certain. But there were occasional sacrifices, mainly of animals, aimed at appeasing certain gods worshiped by the Moorean people...and during wartime and some other occasions, yes, there were probably humans sacrificed here as well, usually enemies of the local chief and people of the settlements, often from other islands."

Pointing to a rocky, table-like structure at the rear of the enclosure, JP said, "that is possibly where the sacrifices occurred at this marae." Gesturing towards a cairn-like small structure, comprised of many layers of flat rocks, he added, "It is claimed by some that each rock piled there represents one person killed during the ceremonies - maybe over hundreds of years. But we can't say for sure."

Eyes wide and focused on the mini-tower of rocks, Cal turned to his sister Meg. "Do you see how high that pile is? That's a lotta rocks!"

Meg shook her head in amazement, and Keely shivered a bit with the horror of what might have occurred in this now quiet, peaceful place surrounded by trees, shrubs and beautiful flowers. Meg grabbed her sister's arms and "mock-pushed" her into the enclosure, and Keely screamed, not at all happy at the younger Webster's attempt at humor. Alex grinned despite himself, recognizing that his kids were probably all getting a little tired and "punchy" after such a long day of touring, along with everybody else in the van.

JP looked around him at the subdued group and said, "Let's take a brief moment of silence to remember all who may have died here." They all bowed their heads, and in absence of human voices, they could hear a small stream flowing nearby, a variety of birds chirping and calling, and the wind, whistling through the trees of this verdant paradise and religious and ceremonial site for so many in the past. And perhaps a scene of death or despair for some - or many - as well.

Their pause was soon broken by JP's voice. "OK, it's time for our last stop, let's get back in the van and head to *Bali Hai!*"

As they returned slowly to the vehicle, Keely looked up at a strange, tree with very twisted branches, one of many like it growing near the marae. "What's that tree called?" she asked JP.

"Great question. I will tell you what it is NOT...a mango tree. It is actually a 'Suicide Tree', and it's called that because it contains a violent, very bad poison, so you wouldn't want to eat its fruit!" Several of the tour members *oohed* or *aaahed*.

"Thanks for letting us know!" said Jess, stepping into the van.

"Yeah, no-go for fruit-o from that tree-o," quipped Alex.

The glares he received from his daughters chastened Alex from trying any more 'dad jokes', *at least for the rest of this tour*, Alex thought. He was really getting punchy himself, still a little jet-lagged. Still, it was all super interesting to him – as a huge history and culture buff.

While JP backed up the van to continue their tour, Alex took a couple more photos, including one of the poisonous tree to add to the brief video he had captured of Marae Titiroa and the traveling group. Then as he stepped in to join the rest of them, he shivered for a second, thinking of the mixed meanings surrounding this sacred site. He was glad to have come, glad to have seen it, but more than glad to be leaving it now, too!

A few more twists and turns preceded the entrance to the final stop on journey, one of their main sightseeing objectives for their adventure around Moorea, and indeed for their whole trip to the island.

"Here we are!" JP said as they rounded the last turn and a small parking area came into view. "*The Belvedere*...which some call '*Bali Hai*' though that's probably not accurate. Let's get out one last time and take a closer look together."

As they walked from the van towards the lookout area, the views of the water and mountains framed by the sun were absolutely stunning. Of course, they were also decidedly different than their previous vistas from *Magic Mountain* and elsewhere during their round the island tour.

"Check that out...both bays, you can see them so clearly...look at the boats wayyyy down there," said Jess pointing to the left side.

"Yes, you can see Opunohu *and* Cook's Bay...and that's Mt. Rotui, right in the center too," said JP.

Meg pulled her brother over towards her while Alex captured some of the sights with his video camera, pausing to take some photos with his digital camera too.

"Do you remember where dad earlier said they filmed the movie *The Bounty*?" she asked her brother.

"Cook's Bay, right?"

"Nope, it was Opunohu Bay...because it looked more 'primitive' when they filmed there." replied his sister.

JP heard them and sidled up to the young Americans, whose other sister and nanny had now also joined them for a look over the rounded railing of the overlook.

"Yes, you are correct, Ms. Meghan! But here's more you might not know." Their guide then shared some additional facts on *The Bounty* and several other movies that had been filmed on or near the island. "Much of what was supposed to be Tahiti in the 1984 version starring Anthony Hopkins, Mel Gibson, and Liam Neeson, and not just the shots of Opunohu Bay, was actually Moorea. In fact, they filmed some of the wide-angle "scenery" and what they call in the industry "establishing" shots not far from where you are standing!"

Alex now joined the rest of the group, and they all took in the majestic view of the two bays, with the jagged Mt. Rotui in-between them. He noticed that there were only a few clouds in the sky above. "We lucked out with it being so clear, didn't we?" he said to JP.

"Yes, we did. Especially in the afternoons, rain is common this time of year, at least somewhere on the island. We've been all around it today, but escaped it. Shall I take one more family photo for you?"

"Sure!" Alex answered. They all bunched together a bit with their backs to the guardrail. After their guide took several shots from different angles, Keely insisted - with the others quickly agreeing - that JP join them for one picture as well. Alex quickly set up his monopod to capture it.

Soon, the Websters moved away to get another vantage point and JP volunteered his photo-taking services for one of the other couples from their tour. Alex helped too by taking a similar picture for them with JP, then stood with Jess as they gazed out toward the spectacular blue waters, the views accented by the deep green foliage of the island's steep canyons.

"Have you ever seen anything so amazingly, strikingly beautiful as this?" Alex asked the Kiwi, knowing how beautiful he had heard her native New Zealand, called by its indigenous people the *Land of the Long White Cloud*, was itself.

"Close, but maybe not quite," answered Jess. "But then again, it's a different kind of beauty. This place is stunning...and I can't wait to get back in that warm water way down there either!"

Alex laughed. He walked over to put his arm around his daughter Meghan's shoulders. "What do you think of this place, Meg?"

"PHENOMENAL, Dad...so glad we came."

Keely stood near them at the railing. "What about you, ready to practice your French some more?" asked her dad.

"I guess," said Keely, smiling.

Cal, from his vantage point nearby, blurted out his preference.

"I'd rather learn Tahitian!"

JP, walking back toward the Websters, grinned. "Well, you already have learned a bit of both languages today," he said in his lilting accent. "And for the rest of your trip, you'll have more chances to learn our local words and culture. Not everyone here speaks English, and in some places on the island, almost nobody does! For now, though, it's time to return to your hotel. The sun will set in only a bit more than an hour."

As they made their way back down the narrow, twisting roadway to the main road near Opunohu Bay, Alex glanced at his watch. It was just past 5 pm, but he felt like they'd been driving for days. *So much to see in so short a time. But what a pretty, very pretty island it was!*

He leaned across Cal to ask the other Webster "clan" members in the back of the bus a question: "Anybody hungry for dinner yet?"

"YES!!" came four enthusiastic replies, nearly in unison.

Laughing, Alex said, "Me too!" and 15 minutes later, they pulled into the driveway leading to the front of the Montcalm.

As they trooped off the van one last time, each of them thanked Jean-Paul profusely for his wonderful guidance and driving on the trip. Alex, last out of the van, leaned over and pressed a couple of 2000 CFP notes in their driver/guide's hand.

"*Merci Beaucoup*, JP. The historical and other details, not to mention all the friendly assistance you shared with us on this trip - all were amazing. We learned so much!"

The other Websters vigorously nodded their agreement.

"Thanks again for the ice cream, JP!" said Meg.

Cal added "And for telling us about the sacrifices!"

This brought a wry grin to the Tahitian man's face.

"Don't you let yourself be one, young man!" and seeing Cal's worried look, he chuckled, "I'm teasing you, of course."

But then, he toned down his smile just a tad. "Please use that sunscreen you purchased today in good health, and wear a hat too - and please respect the ocean when you swim or snorkel. Always do so together, avoid touching the coral, please. And...if you somehow get poked by a sea urchin - well, just ask one of our locals what to do about it," he said, lowering his voice a bit, somewhat mysteriously.

"What do you do if *that* happens?" asked Keely.

"That is one of the secrets of Moorea you'll need to discover yourself - but I hope you don't have to!" replied JP. Then he ceased talking, and turned back to the van, leaving the young Americans to keep wondering as to the answer...

JP still had to return the other two couples to their nearby resort. The three females in the Webster clan called out "*Maururu*, JP!"

"*Aita pea pea*, Ms. Keely, Ms. Meg, and Ms. Jess, Mr. Cal, and Mr. Alex. *Maururu Roa* to all you Websters for coming to visit our beautiful island. Hope you have a wonderful rest of your trip!"

"*Nānā!*" Meg yelled, and the driver turned and smiled back, repeating the farewell message to the girl in return.

As the tour bus pulled away from the hotel entrance, Jess shook her head in wonder. "What a great guy!"

Keely nodded. "I just LOVED his accent."

"And he knew EVERYTHING!" Cal exclaimed, drawing a laugh from the others. And then they trudged with all their bags in hand, back to their bungalow to freshen up before dinner.

Arriving at the room, Alex said, "Hey, remember your suggestions this morning - let's check out the sunset down by the beach before we eat. I'll bring the cooler with sodas, beer, and ice, plus some chips and crackers to enjoy while we watch the sun go down. Sound like a plan?"

"Great idea, Dad," said Meg, and 20 minutes later, everyone had switched to their swimsuits and t shirts. Bearing a nice collapsible cooler full of ice, beverages, cheese, and crackers, they ambled together down to the shore. Setting the bag down under their 'favorite' tree, they all kicked off their sandals and waded into the water to enjoy the warmth amid the lengthening shadows brought on by the setting sun.

Cal munched on French crackers topped by creamy cheese, and sipped from a can of sparkling water/fruit juice mix. "This is the life!"

Alex raised the bottle of Hinano in his hand. "I'll say!"

Jess, Keely, and Meg joined them, and together they all faced the west and raised their cans and bottles in a joint salute.

"To Moorea, jewel of French Polynesia!" said Alex.

"Salud!" said Jess.

"*Manuia!*" added Keely.

Meg giggled and responded showing her already growing familiarity with Tahitian words. "*E*'...Yes!"

Then Jess capped off the toasts, with the sun rapidly falling on the western horizon. She held up her own bottle of Hinano. "This beer is...*maita'i* - yes, that's pronounced *may-tay* - and it's OK even if it's not a Mai Tai!"

Alex laughed and the kids looked at each other, a bit confused before Keely said "I get it, Remember?! *Maita'i* means *good* in this country, even if it's not pronounced like the drink!"

Saturday's sun set soon after on the Worldwide Websters' first full day of adventure - all the way around Moorea. All that was left was dinner back at the hotel restaurant - which turned out to be a very light one. They all ordered salads - given their day had already been filled with lots of eating and snacking. Then it was back to the bungalow, where it took very little to 'knock out' the whole crew, all dead tired from their exciting, exhausting tour around the island. All were asleep, with a couple snoring for all the roosters to hear, within 10 minutes of hitting their pillows!

Chapter 29

Meals, memories, & snorkelin' Websters

November 27, Sunday, morning

Alex couldn't figure out what time it was. His watch was in his pants pocket, and there was no alarm clock next to his bed. Cal was snoring, he knew that much! *But the roosters sure thought it was time to get up,* he cringed. *Earplugs - second note to self.* He pulled an extra pillow over his head and rolled over to return to the dense slumber he'd been in all night. *After all, sleeping in is what Sundays are FOR,* he thought. Alex tried to send his thoughts telepathically to the raging roosters outside. But he did, mercifully, fall back asleep regardless.

About an hour passed before Alex was awakened again, this time by activity in the rooms next door. With the girls up and making some noise, Cal rolled out of bed and went to the bathroom. After he was done, Alex took his place. A few minutes later, he came out to see the connecting door to the girls' room open, yet no sign of the Webster teens. Jess's door was closed, so he wasn't sure if she was around.

"They all went down to see the sunrise," said Cal.

"Jess too?" his dad asked.

"Yep, they left while you were in the bathroom. Let's catch up to 'em."

Alex and Cal put on their sandals and made their way outside in the just brightening light, then onto the now-familiar path out to the beach.

As they walked, Alex noticed it was a bit damp along the path. *Probably rained a bit last night,* he thought. He asked Cal his insights on the trip so far. "Enjoying Moorea, sport?"

"Yeah, it's great! I really like all the maraes and history stuff. And the mountains too. It sure is hot sometimes though, but that's nice when you're in the water. And I wish Mom could be here, but..."

Alex closed his eyes for a moment, flashing back to some of the happy memories of the travels they used to do as a family.

Back then, when the kids were very young and early in his career, they didn't have the money or time (or frequent flyer miles in enough quantity or value) to venture as far as they later did with dad-and-kids-only since the divorce. But they had enjoyed some real family adventures at the Washington and Oregon Coasts, along the Pacific Ocean, and on a few boat and quasi-camping trips to islands around the region, often with their grandparents from Alex's side. As a young couple, they had also ventured up to Canada a couple of times with Keely and her Nana, when their firstborn was still a toddler, then later with all three of the kids for a second, similar trip. Of course, that all happened before the parents' nearly twelve-year marriage was finished.

"Yeah, your mom would really like it here, I'm sure," answered Alex, focusing back on the present and his 9 1/2-year-old son. He looked at the creative, curious kid next to him on the path and really felt the love for his youngest very strongly in that moment. "Hey, we should all get our snorkel stuff rented after breakfast and spend some time exploring the lagoon together today!" Alex said.

"That would be awesome!"

Soon, they passed the now-deserted cafe area by the pool and were coming through the trees to the beach when they saw Keely, Meg, and Jess standing in the shallow water, around 25 feet from shore. They were facing to their right, toward the east, watching the sun rise above Moorea's mountains.

Meg waved, then Keely and Jess did the same. Alex and Cal kicked off their flip-flops and waded out to join them.

"Hey Dad, good morning!" said Meg. "I can feel the fishies swimming around my feet!"

"Yeah, it sure is nice - and I can see lots of fish even from up here above the water," Alex replied. "Hey, on that note - how would you all like to go snorkeling today in the lagoon, after we get done with breakfast?"

"That's a great idea!" said Keely, "I just finished my daily swim practice - about 400 yards out and back while these guys watched, and waded." Jess and Meg gave their thumbs-up to the snorkeling plans as well.

"Perfect...we can all go get fitted for our gear at the Activities hut later. We should probably arrange to keep it for the whole week, as I'd guess the rental rate is a bit cheaper anyway for several days than just one or two. Then we can start exploring around here together today, and later while I'm gone, you four can do some more swimming and snorkeling together here and maybe a couple other beaches nearby."

"Sounds like a plan, Dad," said Meg. They all stood there in the gentle waves for the next fifteen minutes or so, watching the sun slowly rise over the treetops, as the temperature rose. Jess noticed only a very faint breeze.

"It is so peaceful here, I just can't believe this weather, it's wonderful!"

"Yeah," Keely replied to her New Zealand-born caregiver. "And the water is so warm, not quite like bath water, but close enough."

They all nodded and mused in silence on where they were, how surreal it was to be standing quietly in this offshore garden, teeming with plant and marine life just below the surface.

"We are very lucky," said Alex, smiling at the others as he gazed around the island in front of him, and heard the faint, yet steady crashing of the waves against the reef several hundred yards away - behind where they stood on the lagoon's sandy bottom.

"We sure are," agreed Cal.

Jess walked over to him and put her arm around the boy's shoulder. "Glad you passed your final swim class this past summer, Cal...now you can put all of those strokes and holding your breath underwater to good use out here. But don't forget the safety rules, right?"

His father concurred. "Yeah...and that goes for all of you, "Alex said. "Like Jess says, and as JP said on our tour yesterday too, no swimming or snorkeling alone, and if you feel currents, remember to come back in calmly, swimming along the shore and diagonal toward it, if you ever feel any sort of unusual "pull" of the water."

Alex took one last look around, then sloshed a bit of that water on his t-shirt as he high-stepped back through the calm sea toward shore. "Who's hungry for a good Moorean Sunday breakfast?" Four hands shot up at once in response.

That morning's meal, which they joined in sandals and shorts and shirts, was a little different than the previous day's fare. It included - not to be too obvious - French toast, but it was different in taste and texture than they were accustomed to in the US: very small strips of thick, very sweet bread with fresh banana rings atop each slice. Again, there was butter (Alex had seen at the store that Australian butter, packaged in a tin, was very popular here), and this day, there was also ham as well as the usual fruit, pastry options and eggs, both scrambled and over-easy. Each Webster clan member loaded their plates, then went back to fill their juice glasses. Alex and Jess also ordered coffee.

"Another fantastic meal," Jess said after she'd finished most of her breakfast, though still nibbling the last chunks of papaya on her plate.

"That's great for your digestion too, you know," said Keely.

"Really?" said the nanny.

"Yep, papaya contains a natural enzyme, called papain, that is used as an antacid by many people. It's in some of those natural tablets for indigestion you see in the stores. My mom told me about it when we were in Hawaii a few years ago."

Alex sighed to himself. Meg looked down at her lap, and Cal busied himself finishing his French toast and eggs. *Family break-ups are never easy, no matter how many years later*, he thought.

Meg brightened. "So, when are we going snorkeling? And what are we going to do after that?"

"Well," said Alex, as he glanced at his watch, "It's 9 o'clock now, so let's go back to the room, get ready, and say in 30 minutes or so we can go over to the Activities hut and get all our stuff picked out and paid for. Then we can head down to the beach and skin dive out there around the coral for an hour or so, maybe hang out on the sand, under 'our tree' for a while afterwards. Then, I don't know, what do you guys want to do for the rest of your second full day here at the resort? Or on the island?"

"Maybe we could go back into that town we passed, and hike up to the falls there?" Keely asked.

"What do the rest of you think of that idea?" Alex asked, looking from Jess to Meg and Cal.

"Sure, works for me," said Jess, and the younger kids nodded.

"I think that will fill most of our day, and should give us another 'dimension' of the island, plus lots of exercise for sure," Alex observed.

Jess agreed. "I'm for that, 'cause if I keep eating all this rich food and don't stay busy, I'll turn into a whale myself by the time we go home!"

Cal looked very serious and turned to the nanny. "Sorry, Jess, no whales allowed on the plane. Not enough water or space onboard." Then he giggled, and they all laughed, took their last sips of their drinks and pushed back their chairs. Time for adventure, again!

As they headed back to their rooms, Jess glanced casually toward the restaurant's 'bussing' station, across from where they'd been sitting. That's where the plates and utensils were stored and also cleaned up before returning them to the kitchen. She watched as a tall man, who looked to be in his younger twenties, stood there sorting some plates, cups, and glasses. He caught her glance and smiled at her. Jess suddenly realized the restaurant employee was looking directly back at her. She felt her cheeks turn a bit warmer even than the balmy air outside, and quickly shifted her focus to the walkway back to their room.

But she pondered a bit. *Wow, the scenery here is even better than I thought it was!*

Keely grinned and poked her in the ribs. "I saw that!" said the precocious preteen. "He's super cute!"

"Ssshhh!" Jess retorted, "pay attention to where you're walking, no tripping allowed on this trip!"

"Oh my gosh, what a terrible pun, Jess!" Keely shot back, but she was smiling, and so, she saw, was Jess. The other Websters looked back quizzically, but hadn't caught the exchange.

And that is definitely OK, Jess told herself, turning her focus to the day ahead and away from the young server, with whose eyes she had just 'met.'

Alex was pleased when, less than a half hour later, they were all outfitted with more than decent-quality snorkeling gear, obtained at the Montcalm's Activities hut, near the pool (which, given the fantastic swimming and snorkeling in the warm lagoon, they weren't interested in using at all.) Even better, he received the hotel's employee discount, which encouraged him to go ahead and rent all their equipment for a full week instead of bothering with any daily reservations.

Now, they were all armed (and *legged* and *backed* and *faced*) - in other words, *coated*, with the local reef-safe sunscreen, two separate tubes of it purchased at the store the day prior during their circle-island tour. Not cheap at around $30 for both, but worth it and it would likely last them the whole week and maybe beyond.

They settled all their stuff, including towels and their small, collapsible cooler filled with ice and their refillable/insulated water bottles they'd brought on the trip, under 'their tree' on the beach. Alex dropped their room keys into his shorts pocket, then each removed their tops and shorts down to their swimsuits, and began to wade carefully into the water with their fins, snorkels and masks in hand.

Cal spit a bit of saliva into his mask, then adjusted it across his head. The others followed - fog-proofing and securing their own masks, then pulling on their fins once the water was deep enough. One after another, they ducked under the surface to begin their group snorkeling adventure.

Jess had skin-dived/snorkeled in several parts of the world, just as Alex had, with Keely, Meg, and Cal each a little-bit less experienced in order from there. She immediately marveled at the clarity of the water under the surface. Many of the fish were familiar to her - or at least similar to ones she'd seen in Mexico and even the Caribbean. Moors, Tangs, Angelfish, Trigger Fish, one of those super skinny, long Needlefish, and too many more to name - or to know by name. They were everywhere, and she noticed again that the coral actually looked healthier than some places she had visited.

Breathing steadily through the snorkel as she kicked her fins next to the others in the Webster clan, Jess did a quick check from side to side to ensure everyone was proceeding as expected. Seeing all there, including Cal, next to his dad, she made an initial dive down to the bottom to follow Alex, who was already skimming a safe distance above and to the side of a long chain of coral and rocks stretching out several hundred yards along the side of the lagoon, roughly opposite where all their stuff was sitting under 'their tree' onshore.

Keely and Meg trailed their dad by a bit. Though both great swimmers too, they wanted to meander around a bit. Plus, Keely had extra 'drag' on her speed due to the underwater camera affixed to her wrist by its rubber strap. Cal swam next to his sisters at first, but soon he kicked and half-stroked his way toward Jess.

Alex took another dive, and did some power dolphin-kicking using his fins for extra leverage and then surfaced to clear his mask and snorkel as Jess had. Alex had skin-dived like this in enough places to have a routine that he liked to always follow: Swim, surface, survey (by turning around in a circle to see what was around him and where he was positioned relative to a fixed point on shore), then swim again - or continue his activity once the survey step was completed safely.

As he dropped back underwater Alex saw that a higher ridge of rocks and coral was straight ahead. Estimating his depth as well as the strength and direction of the current, he edged a bit closer, peering down in between a couple of large boulders completely covered with coral growths. Schools of various fish swam all around. Amazingly, they weren't that fearful of him - this giant mammal disturbing their daily rounds along the inner reef of the lagoon.

Just as he was about to surface again, several feet further down the ridge, Alex saw something pop out from under a rock to his upper right, around "2 o'clock" if he was using the hands of a timepiece as a reference. After a quick breath at the surface, he dove back down and confirmed what he thought he'd seen - a Moray eel. As he swam closer, Alex saw that the large green/gray eel, maybe 3-feet long and half a foot wide or more, with spots all over its body and with its peculiar jutting jaw and open mouth, was sort of swaying about in a tempting dance, just above the entrance to its lair, waiting for unsuspecting prey to swim by.

Calmly, he kicked his way to the surface, pulled the snorkel from his mouth, and spoke loudly in the direction of his daughters, Jess and Cal. "Hey everybody, come here, I have something to show you!"

When the others had kicked their way to his location from a nearby ridge of rocks and coral, he pointed downward, beneath the surface. "Take a quick look straight down over there."

Meg and Keely dove down first, and Alex could see through his mask - now fixed just below surface to watch them - that they had caught a glimpse of the large eel. They pointed at it with excitement, as he could see from their jerky movements.

After they surfaced and noted "How cool!" it was to see the crafty animal, Keely dropped back towards the moray's nest to take a couple photos with her underwater camera.

Knowing his son and Jess would love to see it too, Alex said, "OK, you two, want to see what we're talking about?"

"Yeah!" said Cal and Jess nodded, then Alex and Jess each grabbed one of Cal's hands.

"1, 2, 3!" the two adults dove down with Cal in tow between them. They took a quick look, Alex making sure as he pointed toward it that Cal saw the eel, which at just that moment darted up and snared a small passing fish in its mouth!

They popped back to the surface together. "WOW, that was AWESOME!" said the youngster.

Jess added "I'll say, that guy is fierce! And huge! Did you see those jaws open?"

"No kidding!" Alex responded, and then taking another break to check their position, laying on his back and simultaneously clearing his mask of a bit of seawater, then "re-coating" it again, he smiled while Cal excitedly explained what they'd seen to his sisters.

"We saw it too!" said Meg

"Yeah, but did you see it gulp down a fish?!"

"Nope we didn't see THAT," answered his oldest sister, and Meg frowned, disappointed she'd missed this part. She dove back down a couple of times while they floated above the site for a few minutes.

"Let's go over there, Dad," Meg said. She removed her mask, and cleared it out with seawater, then like her dad, spit into it and wiped the saliva around it with her finger. While lightly moving her fin-encased feet to stay easily afloat, she pointed towards some large rocks twenty yards further out - on the other side of the lagoon.

Checking the current relative to where their towels and gear sat onshore, Alex nodded and said, "Sure, you want to lead us there, Meg?" and of course, the almost-11-year-old was already gone, paddling vigorously with her fins in a beeline to the new destination.

When they all caught up to her, Meg was diving carefully and repeatedly, down and around the coral reef several feet below the surface. The others followed her along the side of what turned out to be a small rock wall. Just as they reached one end and were starting to turn back toward where they started, Meg popped up, pulled her mask off, and yelled "See the turtle, right down there!" She pointed down below the surface.

At first, none of them could see anything, then suddenly a little, crinkly head popped up, about ten feet away, just for a second, before diving back under the lapping waves. The Websters, mindful of keeping the proper distance so as not to disturb the creature, dropped underwater in unison to see what turned out to be a fairly large, maybe 4-foot long and 3-foot oval/wide green sea turtle.

Alex had seen many of these curious amphibians over the years, and in fact on his first day swimming in this particular lagoon, the previous Friday. But they never ceased to amaze him. Maybe this was the same one? He watched it in quiet wonder, marveling as it gently flapped its arms like wings as it glided over the rocks, head moving from side to side as it made its way to the other side of the rock wall. It dove down and back up once, but he didn't see it eat anything.

Clearly, the turtle wasn't concerned that a bunch of tourists were watching its activities from fifteen feet away. Soon, as they tried to follow from a safe distance, they noticed how fast it was escaping them.

Deceptively quick little guy, Keely thought to herself, as she snapped a couple of photos, and she didn't know it 'til later, but the other Webster kids and Jess had similar thoughts as they watched their "first Moorean turtle" swim slowly, yet steadily out of sight.

Alex surfaced again, observing they were now about 200 yards offshore. He checked the body language, floating position, and faces of the others. "How's everybody doing?"

"Fine," said Keely,

"Great!" gasped Meg,

Jess turned from clearing her mask to answer, "Doing fine!"

Cal managed to awkwardly lift up his mask and reply, "Good, Dad!"

Alex knew that Cal, especially, had to be a bit fatigued at this point. It was not easy to keep paddling, pulling, and diving up and down all over the lagoon. Even he, as an expert swimmer felt his legs getting a bit tired. Checking his watch, he saw it was around 10:45, so they'd been out exploring the reefs and rocks for about an hour.

"What do you say we cross to that other section near the reef, see what we find, then make our way back to shore. We can hang out on the beach for a bit, grab some water, and re-apply our sunscreen?" Alex said.

Hearing no objections, he urged his oldest daughter on. "Keely, you're the swimming champ, lead us over there!" and off she went, Meg trying gamely to keep up, with Jess moving more leisurely with Cal to her side. Alex followed a few yards back of everyone, stroking steadily while keeping his eyes focused mostly on the bottom. He marveled at the seemingly endless supply of different kinds of fish swimming by underneath his saltwater-aided, buoyant body.

When they reached the designated outcrop, Keely had already made another discovery. "Hey everybody, guess what I just saw!? Our first *Humuhumunukunukuapua'a!*"

"Do they even call it that here?" Meg wondered aloud about the Reef Trigger Fish, otherwise known to many as "Humu" - for short.

"I'm not sure," said Alex, "but show us where you saw him."

Keely dove down, pivoting her mask to ensure her dad was next to her. She pointed at a small brown, black, and gold body - loved in Hawaii as the "State fish" - with funny white, protuberant "lips" on its small head and mouth, a flat, oblong shape, with a classic triangular tail.

Alex surfaced, while the others took a closer look at the fish - one of the fastest and most skittish anyone would ever see around a reef here - or anywhere. "Yep, that's a humu all right, great sighting, Keely. Our lucky first humu to add to the lucky first turtle Meg found across the lagoon. A very fortunate first foray into Moorean waters for all of us!"

Keely and Meg groaned in unison at their dad's penchant for alliteration. Jess smiled, and Cal gave a playful punch to his father's shoulder, holding onto his back for a short rest. Noting this, Alex turned his head around, estimated their distance as around 250 yards from their starting point and said "Who wants to race back to shore?"

"I do!" said Meg, and she was off - thrashing towards the beach.

Cal followed close behind, then Jess, all moving at a decent pace. Keeping a careful eye on his son, Alex glanced at Keely. "Let's wait a bit, and then you can go next...but...you KNOW I'll catch you!"

They both watched Cal swim steadily toward the shore behind his other sister, Jess by his side. Suddenly, before Alex could adjust his mask, Keely sprung forward, kicking hard with a somewhat stilted crawl stroke due to the snorkel equipment, speeding straight to the sandy beach.

Alex gave her a head start of around 20 yards, making sure Cal was still making good progress as Jess and Meg led the way, then started after Keely. He began at medium speed, occasionally checking on everyone's positions ahead as he drew closer to shore. Amazed that after many strokes he hadn't yet caught his oldest daughter, he sped up his legs and arms at about the 100-yard point, determined to reach her before they hit the really shallow water and sand.

Just as he almost drew even with Keely, and around the time the others, after quite a head start, were drawing up their legs to stand in the shallows, Alex reached shore. Keely had beaten him by about three yards!

"Wow, kiddo, you have really gotten faster. Great job, but maybe no more head starts needed for you!"

They all laughed, slowly dragged their legs out of the lightly breaking surf and took off their fins, then their snorkels and masks. A minute later, everyone collapsed onto newly spread towels.

"Time for some *sunnin'*" said Jess.

"I'll say," replied a weary Keely, who had really put a lot of effort into her race back to the beach against her dad.

"What? You guys are tired? Wow, I was dog-paddling and relaxing all the way in!" Alex said playfully.

Groaning, Keely pulled her hat over her head and turned over on her stomach. Jess applied sunscreen to the teen's back and legs. "Thanks, Jess!" Keely replied.

Alex turned to the Kiwi. "So, Jess, how would you rate the fish and undersea plant life quality and variety here? You know, compared to other places you've snorkeled?"

"It's right up there with the best I've seen," said Jess, continuing "In some ways it's better, in other ways, not quite as vibrant as places I've been in the Indian Ocean and Atlantic and Pacific, maybe in Mexico, too. But it is incredible, and calm, and warm, and it was great to get that close to that huge Moray Eel - and see him feed, too!"

With Keely protected, and noting that Meg had already put on fresh sunscreen too, while Cal had covered himself and his head with an extra towel, Jess squeezed the other sunscreen tube to reapply it to her face, arms and legs. She turned to the oldest of her 'charges' with a caution. "Don't forget, you might need more sunblock on your face and other parts if you move, Keely," said Jess.

"I will." Then the pre-teen promptly pretended to fall asleep, with faux-snoring and all.

"Let's give her about ten minutes," Alex whispered to Jess, "then I'll make sure she puts more on her face and arms...but now, we should all drink some water. I'm ready for some towel time too!"

After everyone took several sips from their water bottles (Keely joined too after a minute or so of fake slumber) Alex himself slipped into a daydream, and was starting to doze off for a few moments when he noticed someone standing a few yards away on the beach. He pulled his hat up from where it had been partially covering his eyes - and sunglasses - from the super-bright sun. It was a woman and a girl...whom he momentarily recognized as the mother and daughter from family at the airport whose son joined Cal in dancing to the "drumline." He thought back to their conversation on the shuttle to the ferry landing and stood to greet them, but could only remember their last name. "Hi there! Remember us, the Websters? You're the Martinezes, right?"

Mrs. Martinez was a bit startled at first, then turned and recognized Alex and the others. As he struggled to recall their names, Keely stood up next to her dad and called out "Hi, Tiare!"

The girl grinned shyly, making eye contact with her American counterpart, then looked down. "Hi," she replied.

Her mom turned to Alex. "Sure, I remember you. Hello! How are you enjoying Moorea?"

"We're loving it!" said Alex. "By the way, I've forgotten your name.... I'm Alex and you're...?"

"Rai," she answered, "Short for Raiana."

"That's right, now I remember. Well, how are you all doing since your arrival, Rai?"

"We're...enjoying our time here," Rai answered after a brief pause. She wasn't smiling broadly though and didn't sound that enthused. Alex wondered why.

"I really like your swimsuit, Tiare," said Meg, now joining the conversation.

"Thanks, I got it at a shop in one of the towns, um, Maharepa? We went there yesterday." She wore a one-piece with bright colors of blue, green and pink, similar in style and design to some of the pareo they had seen people wearing.

"Yes, my sister owns the shop, so it was a logical place for us to go and find the things we needed for the beach here," said her mother.

"Your suit is very pretty too," said Jess to Rai, "Did you also get it at your sister's shop?"

"Uh huh, yes, I didn't like the ones I had from home, so decided to take a chance on finding a nice one on the island. This one-piece is better for snorkeling and boating, swimming, all the things we love to do here."

"Of course." Jess answered.

"Hey, we just went snorkeling!" blurted out Cal.

"Yes, I can see that!" answered Mrs. Martinez, as she surveyed the collection of skindiving equipment strewn around their four towels on the beach. "We're going to go out a bit later...we were able to borrow some equipment from my sister's house. She and her family live up the road a little ways from where we are staying." She pointed over her shoulder to the east, in the direction of their hotel.

Smiling at Meg and Keely, Rai added, "You look like real swimmers in those nice suits of yours, I bet you move just like fish through the water." She glanced at Cal and Jess, "And the two of you as well...what are your names again? Sorry I have to ask, I wish I was better at remembering names, but I will for next time, I promise!"

Jess stood up and extended her hand. "I'm Jess, the kids' nanny or bab...OK not babysitter, 'cause they're sure not babies! - and speaking of which," she turned to each girl in turn. "This is Keely, she's 12 - and you guessed it, she's a competitive swimmer. That's Meg, she's almost 11, in less than a month, and Cal is heading toward ten years old next March. They are all pretty strong swimmers, though Cal's just getting his real 'sea legs' now. He did great out there in the lagoon today!"

Rai nodded her head. "Love your suit too, Jess. It looks Tahitian, did you buy it here?"

"Thanks, but nope, got it in Mexico, Cabo when I visited with friends last year. I sure am glad it still fits!" she said with a chuckle and a small self-conscious eye-roll in response.

Cal piped up, aiming a question at Rai. "Where's your son?...ummm...."

Meg finished his question. "Linc, right?"

"That's right, Lincoln, Linc's fine too. He's back at our room in the hotel with his dad - Victor - now. Linc's a bit younger than you are, Cal, not quite nine."

Alex suddenly had an idea. "Hey, Rai and Tiare, we were just going to order some food from the restaurant here, as we're getting pretty hungry and it's near lunchtime anyway. How would you like to join us, and maybe Mr. Martinez, er Vic, and Linc can come too?"

The tall Tahitian, or actually Moorean woman averted her eyes just for a moment, then answered with a sheepish look. "Oh, thank you for the offer, but we really need to get back to our room now. Lots of things to do, you know. Family. Other stuff..."

"No problem, or as they say here - a lot, it seems - '*Aita pea pea*'!" Alex replied with a grin, hoping to ease her discomfort with the invitation. He wondered again, *What's up with this woman and her kids?* "How about a rain check, which I'm sure there will be a bit more of (rain I mean) here. But seriously, maybe we can do it another time. We'll be on the island until next Saturday morning."

"Sure, Alex. Thank you again, *Maururu roa*...Many thanks. Maybe later this week will work."

With that, the Colorado visitor and native of the island said, "Bye everybody...for now"

The Websters answered "*Bye*" - except Meg and Keely exclaimed, "*Nānā!*"

With a look of surprise at their correct use of the "goodbye" expression, Rai echoed it back to the girls. Before she and Tiare turned to go, Jess was sure she saw what looked like tears welling in the tall woman's dark green eyes.

Chapter 30

Afareaitu Falls

Alex revisited their conversation from breakfast while the Webster clan walked back to their rooms. "So, what do you all say, should we head into town for lunch and a nice hike?"

"Head to town," said Keely.

"Town & hike," said Meg.

"Town, lunch, and hike," said Cal.

Alex looked at Jess, now brushing some stray sand off her sandals. "What about you, Jess?"

"I'm up for anything. It would be fun to hike and see more of the island - and I bet the waterfall will be flowing well if it's like others I've seen - it rained a little last night."

"Great! That's settled, we'll head into town and then to the waterfall from there. We can pick up sandwiches and take our cold drinks, snacks and stuff up with us in a couple of backpacks. I'll bring one," said Alex.

"Me too," Jess chimed in.

Alex stopped as they neared the Montcalm's main building. "Give me a couple of minutes, I need to check on something at the hotel office. Why don't you all change into shorts and your decent hiking shoes, no flip-flops...oh, and Jess would you please put together a few snacks and drinks to bring? And Keely, can you make sure we bring our sunscreen and insect repellent? I would guess there are mosquitoes up there, and we don't want to get bites or worse on the hike!"

Jess and Keely nodded and returned to the bungalow to get started on their tasks, while the other two kids followed and opened their dresser drawers for clothes to wear on their excursion.

"Hi there" Alex greeted the front desk attendant.

"*Iaorana*, Mr. Webster."

"*Iaorana*, Michel," Alex said, reading the name tag pinned on young man's chest. Luckily, Michel spoke fluent English. "I was told by David Thomson that I could borrow one of the Montcalm's jeeps for a few hours if you weren't too busy. Is that possible? We've had a change in plans, and I do have my International Driver's License if you need to see it." (Alex had picked up one of these on a business trip a little over a year ago. *Now, maybe it would come in handy again*, he thought.)

Michel reached under the desk and pulled out a clipboard with a log on it. "Yes, that should be fine, and you actually don't need the international license here anymore. Things are very slow today, and we've already done our trips to the ferry and airport for the day. Where will you go?"

"My kids and I are just going to do some shopping and climb up to Afareaitu Falls," Alex replied.

Michel nodded. "That sounds like a nice idea, though it might be quite warm this time of day. But the falls should be quite - active - as it rained last evening."

"Yes, it takes around 40 minutes or so to drive there, right, and then around an hour each way on the hike?" asked Alex.

"The driving time is correct, but I don't think it should take that long to climb up and back, unless you wish to swim while you're there. More like an hour, er, both ways, or in combination, up and down from the falls. Oh, and you should park by the gymnasium at the school. Then keep walking until the road ends. When it ends, it becomes a trail. You will see two trees with red arrows and follow the one to the right, probably 10-15 minutes to the falls."

"Thanks so much for the great instructions, Michel. They're a big help so we can get the most out of this hike - and now I won't get lost like I probably would have!"

"*Aita pea pea,* no problem, Mr. Webster, here are the keys, and a map just in case."

Alex signed the paperwork to borrow the vehicle, thanked the attendant again, then strode outside and across to their bungalow.

"Everybody ready?"

Hearing a chorus of "yeses" from the assembled Websters and Jess, Alex said, "Grab your stuff and follow me," as he picked up his backpack with the cameras, and quickly checked the separate large pocket where Jess had placed some snacks and several water bottles.

The whole troop walked around the edge of the reception desk and to the small parking lot behind the office building. They piled into a small SUV as Alex opened the tailgate and dropped their bags in the back.

Alex handed the map to Keely. "Hey Navigator!" he said, with a grin. Then he turned to Jess.

"Jess - hope you don't mind if Keely sits in front to guide me, just the way there, I can figure out the way back."

"Not at all, Alex!"

"Are you surrrrreee, Dad?" Meg asked teasingly, voicing what they all knew: despite his command of facts, Alex had an uncanny knack for getting lost trying to find unfamiliar locations, addresses, and even places close-by when they traveled. (And Alex knew it was true, too!)

"Yes, with Keely as our guide, we'll never get lost!"

"Sure, Dad," Keely said rolling her eyes as Alex backed the car - which they all decided was more like a jeep - around, then headed down the resort's driveway. A quick right turn and they were traveling down the "highway" (only a two-lane road) in the direction of the airport. Their parking and hiking destination was south from there, about 2/3 of the way they'd gone on their tour the previous day, near the 'bottom' of the island, but now reversing their course in an easterly, clockwise direction.

Once they'd driven around Cook's Bay and back near the lagoon shoreline, soon they had traveled past the small lake that sat right before they reached the road to the airport. Keely recognized some of the stores they had passed the day prior. Then, as they headed southward, she saw a few things she hadn't noticed before, like a fishing pier, boat docks, and a number of charming houses. After a pleasant half-hour drive down the coast, alternately in and out of view of the ocean/lagoon, they entered the town of Afareaitu, just as the small roadside sign said.

They pulled into the same shopping spot where they'd enjoyed great ice cream and bought supplies and souvenirs the day prior. After exiting the car, the five of them walked together into the grocery/deli and headed straight to the little sandwich stand near the back. "Old hands" now, they quickly made their selections, and Alex grabbed a couple small bags of chips, a couple of small oranges, and paid for their purchases.

"Can you tell me, are the falls right down that road over there?" Alex asked the clerk.

Switching from French to English, she said, "Oui/Yes, just don't park in front of private homes. Park near school, then walk from there, is best."

"Got it, *Maururu!*"

"No problem," the clerk said with a smile, aimed at all of them.

Less than two minutes after they got back in the car and headed down the designated road, they saw the school and also where the road began to shrink in size just past it. Alex pulled the jeep as far to the end of the parking lot and close to the trail as possible. He stopped under a tree to hopefully minimize the sun beating down on the car while they completed their hike.

As they exited the vehicle, Alex thanked Keely for her "expert navigation skills" and received a wry grin in return. Then he and Jess grabbed their two backpacks, each with fairly small loads of sandwiches and water, plus a few snacks and sweets. Alex, who was lugging another few pounds of camera gear in his pack, hefted it across his shoulders, inserted his arms in the straps, and locked the jeep's doors.

"Let's go find a waterfall!" Keely exclaimed, and they began the trek up the road. As they trudged gradually into the thickening canopy of trees and shrubs, they passed by several houses, some with signs on their driveways reading "*Privé*" or private, and began to notice the humidity more and more as they walked further inland. The jungle started to envelope them, and the mosquitoes were beginning to make their presence known - and not in a good way, if there ever was a good way to experience mosquitoes!

"Lucky we all put on mosquito repellent!" said Meg.

Jess nodded, adding "And sunscreen too!" It was now super humid, though the temperature was only in the low 80's or mid-upper 20's in Celsius. But it definitely felt moister and stickier here than they'd experienced yet on their Moorea trip, likely from the recent rainfall. Certainly, it was muggier than it had been the previous day during their round-the-island tour.

A few more minutes of walking down the sun-dappled road led them to its end, and the beginning of the actual trail to the falls.

"There are the arrows, guys," said Meg, who walked a few feet ahead from the others, and saw the small beacons as she came over a slight rise in the road. Alex stepped up to read the signs.

"OK, we follow the *right* arrow here...shouldn't take more than 10 more minutes to reach the falls."

"Good, because I'm hungry - and hot too!" answered his son.

Cal - and for that matter, all the Websters (and now it was clear that included Jess, too) -were pretty hardy hikers and explorers. They had done lots of treks - some challenging - on family trips and with friends in the hills and mountains of the Puget Sound region. But this climate and their unfamiliarity with the terrain made it a little more difficult. *This is mega-humid*, Alex thought to himself.

"Press on, team!" Alex said, despite the sweat pouring down his forehead, in his favorite drill instructor voice.

"Riiigghht, Dad," Keely responded, more than a bit sarcastically.

They moved mostly in a steady pace uphill, ducking under a few logs, through tunnels of vegetation and low tree branches, and crossing streams a few times. Toward the end, they had to climb over numerous rocks and fallen tree limbs. About ten minutes later, after traversing a substantial pile of rocks, the vegetation mostly cleared out, and they saw the falls up ahead.

"Yay!" Meg exclaimed, "We're here. Now time to wipe my face and neck off - but not too much, I don't want to remove any of that sunscreen OR mosquito repellent!"

"I'm hungry!" Cal whined.

"Yeah, we know, nerd," Meg snapped.

"Shut up, Meg!" yelled her brother.

Alex walked over to his son. "Cal, you know it's not cool to talk to people like that, especially your sister...and Meg," he said, turning to his middle child, "Be nice. No name-calling, OK?"

"Sorry, Dad. I'm just hot and sweaty - and hungry too."

Meg turned to her brother. "I'm sorry, Cal, for calling you a nerd."

"Apology expected," he answered.

Keely and Meg giggled and Jess turned her head away from the family so nobody could see her do the same. Keely made a point this time NOT to correct her little brother's speech, as in her mind she was thinking, *Mmmm that's OK, I know what you meant, Cal.*

"Hey, let's eat first, then explore the falls. What do you think, Alex?" Jess said.

He and the kids nodded, so they found a clear area in front of the wide basin where the water splashed down the rock face from above, making it much cooler and more comfortable as a place to sit. As they plopped down on one of the larger boulders near the rippling pool, Alex and Jess opened their backpacks and handed out sandwiches and drinks to everyone, including themselves.

"Yum, I LOVE these chicken salad rolls! We gotta try to make these and the chow mein sandwiches we got yesterday too, when we get back home!" said Keely.

"I like mine too," said Jess, of her sandwich choice, an avocado, lettuce, cheese and sliced, fried and garlic and mayo-coated sweet potato combination, like the others piled on a French roll.

"Can I taste a bit of yours?" Keely asked Jess.

"Sure, if you let me try yours?"

"Of course," said Keely, breaking off a bit of her roll and receiving a similar portion from Jess in exchange.

"That IS good!" said Keely.

"Same here. They REALLY make fantastic 'fast food' on this island!"

Meg agreed. "Mine's great too, just like Keely's but I put some spicy pepper sauce in my chicken salad, and now it's better than great!"

The others laughed and kept scarfing down their own sandwiches, plucking chips out of the shared bags passed around by Alex and Jess.

As she took a sip from her can of sparkling water and mango juice, Meg finished her sandwich, and announced, "I'm about ready to explore this waterfall. Anybody want to join me?"

"Sure!" Jess said, and Keely and Cal nodded their assent.

Meg and Cal passed their empty sandwich wrappers to their dad (in simple paper wrapping - *Much better than plastic,* Alex thought. *We could learn something from packaging practices here.*) He grabbed Keely's and his own wrappers, then put them all back in the bag that originally had held all the sandwiches. Then he zipped it in his backpack and flung it onto his shoulders, where it also held the camera straps in place. He took some quick pictures (candid ones of the kids' expressions, as he always tried to capture from time to time) and got his video camera ready to record some of the falling water "live action."

Jess zipped up the rest of the wrappers from their lunches in her backpack, and took the last couple of sips of her drink.

"OK team, let's check out that waterfall!" Meg and Cal joined her in front of the waterfall's basin.

"That is really beautiful," said Cal, "Boy does that cool mist help keep the heat and humidity down right here by the falls!"

"I'll say!" echoed his dad.

"I'm going to climb this boulder," Cal declared. He walked towards a huge rock – likely once part of the outcrop backing the falls.

"I'll come with you!" said Meg.

"Be careful!" cautioned their dad. He watched a bit warily as they found footholds on the eight-foot tall and similarly wide boulder, then marveled as the two quickly clambered to its flat upper surface. Alex snapped a few 'candid' pictures of their joint effort to reach 'the summit' of the rock, unnoticed by the two younger Websters.

Meanwhile, a little closer to the basin, their sister was peering upward at the cascading water. "Check that ouuuuut" Keely said, as she craned her neck to see the top of the falls.

"That rain last night must have helped, it sure is flowing nicely," said Alex. He called to Meg, sitting atop the rock: "How high up do you think that is, Meg?"

Taking a careful look and estimating based on her own height of roughly 5'4", Meg figured there were about six or so of her size-worth of water falling from where it emerged over the cliff and rocks to its 'splash point' in the pools in front of them. "Let's see, I'd guess about 35 feet, maybe a little less?" Meg replied.

"Good guess, Meg!" said Jess.

"I was going to say 30-35 feet too," said Alex. "I don't really want to try to climb to their top today, but it sure makes for a pretty picture!"

Speaking of pictures, Alex made sure not to miss the chance for a family photo in this gorgeous place. Something told him it would be fondly recalled by all of them one day in the future. "Let's line up and I'll attach my camera to my little monopod over here, set the timer and we'll get a nice shot of us in front of the falls. I've already got some good photos and video of the waterfall itself, and some audio of the bird calls, too."

"Did you get any shots of these incredible flowers?" Jess asked, as she pointed to a gorgeous native Gardenia shrub, blossoming near some heliconia, aka "red ginger" plants with their distinct vertical blossoms, and what looked to be a few smaller pink and white flowers on various plants all around them.

"Yes, I did snap quite a few, I can show you later, back at the resort. And you know, I forgot to tell you all," Alex added, "Were you aware that your new friend Tiare's name is the same as that beautiful white flower over there with the incredible scent? That's a gardenia, and actually...let me see," he continued, grabbing a small flower booklet out of his backpack. He thumbed first to the table of contents, then turned to the correct page in the mini-paperback. "Here it is: besides the Tahitian name of *Tiare*, it's called *Gardenia taitensis*. And it's the national flower for Tahiti/French Polynesia."

"It smells super-sweet!" said Meg, leaning up to sniff one of the lower hanging blossoms.

"Yeah, it sure does!" said Alex. "You know me and flowers..."

And indeed, they all did. Alex was famous in their household for frequently purchasing (usually inexpensive) flowers at farmers markets or stores and bringing them home for his wife (in the past) and family to enjoy. The blossoms were always beautiful, and almost as often, they were fragrant as well.

But being in this place is like living in a flower garden anyway, thought Keely as she crept through the foliage to join her sister by the waterside. She reached down to feel the water, noting it was surprisingly cool to the touch amid the high surrounding heat. "That's pretty cold!" Keely shouted to Meg and Cal, who stepped down carefully from their perch on what Meg called their "Megarock" to dip their own fingers into the large collecting pool for the falls.

Alex was now trying to find the 'best picture' opportunity and angle, and as he walked around the basin of the falls, turned to gauge the direction of the sun. He found a large flat stone opposite and to one side where he placed the video camera and monopod. He actually had a remote for the video camera, so could easily activate its shutter for a few moments of sound and video of the family in front of the falls. That would come later.

First, he picked up his point-and-shoot zoom camera, focused and adjusted the angle of the lens, and attached it to the monopod, which he leveled on the rock as best he could. "Perfect setting, guys. Just hang on one second, I'll use the remote to take a snapshot with the video camera. Then we'll just use the timer on the regular camera to get a better picture. I'll run over and stand behind you all, so make a little room for me!"

He started to walk over to where they all stood, then realized it would simplify things to set the camera's timer, maybe to 10 seconds, and ask everyone to get set, first, for that higher quality still photo than the digital video camera could produce. Just as he started walking back to ready the device, Meg suggested, "Let me handle it, Dad!"

Alex glanced at her for a second, then figured, *Why not?* He nodded to his daughter. He watched admiringly as Meg jumped forward and adeptly set the camera's timer buttons.

Everything ready, and the 10-second countdown started, Meg quickly rejoined them, Alex situating himself with his arms around the kids. Jess was on the side opposite to him, her arms around the girls' other shoulders and just touching Cal's. They couldn't quite see the countdown on the camera's view screen from ten feet away, but they held "cheesy" smiles as long as they could, and after a few moments they heard a 'click' indicating the digital photo had been taken. Alex ran over, quickly checked the quality, reset the timer and again pressed the shutter button, and they repeated the drill. Only this time he said "Everyone, count down starting now, then say *Tiare!* when it reaches 1 second." And they did!

Alex jumped up. "OK, I know you guys hate doing tons of photos, but just hang here for one moment while I capture some video." He pressed the "Record" button on the wireless remote and heard a slight 'whirring' sound as the camcorder began to record the splashes of the falling water into the pool behind them. "This is Afareaitu Falls here on Moorea," he spoke loudly for the camera, then aimed it at the kids. "Any comments?"

"Oh DADDDD!" jeered Meg, as the rest of them rolled their eyes and laughed. This was an old family joke - Alex (and their mom too) had gotten into the funny habit of saying those words whenever videotaping almost *anything* over the years.

Alex pressed the "Stop" button on the remote. "Great job, everyone! Now I can go home happy!"

"Speaking of going home, since we're not going to swim, I think I'm ready to head back to the car and the Montcalm now," said Keely.

Alex nodded. "Yeah, I agree, what about you Jess, Meg, Cal...seen enough of the falls?"

"Yep," Jess answered, and Cal and Meg put thumbs up to signal their agreement.

Alex put the video camera back in his pack, keeping the point and shoot camera available on his shoulder should there be any compelling 'photo ops' along the rest of the hike. They turned one last time to burn a memorable "mind picture' of the spectacular scenery into their brains, then headed back the way they had come.

The return trip to the car went faster - no surprise there - as they were already familiar with the trail and its main obstacles, and it was mostly downhill. In only about 20 minutes they were passing by the homes they'd seen earlier along the beginning of the path.

"Hey Dad, isn't that a banana tree?" asked Meg. She pointed toward a 25-foot or so high tree with green leaves and what were indeed probably two dozen or more small bananas, still green themselves but pointing upward on several of branches of the plant.

"Yep, you're right, Meg. I read before our trip, somewhere, that they aren't native here, but brought in from outside the islands. Actually, almost all the fruit growing here now was transported, some of it up to 1,000 years ago, by the first people to inhabit this place."

Glancing at the banana trees and other vegetation all around them, Meg sighed. "I bet just about anything would grow in this climate."

"Yeah, for sure," agreed Keely. "It looks like a garden of "mutant" house plants around here, and also at the resort, for that matter.

Actually, almost everywhere we've been so far on this island!" It was a good point - *many of the species that people in North American and other 'colder' climates grew inside their homes were everywhere growing wild on Moorea, just giant-sized*, thought Jess.

"Check out those funny mail boxes in front of those houses, and hey, there's also one back there," Meg said, pointing at the boxes on small posts, about four or five feet in height.

"I'm not...sure those are mail boxes, Meg," said Jess. "But they could be...or for newspapers maybe? But they sure seem extra 'secure' for just that purpose?"

"I'll ask when I'm at the hotel office tomorrow," Alex volunteered. He looked at his watch and realized their first weekend on the island - still only about three days into their whole trip - was coming soon to a close. "It's 2:30 now, what do you say we stop and grab a few more snacks and drinks at that store, then drive back to the resort and cool off with an evening swim and picnic at the beach again?"

"That, Alex, is a fantastic idea!" said Jess, wiping a thick coating of sweat from her forehead and neck.

"I sure could use some cooling off, and cleaning up too!" said Meg, mopping her face with a hand towel she had brought along from the hotel.

They reached the car in less than 15 minutes. After a quick pop in to the store for some more drinks to take back to the room, along with bread, cheese and meat, plus a container of vegetable and sour cream dip (from Australia), they were on the road back to the Montcalm.

As they rounded a corner, perhaps five miles - or 8 km - further, they saw a sign reading *frais/fruits* with an arrow pointing down the road. Keely said "Hey I think that's a fruit stand, can we stop and get some?"

"That's a great idea, Keely, for sure!" Alex concurred.

They drove on until they came to another sign similar to the first one in front of a very skinny driveway. As they ventured slowly down the dirt path, they couldn't see anyone there, and there was no visible activity around the small farmhouse situated further down the trail. But there were bunches of those small bananas, mangos, coconuts, limes, some of the huge *pamplemousse* (grapefruit) they had already tried at the resort, and even some onions and sweet potatoes sitting on a two-tiered, crudely constructed shelving unit just a few feet down the driveway.

"Let's choose one or two of each fruit, then what we don't eat tonight, we can keep the rest in the fridge," suggested Alex.

As they picked the best assortment they could find, Jess asked, "Mind if we add some star fruit too?" She pointed at the unusual yellow and green star-shapes on one shelf.

Alex nodded. "Sure...so how much is this all going to cost? I've got my local money right here. He pulled out a small waterproof wallet where he kept his CFP Franc bills and change.

Keely looked at the "honor system" price list scrawled in French on a small sign near the bench holding the selection of fruit, translated the wording, and then "did the math" in her head.

"All the small fruits are 50, and the larger ones are 75. A bunch of bananas - which they call '*banane*' is 100. The pineapples ('*ananas*') are 250. So, if we add them all up," she continued calculating," we need to pay 640 CFP francs for everything."

"That's about $6.40 in US dollars, a really great deal for all this fresh local fruit!" Alex exclaimed. He put seven 100 CFP notes into the little box the farm stand owner had provided, not worrying about receiving the change back.

They each took a couple of pieces of fruit in their hands, and with their garbage already having been deposited in the refuse container outside the grocery store a few moments earlier, there was room in Alex and Jess's backpacks for it all. Soon, they were back on the road, and they definitely smelled the ripe, fragrant fruits all the way back to the resort.

Chapter 31

Sunset beach picnic - and Jess makes a new friend

When they pulled into the Montcalm driveway to drop off the jeep, it was just about 4:30 pm. Everyone clambered out and headed toward the family's bungalow. Alex took a quick detour to return the keys to the front desk, then joined the others back in their rooms. "Let's head down to the beach in 20 minutes or so, what do you say?"

"Sounds like a plan, Alex," Jess answered. "How about I put together a little collection of fruits and snacks into our carry bag and cooler, and we'll be all ready for our picnic after we jump in the water? It should still be plenty warm enough afterward for us to dry off before dinner."

"That's what I'm talking about! Thanks, Jess!"

Keely offered, "I'll help too. We'll need to bring those small knives and some spoons also. I'll ask if we can borrow a couple of small plates and bowls from the restaurant."

"Good thinking, Keely...how about I run over there with you?"

"Sure, let's go!"

As they walked through the door, the fifth and newest member of the Worldwide Websters was secretly thrilled that the young man she had exchanged smiles with earlier that day was standing at a table nearby, arranging silverware and folding napkins. Only a few people were in the restaurant, as it was still early for most dinner guests.

"Hi there, umm *Iarona*, I mean *Iaorana*!" said Jess. She turned bright red – embarrassed at 'flubbing' her try at the Tahitian greeting.

"Iaorana, and...your accent is so interesting!" he answered, adding "Where are you from? Australia, perhaps?"

"Well, I'm a college, er, graduate student, here with my American 'work family', I'm the nanny for Keely here.

"Hi!" Keely greeted him with a smile.

Jess continued. "I take care of her sister and brother as well. But I'm actually from New Zealand, so you weren't too far off!" Jess cursed her still warming cheeks.

"You are maybe closer to your, real home, I guess, than your current home! Well, wherever you are from, I am very pleased to meet both of you," he said, extending his hand "My name is Julian Bernard, I am Assistant Food & Beverage Manager here at the restaurant. And your name is…?"

"Jess, or actually, it's Jessica. Keely's dad is here working on the hotel's software installation, he's back with the others in our bungalow."

"Oh yes, Mr. Webster, I've met him, when you arrived last Friday, I was in the office doing some paperwork and we were briefly introduced. Will you be sitting down for dinner soon?"

"Actually, we wanted to ask a small favor," said Keely, looking at Julian, then back at Jess, then back to Julian again, a small smile creeping onto her face as she realized the instant, and mutual, attraction she was witnessing.

"So," she explained, "We are going to have a picnic dinner down on the beach tonight, but just snacks as we had a big breakfast here and lots for lunch during our hike earlier today. So, we wondered if we could borrow a couple of bowls and plates, and maybe a few napkins, small knives, and spoons? We're only having bread and cheese and stuff, plus some fruit we purchased at a roadside stand. We just drove back a few minutes ago from the hike we did up to Afareaitu Falls."

"Ah, Afareaitu Falls. Was the water flowing well? Any trouble on the trails? Did you go swimming in the pools there?"

"We had no problems, though it was very humid and hot," responded Jess, fanning her face.

"And the falls were very beautiful," Keely added. "Lots of water flowing, must have been from the rain, we figured. But no swimming…even though it might have been cooler if we did, I'm glad we stayed (relatively) dry on the hike. We're all pool or beach, er, ocean swimmers more than lake or pond swimmers."

Julian nodded. "Yes, it does rain most days here, we are about to head into our very rainy season, though we have had just that light rain last night for the past few days. You are lucky as sometimes the falls are, in dry times, how do you say it in English…only a little bit, um…"

"Maybe just a trickle?" Keely finished Julian's sentence.

"Yes! That is what I meant to say. So, now, for your picnic. Absolutely, I'd be happy to help you! Just give me a moment." Julian reached to the rack near him and collected several small wooden plates, two medium-sized wooden bowls, and the utensils requested. He pulled several napkins onto the table with the other items, then walked briskly through the doors into the kitchen, from which he emerged only moments later, carrying a sturdy wooden picnic basket. Back by his station, he inserted the other items together into the hamper, along with a large red tablecloth.

"I thought this would be an easy way to carry everything for your picnic down to the beach," said Julian. "Do you need cups or glasses?"

"That would be wonderful, thank you so much...Julian, can we have five?" Keely replied, holding up one hand, all fingers extended. He nodded and placed five small hard plastic cups into the basket and raised its handles. Beaming, he presented the package to Jess.

Jess stammered "*Maururu roa?*"

"That's right, Jessica! Or should I say Jess? Now, instead of you're welcome, a Tahitian would say..."

"*Aitapeapea*, right?" Keely blurted out.

Julian turned quickly to the teen and grinned. "That's right, Keely, great job. You are almost Tahitian already!" This caused Keely to blush a little, but not as much as Jess had earlier.

"Thanks so much for lending us this stuff. We will be very careful and bring it back when we've finished our picnic," Keely replied.

Julian nodded graciously. "*Aita pea pea*, Jess and Keely. I hope you have a wonderful time, and maybe I will see you later?"

"Yes, maybe we, I mean you will," said Jess. She smiled broadly as she and Keely left the restaurant and returned to their rooms.

As they arrived at the bungalow entrance, Keely was about to say something, but Jess cut her off. "I know, he's REALLY good looking and very nice too. Maybe we'll have a chance to talk later in the trip. Don't tell anybody though...there's nothing to say anyway!" Meanwhile, some of that redness crept back into her cheeks.

Keely giggled. "Cross my heart, nobody will hear it from me...yet!"

Jess glared at her, but then broke into a grin. "That's right, our secret, Keel. Now let's get everybody down to that beach. The water's waiting, I'm hungry and you know your dad and sunsets!"

With the evening headed toward another spectacular Moorean finale - which itself followed a brief dip in the water and about a half-hour of sipping beverages while watching the sun go down - they all snacked on roughly constructed meat and/or cheese sandwiches, with mayo or mustard slathered on the baguettes they'd purchased earlier.

Keely and Jess had also cut up several pieces of fruit to accompany their other snacks and drinks, though they left the pineapple on the counter in the room to ripen just a bit further (They knew from previous experience that you can tell pineapple is ripe when it's mostly yellow, and smells sweet, sometimes also by when its crown begins to wither.)

The rest of the fruit was refrigerated...it was not too good an idea to leave food out in the tropics, they all knew - because one of the "wondrous" aspects of such areas could be cockroaches. Veteran visitors to such places knew from experience that it was best to keep all their food tightly closed and/or in the fridge, to keep the cockroaches at bay. They had all been initially disgusted by seeing the insects in some of their rooms in Hawaii, Mexico and elsewhere, but you really couldn't avoid them completely, especially after a hard rain. You just had to ignore them and realize, no matter how 'posh' or not your quarters might be while traveling - in such a climate, the cockroaches were *locals*, just part of life in the tropics. And when it came to hotel or resort rooms they decided to *explore*, they didn't discriminate based on price!

As for the picnic dinner - mini sandwiches, crackers, dip, and a beer had made it one of the simple, most satisfying meals Jess felt she had perhaps ever enjoyed. She, Alex, and the kids spent an hour talking and joking about their earlier hiking adventures and just enjoying the splendor of their surroundings as the sun creeped downward, and then suddenly dropped below the western horizon. With darkness looming, they packed up their bags and the basket. Alex shook the sand off and folded their blanket/tablecloth, then slipped it over one shoulder, for the walk back up the path to their rooms.

"I'll go return the picnic basket and thank them for us," said Jess.

"Sure, and *thank you*, Jess - and Keely too - for putting together everything for such an awesome 'beach feast'! I could do this every day! While you carry the supplies back to the restaurant, I'm going to take a quick shower, so I don't have to in the morning before I head over to the office for work," Alex answered.

Later, the kids relaxed before bed, opening their books for a bit. Keely read a book she'd brought along on the trip, while Meg learned about local plants and wildlife from the pocket guide her dad had consulted earlier. Cal sat on his bed in the main room with his school binder open in front of his crossed legs, pencil in hand. "I'm planning my special school project," the boy explained to his dad.

"Cool, that's great, Cal. But it's time for a shower for me, I've got a big day tomorrow. Good night girls!" Alex stepped in through the doorway to their room to kiss each of his daughters on their foreheads, exchanging hugs with each of them.

"Night, Dad," Keely and Meg answered, then went back to their books.

Jess, meanwhile, had stopped by the lobby briefly to read some hotel activities brochures, then walked back into the restaurant carrying the picnic basket. She glanced around, observing that more of the tables were occupied, but it looked like the restaurant was clearing out kind of early...*maybe because it was Sunday night?*

A waiter was over in the corner, and one of his female counterparts was busy arranging new place settings on several empty tables. *Likely for breakfast tomorrow*, Jess thought. As she stood there by the bussing station, couples from two tables signed their bills, pushed in their chairs, and left the restaurant, smiling at the now lightly tanned Kiwi as they passed by her on their way out into the courtyard.

The kitchen door opened and Julian came through it, spying his new friend right away. "*Ahiahi*/Good Evening, Jess. How was the picnic?"

Feeling a bit less shy now than earlier, Jess replied, "It was really special. Great food, gorgeous sunset, and nice dishes - and even the perfect tablecloth for a beach meal - thanks to you, Julian!" she smiled back, while handing the basket to him. "We brushed off all the plates into the garbage bin outside. They are ready to wash. Thank you again, er *maururu*, Julian for lending all of this to us tonight."

"Very happy to do so, Jess...say, do you have a few moments? My duties will end soon... I thought we might enjoy a glass of wine together?"

"Ummm, sure...but I only have a few minutes," Jess said, a bit hesitantly, her shyness returning.

"Why don't you take a seat at any table, and I'll join you in...five minutes," promised Julian, glancing at Jess with a hopeful look on his face matching the rising cadence of his question.

Jess walked to a table in the corner, near the doorway to the patio and pool area. Sitting down, her mind wandered to recollections of their trip to the falls, the beach picnic, then to her plans for the following day's activities. Earlier, down on the beach, she and Alex had briefly discussed the schedule for the upcoming week. He would, of course, be working throughout the next few days, but might be able to join the family for lunch on some of them. Otherwise, they had agreed that Jess could choose whatever options best suited the weather and the kids' 'appetites' for adventure: perhaps a beach day, maybe a bike ride somewhere nearby, definitely setting aside some time for the three of them to work on their school assignments.

Jess had promised she'd check into other activities at the resort that the kids might enjoy during the upcoming "work week." She and Alex concluded they'd be mostly on their own for the next, middle part of their visit while Alex was busy working on the hotel's software project. Jess would also have most of her evenings free from family duties, if desired.

The five minutes was up. Jess stood, turned, and was about to walk out into the lobby to pick up a copy of the activities schedule she'd forgotten to grab, when Julian returned with two small glasses of red wine.

"Oh, are you leaving?" he said, with a slight frown on his face.

"Oh! No, I was just going to take another look at the guest activities list - for the kids. I'm trying to keep them happy and occupied this week while their dad is working in the hotel office."

"I understand. Well, why don't you get one of the brochures, then meet me back here. I can help you choose while we sit outside for a bit. It is still pleasant, and we'll enjoy that glass of wine together."

"OK, be right back." Jess smiled, and hurried to exit through the doorway to the lobby of the resort.

Returning to the restaurant a few moments later, a couple of activities pamphlets from the front desk in hand, Jess almost bumped into Julian waiting right near the door. She reached out to accept one of the glasses he carried, and as he held the door open, they ventured out onto the moonlit patio. It was still not yet 8:00 pm, but getting much darker as it does very quickly in the South Pacific, where they were located, in between the Tropic of Capricorn and the Equator.

They sat down at a small table, in chairs on either side.

"*Manuia!*" Julian said, raising his glass.

Jess clinked hers against it, echoing the toast "*Manuia*...cheers!"

"*Maeva* - welcome, again - to Moorea, Jess. So glad I have a chance to meet you!" said the young assistant restaurant manager.

Jess took a sip. It was a nice, dry red. *Yum!*

"The wine is from France, of course," said Julian. "Do you like it?"

"Yes, very much. What kind is it?" Jess asked.

"It is a pinot noir, from Burgundy region. Have you had such wine before?" Julian asked.

Jess nodded. "Yes, well sort of. In fact, the area where I live now, Washington State, is famous for its fine wine as well, though pinot noir from its adjacent state, Oregon, and especially its region called Willamette Valley, is some of the very best - in America at least. And maybe in the world. Where I come from in New Zealand, the Hawkes Bay region is also known for its excellent pinots. So, France better watch out!" Jess chuckled, taking another sip.

Julian raised his glass in a mock salute. "To New Zealand pinots! So, how long will you be here on Moorea?" he asked.

"Until next Saturday," Jess replied. "It feels like we've been here a long time already though, it's such a beautiful, relaxing place." She changed the topic. "How did you start working here at the resort?"

"I was born here, though my father has French and English parents. I have worked at the restaurant since before the hotel was sold and renovated, then reopened as the Montcalm. I started as a 'busboy' - as you call it - when I was 16, and now, well, almost ten years later, I am an assistant manager. I have learned much about how restaurants work."

"Aha! Your family heritage explains why you speak English so well, and your job experience explains your knowledge of food and wine."

"Yes, that's part of it," Julian smiled, "and also, I spent a year living with my grandparents near London when I was younger, ten years old at the time. That really helped me learn the language, and even some British slang, and to try British food - but neither of these is always a good thing, ha!" He grinned. "I like to stay in practice with guests who visit from America, Canada, Britain, or — even New Zealand, like my new friend Jess." He raised his glass again to her with a twinkle in his eyes.

Jess blushed a bit. (*darn, gotta stop doing that!*) she thought to herself. "Well, same to you," Jess said as returning the toast, adding, "*Manuia* to Julian, who helped make our picnic...magnifique!"

As the two shared smiles and savored the peppery, floral taste of the wine, Jess turned her head and asked, "What is that amazing smell?"

"Ah, that is the frangipani, also called plumeria. See? That tree right there," the Tahitian replied, gesturing toward a medium sized tree near their table, dotted with little multi-petaled blossoms.

"Of course! I have heard of that one - from other places I've been."

The scent was indeed wonderful, and Jess wondered why it seemed even more so at night. She stood and walked over to the tree, placing her nose right next to the blossoms on one branch. Inhaling deeply, she was enthralled by the sweet/spicy aroma. She had to admit to herself that *the atmosphere and conversation were hard to beat too!*

Glancing over to her new Tahitian friend, she took a last long sip from her glass, and set it down on the table. "Thanks for the wine and conversation, Julian. I hope we can speak further this week, but unfortunately, I have to go back to the room now. I'm pretty tired, and big day tomorrow with the kids, you know."

"*Aita pea pea*...you are very welcome, Jess. I am glad to have the chance to share some wine and chat with you – even if not the best in the world, as you say." He smiled broadly. "And I am very happy to welcome you to our island, our nation - from one of its own, me!"

"Ha-ha, well I'm sure you can tell me more about the island and its history tomorrow, or maybe another day this week?" Jess answered.

"We shall plan on it!" said Julian. "Do you have any free time in between your childcare duties?"

"Possibly, but, well, let's see how the week works out...though I'm sure we'll see each other at the restaurant...we'll be here for many of our meals," Jess replied. "Let's just see how things go..."

The Tahitian beamed. "Certainly, oh...but I won't be here tomorrow. It's my day away from work, and normally I have Sundays off work too. But this week, because we have a very busy weekend schedule, I'll have another day off instead, Thursday. Maybe we can find time then for me to show you some parts of the island that tourists don't often see?"

"Sure, Julian. That sounds like fun." She extended her hand. "Thank you very much for such wonderful hospitality. Enjoy your day off, and I know I'll see you soon, and maybe...Thursday too?"

Julian gently accepted her handshake, dark eyes gleaming into hers, and replied, "I cannot wait!"

Jess sauntered up to the family's bungalow and toward the separate entrance to her room around back, but stopped when she noticed Alex sitting outside on a chair outside, one of a pair he'd brought to the patio from inside the bungalow. He was busy typing on his laptop under the single light fixture by the door, and sipping a beer. He glanced up from the screen and waved her over.

"Hey, Jess! Thought I'd come out here and review some project details before bed. Did you have a nice visit at the restaurant?"

Jess was a bit embarrassed, and glad Alex it was kind of dark so he couldn't see her blushing, *which she very likely was,* she thought.

Before she could reply, Alex added, "I had to print out some training booklets in the hotel office, and I saw you chatting with that nice guy at the restaurant, Julian, right? I met him the other day after we got here from the ferry and I was being introduced to the staff."

"Yes, his name is Julian, and he's Assistant Manager of the restaurant. And, umm, yes, he's very nice."

"That's great. Hey, you are welcome to hang out here with me for a bit, would you like a beer?"

"No thanks, I had a glass of wine with Julian...I wasn't expecting it, but it was really good. I think I'll just grab a sparkling water out of the fridge if you don't mind? And sure, I'll sit out with you for a bit."

When Jess returned with her beverage, Alex had closed up his laptop. He was looking up at the stars, super brilliant in this part of the world. "It's amazing how much of the sky, the many, many planets and stars that are visible here. Nice to be away from 'civilization' and all the bright lights for a while, isn't it?"

Jess gazed up with him. "For sure, Alex....and hey, I know I've said it before, but thanks again for bringing me along on this trip. What a nice place to come to - especially when it's so chilly at home!"

"You know," Alex said, "when I was planning this thing, I realized very quickly that as valuable and loved you are in our family, it would have been a real shame if you couldn't join this crazy Worldwide Websters jaunt to paradise, right in the middle of winter! And we wouldn't have it any other way. Besides, I know those *"Three Websketeers"* of mine keep you super busy. But...don't forget, you can definitely have time off too, I'll try to be here for at least some lunches, most breakfasts, and every evening so you can be sure to have some "me-time" to yourself.

Jess grinned. "No problem, Alex. And the kids, they're great, really. We should have lots of fun this week swimming, snorkeling, maybe some other activities. I just grabbed this brochure and saw that there are some cool things to do here at the hotel for kids and adults. I think I'm going to sign us all up for their pareo decorating/tying class on Tuesday. Tomorrow, maybe we'll do some hiking around here and see if we can connect again with the Martinez kids at the resort down the beach."

"Yeah, that would be good - I still am really wondering why their mom, um, Raiana, was so standoffish today. Something seems a bit odd with her, and especially with Tiare, her daughter," Alex mused.

"Well, you never know, traveling can be stressful - and I know *you* know this, but so can kids, and marriage for that matter, though I can't speak directly to that last challenge, not yet anyway. But I do hope to get to know Rai and the kids a little better this week. Maybe we'll figure out a way to bring everyone together - I'm sure we'll cross paths, 'cause, you know, this is a pretty small place, right?!"

"Yes, it is, and that sounds like a perfect plan, Jess." Alex yawned. "Well, I'm gonna hit the hay. Long day tomorrow, hoping we can keep up the great progress we already made on Friday." Taking a last sip to drain his beer, Alex said "Good night!" and stood up.

"I'm going to hang out here for just a bit, Alex. Will we see you at breakfast tomorrow?"

He shook his head. "Probably not. For this first full day of the project, I'll be heading over early. I'll try to catch you all at lunch if it works out. Besides, you've got the money I gave you for shopping and stuff, and everything else you need at the resort can be charged to the room. You can reach me right over at the office if you need anything. For now, see you tomorrow and hope you sleep well!" He stood up and carried his chair back inside as he closed the door behind him.

Jess leaned back in her seat, gazing around and up at the brilliant, star-studded sky. She let her vision adjust for a few moments to make out the faint shapes of the trees and buildings around the bungalow, imagining fancifully that they were animals of various shapes and sizes. She also noted the extreme quiet, punctuated by occasional bird calls and other noises she couldn't quite define. Right now, she thought, was the *definition* of peaceful, though she hoped the mosquitoes would remain at bay so it could stay that way for a while.

Maybe Thursday will work out. It would be fun to see some of the non-touristy stuff here on the island with Julian, Jess thought, as she let her mind wander amid the silence, punctuated by a few calls and rustles among the trees and shrubs. After a few moments pondering the possibilities ahead, she looked at her watch and saw that it was after 9:00. Deciding it was time to head to bed herself, she stood up and circled back around the building, bringing the chair along. She used her key to open the door to her room on the opposite side of the bungalow, so as not to disturb the family.

After a visit to the connecting bathroom between hers and the girls' rooms to brush her teeth, Jess lay her head down on the single-sized bed's pillow. It took all of 30 seconds before she fell asleep, but her last waking thoughts were: *exciting day, lots of activity, and some really intriguing adventures to come...I hope!*

Chapter 32

Monsoon & the marae - a mystery begins

November 28, Monday

Jess heard Alex get up, though it was clear he was trying to be very quiet in his preparations to head over to work at the hotel office. In truth, she had been awake for a while when she very faintly heard him close the door in the room two doors away and leave the bungalow a little after 7 am.

She remembered from the previous night that Alex wanted to have an early breakfast before jumping fully into the software project work. It wasn't the roosters that woke her early this morning - she had put in her earplugs before going to sleep last night. Instead, it was thoughts of her new 'friend' at the hotel. Jess wasn't eager to enter any new relationships right now. She not only had lots of responsibilities and plans for the next several months until she finished her graduate degree, but *even to think of any kind of lasting connection between Julian and her was preposterous. How many thousand miles would separate them anyway?*

Activity in the Webster girls' room next door, actually in the bathroom, broke Jess's reverie. *Time to get going!* She thought, as she began to collect her clothes.

As Keely and Meg finished their morning rituals, Jess did the same, then returned to get dressed. A few minutes later, they were all in the main family room, where Cal was trying to find shorts and a t-shirt and whatever else from among many items he had strewn around the floor.

"What happened here, a typhoon?" Meg said of her scattered brother's messy surroundings.

"Don't say that!" Cal complained. "I couldn't find one of my game cartridges I was looking for ...now I'm trying to find clean underwear..."

Jess stepped over, bent down and pulled up one edge of the boy's suitcase. She extracted a pile of several pairs of fresh undershorts - from where she had packed them. "Here you go, kiddo! You can put the extra pairs in the drawer here. We'll wait outside while you get dressed. Remember, shorts and t-shirts are fine for now, you don't need your swim suit, yet. We'll figure out what we're doing today after breakfast."

It was a quiet morning at the resort's restaurant. Jess glanced toward the front desk when they walked in, but didn't see Alex nor the GM, Mr. Thomson there. She waved at Ravanui, the woman who had picked them up at the ferry on Friday - which seemed ages ago now, Jess thought. The hotel's assistant manager was conferring with the front desk clerk, and she waved back with a wide smile.

Jess walked back to the restaurant down the hall and sat at their table, just inside its door, for a few moments, drinking coffee. She focused her mind on the day's plans while the kids perused the buffet area and pondered the morning's food offerings. She encouraged each of the Websters to try something different for the meal.

"Hey, this could be a fun project. How about we agree to each try something different from the menu each day, OK?"

Keely loved it. "That's a great idea, Jess...we can write our opinions on the things we eat, and then share our descriptions and ratings of all of the dishes and stuff in a report after we leave? We'll be just like those food writers in the magazines and newspapers!"

"I like that plan too," said Meg. "Can we include snacks and candy and other things we buy at stores, and from food trucks too?"

"Sure, of course! It will be a cultural AND culinary experience!" laughed Jess.

"Good!" agreed Cal. "I want to include those amazing chow mein sandwiches on our list!"

"Me too!" replied Jess, with Keely and Meg nodding vigorously too.

Once they'd all finished their breakfast (taking notes of the dishes they'd consumed on the back of a spare single page 'specials' menu they found on a table), they headed back to the room around 9:30 am. Eager to get started on their new project, Keely realized that some sort of tracking system was required to make it easy.

"We need a checklist to keep records on what we ate and what we thought about it. Meg, you want to help me design it on the laptop? We can just use a spreadsheet for now, then later we can put our tables together into a document and share it with our friends and at school."

"Can I help too?" asked Cal.

"Sure, of course you can," his oldest sister answered. We'll put it together...together!" "Meg, you in?"

"Yep, should be fun. We can start now, but it might take us a while to add in everything we've tried already since we got here. It might take us even longer just to *remember* everything, whether we liked it or not!"

Not too surprisingly, it was a while before the kids could agree on the precise format for their 'food reviews'. They did, however, find some templates in the software they were using to get them started. An hour later, the basic outline was finished, and they'd each typed in a few "food entries," starting with what they ate on the plane from Los Angeles and then on to Papeete and during their first three days on Moorea. They had taken turns to recall the specific dishes and snacks, which they learned wasn't as easy to do as they thought. But as they would later find out, they had plenty of time to work on their project on this first Monday in Moorea, because after an "unusual" late morning meet-up, the kids were destined to end up back in their rooms for the balance of the afternoon.

For now, though, the three Websters settled on the categories and corresponding columns of their *"French Polynesian Food Review"* worksheet. Jess, meanwhile, took the 'free' time opportunity to sit in her room on her bed with her laptop and write some offline, draft emails to her family in South Africa and to friends back at school in the Northwest - some of whom were visiting their own families away from Tacoma during this holiday break. She described the trip beginning on Thanksgiving Day, but left out the details of the near-miss of their flight to Tahiti. She did share many of the highlights of their visit since arriving on Moorea the previous Friday, including the ferry ride, swimming at the resort, the tour around the island, and hiking to the falls. And of course, the sunsets, the food, etc.

When she had finished messages to four or five addressees, Jess asked the kids if they'd be OK on their own for a while...so she could go over to the resort and send her emails out, and check for any news from home or school while she was at it. There was no internet service in their bungalow rooms, but she could hook up her laptop in the business center to take care of these tasks.

Keely had a request. "Jess, could you take our laptop with you and print a few copies of our *Food Review* worksheets? That will make it easier to keep track when we're at restaurants, or exploring the island. We have a blank and the sheet we've already been filling out. We can type all of our combined notes into our main worksheet in the laptop later."

"Yeah, no problem. How many copies do you need?"

"Just, ummm...how about seven copies, that gives us each one (if Dad wants to participate, but he might not) and if you want to, then we'll have a couple extra if one gets ruined or lost."

"How about I make ten copies, and we can leave one in the room so anybody who wants to can add their notes, then the others will be available for each person to use all week?"

"Sounds like a plan, Jess. Thanks! I can come with you if you like."

"No, you hang out here, it will be easy. I'll be back soon. Just keep an eye on your brother and sister and wait for me to return."

"No prob, we'll just be working on our notes and maybe our school assignments too," answered Meg, and Keely concurred.

When Jess had left the room at around 10:30, she had no idea it would become such an eventful morning, and whole day, for that matter. It definitely didn't start in the best fashion, which she found once she reached the hotel on her 'brief' technical mission.

Computers and connectivity can be so frustrating, Jess thought to herself. *They never seem to work exactly as expected.* What was troubling her now, about 35 minutes after leaving the bungalow, was that when she sat down in front of the workstation and printer in the resort's business center, she first had to get a sign-in and password to use it. That was no big deal, as she walked back and obtained this at the front desk. The problem was, though there was a cable provided for the internet connection, there wasn't one to connect her computer to the printer.

Now, more than a bit exasperated, she decided to just start by signing on to the internet and sending her stored email messages using her laptop. The problem with that task was she had forgotten her second password for her college email service, which was always supplied for her while using the school's internet service provider. Now, she couldn't even access her school or personal emails - something that had never happened before leaving on the trip! *I must be really tired!* she thought.

She walked back out to the front desk, where they loaned her a printer cable, and also agreed to let her use their phone to call back to school for email support. But *then*, since it was still a holiday week at U of C, the technical service team was slow to respond. *Likely understaffed*, she thought. It was about a ten-minute wait after the initial connection until someone who could actually help her got on the line. After verifying her identity, finally her password was reset and she was able to cause send and receive emails.

15 or 20 minutes later, Jess had breezed through a few messages, replied to a few, left a handful more to read later, and caught up on the weather, news, and a few entries from some online user groups she had joined at school. She also checked the website and internal message board for the college newspaper. Her writing assignments for the following week were already posted, so she figured her editor must have worked over the Thanksgiving weekend. In addition to an article on a lecture series coming to campus in January, Jess also was being asked to write a feature story on some interesting topic of her choice, to be published the week prior to Christmas/winter break.

So, just like the kids, I have a project to get done - or at least started - during my vacation! Jess mused, with a bit of irritation. But then, after a few moments, she realized she was already working on this trip, for part of it, anyway. Besides, she had the perfect subject to write about: *coral reefs and their relative health in the South Pacific.* She could start with info about the "killer" starfish they saw on the beach yesterday, which JP told them was a menace to French Polynesia's reefs. She had also seen for herself - while they snorkeled underwater - just how relatively healthy the coral was here in Moorea vs. Mexico, the Caribbean, and other tropical areas.

Jess decided on a quick comparison to begin the article, then to add research on coral reef health statistics from some good scientific websites, and perhaps include a photo or two from an underwater camera they had purchased and brought along. Then she'd have a pretty interesting story to tell the school newspaper's readers.

Glancing at her watch, she realized that it was already getting towards lunch, and wondered if maybe Alex was going to join them. She decided to visit the hotel office and check in with him to see. First though, she needed to print out the worksheet copies for the kids' food project.

She closed her laptop, and opened up the family's computer she'd brought from the room as well, and entered the login password Keely had given her, then connected the same borrowed cord to the printer.

She had printed two copies of the food list when the printer started flashing a red light on its front panel. "Uh oh" Jess said aloud. "Out of paper...will nothing go right for me today?" It was already almost noon!

She gathered up the two laptops and the cords and strode across the hall and down the lobby to the front desk to ask for some. The attendant asked her to try at the hotel office as they were out of printer paper at the desk! So, Jess ended up right where she would have gone to check on Alex's status for lunch, anyway. But, when she walked around the corner to the office, and knocked on the door, there was no answer.

Jess was just starting to ponder why nothing was seeming to work well this Monday, and what to do next, when Ravanui, the assistant hotel manager who had picked them up from the ferry, and waved at her earlier, came up behind her. "May I help you Ms..... Webster?"

Jess turned. "Oh thanks, and I'm not a Webster...but I am staying with them, and taking care of the kids."

"Of course, I remember now, sorry!" said Ravanui.

"No problem, Ravanui. I'm looking for Alex, Mr. Webster, to see if he'll be eating lunch with us. He said he might or might not, depending on their work schedule," Jess inquired.

"I see...He and Mr. Thomson and two of our other employees went for lunch to a restaurant in town. They should be back by about 13.30."

Jess was very familiar with 'military time', having used this system in her home country. *So, no-go for lunch with Alex*, she concluded. He wouldn't be back for another 90 minutes, at least.

"Thanks, well, that answers that. No problem, I'll arrange lunch for the kids myself. But could you help me with something else? I was printing some pages in the business center and the printer ran out of paper. The front desk asked me to get some here."

"Certainly, follow me." The tall Moorean led Jess into the office area, where she saw Alex's work bag and backpack sitting next to a desk with several computer screens on it in the back of the room.

Ravanui reached into a cabinet above the office's large laser printer there and removed a ream of paper. Here you go, do you need assistance loading it in the printer? I can help you..."

"No, that's fine, thank you. I can figure it out," said Jess.

Ravanui smiled. "Let me know if you have any problems. I will be on a phone call for the next hour, I'm working on some details related to Mr. Webster's software company. In fact, I'm speaking to people in Seattle. That is where you are from, correct?"

"Yes...er I go to college and the Websters live near there, in Tacoma, but Mr. Webster, Alex, has his office in Seattle. He works at LodgeSoft."

The hotel employee nodded. Jess thanked her again then walked briskly, still loaded down with the laptops (which she had placed in her backpack together) and now also carrying the ream of paper. Once back at the business center, she inserted the whole package of 500 sheets in the large printer. Then she re-hooked up the laptop, opened the document, and pressed 'print' - but nothing happened.

What? Thinking something must not be hooked up right, Jess checked all the connections, the computer, the cable, etc. Everything looked fine, but nothing was happening. Finally, after five minutes of re-trying to print, she turned the printer on and off, and pressed the "Print" button on the laptop. *Voila!* It whirred and clicked and thunked and finally began to print the worksheet copies.

"Hallelujah, it's about time!" Jess exclaimed under her breath. She watched the remaining eight copies of the "food review" forms emerge from the printer, then disconnected the cable, returned it to the desk, and headed back to the room. When she opened the door, she figured Keely, Meg, and Cal would be waiting. But they weren't. Searching further in the inner rooms, she found nobody there either.

The kids were gone. But where?

Chapter 33

Where are the Websterkins?

Jess immediately told herself *Don't panic! They are probably somewhere nearby around the resort. It's not a huge place. Maybe they got tired of waiting and went looking for me?*

It was about 12:15 pm, more than an hour and 45 minutes since she'd left them working on their projects in the room. *Darn, I wish I would have come back to check on them instead of having to do all of those crazy printer and computer errands!*

Making a quick circuit around the pool area, she saw no sign of the kids. She stopped at the front desk, but the attendant hadn't seen the children. *Beach,* Jess realized. *That's probably where they are, maybe building sand castles or something?*

When she finished her rapid trot down the path to the beach, passing the bar/restaurant on the way, it was starting to rain. She glanced back towards the hotel and the center of the island, where dark clouds dragged telltale rain showers below them, completely obscuring the view of the jagged peaks they had explored around in the previous days. *Great, now it's about to get very wet.* And just then, the first drops fell onto her head.

It occurred to Jess to ask the cafe staff if they'd seen the children there. She doubled back and walked up to the host station.

"Oh, yes, they were here for a few minutes," the host, who spoke very clear English with a French accent answered. "They sat at a table there with a menu. They asked to borrow another pen, and said they were noting the different dishes they'd eaten," she said, with a smile. "I asked them if they wanted anything, but they said no. Then their friends came and a few minutes later, I saw them walk down to the beach."

"Their 'friends'?" Jess asked.

"Sure, two other children, a girl and a boy, maybe a little younger, came to their table and stood talking to your kids for a while. Then they all left after a few minutes and went to the beach. I'm sure they're still there," replied the restaurant staffer in a kind, encouraging tone, realizing from her expression that Jess was very concerned.

Jess thanked the host and began to walk briskly to the beach, as large blobs of rainwater splashed along the path. Upon reaching the sand, she scanned the beach from left to right. The rain was falling steadily now, but luckily it was still quite warm and her hat protected her head. There were some groups of people leaving the beach and a few more still in the now grayish-blue water. But none were the Websters.

Now Jess was a little more worried, but she still told herself to stay calm. She could feel the heat and humidity, despite the rain. Looking up, she saw the storm clouds were increasing in number, scudding across the sky. Under her breath, she said *"Where are you, Keely, Meg and Cal?!"*

Chapter 34

Figure 8s, a pain in the foot, & a practical p--

The Webster kids had been filling in their food charts manually, on some paper they'd torn from a notebook, for a while after Jess went to the hotel office. Meg suggested they add the dishes they'd eaten at the beach-front restaurant their first day on Moorea.

"Jess has been gone a long time!" said Keely, looking at her watch, which read ten minutes after 11 am. "I guess it won't be a big deal to walk down to the cafe, we can take one of our sheets, fill it out using the menu there, then come back in time for lunch."

"Yeah, that sounds fun!" said Cal, "then we can go to the beach!"

"No, we told Jess we'd stay here, so I'll just leave her a note and let her know we'll be back in a few minutes," said his eldest sister.

Grabbing a sheet of paper, Keely quickly wrote a note to Jess and set it on the little table. It explained they'd be back by noon or 12:15.

They all headed out the door, Meg making quick stops in the bathroom and then to snatch her hat and the scratch paper sheets where they had written out their 'template' for the list of foods they had tried on their vacation. "This should be fine to write stuff down first, then we can put it in the computer later when Jess comes back."

As they exited the room, she pulled the door halfway closed, bent down to put on her flip-flops, and yelled to her sister "Do you have the room key?"

"Yep!" came Keely's answer, and the three of them made their way down the path toward the cafe and beach.

It was still a while before lunch, there weren't any people at any of the tables when they strode up to the small, outdoor restaurant. Keely asked the bartender for a menu, and he nodded to the host, who took three menus and asked the trio, "Where would you like to sit?"

"Oh, we just need one menu, thanks, for a quick project, and maybe just some water if that's OK...and do you have an extra pen we could borrow?" answered Keely.

"Sure, sit anywhere you like, and here is that pen. You can keep it," said the host, with a smile.

The three Websters pulled up chairs to a table under an umbrella, and began to scan and copy down the menu names for each sandwich and drink they had tried since arriving on the island. "This shouldn't take long at all," said Keely, as the host brought over three small glasses of water. Keely called out each item and its ingredients to Meg, who dutifully wrote the details on the sheet she'd brought along from the room.

They were about halfway finished with detailing their past menu selections when Cal said "Hi, Linc! Hi, Tiare!" His sisters looked up to find the Martinez kids from Colorado standing by their table.

"*Bonjour!* How are you two?" said Keely.

Meg added, "*Iaorana!*"

"Hi!" said Linc, and Tiare smiled shyly as she sidled closer to the table where the kids were sipping their waters and completing their list. Another server from the cafe came by and asked the new arrivals if they'd like to order anything. Both Martinez kids shook their heads.

"No, thanks," we're just stopping by for a minute, Tiare replied.

"We're doing a project to keep track of all the foods and drinks we've tried since coming on the trip to Moorea," said Meg.

"Cool," said Tiare, "Can I see it?"

Meg handed her the page. It listed the fish sandwiches, salads, and special tropical drinks they had tried over the past couple of days. "Oh, and add those great chow mein sandwiches too!" said Cal.

"You are right, we definitely need to add those!" said Keely.

Linc wrinkled his nose in distaste. "Chow mein sandwiches? Yuck!"

"No, they are actually really good!" said Meg, and Keely nodded.

Tiare, a bit surprisingly given her earlier hesitance to speak, enthusiastically agreed. "Oh yes, we've had those, chow mein noodles, veggies, and sometimes tofu, chicken, or pork on French rolls, right?"

"Exactly!" said Cal. "We've ordered them a couple of times now. We want to make them when we get home, too!"

"Oh yeah!" Linc said. "Now I remember them!"

"What unusual foods have you two tried since you got here?" Keely asked Linc and Tiare.

"Well, our mom is from Moorea, and she's got sisters, cousins, aunts, and uncles here. We've already been to their houses a couple of times, plus to my aunt's store in town. One pretty tasty local thing we *have* tried is *Firi Firi, spelled, f-i-r-i, twice*."

"They are AWESOME!" said Linc, nodding at his sister and then back at the Webster kids.

"What are *'feery-feery'*? Keely asked, repeating what she thought she had heard Tiare say.

"Well, they're kind of like donuts...hey, we have a bunch of them left over, back in our room. Do you want to try one?" said Tiare.

"Thanks, but we have to be getting back to our room for lunch," Keely said, as she had just realized it was about 20 minutes before noon.

"Oh, it won't take long. We can just run back down the beach to our hotel and get some - then bring them back here," said Tiare, with a hopeful smile.

"That sounds yummy," said Meg,

Cal beamed with his agreement. "Yeah, I'd LOVE to try them."

Keely thought for a moment: *We did leave a note for Jess*...She figured a quick trip would be ok. "Well, how about if we met you half-way down the beach, then we could try them, and you wouldn't have to walk so far back here, either?"

"OK, great. We'll see you midway on the beach between our two hotels in about...15 minutes!" said Tiare with a grin at her brother, who giggled in return. Then she and Linc ran quickly away down the path toward the beach.

The Webster kids sipped the last of their water glasses, brought them back and set them on the bar, and thanked the bartender for letting them use the menus for their research. "We'll be back to eat more another time, *Maururu!*" said Meg. The host waved in acknowledgment from another table where she was seating a couple for lunch. The Websters headed down the path for their mid-beach, food-tasting rendezvous with their new friends.

Keely was a little nervous about running out of time, and she was a tiny bit unsure if she wanted to try whatever a "firi firi" was...but within moments they were already headed down the sand to the meeting point they'd agreed on with the Martinez kids. It was still about five minutes before noon. The wind was starting to pick up, and she saw that whitecaps had formed outside the reef, with more rough water than they'd experienced yet in the lagoon. Looking at her watch again, Keely trailed her brother and sister by a couple of feet as they jogged their way down the beach. She glanced to her right and saw the rocky structure of the marae, looking especially dark and forbidding as a solid wall of slate gray clouds began to cross the sky.

Just when Keely was thinking they might have to turn back instead of continue with the plan to meet the Martinez kids, she saw Tiare walking rapidly towards them across the sand. She held a large paper bag, with Linc following alongside. Keely waved and the two kids from Colorado returned the greeting. In a moment, they reached each other.

Tiare pointed to the bag, "OK, now you get to try Firi Firi!"

Meg was super curious. "What are they?"

"Look inside and find out!" said Linc, with a grin, adding, "I bet you can't eat eight of them!"

"Oh yeah? I bet I can!" Cal said, responding to the challenge as he glanced in the top of the bag. "Wow! Now I know what you were talking about," he exclaimed, as he pulled out a sugar-encrusted donut, actually shaped like a figure 8. "Donuts!"

Meg reached her hand in the bag too. "Yum, and tasty donuts, too. Maybe they should be called "*tasty 8's!*"

Keely followed her siblings, grabbing one as well. "Are you sure it's OK?" she asked Tiare.

"Yeah, of course, my aunt made them, we had a bunch left over from our Sunday brunch. They are a big tradition here I guess...Tahitians and Mooreans like to eat them on the weekends. "

"Yum, they taste like coconut, and boy are they good!" said Meg. Cal was nodding his head vigorously in agreement.

Keely took a bite of hers and loved the luscious, creamy flavor. "What's in them?" she asked Tiare.

"They are made like other doughnuts, but have an even mix of coconut water and coconut milk to give them that flavor."

"They ARE really coconutty - and really, really good," Keely agreed.

Just then, Meg felt a drop of rain on her head, and quickly another. In only seconds, it began to pour with a vengeance. The kids, standing in the middle of the beach, looked for somewhere to hide from the torrents pounding the sand and rocks - and quickly drenching their heads.

Screeching like a wild animal, Linc, wearing his swimsuit, ran straight into the water and started splashing around amongst the rocks and coral while the rain poured down - creating tiny leaping fountains of water on the surface around him. Cal joined him in the lagoon as the girls watched in a combination of amazement and irritation, while getting more soaked by the moment. *It looks like a replay of their wild dancing scene at the airport!* Keely thought.

Glancing at Meg and Tiare, she yelled, "Come on, Cal and Linc, let's get under cover!"

"Yeah, let's head to the trees over there, we gotta get out of the rain!" Tiare cried. She pointed towards a small thicket by the marae walls.

Cal ran back from the edge of the water, and then Linc - in a rush to follow him and the others to get under cover - sloshed unsteadily out of the low surf while the rain swirled and pounded the sea and sand around him. Disoriented by the downpour, he stumbled and put his foot down deep in a hole in the shallow water. Suddenly, they all heard a horrible 'screech!' Already under cover themselves, they turned in unison to see Linc half-running, half-limping toward them, yelling "OWWW, my foot!" as he reached the shelter of the trees.

Careful to avoid entering the enclosure of the marae's ruins, they hid under one of the taller shrubs that offered some, but still minimal, leaves and branches for cover from the steady downpour. The five of them huddled together in a small circle, trying to avoid the relentless, albeit still warm rain. Keely glanced across the marae toward the Martinez family's hotel and noticed that not too far from them, a number of huge construction vehicles sat idle, apparently ready to go to work.

"Let me look at your foot," Tiare said to her brother, and while he winced in pain and hopped on his "good" foot, she lifted up the other to see what had happened. While Linc stumbled a bit to gain his balance, his sister grasped and turned his injured foot to the side, and then she saw the problem. "Aha! You stepped on a sea urchin, several spines of one, it looks like, based on all the 'pinholes' I see in your foot. You're bleeding, but not that bad."

"Oh WOW," said Cal, and Keely and Meg gasped. A small amount of blood was oozing from several tiny holes in Linc's foot. Tiare calmly wiped it away with a now soggy napkin from inside the bag of doughnuts.

"Ow, it stings!" said Linc, as he fought back tears.

"What should we do?" said Keely, more than a little concerned now.

Locking eyes with her brother, Tiare answered, "Well, Linc, you know what to do, just what our uncle told us, right?"

Linc stared at his sister, then down, then at the other kids, and then back to Tiare, and replied, with a combination of fright and embarrassment in his voice, "Really?"

She nodded and pointed. "You can do it yourself, right over there."

Keely, Meg and Cal watched in bewilderment as Linc, seeking a place away from the others' view, limped and almost tripped over the marae's waist-high walls, then hopped awkwardly across the rocks to a tree near a large, nine-foot or so tall boxy structure - a tower of some sort of large rectangular stones with some wood and thatch, made of palms, covering its top. Luckily, the downpour was easing off a bit, but the clouds hadn't yet cleared. The boy winced again, more loudly than before.

Cal jumped over the stone walls in three quick steps and ran to join his friend, calling, "Are you OK?"

"Yeah, but DON'T come over here!" Linc yelled to him.

"Why not?" Cal asked.

Tiare suddenly said, loudly, behind them all, "Because he's peeing on his foot."

Chapter 35

The mysterious box

He's doing what???

Keely and Meg were speechless as they exchanged glances of amazement with each other. They could not even fathom what Tiare was talking about. Cal stood a few feet away from where Linc was, his back to him, and apparently, doing just as his sister suggested. Taking a quick peek, he too was astonished by Linc's actions. As for the reasons why, they were all filled in shortly by Tiare.

"If you get a cut or sting or poke from a sea urchin or a jellyfish or other aquatic animals like them, we're told here in Moorea to pee on it to clean the cut or puncture wound. It's a natural disinfectant. Our uncle told us so, and nobody argued with him when he said it, so I think it's true."

"No kidding? Gross!" said Keely.

"Well, I guess that's one crazy thing I never knew that I can say I learned here!" Meg nodded, then snapped her fingers. "Remember when JP on the tour talked about what you do when you get stung or cut by a sea urchin?"

"Oh yeah!" Keely said, "right as we were being dropped off, he said the 'locals' could tell us what to do. I guess this is it, Tiare!" She turned towards her in amazement.

Once Linc had finished his ad hoc disinfection 'exercise' moments later, he struggled to put a fresh napkin Tiare handed him from the paper bag containing the donuts on his foot to protect the wound. The napkin in place, sort of, he wrapped the now empty bag itself around it for additional protection. Cal decided to join him, and carefully stepped over the rocks in front of the tall tower behind where his new friend was standing.

As he put his sandal-clad foot in a crevice to use as a step up next to Linc, along the side of the tower, Cal heard an odd 'thunk' sound. He bent down and saw that his foot had knocked a fairly large rock out from the edge of the wall. Peering into the place where it had been, with bits of some sort of natural mortar - *or maybe just dirt -* stuck to the edges and the now displaced rock itself, he saw something inside the hole he'd accidentally created.

"Hey guys, check this out!"

"What?" Meg said, as she and the other kids came over to where Cal kneeled by the wall.

"There's something in here, I knocked a hole in this tower thing with my foot!" Reaching in, he flinched. As his sisters jumped back, a small yellow lizard ran onto his arm and quickly scurried into a nearby crevice.

"Yikes!" Keely said, and Tiare laughed.

"That's just a gecko, in fact, it's what Moorea is actually named after! They're everywhere! You haven't seen one in your room or around it?"

"No, we haven't," said Cal, "but that would be cool!"

Keely was curious. "That's where this island got its name?"

"Yep," answered Tiare.

Her brother, limping a bit with his makeshift paper bag bandage, piped in "Yeah, our mom told us the word *Mo'orea* actually means "*yellow lizard*" in Tahitian."

"Wow, that's awesome!" said Cal. He reached his hand back in the crevice. "There's something in here," he grunted as he struggled to free several smaller rocks from the hole. "But I can't get it to budge." He looked up to take a breath from his struggles.

"Let me try," said Keely, and his older sister leaned down to look. She turned around and found a long, stout stick from the ground, then pushed it into the hole, trying to chisel away the pebbles and dirt.

All of a sudden, with one thrust, they all heard a "clank" sound as the heavy stick struck metal, or rocks, or something.

"That's it, you found it!" said Cal.

"Found what?" said Linc, as he edged closer.

Keely wedged one foot in a crevice next to the hole and turned to one side while she worked her hand and the stick she was holding around the object, still unable to see it clearly. Prying the wood back and forth, she thought she could see something dark colored, and rectangular in shape. But it was hard to tell, and much of it was still stuck in the hole.

"I can't get it out. We need better tools. OH SHOOT!" Keely yelled, as she looked at her watch. It was 12:15! "We are late for lunch, Meg and Cal! We have to get back. Jess is probably wondering where we are!"

"But what about the box?" Cal asked, and Tiare, Linc and Meg echoed his question.

"Let's put the rock back in the hole and come get it tomorrow, OK?" Keely replied.

"Yeah! Hide it so nobody else finds it...but how will WE be able to find it again?" Tiare said.

Meg had an idea: "Let's mark the ground near it, with two large rocks - straight across from the hole – but far enough away that nobody else will find it. But *we'll* know. Then we can come back tomorrow with tools, you know, something made of metal, like a screwdriver, maybe a long file or something like that, to pry the box out of the hole. But where can we get tools like that around here?"

"At our uncle's house! He's got lots of tools," said Linc.

Tiare frowned at her younger brother. "How are we going to do that and not let anyone know about our secret...and it is OUR secret, right?" she said, looking around at the other kids. The others nodded, agreeing that was their best option.

"Yes, we have to keep this a secret between just us five," said Meg.

Keely, somewhat skeptical, thought about it a moment, then nodded. "OK, I guess," she agreed. Cal and Linc added their approval as well.

"Not a word to anyone about this, right?" said Tiare, looking at each of the other four.

"Right! - our secret!" they all said as one, arms extended inward from the circle they formed to touch hands together.

"OK!" Keely declared, as she crammed several rocks into the hole while Meg marked the spot with two stones. "There...that should stay. And hey, the rain's completely stopped now too! We gotta get back to the Montcalm, guys!" she yelled to her siblings.

The quintet hastened back from the marae wall and emerged from the trees to the beach again. The rain had stopped except for a few stray drops. The sun again broke through the clouds and the air was downright steamy – it felt hotter now than before the downpour had hit.

Tiare turned to Keely, Cal, and Meg. "We have to go too, and probably need to wash and re-wrap Linc's foot back at the room, but he'll be fine. What time tomorrow should we meet? To pull the box from the hole?

Keely thought for a moment. "How about we say we want to take a walk on the beach to meet you two for lunch? We can plan for noon, and we'll bring a blanket and, I don't know, sandwiches or something. We'll figure it out with Jess. She'll probably have to come with us, but once we get here and have our lunch, maybe we can say we're going to explore or take a hike around your hotel?"

The others nodded their heads, and Keely continued. "Yeah, we'll tell Jess we're going on a walk, maybe to the hotel's bathrooms or the pool, and you," she said, pointing at Tiare, "can come with me to show me where it is. While we're doing that, we'll sneak over and get the box out of the hole with the tools you bring. We'll have to be fast...umm, where are you going to put the tools in the meantime, you know, so we can grab them quickly and go get the box out of our secret spot?"

Tiare grinned. "I'll bring a beach bag, and hide the tools in an extra towel inside. They shouldn't take up too much space. Then when we go to the restroom, I'll bring my bag along, and we can cut through the trees from the pool area at our hotel, pry the box out, put it in the bag, and go back to the beach before your nanny wonders why we're not back yet!"

"OK, well, I hope we can do all that, and...well, that we don't get in any trouble...anyway, we'll see you tomorrow at noon, we hope!" said Keely, turning her heel, grabbing her sister and brother's arms to jog back to the Montcalm.

"That's the plan!" Tiare cried back as she headed briskly in the opposite direction with her brother, who still limped quite a lot with the awkward paper 'package' wrapped around one of his feet.

Stopping a moment, the group's youngest 'co-conspirator' wheeled around. "Don't forget, it's OUR SECRET!" Linc yelled.

Keely, without looking back, raised her right thumb upward, as she and her siblings continued their near-run down the beach toward their hotel, headed straight to where they now saw Jess. She had just started searching for them in earnest, only a hundred yards or so away.

Chapter 36

Dubious explanations & back to the bungalow

"Hey Jess! We're over here!" yelled Keely, as she waved to attract their nanny's attention. The three Webster siblings were approaching the Montcalm's beach from the east.

Jess, hearing Keely's call, turned and saw the kids, stifling her slight anger and heaving a huge sigh of relief at the same time. She waved and began walking to meet them. It was now about 12:25, and the rain had thankfully stopped. Just like in her previously, really concerned mind, the darkness was lifting from the day.

"Where were you guys? I was so worried!"

I knew we shouldn't have gone to the beach! Keely thought. She decided to explain as best as possible why they were late.

When she finished telling Jess how they'd run into the Martinez kids, she sighed. "Sorry that we made you worry, Jess, but we did leave a note! It was kind of an adventure, but we should have asked you before we agreed to meet Tiare and Linc on the beach."

"But, boy those 'figure-8' doughnuts were great!" said Cal. "Until Linc stepped on a sea urchin running from the rain!"

"Yeah, and he peed on it!" said Meg.

"WAIT! What?" Jess said, now quite confused. "Keely, please tell me just what happened? I never saw a note. What note? And Linc stepped on a sea urchin? You guys were in the water?"

"OK, Jess. Let's just sit down for a second and we'll explain everything. We thought we'd have time and it would just be a quick trip to and from the cafe and back, but it turned out differently than we'd planned." Keely pointed toward the restaurant up the path.

When they reached the cafe, they grabbed a table in the corner. The host walked up with a huge smile. "Iaorana! You found them! Welcome back! Would you like something to drink?"

Jess answered for all of them. "Just water please, thanks, maybe something else in a bit" and then turned back to Keely and her siblings. "OK, I'm ready for the details..."

After Keely had finished explaining "the rest of the story" on just what they had been doing, albeit leaving out the details of the box they'd found at the edge of the marae, Jess shook her head. "I asked you guys to stay in the room while I was gone...though I did say I'd be right back, and that didn't happen, I know..." She recounted all the troubles accessing her email and printing out the food list copies.

"Wow. We both kind of had tough days so far. Really sorry Jess for worrying you," Keely sighed.

"Yeah, we're really sorry, Jess," Cal added.

"But wait!" Keely said. "You didn't see the note we left you?"

Jess shook her head. "No, I didn't, and I was really wondering where you were when I got back to the room. It was after noon and you weren't there. That's why I rushed here and to the beach to find you guys!"

"That's so weird," said Keely. She pointed at their food notes, slightly soaked, but still legible. "We left it on a spare sheet of paper...just like this." She picked up the list...and saw more sheets stuck to it underneath.

Turning them over, the oldest Webster sibling suddenly grew very red in the face. "Uh-oh, now I think I know what must have happened. Here's our note...it must have been included with these other sheets accidentally when we left the room at 11:15 or so, and gotten mixed in with our food list. Soooooo sorry!" Keely said, embarrassed by the mistake.

Meg felt even worse, because she was the one who'd grabbed the list from the table - and the message Keely left with it - in haste. "It was me, Jess, I'm the one who picked up the note by accident and brought it with us. It was my fault, not Keely's," she said.

"I appreciate you both taking responsibility," said Jess, "but really, we have a pretty comprehensive failure to communicate situation here, because you were supposed to stay in the room and wait for me, and I then, I know, I took way too long on my errand, and I guess the rainstorm didn't help too much either. Let's just agree that from here on out, we'll agree to do what we say or are asked to do, and if something happens that changes our plans, we'll make sure to let each other know right away. Especially you-all-to-me, OK?"

"Sure, Jess!" said Meg.

Cal and Keely nodded soberly, the older sister noting, "Too bad we don't all have walkie talkies or cell phones or something like that."

Jess shook her head. "I know, but we don't have walkie talkies, and as for phones, we can't use them here anyway, so we'll just have to communicate face-to-face, all right?"

"Got it, agreed," replied Keely.

Jess thought for a moment, and, with a serious lesson learned by all sides, she decided it was time to move on. After all, they were on vacation and no real harm had been done, despite her initial worries. "So, we'll just let this situation go and learn from it, and speaking of learning, tell me about these '*figure 8' doughnuts*?"

"Yeah, they're actually called '*feery feery*'" said Meg, pronouncing rather than spelling for Jess's benefit. "Tiare says that it's one of the main things they eat here in French Polynesia on the weekends."

"They're really coconutty doughnuts. Not stale either!" said Cal.

"And SOOOO good!" added Keely, "they're twisted into shapes like the number 8. Tiare and Linc's aunt made them, I think, and they were left over from their family brunch yesterday. I knew we were getting close to the time for us to be back - like we wrote in our note (that you never got) and we were just going to meet on the beach and share a few with them. Tiare brought a whole bag, and we ate 'em all!"

"I think I did see some of those yesterday here at the resort breakfast table, but they were on the far side next to the bread and I missed trying them. Maybe next time," said Jess. Their drinks had just arrived. "I'm guessing you guys are a bit thirsty, huh? I sure am, stressful times!" She took a sip of her water, "Anybody hungry?"

Keely gave a big sigh and shook her head. "Not me, at least not right now," she replied, still, like her siblings, feeling a bit damp from the previous rainstorm. And a little exhausted too, from all the excitement and confusion of the day - which was still only half over.

Meg also shook her head, and Cal shared his sisters' lack of appetite. "I just want to go back to the room for a while," he said.

"Yeah, me too," Meg agreed.

"Sounds like a good plan to me," Keely weighed in. "Looks like we might get more rain soon too," she observed, noting another large bank of approaching storm clouds. The wind was picking up now as well.

"Great plan," said Jess, "we have snacks there, in case we get hungry later. Let's just focus on school projects and maybe write some letters or postcards, and relax for a few hours until your dad gets off work."

They all finished their drinks, then Jess thanked the server, and explained they weren't going to order lunch after all. They pushed back their chairs and headed to their bungalow. No sooner had they reached its door, and kicked off their wet and sandy footwear, when the skies opened up and it began to pour rain again, even more heavily than it had earlier on the beach.

"Glad we're back under REAL cover!" said Keely, as they pulled the door shut. She looked at the other two Websters, who glanced left and right, keeping the secret they shared from Jess, who had walked briefly into her own room.

Keely grabbed her backpack and jumped lightly on to the bed in the girls' bedroom. Meg took the other side next to her, and Cal parked himself on the bed he shared with his dad in the main room. Jess walked in a minute later and sat next to him at the small desk with her own study materials. *Nice to have some real down-time,* Jess thought, *especially after that little scare today!*

.

Chapter 37

Meanwhile, back at the office...

Unaware of all the 'drama' unfolding around the Websters elsewhere in the resort, Alex was deeply involved in his software implementation project activities. Because of their special preparations before leaving Seattle and also the 'head start' they had gotten the previous Friday after the Websters' arrival on the island, Alex and his team at LodgeSoft headquarters were already ahead of schedule with installation and testing.

Turns out, Bernie, the Information Technology manager on-site and their main contact for the project at the Montcalm, was super-organized. He had already mapped out a 'test environment' for the new software, so they could run it through its paces - meaning its various functions - on a trial basis to ensure every aspect worked correctly - then make quick adjustments as needed. Because of the local coordinator's ingenuity, they were getting testing done two days earlier than they'd initially planned. Alex was very pleased, and so far, his manager Roger Thomson, back at LodgeSoft HQ - not to mention Roger's brother David, on-site at the Montcalm - were happy as well with how the new software install was proceeding.

Alex turned to his project partner. "Bernie, how do things look for the user training next week? I know I'll be gone by then, but I'm wondering if you and Ravi feel confident that you have all the main concepts from the Administrator's Guide down?" Alex held up a large binder, sectioned out by category to cover each software module. "Are you ready to teach the rest of the Montcalm Moorea team how to use the new system?"

Bernie looked up, "I think we're going to be ready, Alex. We've both been studying the manual for the past month while we waited for some of the other 'pieces' of the conversion project to be arranged. We've even practiced two module lessons on each other using our test system. If we keep making progress like we have, we'll be in very good shape by the time you leave to return to the US."

"Before, actually, which is great for all of us!" exclaimed Alex. Bernie grinned and nodded, then finished typing a progress update to his regional IT coordinator from Australia, site of Montcalm Hotels & Resorts Asia-Pacific headquarters.

Lunch, earlier that day, had been an adventure in itself. They had driven to the nearby town of Maharepa and enjoyed fresh seafood and dessert at a restaurant owned by a friend of David's who was originally from Ireland. Alex asked him when they were ordering how he made the jump from the oft-chilly Emerald Isle to Moorea, and Brendan Mahoney, the owner replied, "Well, I just kept going until I found the greenest - but unlike Ireland - *warmest* island I could!"

They all laughed. Alex suspected it wasn't the first time that particular anecdote had been shared with a newcomer.

During their meal, Alex had asked the locals about the island's events and activities, looking for suggestions beyond sites they had already visited. He also queried David and Bernie about the hotel renovation next door - and why it was taking longer than expected.

"What's the real issue with the Hotel Moorea Ra'i?" Alex asked.

"Family matters mostly...that's quite common around here, actually," answered David, with a sigh.

"What do you mean?"

Bernie explained. "You remember when you went on the trip around the island, and you saw the old Fun Club property? Well, there's a similar argument among the family members who own the Moorea Ra'i. They also used to own this land and our hotel. Some of them are from here, others from Tahiti and a few even live overseas now. Some, maybe most of them, favor selling out to a hotel company run by a guy named Pierre Alarie. He's developed a close relationship with one of the cousins involved, and they're working together to convince French Polynesian leaders in Papeete that their plans are sound and appropriate for the site. They gained preliminary approval to move forward with their project, but a "stop" was requested in court by some of the family members who don't agree. So, the project's been on hold for a couple of weeks now."

David added, "And that was the case, up until recently, but we just heard a local judge may be ready to lift the temporary hold shortly, maybe even this week, so I would imagine the work will begin soon."

"What are they going to do with the place?" asked Alex.

"Tear it all down, pave over the marae for parking and outbuildings, and construct the largest resort that's ever been built here, with more than 250 rooms," replied Thomson, "about half of them built over water."

"Wow, that's a huge project. How will it impact your operations?"

The Montcalm GM looked thoughtful. "Actually, it might help us a bit, because as long as tourism stays healthy, with more combined rooms to offer and more guests aware of the island due to greater advertising by our new competitor, it would probably be good for our business too. Their proposed plans do ensure plenty of space and privacy between our two properties, including a wall and trees to separate their expanded site from ours here at the Montcalm."

"So, you're supportive of their plans then?" Alex asked.

David shook his head, and Bernie frowned as well. "No, we're not, or at least, I'm not personally, and neither is Bernie.

"I've lived on this island for 25 years and I know more than most about the history of that property - at least five or six hundred years-plus of cultural and spiritual importance to the local people here. If someone wants to build another hotel - with plenty of suitable sites near here, by the way – they shouldn't destroy and desecrate a revered religious and ceremonial site. But my voice," he finished with a frown, "is small when it comes to economic development, tax revenue, and whatever else is being promised by Alarie and his team."

On the way back from lunch, they had taken a short detour up a small road nearby to the tasting room of the local pineapple (and other) juice factory, which it turned out produced juices and beverages and even wines from a number of Moorea and Tahiti-grown fruits. Alex tasted a few of the offerings, and when they'd returned in David's car to the Montcalm, they also carried a couple of six packs of the juice and fruit drinks Alex had purchased to share with Jess and the kids.

Now, in the late afternoon, Alex pondered the situation with the software installation. He was completing a checklist to share with his Seattle team later, which would confirm their steps and project schedule - once they agreed on it the following morning - *or maybe even tonight?* Alex thought to himself. It was 1:30 in Moorea, 3:30 pm in the Pacific time zone. If he could 'knock out' the basics of the list in the next hour or so, they might be able to be ready to go by end of day for tomorrow.

As it turned out, the tests later that day went very well, so by the time everyone was starting to head out of the office, at around 4:30 pm in Moorea, Alex had received confirmation from his Seattle team on the checklist items, successfully completed local system tests, and all was solidly on track for the next day's packed project agenda.

Waving to Bernie and David as they stepped in their cars to head home, and to Ravi as she wrapped up some final details for guests arriving the following day with the front desk team, Alex was super tired. It had been a very long and active workday, starting around 7:45 that morning, and he'd spent a good chunk of it in the hot, humid air in between rainstorms. He was eager to see what Jess and the kids had been up to, where they had gone, and what sights they had seen. Taking a short-cut through the restaurant, Alex's stomach growled. *Is today the day for that local pizza we all talked about?*

Arriving a minute later at the door to the bungalow, Alex entered with his key. Cal was napping on the bed, with his school binder sprawled in front of him. Jess sat at the desk, and Keely and Meg were studying quietly in their room, the connecting door open. As he exchanged whispered greetings with Jess and the girls, Alex walked back into the main room and reached down to gently shake his son from his slumber.

"Oh! Hi, Dad! How was your day?" said Cal, rising sleepily from the bed and pushing aside his pencil and pen.

"It was great, thanks, buddy. Got lots done, and we're ahead of schedule, which is ALWAYS good. How was your day?"

"Oh, it was fun. Jess got us started on a cool project and then we went to the beach and got caught in a rainstorm and Linc peed on his foot and then we had a drink at the cafe and then we did homework."

"Whoa...what's this about Linc peeing on his foot?" Alex said, as he turned to look at Jess for an explanation. She had a somewhat sheepish look on her face.

Keely, heard them, and came out of the adjoining room just then and clued her dad in on the day's events. "Yep, what happened was, we were on the beach with the Martinez kids, you know Tiare and Linc, and it started raining...I mean, it was POURING! We were going to head for cover under the trees over by their hotel, and Linc, for some reason decided instead to run into the water in his bare feet and swimsuit. He jumped in and was bouncing around and accidentally stuck his foot into a hole and stepped on a sea urchin. Cal ran in to help him. But when Linc came out, it was just a little bloody from the little holes. And then Tiare told him what he had to do - pee on it, which is a natural disinfectant, I think? So, anyway, he went behind some rocks by the marae and did it. We hung around for a bit and made sure we had put some napkins and a paper bag from the donuts around his foot to protect it-but I'm sure he's disinfecting it now back at their room. Then we came back here and met Jess on the beach. Then it started raining again so we just stayed in the room and worked on our school projects and stuff. And that's it, Dad!"

Alex laughed to himself. His daughter surely had the knack for storytelling...*I wonder where she got it?* He was a *bit* worried when he heard about Linc's foot injury. But as nobody had apparently been seriously hurt, he decided not to ask about any of that aspect, instead inquiring, "That's funny, so the Martinez kids DID want to hang out today, but yesterday, per their mom, was a no-go?"

"That's right, Dad," explained Meg. "They came by while we were down at the cafe researching...Oh yeah, we haven't told you yet. We're doing a special project that Jess suggested and keeping a list to share when we get home of all the unusual dishes we're trying, and eating, while we're here on our vacation. Anyway, Tiare and Linc offered to have us try a special, ummm, "delicachy..."

"That's 'de-li-ca-cy' Meg," corrected Keely.

Meg continued. "Right, anyway a local special food, these great doughnuts called 'Firi Firi' which are really just super creamy and tasty, umm, coconut-flavored doughnuts."

"And they're shaped like a figure-8!" cried Cal, excitedly, smiling. "And boy are they good!"

Now it was Jess's turn, "Apparently, the Martinezes had some of the doughnuts left over from a family brunch they attended yesterday and so the kids met them on the beach to try them. And you know the rest from what Keely said," concluded the nanny.

"Well, I'm glad you didn't get TOO wet then. I was busy inside most of the day, but we drove to town for lunch, and there was quite a lot of excess water along the road. For a while after actually too, because of the downpours," said Alex.

"Yep," Jess said. "I asked in the office if you were around - but it was right after you left. No real problems or anything, just checking in when I went to the business center, and then the office, to do emails and print out some copies of the kids' menu checklists for them. You had gone to lunch when I asked Ravanui if you were there. Then it rained a ton, twice! Otherwise, it was a pretty non-eventful day," said Jess, noting grins on the kids' faces as she finished.

"What?!" she said, looking straight at Keely.

"Nothing!" Then, turning quickly towards her father, Keely asked, "What's the plan for dinner, Dad?"

"I was thinking we could try the local pizza. We can order from the front desk and go pick it up, it's only a half-mile or so away. We can also get some salad and drinks, then take it all to the beach to eat it or just have it here in the room. Whatever you guys want."

"How about we bring it here, then sit outside with our table and chairs and enjoy the evening?" said Keely.

Alex thought that was a great idea. The sunset didn't look like it was going to amount to much anyway, as there was a fairly thick layer of clouds still covering the sky. *And*, he thought, *if it starts to look like a beautiful one, it's just a short walk down the path to the beach to see it.*

"Perfect!" Alex answered. "Hey Cal, want to come over with me to the front desk to call in our orders? Then we can head over to the pizza place and they'll have our pies ready when we get there."

"Sure, Dad!"

To Jess and the girls, Alex added, "We shouldn't be long. Actually, I just remembered. We don't need drinks, because I have these," as out of a heavy paper bag, he produced the two six packs of sparkling juice and water he had purchased at the juice factory.

"There are two flavors, mango and pineapple and grapefruit and passion fruit. I can attest they are both great, because I got to taste them at the factory. It's not far from here...we stopped there on our way back from lunch. I'll put them in the fridge and they'll be cold by the time the pizza arrives. I'll probably have a beer, and Jess, your choice - whichever you like."

"I'm jealous!" said Meg.

Alex replied, with a grin, "About the beer? Forget it! You're too young...OH, you meant about the juice factory!" he continued in mock confusion. "Don't worry, now that I know where it is and what they have, maybe we can stop by there again before we go home. Speaking of which, if we keep making progress on the hotel software installation as we did today, I just might be able to finish early and be ready to hang out with you guys full time starting sometime Thursday!"

"That's great, Alex!" said Jess. Despite her enthusiasm, Alex sensed she'd had a very long day too. *I know what it's like to try to keep up with these three*, he thought to himself of his children and their active habits.

"Jess, I think I owe you more than just a beer for today..."

She shook her head. "No, really, it's been a great day, and if I could just have a nice salad and maybe a couple slices of a half-veggie pizza to go with whatever toppings you guys want, that would be great...though I definitely won't turn down the beer, either," she winked at her employer.

Alex nodded knowingly. "Oh, I get it, Jess. BELIEVE me, I do!"

Chapter 38

Bulldozers in paradise

November 29, Tuesday

After the craziness of the prior day - not all of it good, for sure, Jess was ready for one with less excitement. She had taken some time the evening before to wander the property and sit down under one of the very few overhead lights to read part of a book she'd brought along. When she awoke early to a clear sky and no rain (*and no roosters!*), it was both a relief and a reminder that they were in an amazing place, even if not really a 'full' vacation given her child-management duties.

She decided to take a quick walk on the beach before the kids woke up, sliding a note under their door to let them know she would be back soon. It was just before 7 am and they were starting to get into a true vacation routine, meaning no need here to get up early for swim class, soccer practice, or to school. Jess was pretty sure the Webster kids wouldn't repeat the previous day's 'getaway' after they'd made their joint deal to stay closer in touch during the trip.

She almost jumped out of her skin when, as she rounded the corner from her door, Keely stood there in her swim suit, with a towel around her neck. "Daily swim, remember? I promised my coach."

"Oh, sheesh! You scared me...of course!" Jess whispered. "Let's get going so we don't wake the others."

The two made their way together down the path to the beach, and both sniffed and stared through the soft light at the dense walls on either side - comprised of giant plants and flower-bedecked bushes, almost touching them as they walked by. Perhaps it was the fresh dousing by the prior day's rainstorms that made them resplendent with white, scarlet, and pink blossoms. They were incredibly fragrant and buzzing with bees already, even at this hour. Jess couldn't place all of the shrubs' names, but recognized the Hibiscus and Gardenias for their look and aromas, most notably in the case of the latter.

Was that a passion fruit tree, with the yellow and white 'velvety' blossoms? It sure looks and smells like the tree the Hawaiians call "lilikoi," Jess thought as she leaned up to sniff a low-hanging branch. That's what she had seen (and smelled) the prior night on the patio with her new friend, Julian. She reveled in the scents, and the peace, and quiet. *What it must be like to live in such a setting all the time.*

Meanwhile, Keely's mind was on another track. *Would it get boring in a place like this, without the hustle and bustle of a city?* There were certainly quiet neighborhoods in Tacoma, and Seattle too, and for that matter, in most American cities. There were lots of nice parks to get away to in most parts of the growing metropolis surrounding the Puget Sound region, but the sheer silence, only accented by occasional bird calls (and thankfully right now, no roosters!) offered a welcome respite from the clamor she'd grown used to at home.

As they reached the beach, Keely kicked off her sandals, laid her towel down on the sand, and, adjusting her goggles, waded into the water, advising Jess of her workout plan.

"I'm just going to swim back and forth around 50 yards offshore. I'll be counting strokes and estimating the distance. Probably 1,500 yards or so, should take me around 35-40 minutes, tops."

Jess nodded. "Be careful!"

As Keely began her swim, Jess saw the glow of the rising sun touching the sand's edges. It had popped out of the far eastern horizon around 5:15 am, but was only now making its way west over the Moorean mountains toward where she stood. After several minutes of quiet contemplation of the soft linen-colored sand, interspersed with rocks and shell fragments, and the turquoise sea's distant, rumbling wave action against the reef, Jess removed her sandals and waded into the cool waters of the lagoon. The light surf occasionally licked her knees as she made her way toward the east side of the beach.

About ten minutes in to her shore-side stroll, she jumped at a sudden noise, then more that immediately followed. "RRRROAR", "RRUMBLE," "Boom!" It was the sound of heavy equipment being started up, moving and clattering into action. Jess turned her head and saw, off in the distance, far back from the beach, several workers standing around the bulldozers and trucks that had been inactive up to this point since their arrival. *Obviously not anymore!*

Jess frowned in disappointment. *Oh well, all that noise means we'll probably want to visit a few other beaches instead of hanging out here a lot for the next few days*, she thought. *At least unless we are actively swimming or snorkeling in the lagoon. We probably wouldn't hear much of it underwater.*

Reluctantly, she turned around and headed back toward where Keely's towel was placed on the beach, and sat down for a while. Keely was swimming briskly and unaware of the noise further up the beach. She pulled her way back and forth, then repeated the exercise several times across the lagoon using various strokes - just before reaching the small surf line, and far enough out to avoid the main rocks and reefs. Jess's stomach growled. She was getting hungry, *time to try something new for breakfast on this "Tropical Tuesday,"* she thought.

Keely finished her workout and came out of the water about 15 minutes later, and after she briefly toweled off, the two put on their flip flops and headed back up the path to the resort. When Jess arrived at the door to her room, she inserted the key and entered, and was about to open the connecting door to the girls' room when she saw the note she'd left earlier had been removed.

She knocked once and Meg answered, chirping "Good morning, Moorea!" as she pulled on a clean t-shirt.

"Is your dad already gone to breakfast?" Jess asked the youngster, who she could see was getting very tan already, despite all the sunscreen they so carefully and liberally and frequently applied when outside.

"Yep, he left just after 7. He said they're in their main software testing phase and stuff. But he said he was also going early because he was hoping to take a bike ride around the area, maybe down around Cook's Bay and back, at lunch time."

"Cool...is Cal up yet?" Keely breezed by them on her way for a quick shower, waving good morning to her sister with both hands as she entered the bathroom with a bundle of clean clothes in hand for the day.

Jess knocked on the door to the main room. Cal opened it, already dressed in his now trademark shorts and t-shirt.

"Hi Jess, where did you go?" he asked.

"Down to the beach, watched Keely do her morning swim, and guess what?" She shared the unfortunate, and noisy, news. "They've started the construction that Tiare and Linc were telling us about the other day!"

"Oh, no, really?" said Meg, frowning.

"Yeah, but it's not *that* bad, I hope. So far, at least. But it will be louder around the beach for sure while they're working."

Meg stole a glance at Cal, then quickly looked back to the nanny. "No, I'm sure it's no big deal. Hey, you ready for breakfast? I'm *really* hungry!"

Keely opened the door to the bathroom, a huge puff of steam following her out, but she was already showered and changed.

"That was fast!" Jess exclaimed. She also wanted to get changed for their morning jaunt to the restaurant. "Hey, just give me a minute in the bathroom and I'll be ready to walk over. In fact, you guys can go now and grab us a table, I'll be right there and we can see what dishes are featured on their marvelous, Moorean menu today!"

This elicited a groan from the girls. "Oh no, Dad's 'pun disease' is catching...now Jess has it!" said Keely, giggling to her sister and brother.

Chapter 39

Kids plan a 'getaway lunch hunt'

"What are we going to do now! They're going to tear up the marae and find our box, or worse, smash it all up without even knowing it's there!" cried Meg to the other two Websters. They were all in the restaurant, grabbing plates at the breakfast buffet table.

"Calm down, Meg!" urged her older sister. "We don't *know* that they'll be digging up or breaking down that particular area."

"Yeah, but we don't know they *won't* either."

"You're right," answered Keely. "We need to get over there ASAP. But how to do that and not clue Jess into our plans?"

"What about if one of us went over to invite the Martinez kids in person?" Cal suggested. "That would give us an excuse to check things out ourselves. We could also find out if Tiare or Linc have heard anything about the construction and what the workers might be doing."

"Little brother, that is a fantastic idea!" said Keely, punching him lightly on the shoulder, eliciting a wide smile from Cal in appreciation. It wasn't often he got praise like this from his eldest sibling. Usually, and especially in the case of Meg, it was more likely to be a glare or a frown. *But I'll take the positive words and the punch instead, for sure*, he thought.

"OK, so who's going to bring up the lunch idea to Jess so we have our excuse? And who's going to go over there?" Meg said, looking at Keely, who gave her the answer.

"I'll do it, and I'll suggest that I visit the Martinezes to make the invitation in person right after breakfast. I'm sure Jess will think it's OK. And I can take a couple of quick pictures with our camera of the stuff going on while I'm over there."

"What do *we* do?" Cal asked.

"Just nod your heads and agree it's a great idea when I bring it up," Keely said

Meg duly nodded. "Got it!"

Cal concurred, then dug into his eggs and toast breakfast.

Jess walked through the restaurant doorway a moment later, then sat down at their table. The server came over and offered coffee.

"Yes, please!" Turning to the kids, she asked "How's your breakfast? Try anything different this morning?"

"Ummm, not really. I think there's some new kinds of fruit, but this menu is kind of like the one we had on Saturday," Meg said.

"All right, well I'll go pick a few things to eat, back in a minute."

When Jess returned to the table with her own mix of fruit, yogurt and a piece of mango jam-coated French bread, Keely saw her opportunity.

"Hey Jess, we were thinking it would be fun, now that we know them better, to suggest we meet Tiare and Linc, and maybe their mom too, for lunch today at the beach. What do you think?"

"Sure…I guess we could call over to their hotel and find out what room they're staying in, but—"

Keely interrupted Jess's reply. "Oh, no problem, I already know, they're in room 17. Tiare pointed out where it was in the complex yesterday. I thought I could just run over there after breakfast, invite them to lunch around noon, then we could plan together what to bring to our beach picnic. I promise to come back right afterwards."

"OK, but this time no delays, all right? I was really worried yesterday. And no going in the water along the way, Keely."

"Of course not, I already did my swim. Plus, we need time to plan. Also, where will we get the food we'll be bringing?" she asked Jess.

"I was thinking," Jess replied, "if I could trust you guys not to run away again, ha-ha, that I'd rent a bike and ride into town to the little supermarket. I could get some bread, cheese, snacks, fruit, and drinks, and bring it back here. Then we'll make sandwiches and head over around noon, like you said…that is if it's OK with their mom,"

"That's a GREAT idea, Jess!" said Meg, perhaps a bit too enthusiastically. "I mean, that sounds cool. We'll just stay here in the room, doing our homework while you're gone," she added innocently, looking closely at her glass of juice and away from Jess's eyes.

Jess gave Meg a questioning look, but the middle Webster sibling didn't change her expression, so the nanny turned back to Keely. "All right, well I think that's a good plan. If they can't meet there, we can always go to another beach since it might be really loud around here anyway, in fact, are you sure you don't want to go somewhere else? Maybe that beach near the airport? Maybe we could take a cab or something there together?"

"Oh no, we'll be fine and we'll just walk further down the beach from their hotel, away from most of the noise." Keely wiped her mouth and pushed back her chair from the table. "Why don't I head over there now, I'll be back in a jiffy," she said, and started down the path to the beach before Jess could question her further.

"Hurry back!" Jess called after Keely as she strode away, then turned toward the other Webster children. "OK guys, well, let's enjoy the rest of our breakfast while your sister's gone, "she said, while gratefully accepting the steaming cup of coffee the server brought to the table just then. Jess added a healthy pour of milk then took a huge sip - much needed to counter some of the cobwebs still in her head from her early morning wake-up and walk.

Keely didn't bother to look back as she hurried out to the beach. She was focused on getting across the sand and to the edge of the marae as fast as possible. She felt the camera in her pocket. *But how is taking a photo really going to help if they're tearing up the marae?* she thought.

She removed her flip flops to increase her walking speed once she reached the sand, and could really hear the clatter of the heavy equipment now. She strained to see just where the machines were operating, and as she drew closer to the adjoining hotel, she let out a huge sigh of relief. *Looks like they're working more toward the front side of the property, near the road, right now*, Keely mused. *I hope they stay there!*

Reflecting on their secret plan from yesterday, she suddenly realized that it would have been smart to bring a large bag or something with her, and maybe to try to get the box free by herself while she had the chance and was passing so near it. *Darn! Wish I'd thought of that...but...maybe it's too hard to pry it out by hand anyway, without tools.*

She decided it was best to stick with the plan, but she noted the need to hurry - and hoped those bulldozers and workers didn't come near the secret box's 'hiding place!'

In a couple of minutes, Keely was just arriving at the outermost buildings of the neighboring resort. She started walking past the first and second buildings, looking for room numbers. *There!* She saw #17, with a neat little walkway lined with rocks and plants. *This place isn't as pretty as the Montcalm*, she observed. But actually, its abundant flowers and plants looked older, taller, and bushier than the ones at the Websters' hotel. Stepping in front of the door, she knocked firmly.

"Who is it?" came a voice from inside, then it opened, and Mrs. Martinez stood there, with a somewhat surprised look on her face.

"Hi, Mrs. Martinez, it's Keely Webster, remember me?"

"Of course, Keely! Come on in!" she said as she stepped back to allow Keely to enter, then pointed toward a large living room leading to a full kitchen area. "The kids are in here, working on their school assignments."

Keely walked into the room and Tiare looked up, even more surprised than her mom. "Hi...I didn't expect to see you *here*, Keely!" said Tiare.

Linc, with a fresh bandage on his foot and lounging on the couch, was also curious about her pop-in visit, as it showed on his face.

"Yeah, well, I thought it would be nice to stop in and invite you all to lunch today, like we talked about yesterday?" Keely ventured, looking first at the kids and then at Mrs. Martinez.

"Umm...lunch? Oh, I am sorry, we have other plans today," the woman answered. "We have to go into town."

Tiare pleaded. "Mom! Can't we just have lunch with them, and then go? Or maybe you can go without Linc and me?"

Keely decided to jump into the conversation: "Sorry you can't make it, Mrs. Martinez, but we will be with our nanny, Jessica and I'm sure it would be fine if Linc and Tiare joined us - even if you can't come yourself. We'll just be out on the beach in front of your hotel...and we'll bring all the food. You don't have to do anything!"

"Well, I guess it would be all right, but of course we can send the kids with lunch from here, we've got lots to make sandwiches with and we have some cookies my sister made, and drinks. But we don't have quite enough for everyone though...."

"Oh, that's no problem at all, Mrs. Martinez, we have all of our food covered and could even bring extra."

"Well, you can certainly share the cookies," answered the Tahitian-American with a smile.

"Sure, that sounds awesome!" Keely replied, "and *we* can share some of the fruit we bought on the island. We got it after climbing to Afareaitu Falls the other day. It will be fun!"

"Yeah, Mom. It will be fun!" added Linc, moving to his sister's side as both vigorously bobbed their heads in agreement.

"But you must stay out of the water and be safe!" their mother cautioned.

"We will! I can't go in anyway with this bandage that I've still got to wear 'til tonight," said Linc, glancing at his sister.

"OK then...what time will you and the others be there, Keely? Should the kids just meet you in front on the beach? I probably won't be in the room then because I have to leave to go to town at 11."

"We'll meet out front at noon if that works?"

"Perfect!" Tiare said, and as her mother turned to look in the fridge for the supplies needed to start making lunch, she grinned at Keely. Keely quickly returned the look and headed toward the door.

"OK then, sounds like a plan. We will talk to you later, Linc and Tiare, and love this place, Mrs. Martinez. See you soon!"

The kids' mother returned the well wishes and walked Keely to the door. As it shut behind her, Keely pumped her fist in the air.

YES! she said quietly to herself. *The first part of the plan is set. Now we just need to make sure we have the tools, and enough time, to get that box loose after lunch!*

Chapter 40

Family fights...and back for the box

When Keely returned to the bungalow, she first verified - along the way - that the location of the mystery box was still 'safe' from the construction equipment. *Interesting*, she pondered on her walk back from the Martinez family's hotel. She had looked the words up at a Tahitian language website while using the hotel office internet for a while the previous afternoon, and "*Moorea Ra'i*" - or at least the second word after the island name, meant "sky" in Tahitian. *So, Moorea Sky was its name, if translated to English.*

Hmm, I wonder if Mrs. Martinez's name Raiana has something to do with 'sky' too? Keely was always interested in the etymologies, or origins, of words she learned. She rounded the corner and turned up the path from the Montcalm's beach. When she arrived at their bungalow, she entered to find her brother and sister playing video games and reading, respectively. Jess was in her room, and Keely knocked lightly on the open door to let her know she was back from her invitation errand.

"Well, is the lunch on for today?" Jess asked.

"Yep, all set for noon over on the beach by their place. And I saw that the construction is right now only happening on the outer parking lot at the Moorea Rai, so it shouldn't interfere with our picnic," Keely said, stealing a quick glance back at Meg and Cal, who stood behind her. She noted their eyes moving away from her and to Jess - who luckily had her back turned at that point as she searched for shorts, socks, shirt, and non-flip-flop footwear for her planned bike ride and grocery run to town. "Oh, and it'll be just Tiare and Linc...Mrs. Martinez has some errands to take care of in town, but she'll send them with lunches, and home-baked cookies for all of us too!" Keely added.

"OK, too bad Rai won't be able to join us, but oh well. Anyway," Jess continued, as she filled her water bottle from one of the large plastic ones they had sitting next to the fridge, "it's 9:30 now and I'm going to pick up my rental bike from the hotel in a few minutes. The grocery store at the end of Cook's Bay is only about three miles away. So, I have plenty of time to ride there and pick up our lunch stuff and still be back in time to change and head over with you to meet the Martinez kids before noon. I hope I'll be able to fit all the stuff I buy in my backpack! Meanwhile, the three of you should work on your projects while I'm gone. And nobody leaves this room, please, until I get back. I won't be gone more than an hour and 15 minutes, tops."

"Sure, Jess," said Meg, and her brother and sister nodded as well.

"See you all soon!" Jess had put on some light blue jean shorts, a t-shirt and her sneakers for the ride into town. She closed the door behind her and walked across to the hotel to pick up the bike.

As soon as Jess was out of sight, Meg and Cal shot several questions to Keely at once – mostly about the plans they'd made the previous day.

"So, tell us what happened!"

"Was Tiare and Linc's mom nice?"

"Did she have any problems with our plans for lunch?"

"She was very nice...but she won't be with us, as I told Jess," answered Keely. "So, we move forward with the plan. I just hope that Linc and Tiare have gotten the tools we need to get that box out of the hole in the rocks!"

"Yeah, me too," said Cal.

Jess returned just after 11 am, looking a bit disheveled and sweaty after her ride. "I pushed the pedaling pretty hard," said the nanny. "It was hot, but hardly any hills, and mostly it was the humidity that got to me. I'm glad I did it though, it was an interesting ride, around Cook's Bay and along both sides of the lagoon shore. Almost no traffic either. I took some time to browse around the store. And the hotel didn't charge me to rent the bike, either, 'cause of your dad's business here. Bonus!"

As she removed the items from her backpack onto the table, the kids saw sandwiches wrapped in paper, a couple bags of unfamiliar chips - from what looked like France based on the wording, and plastic plates and forks. Jess also pulled out a large container of salad with a separate small container of dressing. All of it but the utensils and chips went into the fridge with their drinks and some fruit that would make up the rest of their picnic lunch.

"I decided on ham and cheese for you guys, cheese only for me, plus salad and chips. How's everybody's homework going?" she asked.

Keely answered first. "Pretty good. I'm working on my idea to cover a major social issue here, which is my French class assignment. I'm thinking maybe I'll talk about the problems with reefs being destroyed by that crown starfish and harsh chemical sunscreen some people wear. But I'm still not quite sure," replied Keely.

"Ha-ha! That's something I was going to include in a story in the college newspaper. Maybe we can work on it together, Keel?"

"Sure!" answered the pre-teen, with a surprised grin.

Meg weighed in on her project as well. "I've got to come up with a *colloquialism*. I'm planning to cover "*Aita pea pea*" and how it became popular, but I need some written and video examples of how it's used. Maybe I'll ask Tiare's mom or somebody at the hotel about it and can video them saying the word in a sentence? I should have asked JP when we were on our trip...or how about your new friend, Jess...what's his name? The guy working at the restaurant?"

Jess blushed a bit. "Ohhhh, you mean Julian? Yeah, I'm sure he could help you out. Let's ask him if we see him at dinner. Oh, your dad left a note that he'd like to eat with us at the restaurant tonight. He expects this to be his busiest day yet on the project, but he's also hoping to take a bike ride for exercise in the middle. I think we'll head over around 7:30 or 8. You guys might want to eat a bit more at lunch, but it's up to you, just be aware of the long wait 'til dinnertime."

Keely nodded. "We'll be fine, swim suits on underneath, plus we have lots of snacks and fruit that we brought and also bought here on the island - in case we get super hungry between lunch and dinner."

Forty minutes later, after she'd showered and changed clothes from her ride, Jess began to gather all of the lunch elements together. "Are you all ready to go? It's pretty sunny and hot again today, so you better put on sunscreen now before we leave."

Soon, they were back on the path to the lagoon, each wearing shorts, flip-flops, and hats. Megan brought her dad's video camera and case along, thinking she might be able to film some shots and sounds of the beach and maybe someone saying "*Aitapeapea*," too.

"Hey, you could always ask Mrs. Martinez, she was born here on Moorea," suggested Jess. "But, oh yeah, I forgot she won't be there at lunch today. That really is a bit disappointing...I was kind of looking forward to talking some more with her. Oh well, I'm sure we'll still have fun."

They noticed that the beach was more crowded than the same time the prior day, and Meg had a theory why. "These are all the people who missed swimming and sunbathing because of the storm yesterday, I bet."

Jess nodded. "Good point, Meg. It's definitely a hotter day today, with only a few clouds to cool things off. Not much breeze, either."

When they had walked to the midpoint of the marae walls, they saw Tiare and Linc waving at them, both carrying small bags. Tiare also had an extra, larger beach bag hanging from her left shoulder.

"Hey!" Keely shouted as they waved back at their two friends, then quickly joined them in front of their hotel.

"Hi Linc and Tiare! All ready for our lunch picnic?" asked Jess. "Looks like you brought LOTS of stuff, do you want to set it down?"

"Oh, yes, hi Jess, thanks for inviting us, and no big deal about all the stuff. We have sandwiches and fruit and drinks. And my mom sent along some cookies that my aunt made."

"Yay, more local goodies!" Cal exclaimed.

Tiare laughed. "Yeah, our Moorean family sure loves to eat sweets! I wonder if it's 'cause of the French and other explorers who came here, or do you think they already had 'sweet tooths' in their ancient society?"

Meg threw up her hands. "Who knows, but if those cookies are anywhere close to as good as those Firi Firi doughnuts you shared with us yesterday, I may never go home!"

The six of them walked with their bags to a cooler section of the beach, under a large tree, spread out their blankets, pulled out the various food items, and sat down to eat. As each munched through their lunches, Jess casually asked about Tiare's mom not being able to join them.

"Oh yeah, she's having this big meeting tonight, and I think she needed to get some papers ready or something."

"What's the meeting about?" asked Keely.

"Well, I'm not sure of all of it, but it has to do with this hotel and a builder who wants to buy it and tear it down. You know all that construction out front? That's just the first part - but their plan is to replace all the buildings with a huge new resort. My mom and some of her family are against it, but other members of her family are for it - mostly her cousin, one of my aunt's sons. I guess he has a job with the developer, actually. Anyway, he's trying to get everyone in the family to agree to sell our land, which," she pointed and extended her arms from the far east end of the beach, then to the road, and then across the marae towards the edge of the Montcalm, "is all of this, and it has all been owned by my mom's family for hundreds and hundreds of years."

"Wow, Tiare, are they going to pay you lots of money for the land?" Cal asked their new friend.

"Yeah, I guess, but my mom and her other sisters and some cousins aren't happy about destroying this whole property - and especially the marae, which is sacred, you know, to her family and the people who once lived here. They want to do a less, umm, destructive kind of fix-up of the hotel. But the developer is offering so much money that there might be no way to keep it from happening. That's why - you may have noticed - my mom (and my dad too) aren't very happy right now. In fact, this whole trip so far. Too bad - it could have been a nice vacation for all of us."

"Really sorry to hear that, Tiare," said Jess. "I'm amazed that anyone could just destroy an ancient site like the marae...isn't there some historical society or rules or something that they have to get approval from first?"

"Yes, my dad says the planning department, or whatever it's called, is more interested in the money they'd make from the new resort - and one of its main members is a friend of my uncle's. He says that there are dozens of marae around Moorea, and we can't afford to keep this one, I guess, given what he calls its 'prize...I mean prime tourist location' (she rolled her eyes) on the water here."

They all sat and thought about Tiare's comments while they continued eating their lunches. Suddenly, Keely remembered their "mission." She turned to her new friend.

"Hey, Tiare, can you come show me your hotel's restroom? I really need to go - after all this fruit juice and water I've been drinking today."

Glancing at her nanny, Keely asked, "Is that OK, Jess?"

"Sure, I guess so. If it's OK with Tiare."

"Yes, for sure!" the younger girl answered, and then, "Oh! I just realized I forgot to bring those cookies we were talking about. Let's just go to our room and grab them from the fridge, Keely, while you go to the bathroom there. I have a key. We can be quick."

In three seconds, the two girls were up and gone, Tiare carrying her backpack. "Back soon!" said Keely as she and her new friend from Colorado walked hurriedly out of sight.

Chapter 41

A tough extrication, and Keely's in the doghouse

As they moved into the trees around the corner from where they'd been sitting, Keely asked Tiare urgently, "Where are the tools?"

"Right in our room," she replied. "They were too bulky to put all of 'em here in my bag. But don't worry, we'll have more space once I get rid of our towels and lunch leftovers. Plus, we just need to get the tools over to the marae and our hiding spot, get the box out of the hole, then we can take them back to our room when we're finished."

"All right.... I guess that will work."

They drew near the door to the Martinezes' hotel room. As Tiare turned the key in the lock, they stopped for a second, listening. She grasped the doorknob, then opened the door, both relieved that - even though they didn't expect it - nobody was inside.

"Hey, where's your dad?" said Keely.

"He's with my mom now, but earlier he was checking out some of the properties around here. He works as a construction manager but also invests in houses and stuff at home, so he wanted to look at a few places for sale here on Moorea."

"Got it," Keely said. "I'm going to use your bathroom. You get the tools, then we have to run super-fast over to the marae and get the box free."

"No prob, they're hidden in my suitcase in the closet," answered Tiare. When Keely had finished, she came out to see that Tiare was carrying a much bulkier-looking bag than she'd had earlier at lunch.

"Do you need help carrying it?"

"No, this is fine, it's just that the screwdrivers and the small pry bar thing in here (and a hammer too) are awkward, you know?"

"Right...well, OK, let's go!" And off they went to the marae.

The two American girls hurried through the trees and began to emerge into the clearing. Once there, they saw their destination: the little tower of rocks on the edge of the marae, easier to locate than they'd thought the previous day. Keely stuck out her hand to stop Tiare, taking a moment to gaze all around them. "Do you see anybody?"

"Nope, we're good!" answered Tiare, as she did the same.

Reaching the hiding place, Keely knelt down and quickly began removing the rocks they had stacked in front of the hole holding the box. Next, she reached in to Tiare's bag to grab the pry bar, and used it to loosen the first stone from the top of the hole.

"Aaaargh, it won't budge! Let me try the bottom side of the hole," and she wedged the long flat bar into a crevice near where two rocks met, pushing hard and moving the tool sideways and back and forth. The rocks shifted just a little.

"Keep trying!" urged Tiare, as Keely continued her efforts to pry the blockage loose.

"I don't want to damage the tower, though. That would be really bad! Hand me the hammer, quick!" said Keely, and Tiare obliged. The older girl took the nail-remover side of the hammer and pulled on the inside of the hole, trying to find a way to carefully wedge the rocks that way. They moved just a bit more, which gave Keely more hope.

"If I could just get inside this little crevice between this rock here," pointing to one large stone and a smaller one below it, "and this other one, I think I could get them both out."

"How about the screwdriver, that would fit there, wouldn't it?" suggested Tiare.

Keely grabbed the tool from her friend and wedged it carefully, further and further, into the gap between the rocks. They began to slide, just a little.

"Hey, while I do this, you take the pry bar and pull from the inside, but be careful!" Keely told Tiare.

They both went back to work, one pulling from the inside, the other separating the rocks from outside.

Keely yelled as she felt the rocks breaking free. "It's MOVING, it's coming ou...!" Suddenly two large rocks blocking the hole came out all at once and the two girls grunted as they fell backwards onto hard ground with the momentum. Luckily, neither rock fell on their legs, and the tower structure was still intact.

"Whew, that was HARD," said Keely, wiping drips of sweat from her face. She peered into the hole and groped around a bit. "I see the box, but it's tough to reach from the angle I have to use to get my arm in there. Did you bring a flashlight by any chance? It's quite far down there now, I think it broke free and fell lower in the hole when we pulled out the stones."

"No flashlight, sorry," said Tiare with a frown.

Keely looked closely at her friend, smaller and thinner than her, with skinnier arms, but almost as long. "Can you reach to the bottom and grab the box?" She pointed from the top of the hole into the darkness below. "I can just barely see it. It's sitting on sort of a ledge, lucky for us!"

"Let me try," said Tiare, and she reached into the hole as far as her arm could go. She could just touch the box with her fingers, but it was sitting mostly flat on the ledge, and she couldn't feel anything to grab on its surface. "Shoot, it's sitting there but I can't grasp it, you know? WAIT! I have an idea!"

She picked up the pry bar again and inserted it gingerly into the hole in the rock tower. Maneuvering it to one side then down towards the box, she felt and heard it scratching the metal top, then the edges. "I just need to get it a BIT to this side...." Tiare grunted with the exertion, sweat pouring from her hair onto her t-shirt, which was now covered in dust.

Keely suddenly glanced at her watch. "Oh wow, it's been 25 minutes since we left everybody at the beach. We are seriously running out of time!"

"I've almost, almost, GOT IT! Just a sec while I use the pry bar to tilt the box upward.... THERE!"

"You got it???"

"Almost!" Tiare carefully pulled the pry bar back out of the hole. "This is the tough part...I need to reach back in and grab the edges to pull it out, but I can't knock it back over or we'll have to start again!"

"OK, go for it!" said Keely.

Tiare carefully reached over the top and inside of the hole and down toward the box, ever so slowly as to not knock it over from where it was tilted up on its side. "OK, I can feel it...moving my hand to the side, grabbing both edges now...."

Keely watched breathlessly as Tiare slowly begin to lift the box up toward the hole at the top, still not very wide at all, but *maybe*, she thought, *it would be wide enough?*

"Almost got it...aaaahhh this is heavy, it's hurting my wrist!" cried Tiare.

"I'll help!" Keely said and she carefully reached in to where Tiare's hand was bent like a claw holding the box vertically, only a few inches from the opening. She found just enough space for both their arms to fit through, and extended her fingers to the other side from where Tiare had a tenuous grip on one side of the box. Feeling the metal, she moved her hands and fingers across its surface...THERE. She grasped the opposite edge of the box.

"I've got the other side. Now we just need to pull it up together. I'll take the bottom edge, you take the top, slowly...and careful not to cut yourself on this sharp lava rock!"

Tiare began lifting her arm and wrist, clutching one edge of the heavy box, toward the hole at the top edge of the hiding place. Meanwhile Keely was stretched as far as she could reach to stabilize the bottom of the box and slowly raise her own arm and hand to match Tiare's movement above.

"I see it, we've almost got it!" said Tiare.

Sure enough, the top edge she was grasping was now visible at the edge of the hole. With renewed vigor, Tiare kept pulling upward and Keely pushed and held it from the bottom, at the same time. "We just have to get it braced up in the opening to get it out of there!" said Keely.

Tiare pulled the box a few inches out of the hole and began to balance the edge on the rocks there. Keely, at the same time, was also lifting it (at a very unnatural and painful angle to her arm).

"OK, I can't move my side up any further, because the box and your arm are blocking it. Can you move it to the side of the hole a little, and hold it for a sec while I pull my arm through the small space on the other side?" Keely asked Tiare.

"I'll try!" Tiare felt the fatigue shooting through her wrist as she swung the back edge of the box a bit toward the rear of the hole.

Now in a better position, Keely was encouraged. "OK, I'm going to slowly let go, do you have the box balanced a little more on the edge?"

"Yeppp...just barely!" said Tiare, under some real strain now. Carefully removing her hand, Keely saw the box start slipping, just a bit, back into the hole.

"HOLD IT!" she yelled and then in one quick movement, pulled her hand and arm out of its prior place under the box and grabbed right in between Tiare's wrist with her own. "GOT IT!" she cried.

They began pulling the box up and out. But it wouldn't budge.

"It's at the wrong angle!" said Keely. "Let's tilt it up a little the other way, and try to pull it straight out!"

She used a second hand to pull on one side while Tiare held the other edge. Slowly, they were able to get the edge facing straight out. Then with all four of their hands, they pulled it directly out until about half of the box was sitting on the rock ledge above the hole.

"Keep pulling.... now lift it straight out!" said Keely. With less than an inch to spare on either side, the box finally came free. They had done it!

"Wow, this is pretty heavy!" said Tiare, as the two of them carefully moved the box to the edge of the rock tower, then onto the ground.

"And it sure was hard to get outta there!" said Keely.

"I know!" agreed Tiare. "And look at us!" She pointed to her arms, shirt, shorts, noting all the dirt and dust coating them. "You've covered too!" She grinned at Keely's face and arms and clothing, all coated in reddish brown dust from the ancient volcanic rocks.

"We've gotta get this out of here and back to your room fast!" said Keely, with a frown. "We've been gone more than half an hour, and we're filthy! Jess is going to wonder what's up!"

The two girls carefully maneuvered the box into Tiare's over-sized beach bag. Then they placed the tools on top and around it. It would barely close, *but no time to worry about that!* thought the young Coloradan. Together, they began walking back toward the Martinez family's room at the Moorea Ra'i, careful not to trip as they lugged the bag between them all the way.

They had just come out of the trees and were heading to the building and #17's door when Keely gasped. "Ohmigosh! There's Jess and everybody, right by the pool!"

"Did they see us?!" Tiare asked frantically, as they moved as quickly as possible with the heavy and increasingly awkward load between them. Soon, they were in front of the door to Tiare's room.

"I don't think so, but we gotta hurry. Jess will be asking lots of questions!"

Tiare pulled out her key, turned it in the lock, and quickly moved inside holding one handle of the bag while Keely held the other.

"OK, bring it over here!" Tiare said, moving toward her closet.

When they reached the closet door, they carefully set the bag on the floor. Tiare opened her beach bag, removed the tools, set them aside, then said "Help me put the box in my suitcase."

Keely grabbed one end while her friend took the other. It didn't seem quite so heavy now. They lowered the metal container into the medium-sized travel bag, then Tiare set the tools on top, and closed its lid. Shutting the closet door, she said, "Now we have to get all this dust off of us and get back pronto to everybody else!"

As they hurried around the edge of the building near the pool area, Keely and Tiare waved to the others, much cleaner after a rapid wipe-off in the bathroom with the towels there, but still sweaty after their difficult undertaking to remove and bring back the mysterious box.

"Where were you!?" said Jess.

"Oh, yeah, sorry, we went exploring around a bit, checked out the gift box...I mean gift shop, here at the hotel, you know, by the front desk," said Keely, making up a story on the fly, and feeling really bad at the same time about lying to Jess.

"Well, I was a little worried, and this is two days in a row, Keel," Jess said. She looked a bit sad and, Keely thought, probably disappointed with her.

"I'm really sorry, Jess," said Tiare. "It's all my fault. I didn't think it would take that long, but we started looking at some of the clothes and souvenirs there and lost track of the time. But we have the cookies!" she said, holding up a full bag of her aunt's concoctions.

"Well, I guess it's ok...Tiare, are guests allowed in the pool?"

"Ummm, sure! That's no problem, and a good idea! Let's hang out for a while, cool off and stuff," she said, looking sideways at Keely.

As Keely returned her gaze, she saw Jess raising her eyebrows a bit. *She knows something's up!* thought Keely. Meanwhile, Meg, Cal, and Linc were jumping around in the pool.

Keely smiled at Jess a bit ruefully. "Yeah, swimming sounds like a great idea, but first I need to rinse off a bit, all this running around and shopping stuff is making me really sweaty!"

Chapter 42

Dinner with Dad & future plans

"Boy, that was a long day. But so worth it!" said Alex, sighing as he took off his dress slacks and replaced them with a pair of shorts for dinner.

Cal was across the room, playing video games while he sat on the bed. "What happened?" he asked his dad.

"We got most of our system testing done. Now it's just some wrap-up details, probably one more run-through and a test transmission tomorrow night. Once we check it out in Seattle, then confirm the details back here on Thursday morning, this new software will be ready to roll for the Montcalm! But...I didn't have any time for a bike ride today, unfortunately. Maybe tomorrow, we'll see."

"Great job, Dad! Does that mean you'll have time to hang out with us for sure on Thursday?"

"It's looking that way...fingers crossed that things keep working as smoothly as they have. Hey, what did you guys do today?"

His son quickly shared the day's summary. "We had lunch with the Martinez kids over by their hotel. Went swimming there too, in their pool. It was OK, but the pool wasn't heated, so it actually seemed a little colder than the ocean! Then we came back here."

"Hmmm, were their parents there with you?"

"No, but Jess was...she came with us to lunch, and she even rode her bike to town to get stuff for our meal!"

I really need to give Jess more free time and some special reward for the fantastic job she's doing, thought Alex. "That was really nice of her, I hope all five of you thanked Jess for everything," he said.

"Oh yeah, we did, for sure." Cal's voice dropped to a whisper. "Hey Dad, maybe we can buy something really nice for Jess before we go home. Maybe a present from all of us, you know, a souvenir or something? A cool gift she'll really like and can take back home to remember this place."

"That is a great idea, Cal," his dad whispered back. "Let's find some time later to talk to your sisters and start getting some thoughts together on the perfect thank you present, just for Jess!"

The girls sat outside Jess's room on chairs pulled from the front patio. As they wrote in their notebooks their dad peeked out the door.

"How are you two doing?"

"Good, Dad!" said Meg.

Keely thought for a moment. "Well, except I made Jess worry a little when I was gone exploring around the hotel next door for a while with Tiare today - she knew we were going after we finished lunch at the beach there, but we were gone longer than we had planned. I've already apologized to her, but I just wanted to let you know."

"I'm glad you told me, Keel. Integrity is what it's all about. People need to know they can depend on you to do what you say you will. Jess really has a tough job taking care of you guys and all the details each day. Plus, other kids too, today!"

Keely nodded and looked down. She felt a twinge of guilt about the secret she and the others shared - which was kinda frustrating since they still hadn't even opened the box yet. Tiare had whispered to Keely before they'd left her hotel that she'd try to bring the box over tomorrow. But things could change...

She jerked her head back up when her dad asked, "Where's Jess?"

"Oh, she just left while you were changing, went over to the business center to make a few more copies, I think. Should be back in a few minutes."

"Well, then this is a good time to share an idea your brother suggested just now."

They all gathered around their father. "Let's find a nice present, a really nice one, for Jess, to help her remember her time here on Moorea, and also to thank her for all the great things she does for all of us - you guys especially."

"That sounds perfect, Dad!" Meg said.

Keely agreed. "What were you thinking of getting her, maybe jewelry, or clothes, or artwork, food, or something like that?"

"Yeah...maybe a nice outfit, or a necklace or earrings or something made here. Something she'd really like - not too extravagant. You know Jess's style and size, right? How about we all go into town on Thursday, find a place that sells those sorts of things, and pick it out together?"

Keely quickly thought of another idea to make the plan work. "We'll tell Jess we're just picking up supplies while she takes the morning off."

"Yep, and also, I was thinking - if everything works out as I hope it does with our software project setup - that we could go explore that motu on Thursday. You know, the one we saw on our round-the-island trip our second day here. We could have lunch and then snorkel and swim near the restaurant out there? Jess can join us too, of course, if she wants."

"LOVE it, Dad, this will be cool, and I can't wait to go out to the motu...I remember its name - *Tiahura!*" said Keely. The other two Webster kids beamed with approval as well.

Just then, Jess walked toward them from the hotel lobby area. "Hi Alex, how was your day at work? Is the project going as planned?" she asked.

"Better than expected, Jess. Great, in fact. Bernie and his team here and our staff back in Seattle are working well together. Lots of questions back and forth, but everybody's well-prepared, collaborating closely, sharing ideas to make things even easier than we'd expected. Also, our testing has gone faster than planned, and I was telling Cal and the others, I'm hopeful that we'll be all but done by Thursday morning."

As Jess nodded, Alex added, "Fingers crossed they are, because I thought we could go have some fun together that day - head back to the motu we visited last Saturday, and have lunch, explore the waters around there with our snorkel gear.

"Also...I heard from Keely that she freaked you out a bit today. We talked about the importance of staying in touch. Sorry about any worry she caused, and as you already know, she's sorry too." Jess looked a bit embarrassed, so Alex quickly changed topics.

"Actually, I almost forgot, I was already planning to suggest you take Thursday morning or all that day off. Hang out here at the Montcalm, or rent a bike, maybe, or you can just take a few hours to do whatever you want. I'm going to run into town that morning and try to pick up some Moorea gifts for my team members and family before I forget, and the kids will come with me. We should be back by noon or so, then we'll head down to the motu and check out its offshore restaurant and the beach club. Maybe we can swim and snorkel for a couple of hours. It'll be a blast. What do you think...want to explore on your own, or come with us?"

"Sounds fun, thanks, Alex for the time off...and thanks for talking with Keely. She's fine...she knows that I just want to make sure she's safe, and she - and Tiare also - did apologize to me afterward. So, I'm cool, but I'm glad she told you," Jess added, glancing at Keely with a smile - and receiving a grin in return.

"Well, that's settled then! Let's go eat!" Alex said, and they all headed out the door to dinner.

Each of them had something a bit different at the Montcalm's restaurant this meal, including a bowl of poisson cru shared between Jess, Alex, and Keely, who liked her first try of the tasty local concoction. They shared a huge, family-style salad with fresh local greens, dressing, and some very tasty, sweet little tomatoes. Of course, there was plenty of bread and butter plus a large bowl filled with star fruit, mango, and pineapple slices.

Dessert was a banana-coconut pudding with macadamia nuts and little, colorful macarons, made on the island by a French baker who supplied the Montcalm as well as his own shop. While the others finished eating, Jess excused herself to use the restroom. As she walked towards the other end of the restaurant, she saw Julian busily coordinating a large group table's order. The Tahitian smiled widely and held up a finger as if to say "Wait a moment," so Jess walked over towards his workstation.

A moment later, Julian came over to greet her. "*Ia ora 'oe i teie po...* Good evening, Jessica!" he said, translating to help her understand.

"Same to you, Julian. How was your day off?"

"Oh, it was fine, but I was asked to come in early today to help out. That's ok, because now I will have more free time on Thursday. How have your last couple of days been? Any more fun adventures to talk about?"

"Well, the kids have definitely been keeping me busy, and we all got caught in that rainstorm yesterday, but we're fine."

"You are getting more tanned skin, I notice," said Julian.

Jess laughed, "I KNOW, no matter how much sunscreen I put on too. The sun is intense here, and so is the rain, as we all saw!"

"Yes, it is!" He lowered his voice. "I have to go back to work now. Do you have time this week – maybe Thursday – to see more of the island?"

Jess smiled. "Well, I just found out I've got Thursday off, but I don't want to miss the family's trip to the motu and the cafe there that afternoon. You know, Tiahura, on the other side of the island, past Opunohu Bay?"

Julian smiled widely. "Of course, I know Motu Tiahura and the restaurant there, it's called "*Haari*," which means "coconut" in Tahitian. What if you could go there AND spend time with me exploring the coast?"

Jess leaned forward as Julian continued. "I have a small motorboat, and we could launch it right near there, then cruise down along the west side of the island for a while. We can come back to meet your 'family' at the dock across from the restaurant, by the parking lot. The boat has plenty of room for six. I can ferry us all across and you and I can swim and snorkel with the Websters there too. It will be fun!"

"That sounds like a blast, Julian!" Jess said. "Let me clear it with Alex, and I'll let you know. But first, I have to - you know - go..." she said, looking towards the restroom door.

Julian chuckled, waving toward the restroom. "Of course! I will look for your sign *oui* or no when you return to your table. Actually, what we say in Tahitian is "*E*" for "yes" or "*aita*" for "no." And if it's "*E*" - which I hope very much it is, I will pick you up after breakfast on Thursday!"

Jess grinned. "I already knew SOME of those words, but thanks for reminding me anyway!"

After Jess came back from the restroom, the kids were finishing up their meals. Keely yawned, looking especially sleepy - *probably from her busy day and all of the running around with Tiare*, thought the nanny.

Turning to their dad, Jess mentioned Julian's invitation. "My new friend Julian, the Assistant Manager here at the restaurant, invited me to cruise around the island with him on his boat. We'd be leaving from here in the morning, and he offered to transport all of us out to the motu later. He has plenty of room and then, I can come back here with all of you after we eat lunch and snorkel and stuff. Does all, or some of, that sound OK?"

"Of course, Jess, and that'll be great if Julian can take us out there - and join us for lunch too," he answered, grinning. He looked over toward the far table where Julian was staring at Jess.

Jess raised the thumb and forefinger on her left hand, and used the forefinger of the other to make a crude "E" shape, holding it up for him to see.

Julian clapped his hands and smiled, responding with two thumbs up.

Jess blushed, smiled, waved, and nodded her head enthusiastically.

The plans for Thursday were set. *So much for needing to speak the language to communicate!*

Chapter 43

Pareo production and a Tama'ara'a invite

November 30, Wednesday

The Websters' sixth day in their island paradise dawned, not surprisingly, warm and, for the second morning so far on the trip, a little wet too. But the rain that fell during the night had mostly stopped, shortly before everyone arose to the cacophony of the newly-energetic, and apparently freshly moistened lungs of the nearby roosters.

"If that isn't a reason not to keep chickens around the house, I don't know what is!" growled Keely, rubbing her eyes and bellowing a huge yawn, which soon spread to her sister, also rising out of a deep slumber. She and Meg had gone over all the events of yesterday last night while lying in bed, before she fell asleep quickly after - not surprising because Keely was completely exhausted by the exertion and mental stress of their "box-removal" mission.

"So, do you think we'll be able to get the box open today?" Meg asked her older sister, careful to keep her voice down so Jess wouldn't hear them from the next room.

"Gosh, I hope so, but how we're going to get together with the other kids to do it, I have no idea. If it keeps raining, we might be stuck doing stuff inside. But I hope not," Keely answered. Just then, Cal knocked on their door.

Opening it, the girls saw that he was alone in the bungalow's main room. "Dad left for breakfast a while ago," Cal whispered, "so the coast is clear. Now, can you tell me Keely, how did you and Tiare do with the box, did you have any trouble getting it loose from the rocks yesterday?"

Keely explained what she had already told Meg, whispering, "The big question is how to get it open, 'cause the lid might be rusty, or stuck, and also where - and when - will we try?"

"And *what do we need* to do it?" Meg whispered back. "I guess if Tiare and Linc still have their uncle's tools in their room, they could help us. But it might require some serious creativity *and* strength to get it open!"

Keely perched her chin on her knuckles. She thought aloud, speaking quietly. "Hmmmm...how to get it open, without breaking it - even if we could do that - it's solid metal, maybe brass, even if it is super tarnished or rusted. I hope it doesn't break!"

"What about if we try to 'pick' the lock on it, like in detective shows on TV?" proposed Cal.

Meg glared at her brother. "I'm not an expert lock-picker, and neither is Keely. Are you?" she asked haughtily.

"No, guess not," he answered, somewhat crestfallen. "But then how are we gonna get it open?"

"Shhhh! That's going to have to wait," said Keely. "Plus, we don't even know if we'll be able to *talk* to Tiare and Linc today. And right now, we have to go to breakfast."

Just as she said this, Jess came out of her room, looking ready to roll. "I'm hungry! Are you guys? How did you sleep?"

"Fiiiiiinnnne," said Keely, stretching out her response along with her arms, in a reflection of the fatigue she still felt from yesterday's secret box-removal operation. And her arm was pretty sore too. *So is my wrist!* she realized to herself. *No doubt Tiare's hurting too!*

The others nodded, looking a little bit more awake than Keely. Jess grinned and put her arms around the shoulders of all three Websters. "Let's go and add some new dishes to your lists of marvelous meals on Moorea!"

After a pleasant, uneventful breakfast, the clock read 9 am. Jess shared the idea she'd mentioned to the kids' dad the day prior. "How about we try an activity here at the resort? I saw a list of classes on the bulletin board, might be fun to try one. See? Over in the lobby, on the wall."

They followed Jess into the reception area, and near the concierge desk was a single sheet of paper with some nice tropical graphics. "Check this out - '*Pareo-Making for beginners*' - that sounds really awesome, and we could each have our own custom-made souvenir of our trip when we're done!" Jess exclaimed.

"That could be pretty cool," said Keely, and Meg and Cal nodded, and shrugged, respectively.

Jess saw the boy's lackluster response.

"What, Cal, do you think you won't like the class?"

"Nahh, it's just, I'm not that great at art, so I don't know how good of a pareo I could make, and plus, I don't even know how I'd wear it."

"Hey, that's what they teach you in the class, and I bet they would show you how to put it on too," encouraged Jess. She put her arm around his shoulders.

"OK, I guess," the almost ten-year-old replied, though he still didn't look that thrilled by the prospect.

Jess asked the concierge for the sign-up sheet and was handed a small notebook turned to a page with a list of attendees for that day's class. She filled in their names and room number, noting that there was a cost of CFP1500 (about $15) for each pareo made. "Would you like me to charge this to your room, Ms. Webster?"

"Ummm, sure," answered Jess, adding, "My last name is Forrester, but just Jess is fine," as she smiled at the young Tahitian.

Jess remembered a thought she'd had. "Oh, what if we need to add anyone to that list, can we do that?"

"Oui/Yes. The maximum number of students for this class is ten. Right now, we only have seven, which should be fine."

"Sure, I was actually thinking more about just making a second pareo myself, so that's no problem, or *"aita pea pea,"* she grinned.

The concierge laughed. "You are really good at our language!" she replied, as Jess took out a 2,000 CFP note from her personal funds that she'd had Alex exchange for her. "I want to pay separately for this one," she said, as the concierge got up to ask the front desk attendant to provide her change.

As the woman handed a 500 CFP bill back to Jess, Keely poked her lightly in the ribs, and whispered, "What if we made an extra one for Dad and gave it to him as a present?"

"That's a fantastic idea, Keely!" Jess replied.

"Totally!" said Meg.

Cal brightened considerably. "He'll be so surprised. Cool!"

Turning to the concierge, Jess said "Please make that six pareos, or maybe that's pareo for plural too? Sorry, six total, with five paid for from our room tab."

Back in the room, everyone flopped on their beds, letting their ample breakfasts digest a bit. Keely jumped up a few minutes later and leaned into Jess's room. "Hey Jess, you know I need to swim every day, right, like I promised my swim coach? Can we go down to the beach in the afternoon, maybe?"

"Sure, that should be fine...how about when we get done with the class and eat lunch. Sometime around 1 or 1:30."

"OK, cool. Thanks, and thanks again for being so understanding after I was so late yesterday."

"No prob, Keely," Jess replied with a wink of her left eye.

A few minutes before 11 am, they all left to meet down near the pool, in the same clearing where Jess had shared the glass of wine with Julian a few nights before. It was a large, grassy area, and several portable tables were already set up, with materials for their projects on each, and what looked like seven separate pareo preparation stations supplied and ready.

Two women were already there, standing near one of the tables. The Websters and Jess headed over and took a quick look at the paint, fabrics, and other materials. Just then, they heard a women's voice coming from behind them. "*Ia Orana* and *Maeva* to our pareo-making class, everyone!" and recognizing its source, but thoroughly surprised, Keely whirled around.

"Mrs. Martinez!" she exclaimed.

"Hello!" chimed in Meg and Cal.

Jess also smiled in surprise. "Hi, Rai! I had no idea you'd be teaching this class!"

"Yes, I'm actually filling in for my sister, who would be here except she's away on business in Tahiti today. I have made many, many pareo in my life. So, I said I'd be happy to sub for her as teacher, and here I am!"

She turned to greet the rest of the students. "I guess we have some happy pareo-makers today! By the way, as you may have just heard, my name is Raiana, but you can call me Rai."

Glancing behind her, Cal asked her, "Are Tiare and Cal here too?"

"Yes, they are getting some more supplies from the car, they'll be here in a minute."

Meg, Cal and Keely looked at each other. Cal couldn't help his jubilation that their friends would be taking part too. "Score!" he cried.

As if on cue, Tiare and Linc came around the corner from the parking lot, bearing two fairly large cardboard boxes.

"HEY!" Linc yelled at Cal with a grin. The two boys, with similar energy to what they had shown during their goofy joint dancing routine upon their arrival five days ago, slapped high-fives with each other. Tiare's response was more subdued, but she was still thrilled to see her friends, judging by the massive grin on her face.

While Jess officially 'checked in' with Rai, she shared their desire to decorate two extra pareo.

Keely and Meg took the opportunity to get an update from Tiare.

"Is the box safe - still?" asked Keely.

Meg added, "When and where do you think we can open it?"

Tiare nodded, then shrugged her shoulders. She whispered back. "Let's see if we can go swimming or something later, but I'm not sure how we can get away again..."

"Yeah, I am pretty sure I don't want to try," said Keely, explaining that she didn't relish getting in any more trouble with Jess.

Rai and the others present were finishing up the check-in process, so the girls broke their 'huddle' to pay attention. Rai outlined the session details, showing them the materials and fabric paints they'd be using to create designs and colors of their choice for their pareo (at this point she explained to the students that the plural was the same in Tahitian, usually spelled with a 'u' at the end, so, *pareu*).

"Your creations can be made from pre-dyed or plain fabric, and once complete they'll dry quickly, no matter what colors or designs you add to them. We also have stencils here of several of our native or local symbols, plants, and flowers, like the breadfruit, or "*Maiore*," and of course, the *Tiare*," she explained, beaming at her daughter, which brought a blush from the eleven-year-old. "And we have extras, so if you make a mistake, don't worry too much. Just take your time. I'll show you how to do it and be right here to help each of you."

Rai glanced at each of her 'pupils' in turn. "So, everybody ready to get started? Oh, almost forgot!" She removed a couple of plastic film-covered wood plates from one of the boxes Tiare and Linc had carried from the car. "Here are some snacks, you are all welcome to try any of them. Some fresh and dried fruit, cheese, crackers, and when everyone's tried these, I've also brought some local cookies made right here on the island by my sister."

Supplies and snacks at hand, each student began work on their pareo painting. What an adventure it turned out to be!

Keely and Meg watched closely at first as Rai demonstrated how to align the stencils with tiny pins to apply the fabric paints inside them onto the fabric. She then showed how they could add flourishes of color elsewhere as desired, by carefully painting around the stenciled figures or using a reverse stencil to 'color wash' whole sections with a foam brush. Rai held several pre-made examples and varieties up for reference.

Keely was eager to get started, as was Meg. Soon, they were busy aligning their chosen stencils from among many firm paper options, positioning them over the roughly two-meter x two-meter fabrics in front of them on the tables. With no wind, it wasn't that difficult to be precise, and with heavy canvas 'scrap' fabric covering each table, no paint could leak through to the surface below, or onto the ground.

After about ten minutes, Keely announced that both she and Meg were now ready to create their color schemes. Gazing over towards Jess and Cal, she saw that Jess had two sheets of fabric in front of her. She was also helping Cal pick and align his stencils for his shirt.

Rai walked over to see how they were doing. "Looks good. Now you take the paint, squeeze and brush a little on the section where you want more coverage of a certain paint here, then use large or small brushes to apply the paint to the fabric elsewhere. Like this." She demonstrated on Keely's sample pad next to her pareo.

Looking at the example that Rai had brought, as well as the traditionally-designed pareo she had worn to teach the course, Keely decided to include shades of blue and red in a simple, small, repeating flower pattern, all on a light blue background. Meg, meanwhile had opted for a tie-dye look, and Rai explained to her how that effect could be achieved via rolling the fabric into knots then, at strategic points, dipping it into different colored paint buckets. She gave Meg four small plastic pails to use for her chosen colors of pink, yellow, and blue, with a little green too. Cal chose big hibiscus flowers for his pattern, using teal and blue, on a gray fabric, to match his favorite football team's colors.

They both completed their own pareo(s) (they couldn't keep from referring to them using the English plural 's') around 25 minutes later.

"That was surprisingly easy!" said Meg. She and her sister walked over to see how Jess was doing.

"Wow, that's amazing, Jess! Both of yours are beautiful, but they are so different!"

"Thanks, Keel. Yeah, this first one is for me, it's got some of my favorite colors (blue, purple, and green) in a simple floral design." Pointing to the other one she was painting, which had another "take" on Tahitian traditional themes in its look, she nodded to Rai, who had just joined them at the table. "This one was suggested to me by Rai - it combines symbols of the ocean, the fish, and *mana* - the life force above all - on one garment, all in blue, pale yellow, and red on the gray pareo. It's a gift for a friend I met here...ummm...because he's been so nice and he's taking me/us out on his boat, and, you know," she said with a blush.

Keely, for once, didn't tease her about it. But she did smile at her. "That's really cool, Jess. Beautiful idea!"

Meg added her own praise. "Yeah, I really like it too, Jess!"

Keely continued, "Would you be able to help us make the one for Dad? We'd really like to put a pareo together that matches what he likes, you know, his favorite colors and in a nice, simple design?"

"Sure, but I tell you what, let's talk to the expert," Jess said. She gently called to Rai at the next table, where she was helping another 'pareo-maker' with her painting, "Rai, we need your input on how to create a very special pareo."

"I'm happy to help, just a moment and I'll come over."

In a minute, Rai was by their side, again expressing her admiration of Jess's surprising pareo-design expertise. "I really like how both turned out." She pointed at the one for Julian. "Your friend will love how the three themes are so nicely combined on one garment. The way you've got them arranged and spaced on the fabric will also work well when he ties it around his waist. We usually show some of the ways pareo can be tied/adapted to various shapes and sizes at the end of the class, or you can learn a lot just in attending a "*Tama'ara'a*", it's sort of like what the Hawaiians call a "luau," she explained.

Meg beamed at a recollection of her own. "Really? That sounds like fun. We saw where they hold them on our trip around the island last weekend. At Kiki Village?"

"Oh, you mean "Ti'i Village?" smiled Rai, continuing, "Yes, they have very nice shows there, maybe a little touristy but very interesting anyway, and I know they have good food because I am friends with (or related to) some of the people who prepare the dishes for them. And who participate in the dances, too. I was raised learning how to dance in our traditional manner, called "*Tamurei*" or "*Ori Tahiti*."

"Is that like *hula*?" asked Jess.

"Well, there are some similarities, but really, they are quite different. Our dances are much more...ummm...active than the typical hula movements, at least most of them, but some versions, like what we call "*aparima*" are slower, you know, more umm," making eye contact with Jess, "sensual in nature."

Rai stopped, and changed topics. "Hey, I came over here to help you with something special, right?"

"Yes, we're trying to make a really cool pareo that my dad will like, kind of masculine, simple, with some really interesting design that reminds him of our time in Moorea - and if we're lucky, one he'll actually WEAR!" laughed Keely.

Rai clapped her hands together, smiling at the trio from Tacoma. "Perfect, what a great idea, and I have some really good suggestions for you." She quickly walked to the main table, and came back to them bearing a couple of new stencils. "Here are some designs he might like, I know he swims a lot, right?" she asked.

"Yes, Dad loves to swim in the ocean, listen to the whales, see the turtles and the fish and other sea life," said Meg.

"Then here is what I recommend," Rai answered, setting down two stencils. Suddenly, Tiare and Cal dashed to the main table, and picked up two others. Their mother smiled when they returned.

"Place these stencils alternately in threes along the edge of the garment. You can use this nice flower one to put in the center, then pick your colors to express his favorites. So, you will have the ocean, the whale, and the turtle symbols and also a flower in the center. Then maybe some 'swirls' like this stencil shape around the edges, or mountains, like Linc has brought - here. What are your dad's favorite colors?" she continued.

"I think he really likes blue, green, and maybe black or gray, like Jess has made for her friend's pareo. Can we do those on a white pareo, maybe?" Keely inquired.

"Sure, or what about just picking a white pareo, stenciling the figures in navy blue, green and then blue again along each border, then painting the center symbol in either blue or black too?" suggested Jess.

"That is a great, idea, Jess! You really have a true eye for pareo fashion!" grinned Rai.

"And I think you should have green mountains along the side, he loves climbing mountains on his bike, especially!" added Cal.

With the design settled, Rai helped Cal finish his "*Seahawk*" themed pareo. Meanwhile, Meg and Keely, with some assistance from Jess, used their newfound skills to create their special gift garment for Alex.

With their completed designs hanging to dry on lines hung up between trees at the edge of the lawn, Jess and the kids used the hose and portable sink provided to clean stray paint off their hands.

Rai saw they were done, and motioned them to follow her to a corner of the work area. "Earlier, when we were talking about the Tama'ara'a, dancing and all, I thought of something fun. But I wanted to make sure you had time to complete your projects. Now, I'd like to invite you to experience some of our Moorean culture for yourselves.

"You all have been so nice to Tiare, Linc and our family, how would you like to join us at a special party, our own tama'ara'a, over at the Moorea Ra'i, where we're staying, tomorrow night?"

"That would be awesome!" said Keely, and Meg and Cal bobbed their heads in agreement.

"What a generous offer," said Jess, "I'll need to check with Alex, but I'm pretty sure he's planning to finish up his project by tomorrow morning. We'll be going to Motu Tiahura for lunch and snorkeling, but should be back before evening. I'll let you know for sure by tonight, OK?"

"Of course, Jess, that's fine, no pressure. It will be just our extended family and all of you if you can come. We'll start the festivities around 6 pm, right before sunset. But we'll be preparing food and tables all day, roasting meat in the traditional pit and everything else, sort of like you may have seen in Hawaii, but with quite a few dishes that you may not have tried yet."

Rai then capped off the class by demonstrating several of the most popular ways (of hundreds, she said) to tie a pareo, no matter what gender was wearing it. They all tried with their own, now fully dried creations, and laughed at some of the results. But by the time the class ended at the bottom of the hour, each student was able to figure out at least a few basic ways to tie their own garments.

"Do we have to wear these to the party tomorrow night?" Cal whispered in Rai's ear, with more than a little worry on his face. What he didn't tell her was that he was wondering how he'd be able to hide his underwear if he didn't get his own pareo correctly tied around his waist.

"Only if you want to, Cal, or you can just wear shorts or pants and any shirt, it's just family, very casual. Just be festive!" Rai whispered back with a wide smile.

Linc leaned over and quietly spoke to his friend. "Have you ever heard of those Scottish kilts? You know, just like with them, you don't wear any underwear with pareos either!"

Cal turned crimson. "NO WAY!" he retorted. He decided then and there that his wearing of a pareo would be limited indeed!

Linc started laughing so hard he almost fell down, then his sister joined him. Seeing quizzical looks on the faces of the other Websters and Jess, Tiare explained more about their under-pareo options. "You can wear a t-shirt or underwear or even a swim suit underneath your pareo if you want, I can show you how to do it," Tiare said to her new female friends in the group.

Rai turned to Cal and put a reassuring hand on his shoulder. "If you decide to wear yours tomorrow, you can definitely hide your underwear beneath your pareo. I can help you tie it if you like, then just put on some fun shirt on top and you'll be comfortable - and look great too!"

Cal uttered a huge sigh of relief. "I am really, really glad to hear that!"

Chapter 44

The waiting game continues...

The Websters helped their new friends pack up and carry the boxes of paint and other materials back to their car. Jess noticed that the small hatchback Rai drove wasn't as new as a typical rental car, and it had an unfamiliar nameplate.

"I've never seen a car like this," she mentioned to Rai as she was closing the rear door.

"Yeah, it's my sister's. She's letting me borrow it for things like this class and some meetings we have to go to - most are at her house anyway, while we're here. It's the one we brought over on the ferry, a French car, imported here like most of the automobiles in the islands. I think they get a lower price advantage due to French Polynesia, you know, being sort of an extended part of France."

"That's great to have a car, makes it convenient when you have to go somewhere, visit the sights and shop and stuff," replied Jess. She noticed Rai frowning.

"Uh huh, I just wish we only had the concerns of tourists, instead of potentially our family losing...Anyway, yeah, it is convenient for sure."

Turning to face the New Zealander/Tacoman, Rai changed the topic. "SO glad you all might be able to make it to the feast tomorrow, Jess. Let me know if you can, maybe by calling our hotel, or either way, just show up if it works with your family's schedule. We'll have plenty of food and everything either way. Oh, and thanks again for taking the class."

"Will do, I'm sure we can swing it, but will confirm. And thank *you*, Rai, this class was incredibly interesting - and fun too. And look at the beautiful works of art we all were able to produce! Such a gift of knowledge and creativity - and now we have something stunning to wear - or give to others. Alex will love his from the kids, and...my friend will like his too, I'm sure." She looked down at the simple, striking design she'd created for Julian's pareo.

Rai nodded her approval, then her lip trembled a bit, as she replied. "You did very well, Jess, especially for a first-timer. Me, this...all this island art and culture...was a big part of my life once...and I just really like to share it with people - when I can..." Her voice trailed off, mist welling in her eyes.

"OK!" Rai lifted her head and forced herself to shift focus to Linc and Tiare, now circled around and in apparently deep conversation with the Webster kids. "Tiare, Linc, time to head home!"

"Hey, Mom?" Tiare asked, as she strode up to the car, "Could we hang out with these guys for a while then walk back via the beach to our hotel and meet you there? You can park the car and we'll help you unload it when we get back."

"Umm," glancing at the Websters' nanny, Rai inquired, "Is that OK with you, Jess?"

"Oh yeah, no problem, I mean *aitapeapea*, Rai. That will be fine. I'll make sure they all get back there in the next hour if that's OK?"

Rai nodded. "*Maururu roa*! Except I forgot, I will actually be dropping the boxes back at my sister's house now - but I'm sure one of her kids - my nephews or nieces - will be there to help me unload it. It's not too much to handle since the tables stay here at the hotel anyway. They will pick them up and store them inside after we leave. I should be back at our room at our hotel by..." She paused to glance at her watch, "around 3:30 at the latest."

"Great, that will give Keely time to get in her daily swim - she's required to per her agreement with her swim coach back home. How about if I take all the kids to the beach at the same time?" Jess asked.

Rai was thrilled with this idea.

Keely, Tiare, and the other three kids? Not so much, but they didn't dare share their concerns of missing the chance to sneak away and open the secret box!

Each smiled, instead. "Sure!"

"Great idea, Jess!"

"Thanks, Mom!"

Time for Plan B, Keely thought...

After their mother left, Tiare and Linc hung around in the bungalow while the Webster kids and Jess changed into their swimsuits in their respective bathrooms. "I really like these rooms!" said Tiare, noting the mix of the clean lines and modern conveniences along with the authentic Polynesian decor around the main and connecting rooms, including local crafts and prints on the walls and the bright colored, floral bedspreads - even the beds themselves, constructed from what looked like local wood.

Keely, having changed in the bathroom, walked in, followed shortly by her sister. "Yeah, it's nice and peaceful around here for sure," the oldest Webster sibling responded. She lowered her voice. "Now, how are we going to get that box open? And when?"

"Bigger question...do we still have the tools?" whispered Meg.

"Yes, they are still in the closet with the box," answered Tiare. "But we have to find a way - and a private place where we have enough time - to get it open."

"Simple," said Meg. "How about you two just open it - if you can - using the tools you've got. We'll hang out down by the beach after walking you part-way back to your hotel. We'll wait there to see what you find."

"NO," insisted Keely. "We have to do this together. Either we find some way to open it today, or what, we wait until tomorrow? Maybe before the party?" She looked at Tiare. "How about right before the party starts, but soon after we get there?"

"I think Keely's right," said Tiare. "This is a team and we've worked so hard to get the box out already, let's not stop now. I vote for tomorrow. We wait until we all are together at the tama'ara'a.

"Maybe we can find an excuse to go back to your room again to pick something up?" said Keely.

Tiare shook her head. "Naah, we tried that once, didn't we? It might look suspicious."

"Well, then," countered Meg, "We will just have to find a way to NOT make it suspicious. We need to see what's in that box. And we need to do it soon!"

Chapter 45

Alex hits the road & "constructive criticism" of a kind

November 30, Wednesday, Montcalm office

Alex was thrilled, and now more than "cautiously" optimistic that the work project that had brought them all to Moorea would be completed not just on-time, but ahead of schedule. They had finished several tests and transmissions thus far, and the team in Seattle was actively reviewing the results with the Montcalm's regional tech team as well as Bernie Tetuanui, the local manager of the LodgeSoft software implementation.

Glancing at his watch, he saw it was already 11:45 am, local time. Alex decided he could get a couple more emails sent to other clients in the US, then just before noon stood up and walked over to Bernie's desk.

"Hey Bern, I'm going to take that quick ride I mentioned yesterday, is it still OK to borrow a bicycle from the hotel?"

"Absolutely, Alex, and have fun...we are way ahead of schedule. Your team in Seattle says all the tests and transmissions have worked out. I'm completing some internal documents and instructions for our team now, and I expect to be finished up with those by end of day today at the latest."

"OK, then, I'm off to the Activities Center to check out a bike. Thought I'd ride to town, then back down and around the property next door and the marae grounds. Haven't ever seen them up-close from the shore-side of the island. I'll see you around 1:30," Alex said.

Grinning, Bernie gave a thumbs-up and said, "Take your time and enjoy the ride, we'll be ready when you get back!"

Soon Alex was on one of the resort's simple, cruiser-style, one-speed bicycles, still wearing his casual work clothes. His backpack (containing his ice and water-filled Contigo bottle, but with plenty of room to spare) was over both shoulders, with one of the Montcalm's loaner bike helmets strapped on his head. As he rolled out of the resort parking lot and turned onto the main road, he made his way eastward, passing through the village of Pihaena after only a few minutes of pedaling.

He kept up a reasonably brisk speed, spinning the bike along the west shore of Cook's Bay and past the hamlet of Paopao and around the inlet's other side. He decided not to stop and continued toward his destination: Maharepa, just beyond the other side of Cook's Bay toward the airport.

Reaching the head of the bay and then passing a few small resorts and one larger one, but mostly with the road to himself - he was acutely aware of all the interesting sights and sounds along the route. There was almost no traffic, with cars passing him only occasionally, and usually quite slowly, given the very low speed limit. He smiled and waved as he passed a jogger - *looked like a tourist*, he thought - trotting (and sweating) in the mid-day heat on the other side of the road.

Hearing a loud cry, Alex lifted his head from his deep thoughts and saw a large bird "greeting" him from the gently swaying trees above. Smiling upward at the notice he'd received, he wondered how he'd never thought of coming to Moorea before. Quickly, he reminded himself that in his post-college life of only just over 20 years, he, and the kids too on some trips, had been very fortunate to travel to many interesting or scenic destinations. Though French Polynesia could certainly be classified as both, it was far away from his usual client software installation locales.

So glad I got this opportunity - and that we could work out bringing the kids and Jess along - with the holidays making the timing that much easier, he thought. Just then, the bird which had called to him took flight. He saw it had sort of a headdress, almost a "mullet" in gray on top, but beautiful stripes of red on its underside. *What had its message been?*

Continuing on, Alex occasionally glimpsed the shoreline as he crossed by a few stores and commercial buildings. After almost 30 minutes of steady, solid pedaling averaging around 12-15 miles - or about 20-24 kilometers - per hour, on mostly level land (but including one fairly steep hill), he saw signs of Maharepa town ahead, with more houses and cars appearing as he now cruised alongside or within view of the lagoon, small waves lapping onto the shallow beachfront just to his left in one section.

Here, he noticed the grass and brush grew right up to the water's edge. Out in the lagoon, a lone paddle boarder stroked slowly toward the entrance to Cook's Bay, near the reef line that surrounded the island.

Alex liked to make every ride a *workout*, and he had strapped on his Garmin GPS device to the bike's handlebars to measure his distance and speed. The tall American checked its display and pressed the "stop" button as he turned off the road into a small parking lot in front of some stores. *Time for some quick shopping*, he mused, *and maybe some big gulps of water too, before I ride back. It's HOT around here!*

The tiny supermarket he entered was much cooler inside, with a big fan blowing from its back door. Alex walked gratefully past the refrigerated coolers there and spied his first 'quarry', a six-pack of Hinano beer and some more sparkling juice for the kids. Everyone liked this latter beverage as a thirst-quencher. He grabbed a sandwich, a lime and lemons to take back, and a small bag of locally-produced cookies.

After he paid for his purchases, Alex walked outside, hot as it was, and sat down at a small table. A tree's generous branches provided at least some respite from the burning sun. *I'm starting to get a little more used to this heat and humidity*, he thought as he munched on the sliced ham and cheese sandwich and drank from his ice-cold water bottle.

Soon, it was time for the cookies, which he downed in short order. He disposed of all his food wrappers in a garbage can outside the market and walked over to an adjacent shop displaying local crafts and clothing in its windows. Glancing at his watch, Alex told himself, *you have five minutes to look - then you have to get started back to the Montcalm.*

Admiring some dresses to one side of the store, Alex reached up to feel the fabric, surprised at its softness and marveling at the intricate designs of many colors. Moving on to the glass counter along the other side of the store, a large selection of Tahitian Pearls and other jewelry beckoned. As he peered down at the natural stones - primarily from distant islands of French Polynesia, he vaguely recalled reading in some guidebook or website - he saw all sorts of mounting options were offered, including necklaces, bracelets, amulets, and rings.

The sales clerk greeted him with a friendly welcome, "Bonjour!"

Alex replied, "Hello!" She quickly ascertained his nationality, then asked, "May I show you some pearls?" in heavily accented English.

Alex shook his head - *no need in my life for pearls of this quality for sure*, he thought. At least not now. *Who would I give them to?*

With his self-imposed counter-shopping time limit of five minutes now reached, Alex smiled at the clerk and said "*Maururu,*" then "I'll be back!" He walked outside to his bike, leaned against the store's exterior wall. Quickly mounting it, he hopped on one leg while starting the pedals with the other foot, then cycled back out of the parking lot towards the resort. His backpack was, of course, with the liquid containers he'd purchased added in, a little heavier than before, but he didn't mind. *Time for a little weight workout on the legs,* he thought.

Soon, Alex had retraced his earlier route in reverse and was almost all the way back through Pihaena when he saw a familiar sign reading, "*Juice Factory - Free Samples.*" Checking his watch, he saw it was still forty minutes before he was expected back at the office by the project team,

"Why not?" Familiar now from tasting some of the factory's delicious samples with the Montcalm team during their earlier lunch outing - he decided to purchase a few more of the local beverages.

It was only one minute more of pedaling through tall, fragrant shrubs until he reached the factory. Sliding off his bike, he smiled and asked the smiling host which options were available to taste.

Reaching under the counter, the attendant, different than the woman who had helped the resort group earlier in the week, placed five tiny paper cups in a row. He began pouring from one bottle to another down the line. "You try these...ananas, pineapple, first?" he asked.

Alex took small sips of each. He mentally catalogued his favorites.

After he was finished, the server asked "Which you like best?"

Alex pointed to #4 in the line of mini-cups.

"Aahh - that is hibiscus and lemon, great choice!"

"Do you make all these juice varieties right here?" Alex asked, just to confirm his understanding from the first visit.

The host nodded, and replied in excellent English. "Yes, we do, and we supply to much of French Polynesia right from our factory." Then, pausing for a moment, he said "We make adult drinks, with alcohol in them, too. Would you like to try?"

Alex thought a moment, then realized, as he was both riding a bike and also had to go back to work for what could be a busy end to the last full day of the project, he'd better pass. "No thank you, I wish I could, but you know, I have already tried a few of them two days ago. May I have a bottle of the sparkling fruit wine and also one bottle each of the Hibiscus Lemon and also the Passion fruit, Mango and Guava juices?"

As the host gathered Alex's purchases and he paid for them in cash, he realized his backpack was getting very full. *But I only have a mile or two back to the resort*, he thought. *I can certainly handle a load like this for that long!*

It was true - Alex had a habit of bicycling out to get groceries on trips with the family - when he had a bike to ride - or even by himself, and he often loaded the bags or backpacks he had up to or beyond their capacity, resulting in some fairly heavy weights and hard pedaling at times, especially when steep hills were involved. He liked the double duty of exercise and completing errands, but sometimes he was under time constraints to do it.

This time there was no such concern, as it was only five minutes after 1:00 pm, so he found no reason to rush. His pedaling soon brought him near the entrance to the resort next door to the Montcalm, with the rakish sign "*Moorea Ru'i*" out front. He heard the noise of heavy equipment, signaling the construction work now underway there. Alex wondered for a moment if he should even bother riding down the path and possibly running into further delays. Out of curiosity, he decided to check out more of the property while he had a bit of time.

Rolling up towards the hotel lobby, which he thought was "quaint" but, as he'd heard, appeared in need of a renovation. He passed slowly down the circular driveway and then along the small lane traveling past the buildings that housed the hotel's guest rooms. He had just reached the beach, a couple hundred meters down the path, and had begun his return toward the entrance/exit point when he saw a worker sitting in the cab of a large bulldozer. The machine stood, engine off, near the side of the large marae, the multiple-stone-ringed monument they had briefly explored while walking on the beach.

Next to the bulldozer stood a tall, Tahitian-looking man with short sleeves which revealed some impressive arm tattoos. He seemed to be arguing with a slim woman whose back was to Alex as he rode up alongside. Suddenly, as he passed the two people, he glanced back at what sounded like some very angry conversation. Just then he recognized one of them. *That's Rai Martinez! I wonder why she's so upset?*

He judged quickly, with some relief, that their new acquaintance from Moorea, and now Colorado, was in no imminent danger - as she had already walked away from the guy and the bulldozer and toward the hotel buildings. Alex pedaled onward, as he didn't want to be late back to the office, but he shook his head inside his helmet. *Wow,* he thought, *she seemed really upset, and so did that guy. And that wasn't her husband, so who was he? Something weird's going on over there.*

Chapter 46

Rai's breakdown

Around the time their dad was finishing his ride on this pleasant Wednesday afternoon, the "pareo-creators" were hiding their custom-designed frocks in their bungalow rooms as a surprise to be shared with Alex and Julian later. They then headed down the path and over to the beach in front of the Moorea Ra'i.

A slight breeze had arisen, and Jess was relieved. "Just when you think it's too hot, that wind picks up and keeps it manageable, you know?" she said to Keely and Tiare as they walked side-by-side across the beach toward the latter's hotel.

"Yeah, I'm starting to get used to it," answered Tiare. "It gets pretty hot in Denver, but this is a different kind of heat. Much more humid. And knowing that the beach and the warm water and all the tropical fish and stuff are right there when you want to jump in and join them is pretty nice. Not something you can do in Colorado!"

Meg, trailing behind the others, picked up a rock and threw it as far as she could into the lagoon. She was loving the trip thus far, but missed Tacoma and her friends just a bit. She knew soccer would be there for her when she got back - well maybe not until spring, but her teammates would welcome her home. Meanwhile, she thought about the secret box. Now that they had agreed not to try to open it until tomorrow, her imagination was running wild on what they might find inside. *Maybe we could shake it around a little to see what's in there,* she thought. She glanced at her brother and Linc, walking and talking together. *Luckily, they haven't - yet - blabbed our secret!*

Cal and Linc were actually trading stories on things typically important to almost 9–10-year-olds, like video games, sports, and action figures. Cal was also sharing some key facts he'd recently learned about Moorea with his new friend. "How do you like it here, Linc? Especially since your family is from here, er your mom at least."

"It's pretty, and it's hot, but I really like it. There's lots of things to explore, you know? - as long as I avoid stepping on sea urchins, that is!"

"Yeah, that was scary!" Cal agreed. "How long is your family going to be here?"

"I think another week or a little more. We were supposed to leave earlier...but with the family fighting and the hotel and stuff, I guess we might be staying a bit longer..."

"What's going on?"

"Um, I don't know really, just that argument about selling the land or not, and my mom is all upset about the big plans to tear down part of our hotel. And hey, I heard they are even talking about putting a parking lot on part of the marae where we found the box!"

"Wow, I hope not, it's a cool place."

"Yep, that's how my mom feels, and I guess most of our family too. But I'm not sure what's gonna happen."

Jess looked back to see the boys chatting, and glanced at Meg, deep in thought and tossing stones. She slowed down to allow Meg to catch up as they approached the beach in front of the Moorea Ra'i.

"Hey kiddo! How are you feeling today?"

"Great, just thinking a little about home. I'm really happy I'm here, but I do miss my friends and mom and grandma and grandpa."

"Sure you do, that's understandable," said Jess.

"What about you, enjoying the trip?" Meg knew their nanny had been very busy... like almost the whole time since they'd arrived.

"Oh yeah, this place is awesome," said Jess. "It's not always a picnic, just because of my duties with you guys and that crazy day when nothing would work with the computers and copies I was trying to make. But if that's the worst of my problems then I've gotta be thrilled, you know? It's so different here - a little hot - especially compared to what I'm used to at home in New Zealand of course - but I love the landscape, the water, the mountains, the culture, and even the language differences."

"I bet you love something else too," Meg said with a wink. "And his name is Julian, right?"

Jess turned bright red, even in the sunshine. "Oh...well, I wouldn't say *love*, but he is pretty cool. We'll see...I'm not really looking for a boyfriend, but we *are* going out on his boat tomorrow and I'm looking forward to seeing the island from the water, and...seeing him too, yeah."

Meg went on. "Well, tomorrow's gonna be a fun day for sure, with you going out on the boat, and us meeting you down by the motu so we can snorkel and have lunch, and then we'll all be at the 'tamarawah' or whatever it's called, tomorrow night. Whew!"

"Yeah, I need to remember to tell your dad about the invitation, and I wrote it down to check the pronunciation. It's called a *"Tama'ara'a."*

Jess looked around as they arrived at the nearby resort's beachfront.

"OK, here we are, let's find a good place to set down our blanket while you guys...hey, wait, isn't that Mrs. Martinez, Rai, right over there?" she said, pointing across the property, near the marae.

They glanced up and saw Rai walking toward her hotel room.

"Yeah, it is," said Meg, as the others followed her gaze.

"Let's run over to the room and see if she still needs help, I didn't expect her to be here," suggested Tiare.

Jess agreed. "Sure, I'll stay here to hold down the fort while you all help Mrs. Martinez. I want to do a little writing on postcards for my friends and family so I can send them before we leave. Don't be long and come back right after you finish unloading the boxes for Tiare's mom," she said, looking at the three Websters and making eye contact with each.

"We will!" said Keely, and off the five of them dashed to the Martinez family's room.

When they reached the door to the hotel room, it was ajar, and Tiare led the way, quietly opening it and entering the room, followed by the others. "Mom?" she said, amid the troubling sound of crying inside.

"Is everything OK?" Tiare continued, as Linc came forward to join her in the room and the Webster kids lagged behind by the doorway.

Raiana turned around, her eyes rimmed in red. "Oh, yeah...I just had a bit of a quarrel with my cousin...it's nothing."

Her daughter was concerned. "Why, Mom? What was the argument about?"

Rai, clearly uncomfortable, was short in her reply. "I don't want to talk about it right now, OK?"

Tiare saw her cue to change the subject. "Sure, Mom.... Hey do you still need help with the boxes in your car?"

"No, thanks. I already brought them in here myself...I just was so mad I wanted to do something productive. You guys can go hang out at the beach...Is Jessica with you?"

"Yeah, Jess is back there saving us a place on the sand, and writing to people back home," answered Meg.

"Well," the Tahitian-American woman said with a strangely 'formal' tone, looking at Tiare and Linc, "if it's OK with Jessica, you two can join them back there. I need to lie down for a while. Maybe do a little thinking, and resting, just for a bit...." Her voice trailing off, Rai turned away.

Tiare, sensing her mom's very unusual, exceptionally high level of stress, stepped forward and wrapped her arms around her waist. Her brother followed her, while the Websters looked away, slightly embarrassed but feeling sad for the situation vexing Mrs. Martinez.

"Sorry about everything, Mom. We'll let you rest for a bit, and if Jess says it's any problem to hang out with the Websters there, we'll come back. Otherwise, I think we'll be down at the beach for a couple hours. Love you!"

With this, Tiare's mom seemed to recover a bit of her normal self. She forced a smile at her two children, then nodded to the Webster kids. "Love you too. Have fun you guys, and make sure you listen to whatever Jess says while you're at the beach!"

Chapter 47

Plans come together

When Alex returned to the Websters' bungalow from the hotel office on Wednesday, it was a bit later than usual for the project thus far. *Of course, that was a good thing*, he thought, because it signified that they had wrapped up virtually all the details for their software implementation with only a handful of last-minute checks and follow-up steps remaining, all scheduled for the next morning. Since Seattle was two hours ahead of Moorea, that would give ample time for LodgeSoft's HQ Implementation/technical team to figure out any issues before he and Bernie and the local Montcalm project staffers were due in the office. Hopefully, all would proceed as planned, leaving Alex time to do some quick shopping with the kids before they continued onward to their planned adventure at Motu Tiahura.

"Hi Alex!" Jess greeted him as she stepped up to the open door to the family's main room. "I was just over at the restaurant talking with Julian about our plans for tomorrow. He's all set to pick me up at 8:30, right after breakfast. How was your day?"

"Amazing...we're ahead of schedule as I had hoped, and with any luck, we'll have everything wrapped up by mid-morning at the latest. Then the kids and I will be clear for the rest of Thursday, to drive down and meet you and Julian for the trip to the motu. Did you tell him he was welcome to join us for lunch?"

"Yes, I did and he's excited. He's already planned a couple of stops for us on his boat before we meet you at the beach across from the motu and the restaurant. Oh, and speaking of plans..."

Keely, Meg and Cal popped out of the girls' room, where they had been wrapping their dad's special present. "Yeah, Dad, we've been invited to a "tamarando" by Linc's mom!" said Cal, excitedly, in the process mangling the Tahitian name - in a completely different way than any of the others had thus far - for the upcoming family fest.

"Actually, Jess finally looked it up and shared the spelling and pronunciation with us," said Meg, pulling a piece of paper out of her pocket, "T-a-m-a'-a-r-a'-a" which I think is 'Tom-ah-ara-a.'" Mrs. Martinez said it's kind of like a Hawaiian luau, but Tahitian (or Moorean here), and there will be lots of good food and music and dancing, but different than we've probably seen before."

Her older sister added a clarification. "Yeah, Dad, remember how in most of the luau shows we've seen, they often have the dancers and music from Tahiti and other Pacific islands as part of the program? Well, this will be ALL about Tahiti, or at least focused on the islands here in French Polynesia, and it's mostly Mrs. Martinez's family and friends putting it on. Should be REALLY cool!"

Alex looked at Jess. "Do you think we'll still have time to get there after our motu trip tomorrow?"

She nodded. "Oh sure, we don't have to arrive there - near the beach in front of the Martinezes' hotel - until 5:30. If we get back here to the bungalow by 4:00 or 4:30, that should give us plenty of time to shower, change, and walk over for the event."

"Well, that's exciting. I'm really glad because with all of my work stuff, I forgot to set up a visit to that 'Ti'i Village' place we saw on our round-the-island trip last weekend. Now we can enjoy an even more authentic - I bet - meal and show with Rai's local family sharing their traditions. "But," he continued, pausing for a moment, "you know that saying about **never** showing up empty-handed to a party. We'll have to figure out something to bring to thank them for including us in their celebration."

Just then Alex recalled his earlier sighting of their Tahitian-American friend during his ride. "Hey, by the way, how did you connect with Rai and the kids for the invitation? I thought maybe she might not really like us much based on our past interactions. I guess I read that wrong?"

Jess smiled, and explained. "Great question, and here's what happened, Alex. I registered the kids and me for a pareo-making class today here at the Montcalm. When the instructor showed up, we were all surprised to see it was Raiana! Turns out, she was 'subbing' for her sister. Apparently, she was raised to learn all the traditional Tahitian/Moorean dances and customs - AND she's an expert pareo-designer. So, she's a great cook, designer, and probably a fantastic dancer too!"

"Very cool!"

Keely spoke up. "Dad, there's something that is really upsetting Mrs. Martinez. We're not sure exactly, but we saw her crying this afternoon when we dropped by to help unload her car at their hotel."

"Yeah," chimed in Meg, "We thought she wouldn't be back there until later. We were going to swim, but then decided not to after all."

"AHA!" Alex responded. "I was wondering what was up! Well, I may have one clue toward this mystery..."

Before he could explain, Cal piped up with his own input: "I know what's wrong! It's about them selling the hotel and Linc's cousin or Mom's cousin Tawna...never mind, I can't remember how to pronounce his name. But that's who's making her upset. Linc says she's been fighting a lot with him over the construction and stuff."

His dad looked thoughtful. "Hmmmm...that makes a lot of sense, Cal. That's probably who I saw with her over by the marae on my way back to the office. But by the time I realized who it was and looked back from my bike, Rai had begun walking to their room anyway. Then, when I returned to the Montcalm office, I asked David, the GM and Bernie, my IT partner for the project, if they knew anything more about the situation. They said that it might have something to do with approvals for the hotel's new construction. Someone just filed a request in local court to block the work from being done - David says they got a judge in Papeete to agree to hold construction up for two weeks. I wonder if that's what she was arguing with that guy about?"

"Not sure," said Jess, "but maybe we'll find out more tomorrow. I'd imagine most of the family will be there at the feast and show. I just hope everything's OK. Rai was so thankful for the time the kids and I have spent with Tiare and Linc - plus signing up for her pareo-making class - that she really wanted us to join them tomorrow, and learn some more about local culture and cuisine with their family and friends."

"Sounds like a plan," Alex replied, "though I'd suggest we all just keep our thoughts on whatever this conflict is about to ourselves unless Rai brings up the situation. We don't want her to be even *more* uncomfortable, right?"

The others nodded, and Alex changed the subject to a brighter topic. "Right now, though, I'm super hungry. What do you say we grab some to-go snacks, salads and drinks from the cafe and head down to the beach for sunset?"

Chapter 48

Work wraps up

December 1, Thursday

Alex was up and out of bed early, then dressed in his tropical business casual office attire, maybe for the last time on the trip, he thought. *I really hope all worked out as planned with the final tests and transmissions. Would love to have a nearly full day to spend with the kids.* Then he remembered just how activity-packed this day would be indeed - they'd be going to the luau, or actually *tama-whatever,* he corrected himself, after returning from a half day at the motu. And shopping for Jess before that! *But none of that can come before we complete the software project that brought me here.*

He quickly went into the bathroom and brushed his teeth, then wet down and ran a comb through his hair. He'd showered the previous night, after Keely had convinced him to go for a short swim with her at sunset – in order to get a few more laps in to meet her daily practice "quota" as prescribed by her coach back home.

Walking back into their room, Alex smiled. A faint snoring was coming from Cal's side of the bed. *The kid's wiped out, hope I can sneak out of here without waking him up!* Grabbing his backpack, computer, and notes from the previous day's business conversations, he headed quietly outside and closed the door behind him. It was 7:00 am. Just enough time for an early breakfast - then a status update call with the Seattle team before he joined Bernie in the office for their final project meetings.

Yawning his way down the path to the restaurant, Alex realized he too was tired. *This place is so relaxing, you just want to sleep with the peacefulness, the heat, the humidity...I need COFFEE!"* Soon afterwards, he had a cup of good French Roast and some light cream, with his computer open on the table. Looking around the restaurant, Alex saw he was one of only two or three people eating at this hour. *All the better to get stuff done, get on that call, and finish up our work before 10!*

Alex wolfed down a light breakfast while reading the week's sales reports on his computer, then arose from the table. Gathering up everything into his backpack, he walked to the small "phone room" just inside the office door past the lobby, where he could speak privately with his teammates in Seattle.

"How's it going?" he asked Cynthia Nguyen when she answered his call.

"Great, in fact fantastic. Everything is working, all the tests turned out great. We should be able to wrap up this morning during our meeting in...about an hour. Also, Alex, I don't know what you did to 'school' him, but Bernie is really, really good...super organized and creative. He's already shared his training plan – adapted from one of our templates for the staff there. I'm betting this goes down as the smoothest *Chain-Linc* system implementation ever!"

"Great news indeed, Cyn. Glad we can finish up early because, frankly, it will be nice to have a couple days to actually relax and enjoy this place a little more before we board the plane home. Speaking of...guess what? We're going to this small islet off the coast - called a motu - for snorkeling and lunch at a small, but apparently very good restaurant there. Then we're going to the Tahitian version of a luau this evening!"

Cyn was impressed. "Sounds like a lotta fun, Alex."

"Yeah, it's called a *Tama*...umm, anyway, it's a huge family tradition here. We're going at the invitation of a couple and their kids staying at the resort next door who we ran into at the airport and a few times since. The mom is originally from Moorea, and they live in Denver now. It's going to be a blast I'm sure, a fun feast and dance party. I could use some simple excitement and a nice Mai Tai!"

"Well, sounds like you're going to have a lot more fun than I'll be having tonight, if I can get home before the snow hits, that is. They're forecasting 4-6 inches out where I live."

Alex knew her home was in the Cascade Mountain foothills east of Seattle, but still he was surprised at such significant snow falling in the area before Christmas.

"You're kidding! This is pretty early in the year for that much, but...I guess it's not *that* uncommon to have a snowstorm so soon after Thanksgiving...Well, I know we'll talk later, but tell you what, if the Montcalm agrees that we're all good to go this morning, I want you to be on your way home, Cyn, by early afternoon, OK? 2 pm at the latest. Go home and relax, get ahead of the snow there, and take the weekend off. That's what I plan to do!" Alex was insistent, and his colleague was very appreciative.

"Oh, that's awesome, Alex! I'll definitely aim to get out of here early. And I'll be thinking about tropical sands and calm waves instead of cold and wet snow falling on my face. You are lucky you are where you are!"

"I know I am, believe me. Thanks again, Cyn for your fantastic work. I'll be talking to you and the team, along with the Montcalm Moorea staff in... (he looked at his watch) ...about 40 minutes."

The time sped by as Alex dealt with a few emails related to other customers and projects. Nine o'clock rolled up quickly. As expected, the project wrap-up meeting went fast, and after all sides agreed that the software was working as hoped and the local Montcalm staff were ready to start their self-directed training, Alex patted Bernie on the back and said "Great job, Bern. One of the very best implementations we've ever done, and I've heard some nice compliments from Cyn Nguyen and our headquarters team on your preparation and leadership - and for your creative new training ideas too!"

"Thanks, Alex. Just make sure you tell my boss for me, OK?" he reminded the Seattle software sales head with a wry grin.

"Oh, you bet I will, I'm going to check in with David before I head out for the rest of the day. Going to Motu Tiahura with the kids and Jess and her friend for lunch and snorkeling. He has a boat and will take us over there. Then tonight we're heading over to the Moorea Ra'i for a *tama'*...party." Alex hesitated, trying again to remember the correct term, but Bernie filled in the gap in the word.

"Oh, a Tama'ara'a. Cool. You'll have a great time. Can't wait to see the pictures. And the food! look forward to hearing about it. You *will* check back in with us before you leave Saturday, right?"

Alex nodded. "Of course, I will...we need to have a celebratory *Hinano* or cocktail of some sort, right? I'm hoping we can all do it tomorrow, Friday, in the late afternoon? We'll be enjoying our last dinner here tomorrow night, then leaving Saturday morning for Papeete, then later on we'll be heading for home - by way of LA, same way we got here."

Alex picked up his bag, waved to the rest of the small office staff, and walked across the hall to the GM's office. Leaning in he saw that David Thomson was on the phone. Thomson, noticing Alex, said, "Hold one moment please," to the other party on the line, then cupped the phone to his hand. "Success?"

Alex nodded and gave a thumbs-up. "Success indeed. Bernie's awesome - really helpful to our team and a great project planner. You are ready to go for training. The software works and all the tests went well. Tomorrow afternoon, after we check for any last 'bugs,' we're going to celebrate, OK David?"

The Montcalm's GM replied "Absolutely, Alex!"

"Still OK to borrow the jeep?" Alex wanted to ask permission again, just to be certain, and also polite - and he got instant confirmation from Thomson.

"Of course, no problem." He waved his hand, urging Alex out the door. "Now get out of here and have fun on this beautiful island with your kids. Talk to you tomorrow!"

Chapter 49

Special gifts, and onward to the motu

Probably an hour or so earlier than Alex was wrapping up his morning in the Montcalm's offices, Keely and Meg had been finishing their breakfast when Julian stopped by to pick Jess up for their boat ride. *They make a cute couple*, Keely thought, dressed in shorts and shirts with their swim suits underneath and sporting flip flops on their feet and (Jess at least) heavily lathered with sunscreen. Wearing hats, of course, given they'd be out on the water under the hot sun much of the day.

The Webster girls waved goodbye as Julian's small truck left the parking lot. Then they turned to each other and grinned: "Shopping and surprise time!" said Meg.

Keely 'high-fived' her sister and they walked back to the bungalow. They needed to gather all the supplies for their own voyage to the motu - after their shopping trip with Dad along the way. Cal was already there, having finished his breakfast a few minutes earlier.

"Keel, I've got my fins, mask and snorkel, and my towel. What else do we need for this trip?" he asked his sister.

"I think that's pretty much it," she answered. "I'll throw some drinks and ice in the cooler right before we leave, and I've got the sunscreen for all of us too. Meg, make sure you've got all your gear, and don't forget to bring an extra big towel, we might need it out there. I'm going to bring this beach umbrella I found in the closet; it could really come in handy to shade us a bit more from the sun."

"Check. Now, we've got just over an hour before dad said he'd be back from the office. Let's talk about our plans tonight," Meg suggested.

"Right, good idea." Looking into her little brother's eyes, Keely cautioned him. "OK, Cal, you *must* keep this a secret, you know?"

"I know, I will, cross my heart," the nine-year old answered, albeit with a bit of a sour look on his face. "I've kept the secret so far, haven't I?" he countered.

"Yeah, you have, sorry for doubting you. I just feel kind of bad about having so many secrets at all. I sure will be glad when we can tell everyone what we found," Keely said.

"You mean, when we find out *what* we found, right?" clarified Meg, with more than a bit of sarcasm in her voice, as they still didn't even know what was in the box.

"And that's why we need a plan," Keely answered. "We have to get that box open tonight at the party. And we will have to be really careful and a little sneaky to do it!"

The three of them huddled up for a quick discussion on just how they'd make the plan happen, with the help of their friends at the Moorea Ra'i. With only a couple days left on the island, time was running out for them to solve the mystery.

The Webster kids were sitting outside the bungalow working on their projects for school, and updating their respective lists of foods and dishes they'd eaten on the trip, when their dad walked up the path from the hotel office just before 10 am. He had a big smile on his face.

"So, I guess the project worked out as you expected, huh Dad?" asked Meg.

"Yep, all done and wrapped up with a bow...or something like that. It went really well and I'm raring to go. Did you gather all our gear together for the motu trip?"

"It's in the bag!" Keely answered with a giggle.

"Then, saddle up and let's hit the road. Shopping for a gift for Jess first, then onward to Motu Tiahura!" proclaimed Alex, spotting and grabbing his wide straw hat that would come in especially handy out on the water and at the beach. He went into his and Cal's room to change his clothes and gather his supplies together for their adventure. A moment later, all loaded up with bags and backpacks, hats and sunscreen, the four of them walked quickly toward the Montcalm parking lot and their borrowed jeep. *Another big day for the Worldwide Websters, indeed.*

Alex explained to the kids that they'd be doing a bit of 'doubling back' to get their shopping done before returning the way they came, then further west to the dock where they'd 'set sail' for the Motu Tiahura. But it wasn't that far out of the way, and they had plenty of time.

They arrived in the town center of Maharepa less than fifteen minutes after leaving the Montcalm. Alex pulled into the same parking lot he had rolled into the day prior. This time, though, he was glad to be behind the wheel of a car, instead of pedaling on two of them. *Lots to do, and stuff to carry*, he thought.

As he and the kids exited the jeep, there was a sense of anticipation... for the rest of the very packed day of activities. But first things first: they needed to find something nice for Jess.

A few minutes later Alex heard the words every father or significant other or spouse loves to hear. "Oh, they're spectacular!" Given the location, one might have thought Keely's enthusiasm was directed at the scenery. But she was actually talking about the small, yet attractive Tahitian pearl earrings he held carefully in his hand. They had just walked into the same store Alex told them he'd visited while on his lunchtime bike outing the day before.

"Wow, Dad, that's a great choice!" Meg echoed her sister's praise of the small globe-shaped earrings selected by their father. "I had no idea you had such, uh, a sense of style."

"Yeah, Dad, they are really pretty," Cal said as he turned from where he'd also been examining the jewelry in the glass showcase.

"Do you think Jess will like them?" Alex asked his three children.

"Oh, absolutely!" Keely responded with vigor, then, winking at her sister she pointed to a rack of pareo across the store. They had similar colors and patterns - evocative of the island's tropical setting - as their own custom creations (and Jess's too.) Likely an excellent match to earrings like the ones their dad had selected, too.

Following Keely's gaze, Alex commented, "I didn't want us to go overboard. I hope Jess has a nice dress or something to wear with these."

His daughters exchanged knowing glances. *No problem there!*

The sales clerk walked towards them and nodded at the earrings in Alex's hand. "Great choice. These are made locally."

The colors of the earrings, shimmering in the light diffused through the shop's windows, seemed to change as he rotated the lustrous pearl pieces - almost steely-black but also faintly reflecting a rainbow of other hues - in his hand.

"Perfect present!" Meg declared, and the others enthusiastically agreed.

Alex handed the earrings to the clerk, and while she selected the appropriate box from beneath the counter, he turned to the kids.

"It's a little bit more than I wanted to spend, but I think it's a perfect way to tell Jess how much we appreciate her, you know?"

Keely agreed, adding "For sure, Dad, such a nice memory for her of our visit here, handmade, and um, naturally grown in the islands. Jess'll be amazed, and I know she likes pierced earrings best."

As she finished wrapping up their gift, the clerk smiled at the Websters. "You have made a very fine choice. A woman in the next village makes these herself, using pearls from islands here in French Polynesia. Here is a card with more information on their origin."

Picking up the card, Meg read to the rest, doing a surprisingly good job with the pronunciations: *"Tahitian black-lipped Pinctada Margaritifera oysters are where these pearls are grown, and specifically, these pearl earrings are from the 'Gambeeair' (Gambier) Islands of the 'Tooahmowtoo' (Tuamotu) archipelago. Mangareva is the island where they are finished and strung."*

"That's right!" said the clerk, adding with a wink, in very fine English, "Some say Tahitian pearls are a symbol of hope for the broken-hearted, or that they can help heal any ailment and ward off negative energy!"

"Well..." Keely stated, "I don't know if she's broken-hearted, but Jess definitely has been alone for a while now in terms of relationships. But who knows, maybe that changes after today?" She let out a giggle and beamed at her dad and siblings. Of course, she was alluding to Julian and his trip on the boat with their nanny, exploring around the island before meeting them all at the motu later that morning.

Moorea is a magical place, Alex thought. *You never know....*

His momentary reverie was interrupted by a request from Keely. She held up a small paperback book she'd found on a shelf. It was titled "**Getting to know French Polynesia.**"

"Can we buy this? It would help me with my school project, and I'm sure it would be useful for Cal and Meg's projects too."

"Sure, Keel. Cal, Meg, you two agree, everybody shares the book?"

"Fine with me, Dad," said Cal, and Meg nodded as well.

"Please add this to our total," he asked the clerk, handing her his credit card. He turned to the kids. "We'll have another chance to shop before we leave on Saturday. That's when we can pick up souvenirs and small gifts to share with family, friends, and for me, my colleagues at the office in Seattle."

Leaving the store with their purchases, Alex and the kids piled into the jeep, ready to make their way back toward the west side of the island and the rendezvous with Jess and Julian. But first, they decided to make a quick stop back at the bungalow and hide, in Alex and Cal's dresser, their special gift for Jess. Soon they were back on the highway heading west, to Motu Tiahura.

Chapter 50

Voyage beyond the reef

Winding their way along the road in their borrowed jeep, now traveling down one side of Opunohu Bay inland toward the soaring, jagged mountains, and then back around the other, the Websters came to the town of Papetoai within a few minutes. They passed the turnoff for the trail up to Magic Mountain viewpoint - the place they had visited during their round-the-island tour the previous Saturday.

For the first time since that tour, they were heading back to the far northwest side of the island. Soon they saw the beaches fronting the once-posh and now abandoned *Fou de Joie/Fun Club Moorea* resort. As they entered the parking lot facing the motus offshore at Tiahura Beach, they saw a few boats and small watercraft, including motored, sail, and human-powered versions traversing the lagoon. A couple small huts advertised boat, paddleboard, and snorkel gear rentals, and one had a sign for the restaurant - *Haare* - that they would be visiting on the motu.

Alex pulled the jeep into a parking space near the lot's edge, not far from the small dock and boat launch area. "I'm really glad I asked David Thomson to help us make reservations for the restaurant out there. He and the other staff members I talked to at the Montcalm say it is often sold out, and of course it's only open for lunch, and only five days a week anyway. And even better, we have our own transportation already arranged with Julian, and Jess!"

As if on cue, right when Keely, Meg, Cal, and their dad exited the borrowed vehicle, they glimpsed what Alex estimated was an 18-foot runabout coming through the small break in the reef offshore.

"Hey Dad, I see them!" said Meg.

"How do you know it's them?" said Cal, her brother just a bit skeptical because his middle sister was sometimes known for jumping to conclusions and false alarms.

"She's right, see Jess's hat? It's definitely them," said Keely.

Meg gave her brother "the look" for challenging her comment. Then she and the rest of the Websters waved in unison, and received an enthusiastic wave back from Jess. She was sitting next to Julian as he expertly piloted the boat, at very slow speed, toward one of the handful of mooring spots open at the end of the dock.

"Everybody, don't forget your backpacks. Cal, can you carry this bag, and Keely and Meg, can you grab the towels and snorkel gear?" Alex had his own backpack and their small cooler in one hand. With the other he reached in to grab his straw hat - one of the types sometimes called a "Tahitian" and commonly worn here and in many parts of the globe. While locking up the jeep, Alex also did a quick scan of each of his children to confirm they were appropriately attired for the coming time in the hot sun - including hats, sunglasses, water shoes and of course, lathered in their local reef-safe sunscreen. It was times like these when being a single parent became especially exacting and even more challenging than usual. *Can't forget the key things*, Alex thought.

"Hi everybody!" Jess cried warmly as Julian waved one hand, the other turning the steering wheel as he guided the boat alongside the dock, inflatable rubber fenders hanging on one side of its front, or bow, and rear (stern) to protect its hull from the rough wood surface.

As the others returned Jess's greeting, Alex reached out to take the stern mooring line Julian had coiled and tossed to him. He affixed it with a 'cleat hitch,' making a couple of loops and tying the line via a non-slip figure-8 pattern around a cleat on the dock, while Keely grabbed the other from Jess, who was kneeling on the bright white cushions in the 'cut-out' seating area at the bow of the boat.

Julian stopped the engine, climbed out, and took the forward line from Keely with a quick smile, holding the bow loosely near the dock. With no real waves, and only a light breeze, 'docking' in the lagoon was an easy exercise this day, probably on many days in Moorea.

"*Ia orana!*" said Julian, shaking Alex's hand and grinning at the Websters, all decked out in shorts, shirts, and hats for their adventure. Their Tahitian/French captain wore no shirt on his deeply tanned torso, but did sport some durable below-the-knee board shorts and sunglasses.

"Iaorana to you two too!" answered Keely, to the smiles of the others.

"Welcome aboard the *Mateata*! Are you ready for a fun boat ride?" asked their host.

"Yeah!" said Cal, with two thumbs up to accentuate his answer.

"Great, let's get you all and your gear into the boat. You won't need your fins where we'll be snorkeling in between the motus, but you will need your water shoes - but not until we get to the motu. As you can see, we have seating in the back - or what we call '*en poupe*,' for two of you..."

Cal giggled at the translation from French, and Keely rolled her eyes.

"It's not the same kind of 'poop,' she said semi-sarcastically to her brother. "It's French for 'rear' of course!"

Meg grinned widely while her dad and Jess chuckled quietly. Meanwhile, Julian continued his instructions, pointing to the boat's bow.

"I know you are all great swimmers, but we have life jackets at each seat for you to wear when we are out on the water. There is room for two to sit up front, so with Jess next to me...," grasping her hand and eliciting what Keely clearly observed was a blush from their nanny and new honorary Worldwide Websters family member, "there's plenty of spaces for everyone! Just find your favorite spot to sit and we'll take the boat out for a quick ride beyond the reef. If that is OK with you Mr. Webster, *E?*"

"Of course, that's an awesome idea!" answered Alex. "The good news, Julian, is we're all 'seasoned sailors' with lots of experience boating with the kids' grandparents, exploring the waters of Puget Sound where we live, plus trips to California, Hawaii, British Columbia, Canada, and a few other lakes and rivers too. By the way, our reservation at the restaurant out there isn't until 1 pm, so we've got plenty of time yet. Plus, I know everybody would love to see what Moorea looks like from the water on this side of the island!"

"'*Aita atu ai!*' Fantastique!" replied Julian, as he helped first Meg, then Keely onboard. Cal insisted on stepping over the side of the boat, or gunwale, on his own, and accomplished the feat surprisingly deftly, Alex noticed with pride.

With all his passengers save Alex in the boat, and with their bags and backpacks stored underneath the seats and near its stern, Julian started the engine. Then, crouching a bit to maintain balance, he stepped between Keely and Meg, who had grabbed the prime seats forward, and pulled in the mooring line Alex handed him.

Meanwhile, Jess had unfastened the rear line and quickly stepped back on the boat with it coiled in her hand. Alex followed, lightly pushing the dock away as stepped aboard. In a moment, with everyone seated, they were off, *putt-putting* slowly through the lagoon towards the break in the reef. They could see it in the distance, marked by a chain of continuous surf beyond it, several hundred yards from shore.

As they neared the outer reef line, they observed the ocean waves breaking in decent-sized 'sets' just past its border. *Not too large, about a 2–3-foot face*, thought Alex. He was never a real surfer himself but had learned the basics of the sport (as had Meg on one trip to Hawaii's Big Island) and had also done lots of body-boarding, mostly while at college in California. Alex had read that surfing was pretty big around the island, including even some major competitions. He turned to their captain.

"Julian, do you surf?"

The Tahitian nodded. "I have many times in the past, but not so much anymore. It's very popular around here, and in fact if we headed further down the coast on this west side, there are some big waves sometimes and a surf camp is located about two-thirds of the way toward the other end of the island from where we are, near the town of Haapiti. But it's also mostly only for experts, you know? There's no completely 'safe' or easy place to learn how to surf here because most of the waves break outside the lagoon and into the reef openings."

Jess piped in. "Yeah, we just went down near there this morning, and I can tell you it's spectacular to see the mountains from that side of the island. Such an unusual perspective from the water. Also, there were quite a few surfers by Haapiti, and we jumped in the water nearby, but out of their way, to snorkel for what - 20 minutes? She looked at Julian for confirmation. "We saw lots of fish of all kinds, and Julian pointed out some of the towns and special sites and landmarks along the way. It only took us about 15 minutes or so each way to cruise down there and back."

Julian, nodded, then looked up as he gazed over the bow of the boat, one hand on the steering wheel. "Now, my American friends, we'll go in the other direction first, then return to Tiahura Beach and the motu after a quick trip...to your hotel!"

Meg asked a question her dad had mentioned to her earlier, but had forgotten to pose to Julian. "What does the name of your boat stand for in English? I saw it on the side when you pulled in to the dock."

"Ah...*Mateata*, it is Tahitian for "cloudless sky," and that can be a person's name, usually for girls here, as well."

"Cool, I like it! Everybody loves a sky with no clouds, right?" responded Meg.

As they all gazed back at the magnificent green peaks looming above the retreating shoreline, Keely paged through her new book, which she'd brought along on the trip. "Is that Mt. Parata?" she asked Julian, extending her finger towards a sharply-pointed peak that rose above the others.

Glancing back, as he piloted the boat carefully through the space between the last and tallest set of coral reefs, the young Tahitian answered, "Yes! *Ohipa maita'i*...Good eye, Keely...it is the most prominent of the three mountains you can see towards the beach we just left. The others on the, um, right side and left side of it are Matotea and Tautaupae. They are each taller than 700 meters. Tautaupae is highest."

Keely confirmed from her book and explained to the others that the former was 714 meters in elevation, while Tautaupae was 769 meters high at its summit.

"How tall is that in feet, Meg?" Alex turned to his younger daughter to run the calculations, which he knew she could almost do in her head.

Watching the 'wheels turn' in her brain, her dad didn't have to wait long before the not-yet-11-year-old answered. "Umm... let's see, meters are just under 3.3 times the length of a foot, so, for the tallest one, let's say 770 times 3 plus a little, or around 2,500 feet tall?" she answered.

"That's tall! Have you climbed all the mountains here, Julian?" asked Cal, from his seat at the rear of the boat.

The Tahitian shook his head. "Oh no...some of them are actually very dangerous, almost un-climbable - is that a word? Sorry, in English - how do you say that? In fact, for some of our mountains here, this is the truth: there is no written record of ANYONE ever reaching their summits on foot. I have climbed Rotui, which you see there," he pointed toward the familiar peak they had seen from the Belvedere lookout during their tour, "and it is hard to do but possible, and then Three Coconuts Pass from the Belvedere and across the island. But not any others of great size. I don't want to work so hard, you know?" Then grinning at Jess, he concluded, "Also, I want to have a long and happy life!"

"No arguments with that here!" laughed Jess. And yes, it looked like she was blushing, again. Keely and Meg, and their dad, all noticed.

Julian continued. "I thought it would be fun to show you the Montcalm from the water, including the entrance to Opunohu Bay, then we'll come back and head out to the motu for our lunch date."

Cal answered their captain with a crisp 'salute.' Julian gave the young American a hearty 'thumbs up' - and a salute and a grin – in return.

Heading east, they soon crossed the large opening in the reef leading to Opunohu Bay, Julian explained that the waters outside of the 'mouth' of the picturesque inlet were called *Tareu Pass*. He steered the boat behind the reef opening, heading further eastward towards the beach in front of their hotel, although they remained several hundred yards offshore from it in the shallow lagoon. Spying 'their tree' on the Montcalm's distant beachfront, Meg suddenly remembered a goal she'd set for the day's trip.

"Hey Julian, can I ask you a question? I have a school project to research colloquialisms, which are, you know, local sayings in a particular language or culture, and I chose "*Aitapea pea*" for my project focus. I want to record your answer, if possible, too. Is that OK? Also, I have another question: Have you always said this, or was there a time you remember not saying it?" She quickly took the video camera from her dad's bag, turned it on, and got ready to 'shoot' Julian's answer, if he said it was OK.

"Sure, Meg I can do this...*aita pea pea!*" He laughed along with the rest of them. As Meg pressed the 'record' button, he then continued, "Hmm, since I was a little boy, we have said "*no problem*" or "*don't worry*," even "*do not fear*" and in all ways we say this - if we were speaking in English - we say in Tahitian "*aita pea pea,*" Julian answered.

Videoing his answer, though the boat was bouncing and rocking just a little, and thus the camera too, Meg followed up, "Is there any time you should NOT say it to people, any special situations?"

"Well, when someone dies, or something bad happens to them, that is one time not to say it, it is considered...unrespectful, or disrespectful? You don't say this to a person or their family in such a situation."

"Of course, that's the same where we come from, right, Dad?"

Alex nodded as Meg thanked Julian for his contribution. She turned off the camera and jotted down some notes with a pen in her small notebook which she pulled from her backpack.

They now ventured a bit closer into shore. Julian slowed the engine to a mere 'putter', generating nearly zero wake from the boat as he pointed its bow toward land. They remained offshore in slightly deeper water, but could clearly view the Montcalm property. A couple dozen sunbathers, swimmers, snorkelers, kayakers and body board loungers were enjoying the mostly still, clear, and warm lagoon.

"There is the Montcalm...and to the east, you can see one of our ancient marae next to it - just before you reach my family's resort, the Moorea Ra'i. It was an especially large temple and meeting center in ancient times, and in fact my extended family has owned and lived on this land for many centuries."

The Websters looked at each other in surprise. Keely exclaimed, "What did you say??? That's funny, our friends Tiare and Lincoln Martinez's mom says it's also *her* family's place. Do you know them?"

"Of course! Raiana is my aunt, my mother's sister. I will be seeing them tonight at a family party we're having," answered Julian. "I didn't know you knew Rai and her family. How did you meet them?"

Jess was flabbergasted too. "OK, you know what is even funnier? - the Websters and I were invited to what must be that same party you are talking about, tonight!" she told him. "When I said earlier that I was going to a luau-like dinner at another resort, I had no idea it was *your* family's too! How amazing...small world!"

"Well, even more amazing than that," smiled Julian, "I will be dancing and playing music tonight with the other members of a local performing group as part of the party - which you may know by now is called a -"

"Tama'ara'a!" yelled Meg and Keely, almost at the exact same time, drawing a laugh and genuine surprise from Julian.

"Wow, this will be exciting, what kinds of dancing?" asked Cal.

"We have several different 'routines' that we perform together, but all are from here in Tahiti. We wear costumes and it's lots of fun - and great exercise too," said Julian.

"Well, I can't wait to see *that*, does anyone else in the family dance?" Alex asked.

"Oh, I am sure Rai will be dancing; I'm not certain if you know any of the others who will join us though. But you'll meet them all tonight, believe me. If you've been invited to one of our family's tama'ara'a' celebrations, you're not just friends, you're part of the family too!"

As Julian slowly brought the boat around to port, heading back out toward the mouth of Opunohu Bay and gradually increasing speed across it in the direction of Motu Tiahura, Keely was thinking of their secret box, and how she was feeling more and more ready to not keep it such a secret anymore. She leaned over to Meg, seated next to her on the other bow cushion while the others chatted with Julian about their surprising and serendipitous discovery.

"I think we should tell Dad and Jess and the Martinez's parents about our box. I'm tired of keeping it secret and I don't like lying about what we've been doing."

"I was thinking the same thing!" her sister whispered back.

"I'll make sure Cal's onboard with our decision, then we'll talk about it with Tiare and Linc tonight and figure out how to tell Dad, Jess, and their parents when we are at the party."

Just then, as they had almost reached the edge of Opunohu Bay, they passed the reef opening again to return toward their lunch destination. Cal pointed ahead of the boat. "Look!"

Swimming across the opening were a dozen or more dolphins. They dove, jumped, and sped past the boat in a churn of activity.

"Those dolphins are probably chasing a school of fish," said Julian. "And also, they are good luck. We believe they are wise and powerful. When we see them, our culture says it means we are protected, and they help us also to make good decisions."

Keely grinned in amazement and winked at Meg, "How true that is, Julian!" and they both erupted in giggles.

"What's up?" said their dad.

"Oh nothing...we just really agree, seeing the dolphins crossing our path is making us wise - and hopefully bringing good decisions - and good fortune - for all of us!" Keely replied.

Julian maneuvered out past the reef again, then increased the engine's speed and soon they were in what he told them was *Ta'atoi Pass*. Shortly after, they again crossed over the break in the outer coral and wave barrier and they could see the town of Papetoai in the distance. The first of three motus, *Inora*, was the smallest, and as they neared Motu Tiahura, where they'd be having lunch and snorkeling soon, instead of heading back to shore they motored out, very slowly, to the edge of the reef around it part-way to the third and largest motu of the group, *Fareone*, on Tiahura's west side. There, Julian idled the engine for a moment to let them all drink in the view.

"The perspective from out here is really different than from land, looking back at the shore and those...I'd call them 'towering' mountain peaks. The greens and blues are out of this world!" Alex observed.

"I bet you really love living here, huh Julian?" said Cal, to their captain.

The native Tahitian took a moment before responding to his American guest. "*E!* or *oui*...Yes, I really do, though it has changed much in recent years. It is also quite expensive to live here, but there are some government policies that help make it less so for those of us who are born here. Still, it is such a beautiful place to call home. And I'm very glad to show more of it to you - especially from out here on the water."

"Moorea...is magnificent," said Meg.

Keely nodded, then added, "And it is awesome that you could take us out to see it from here, Julian. So glad you met Jess!"

"So am I, Keely," replied the young Tahitian, with a wink.

Peering in front of them between the two motus, Fareone and Tiahura, they saw a couple of snorkelers meandering through the shallow water that separated the two islets. "There's a really nice coral reef throughout that area," Julian said, pointing. "I'll take you over there - we can drop in along the beach or even swim across to the other motu - after we eat lunch."

"That would be super cool!" said Meg.

As Julian helmed the *Mateata* eastward again, back between the reef and the motus, they passed along the shore side of Tiahura and soon approached the landing area for the *Haare* restaurant. They caught a glimpse of several tables of various types and shapes waiting for patrons all set up along the beach, facing back towards the main island of Moorea. Nearing the restaurant's shuttle landing area - really just a place to pull the boat up onto the beach - they could see the 'taxi' boat had just dropped off several passengers.

As its previous 'occupants' sloshed through the water carrying their day bags, the shuttle boat headed back to the dock onshore. Julian guided the smaller *Mateata* at a very slow speed toward the beach, aiming for a spot about thirty meters northeast of the main landing area.

As Julian cut the engine, they all felt the craft nose gently into the sand. "Here we are!" he announced. "Time to unload all our gear...Mr. Webster, er, Alex, would you step off the boat and help the others while I cover our seats and anchor the boat onshore?"

"Sure...*aita pea pea*, Julian!" the American replied, as he positioned his own gear next to the side of the boat, and expertly stepped up and over into the warm, shallow water and sand below, which reached just above his calves.

"Jess, kids, grab your gear, and remember, we don't have to move it all at once. Just hand it to me, a little at a time. I'll hold it until you get off the boat, then you can carry it to shore or put it on your back."

As everyone had again donned their soft water shoes, the process was quick and easy. Cal came first, extending his bag over the side to his dad as he slid one leg and then another over the railing to step into the warm lagoon. As he plowed through the shallow water toward shore and the others began to disembark, the nine-year old suddenly yelled out "HEY, look! It's a stingray!"

Meg was slipping over the side of the boat with her dad's help. She looked at her brother and cried out, "Where?!"

"Right over there, see!" Cal was pointing to a spot about 15 feet away, where a ray about one meter long including its tail, was slowly swimming along the sandy bottom.

Meg scooted to the side of the boat to see for herself.

"Wow!" Keely shouted, as she and Alex looked to where her brother was pointing. "Are there a lot of them here? Are they dangerous?" She looked worriedly at Julian as she tentatively hoisted herself over the edge.

"Yes, and no... they are usually friendly, but you must treat them gently - and they will sometimes swim up to you too," he answered.

The *Mateata*'s skipper finished dropping the anchor off the bow to hold it in place temporarily. He then pulled a heavy blanket from under one of the seats to cover them and part of the boat, to keep the sun from damaging the cushions and super-heating them to almost skin-burning temperatures at the same time. They would be on the motu for a few hours, so *better safe than sorry*.

As Julian stepped over the side with a large pack containing his gear, he reached up to grasp Jess's hand. She smiled, shifted her two bags into the other hand, and neatly flipped first one then both legs over the side to join her friend in the shallow water.

Alex was now ready to join them. He leaned across the gunwale, grabbed his backpack, and swung it over his shoulder, then picked up the two small bags containing all their remaining stuff. They sloshed to shore, ready to see just what the Haare restaurant, and Motu Tiahura, were all about, as the next chapter in the day's adventure.

But first, once the Websters, Jess and Julian reached the beach, Julian and Alex waded back in to the shallow water. Julian lifted and carried the anchor while the two of them pulled the boat firmly onto the shore. They used their hands and a small stick to bury the anchor in the sand, though, Alex noted, there was almost no wind and not much of a current on this gorgeous, sunny day to move it anywhere. "I guess you don't usually need an anchor around here, right?"

"No, but winds change quickly. It's always good to be safe."

Alex nodded as the group walked up the path leading to the restaurant. It looked about as laid-back as he expected - a low-slung series of woods building with thatched roofs and an open kitchen in its center, to the rear of the property, smoke rising from its roof. Up-front were around 10 four or six-seat tables, mostly of the former size.

Approaching the casual, no-door entrance, their hostess greeted them with a wide smile. "*Iaorana e Maeva! Bienvenue au Haare* at the Beach!"

"Ia Orana, Maururu," said Keely, and Julian looked at her approvingly for how comfortably she handled his language after less than a week on the island.

He turned to the hostess. "Ia Orana! Hello, Pua, this is the Webster family. They are good friends of mine from the US and they have invited me to join them for lunch. Do you have one of your nice beachside tables for us?"

"E, Oui, of course, Julian", she answered, checking off the reservation in her book, then, in halting English, "Come this way please."

Pua led them to a quiet spot over to one side of the restaurant area. When they got to what was essentially a standard wooden picnic table, they saw it had a perfect view of not just the distant Moorea shoreline and the dock they had departed, but they could also just barely see what they all knew - from their round-the-island trip earlier in the week - were the remains of the Fun Club resort. Lively tropical music was playing from speakers on the deck of the restaurant.

As they took their seats and surveyed the surroundings, Jess sighed. "This is great!" She beamed at Julian and the restaurant's hostess.

"I'll say!" said Alex. "We are very happy to be here, thanks much, Julian for bringing us."

Pua then handed them several menus, and explained, with Julian interpreting a bit along the way, that they would be able to keep the table they had reserved all day or they could leave and explore the island once they were finished. Meanwhile, she asked that they order their drinks and lunch appetizers and entrees now, explaining that they then were free to come and go, to swim right off shore from their table, or maybe even take a short walk. Their dishes would follow the drinks by probably 20-30 minutes, as it was quite busy. "Please relax, and enjoy our beautiful place!"

"Dad, this is *A-MAAAAzing!*" said Keely, as she plopped into her seat. The others nodded enthusiastically, as they announced their drink selections around the table. The Webster girls both ordered virgin (non-alcoholic) pina colada (pineapple coconut blend) drinks, Cal chose the restaurant's fresh lemonade, and Jess, Julian and Alex all ordered local beers. They also took a quick look at the menu and by the time Pua had returned with their drinks in about ten minutes, they were ready to order their lunch entrees.

Moments later, after giving her their meal orders (and following a couple of suggestions from Julian based on their general food preferences), they all agreed it was quite warm, and thus a perfect time to 'test the waters.'

So, they pushed back their rattan chairs and waded right into the calm lagoon, gazing across towards Moorea.

"This...is the life!" said Jess, sipping on a tall, frosty beer and holding out her mug in a salute to Julian.

"Yes, it is," he answered. "*Manuia!*"

With that encouragement, six hard, clear plastic glasses were lightly 'clunked' together, with all toasting in Tahitian - in unison - while they splashed their toes through the warm water and soft sandy bottom of Motu Tiahura.

Chapter 51

Lunch - 'islet style", and a deeper dive

"That lunch was killer-good, wasn't it?"

Meg directed her comment to her dad, but they all agreed, having finished their meals at *Haare*, the restaurant out on the motu. She had enjoyed some grilled skewers of local fish (mahi mahi) and though they had each at least tasted a small portion of the poisson cru as an appetizer, all the dishes served had been tasty and expertly prepared. From Cal's and Alex's grilled fish with garlic and coconut dressing, plus a side of fries each, on through the very fresh salads selected by Jess and Keely (Curry with carrot, tomato, turnip, onion, bell peppers and, of course, coconut for Jess, and a Thai Papaya salad with mostly the same ingredients, plus ginger and lime for Keely), it was all amazingly fresh. Julian, funny enough, had ordered a double cheeseburger and fries, which made all the visiting family members chuckle at the irony of a Tahitian choosing to 'eat American style' here in paradise!

Now, after re-applying their local reef-safe sunscreen all around and securing their bags in a convenient place offered by their server (at Julian's request) inside the restaurant, the Websters, Jess, and Julian were heading as a group to the other side of the motu, not overly full from their meals but certainly well-satisfied after the relaxing, reflective experience of eating lunch at a tasty restaurant on a tiny island.

It wasn't a long walk to the west side of the motu to check out the reef area they'd seen earlier from the boat. They each toted their skin-diving gear in their hands, and once there, left on their water shoes to protect their feet, grabbed their masks and snorkels, and after rinsing them out in the traditional (spitting) way, began their undersea, or at least, under-the-lagoon adventure on Motu Tiahura.

Julian and Jess led the way, and the rest of them followed behind and to either side as they gently paddled and stroked out into the very shallow waterway between the motus. They knew to carefully avoid touching any coral, but they were so surrounded by it only a few feet below the surface that it required some careful maneuvering for the first 20 feet or so to stay safely away. Luckily, they were very buoyant in the water and were able to float just below the surface.

The two Webster girls held hands as they swam slowly along, and Alex gently grasped Cal's arm as well, to help guide and help him avoid a painful bump into any sharp protrusions that might hurt both him and the coral. It wasn't one minute later that the excited 'pointing' and exclamations began...Cal first, noting the unusual fish poking his head out between two rocks about six feet below them. Alex looked underwater and nodded. He shot a quick photo once he'd aimed his waterproof camera, dangling from his wrist by a rubber wristband so it'd be ready when needed. (Later, they determined what they'd seen was a *teardrop butterflyfish*.)

As they continued to explore the reef and rocks along the shallow passage between the motus, they were rewarded with probably five or more species of fish and plants they hadn't seen in their previous snorkeling near the shore by their hotel. Bright blues, yellows, stripes of many combinations, the sun revealed them all in their splendor. Some larger, some smaller than they'd experienced before. Some faster, and some almost plodding, ignorant of the human faces ogling them behind their face masks above. The snorkelers were able to come close, but not too close, perceived no doubt as strange creatures from above interrupting the much more natural swimming-as-part-of-daily-life below.

Meg, with an underwater camera like her dad's attached at her wrist, took a few, select photos under the surface. She and the rest of the Webster group quietly explored all around the rocks and undersea plants, even catching a glimpse of another turtle, quite a distance away.

Until the scream...

"Oh my God!" came the cry after the initial shriek. Alex popped his head up and removed his snorkel and mask, quickly swimming over to where Meg had done the same and was treading water. Soon they all had their masks lifted, snorkels out of their mouths. "Shark, it was right there!" Meg gulped, as she pointed.

Julian suppressed a smile and quickly put his gear back on and ducked his head down. He popped back up, then gestured to Alex.

"Follow me, and let's see if we can get a quick photo."

The two men, with Jess floating stationary next to the three kids as they went, swam a few meters in the direction where Meg had pointed, and the kids could see their dad raise his camera underwater and click the shutter a couple of times after they stopped and looked straight down at the sea bottom. In a few moments, they came back and lifted their masks, smiling.

Alex spoke first. "You're right Meg, that was definitely a shark, but it's a *black-tipped reef shark*. They are generally harmless and usually only about four to six feet long. That one was on the smaller side, but it was just swimming along, maybe looking for food, like they tend to do wherever you see them. They don't typically bother humans and mostly roam right near the bottom. I didn't say anything at the time, but I saw one similar to it on my first day in the water, in the lagoon by the hotel. I also saw one during an early morning swim on the Big Island in Hawaii, on my first trip there a few years ago. It was at 'A Bay' - Anaehoomalu Bay, on the Waikoloa coast ...But don't feel bad about screaming, the first time I saw one, it scared me too. Boy did I swim back to shore fast!"

Julian laughed, adding to Alex's comments. "Yes, reef sharks are common here, but they are pretty shy around people, like Alex says. There *are* much bigger sharks here, but they are mostly offshore, beyond the reef. I really doubt we'll see any of those more dangerous types on this trip."

With everyone calmed down a bit, they resumed their explorations. After a few meandering trips from one segment of the lagoon to the other, they surfaced to maintain their position across from where they had entered the water.

"OK, Cal," Julian said, looking at the youngest in their group. "How would you like to see some stingrays?"

"YEAH! Where?" answered the boy.

Julian gestured in direction of an outcrop on the shore side of the neighboring Motu Fareone. "Just follow me...to that point over there...we'll have to swim about 100 meters, but it's not very deep water."

They all paddled and stroked to a section of land that jutted out from the motu, and within a few minutes, even without fins on their feet, they had reached the area Julian had indicated.

As he slowly returned to vertical, Julian motioned the others to do the same, while keeping their masks on. He shuffled his feet a bit on the sandy bottom, and some of it swirled around. "Cal, gently move your feet back and forth, like I'm doing."

After the two of them did so, not 30 seconds later, they looked down through the sand, stirred up a bit in the otherwise crystal-clear water, and saw three stingrays gliding slowly towards them.

"Don't be afraid, just stay still and watch them swim around you for a bit. You can also duck your head down with your mask on, but be careful not to step on them. See how gracefully they move?"

"Can we touch them?" asked Keely.

Julian shook his head. "No, that's not a good idea, because the barb on their tail is definitely not something you want poking in your arm or side. But they are really quite - how do you say it in English - *peaceful*?"

"Maybe 'docile'?" suggested Jess.

"Yes, docile, thank you, Jess. They don't want to hurt you; they are just curious. You see, stingrays are normally nocturnal, they sleep during the day, and feed at night. But they feel your presence via electrical impulses you send out. They wonder what you are doing, so they swim up to you when you are near them, like we are."

"Should we feed them something?" asked Meg.

The Tahitian again shook his head. "No, we don't need to, and really, that is not a good thing because it disturbs their natural feeding patterns and instincts. Many people do feed them, but that may be why more of the stingrays are now present during the day than in the past. Unfortunately, some of them have been hurt by getting attacked by other fish, predators, and sharks, because they often come together in groups when they are curious like this. So, it's better to just enjoy them, watch them, and then leave them alone to swim as they like. They will have plenty of food tonight."

"What do they eat, Julian?" asked Keely.

"Mostly crabs, oysters, barnacles, squid... other sea animals like that."

They all watched, gently moving their feet on the bottom, as two more rays, one quite large, came closer to the group of snorkelers. They gasped with delight as the animals swooped toward and around them like giant birds with very wide wings.

"Oh, they are soooo cool!" said Cal.

"That one is all purple-colored, and that huge one there, it is kinda pinkish. It must be 4 feet wide. Wow!" added Meg.

She ducked her head under, with her camera poised, for a few moments, then popped back up. "You have to see this, guys...there are around six swimming all around us. Duck down and check them out!"

For the next 15 minutes or so, they all watched and marveled at the grace and curiosity of their undersea friends, taking a few photos when they could, but keeping their distance without reaching out to touch, just to be safe - both for themselves and for the stingrays too.

There didn't seem to be much interaction between the reef fish and the rays, Jess noted. Alex observed this as well when they had all surfaced and returned to an upright position.

"These rays are some of the most interesting, graceful creatures I have ever seen! They just kind of 'do their thing' in the water, and they seem very friendly. I guess they sting only when threatened, right?"

Julian nodded. "Exactly...they must be frightened somehow or attacked before they will flip the barb on their tail - and there are also often barbs, or *blades*, on their backs- usually against a predator, maybe a dolphin or a shark. But also, they don't attract that many predators. That's why it is important not to disturb them too much or feed them unnecessarily. Doing so could bring bigger fish or other, you know, attackers, and that would upset the balance of life here for the rays - and maybe even be harmful to their predators."

"Thanks so much, Julian, for bringing us out here," said Alex.

"And for all the great information too," added Jess. The kids all nodded in agreement, snorkels hanging to the side, and their masks getting a bit foggy as they bobbed up and down in the calm lagoon.

"I'm happy to do so. Please share what I've told you with your friends back home. Oh, I forget to tell you that there are even larger Manta Rays not too far from here too, and yes, big sharks also as we discussed. But I guess those we can save for your next visit to Moorea!"

"For sure, Julian...they're on the list for Worldwide Websters Moorea Trip 2.0!" joked Alex.

"Dad, I think I want to talk about stingrays and what we learned when I get back to my class in school," said Cal.

"I'm sure you will, son. Keely, Meg, Jess and I got some nice photos we'll share with each other later. Speaking of that, is it 'group photo time'?

Not one of them groaned about another picture at this point - *you just couldn't have too many reminders of such an amazing trip*, Jess thought. Lucky for them, when they were back on the beach at Motu Tiahura and had removed their gear, a nice couple nearby offered to take a few photos of the whole group, using Alex's camera which he'd stashed in its bag on the beach under a tree. The gorgeous lagoon and motu trees served as the perfect background.

It was getting towards 3 o'clock, Alex noticed as he checked his watch.

Looking at Julian and Jess, he said "Probably a good idea to start heading back to the boat and then our car. We still have plenty of time, but I know we'll all want to shower before the party tonight."

"Yeah, the tama...rama...tam.."

"'Tama'ara'a'" is how you say it, Cal!" chided his oldest sister, as she jokingly punched him in the shoulder. They all laughed, and leaving the aquatic wonderland behind, they proceeded along Motu Tiahura's shore, to the restaurant to pick up their gear, and then back along the beach and into the boat. In about 25 minutes, they had returned to the dock where Julian had first picked them up.

Jess was last, other than its skipper, to leave the craft, having handed everyone their bags over the rail after they had disembarked. Turning to 'Captain' Julian, she squeezed his arm and smiled. "Mauruuru for such a wonderful time today, Julian. It was incredible going out on the *Mateata* with you and seeing a whole different side of Moorea!"

The Tahitian grinned shyly, then gazed into the eyes of the New Zealander - who had journeyed to his home by way of America. "Mauruuru Roa, Jess. *Te ite nei au ia outou i teie pô*, See you tonight!"

She kissed him quickly on the cheek, then stepped off onto the dock, waved, and the Webster contingent walked with their gear to their parked jeep. When Julian waved from the boat, Jess smiled, waved back, and turned and jumped in the rear seat of the jeep next to Cal for the drive 'home' to the Montcalm.

Chapter 52

Conchs and conversation

The Websters and Jess took turns showering upon their return to the hotel bungalow. Everybody's skin was dry from the salt and tinted a bit pink, showing signs of just a little too much sun as well - difficult to avoid even with frequent sunscreen re-application considering all the activities involved with their visit to the motu. However, cool showers – and aloe vera gel - will refresh anybody, especially when a party is on the horizon.

"Everyone almost ready?" Alex called, knocking on the girls' door.

"Just a couple more minutes, Dad!" Keely yelled back.

Taking a look at herself in the mirror, Keely was pleased that her dress from their last trip to Hawaii still fit pretty well (it had been a bit too big for her when they bought it), and it worked just fine with her sandals too. Meg wore a combo that she'd put together using her new pareo for the bottom and a nice pink t-shirt for the top.

They both turned when Jess came through with a rap on the door. "Knock-knock!"

"WOW," exclaimed Meg. "You look awesome!"

"Mauraru!" Jess answered with a giggle. She was wearing a loose-fitting dress she had picked up on her trip with friends to Mexico, a sheer tropical print in blue that accentuated her eyes.

"I thought you might wear your pareo tonight. But that's gorgeous! Julian won't know what hit him!" Keely said, which of course embarrassed Jess a bit.

Turning a bit redder even than her light sunburn, she answered, "Oh come on, Keel, we're just, well, we've just gotten to know each other, you know? But thanks!" She took a look in the mirror and, then glancing at each of them, declared "I think us girls are ready to party!"

Meg and Keely laughed and high-fived Jess together, Meg shouting "*Tama' ara' a, here we come-ah!*"

When they came through the door to the bungalow's main room, Cal and Alex were also in the best clothes they'd brought on the trip. Cal wore a floral print shirt purchased from a past-season clearance rack prior to leaving Washington, and Alex sported a blue, white, and maroon reverse-print Aloha shirt from a previous trip to Hawaii.

"You all look incredible!" said Cal, complimenting Jess and his sisters on their outfits.

Alex added, "I can't disagree, wow!"

"Not so bad yourselves!" countered Meg.

"So, why don't we take this 'mutual admiration society' out of here and over to the party next door?" Jess suggested. She took a sip from her water bottle, then led the way down the path to the lagoon.

The sun was still bright when they reached the beach about five minutes later and started the short trek along it to the Moorea Ra'i. A few people were taking the opportunity to enjoy the lagoon's charms one last time before sunset, some with snorkel gear. Keely's mind wandered back to the magic of swimming with the rays, as they calmly and gracefully swooped around their whole group out at the motu. *Not sure I can ever duplicate THAT experience again!*

It wasn't quite 5:30 yet, so despite a very busy day, their timing had worked out well. Alex hadn't wanted to arrive 'empty-handed' so he carried in his arms a small bouquet of local flowers and a bottle of wine they had purchased before returning to the hotel. Everyone else was now refreshed and full of anticipation for the evening ahead.

"That's a really cool ensemble you're wearing, Meg. I haven't seen it before," he said.

"I know! I MADE the pareo myself, in our class. Glad you like it!"

Jess and the three Webster kids exchanged quick, conspiratorial grins as Alex momentarily gazed out into the lagoon. They savored, together, the secret they held (although not the one about the box, in this case). Instead, they were excited about the custom pareo they had created for their dad during the class with Rai Martinez. They planned to present it to him the following day - their last full one on the island. Of course, the kids and Alex were thinking that there was a beautiful piece of local jewelry waiting for Jess to discover it as well. Tomorrow looked to be another day of gifts and fun surprises.

As they rounded the corner of the beach a few minutes later, they saw a transformed landscape in front of the pool area of the

Martinezes' hotel. Several large round tables were surrounded by 8-10 chairs each on the beachfront lawn, partly filled at this point with guests - presumably from Rai's local extended family and friends - and each with a colorful centerpiece of fresh flowers and leaves. The tables were arranged in a semi-circle in front of a substantial wooden platform. Alex recognized the components of a small but powerful sound system, with several microphones on the stage and speakers to its sides. Tall electric lights stood on either side to spotlight what were clearly going to be a few - or more - performers. These were connected by extension cords leading behind the performance area. *Clearly, they had parties here fairly often*, he surmised.

Almost as if on cue, as the Webster clan arrived at the tables, three men walked up onto the stage. One held a guitar, one carried a ukulele, and the other set a large instrument - what looked like an oil drum with a long neck and strings - onto the floor in front of him. The lead guitarist approached the forward mic, tested it, gave a brief intro, then they started playing a soft Polynesian-themed tune. The gentle ukulele's sound complemented the guitar, and the strange-looking oil drum setup was plucked expertly to set a perfect rhythm.

And the party was on!

Raiana Martinez stood next to a small building where Jess guessed much of the food was being prepared. She admired the Tahitian-American's dress - a gorgeous near floor-length frock in a floral print - and the crown of red and white flowers, interwoven with deep-green leaves, that encircled her forehead.

Glimpsing the Websters, Rai broke into a huge smile and strode over to them. Tiare, wearing a striped blue and green thin cotton dress, and Linc, in shorts and a polo shirt, plus flip flops, followed along with their father, Victor.

"Ia Orana! Maeva! Welcome, Websters. So glad you could join us this evening for our family get together. You all look beautiful...very Tahitian!"

"Mauruuru roa, Mrs. Martinez, you look great too! We are super excited for our first-ever tama'ara'a," Keely said, speaking the last word somewhat haltingly, but correctly this time, albeit with a crooked grin.

"That's great, Keely! You pronounced all those words perfectly!"

"I knew those Tahitian lessons would pay off!" joked Alex.

Vic wore linen pants and what looked like a new, yet somewhat subdued floral print shirt similar to Alex's. He chuckled along with his wife. "Maybe you should teach all of us, Keely...I still am working hard to learn and I've been married to my Tahitian, er, Moorean wife for 15 years!"

"Sure, though my sister Meg is pretty great with languages too," Keely answered with a giggle.

Meg, taking Keely's compliment in a different direction, asked Rai a question: "Hey, Mrs. Martinez?"

"You can call me Rai, Meg, and of course you all can. We're definitely not stuffy in this family, as you'll find out even more tonight!"

"Can't wait! And thanks. Well, Rai, I was wondering if you, and maybe others from your family, can help me with a school project. I need to define and research, and do some video interviews, on a colloquialism - a local saying - used in this country. I already chose the phrase '*aita pea pea*' - which is pretty common in many languages and as we know it in English: '*No Problem.*' Would you be willing to tell me, you know, how and when you use this expression? And even maybe when you *wouldn't* use it?"

"*E* (yes), Meg. Aita pea pea. Happy to help you!" Rai answered with a laugh and a wink to Jess and the others, who beamed at her response. "Seriously, though. Let's walk over by the beach for a moment - where it's a bit quieter - and you can interview me there. Even better, we can ask a couple other people I see are here, local family members and friends of ours, and I'm sure you can find a few more to ask after that!"

Cal watched his sister walk with Mrs. Martinez over to the edge of the seating area nearer the sand, with Alex's video camera in hand. This reminded him of his own project, and he got a bit worried. "I'll need to ask a few people about that "*Heiva*" thing in Papeete. Maybe they'll know someone who has gone to it?"

"Are you kidding, Cal? Just about everybody you see tonight has competed in the Heiva at some point - it's the biggest event they have around here!" Tiare, who had just stepped in to the circle formed by the remainder of the Webster kids and her brother, assured him that he'd get help for his school project too.

Cal looked relieved. "That's great, Tiare. Could *you* tell me more about it? Were you ever in it?"

"No, but several of my cousins, aunts, and uncles have been. You can meet them tonight. Let's see..."

Just then they heard a strange, and progressively louder, sound, coming from over by the lagoon. It was almost like a wild animal had arrived at the party!

Looking all around them for the source of the noise, the Websters couldn't see anything. Then, several people at other tables pointed upward. Way up in a palm tree, right near its very top, they saw Julian, bare-chested but covered by a pareo which was draped in layers around his legs, just to around knee level. He was blowing into one end of what Alex realized was a conch shell, and turning with each blast to face the four compass points. Once finished, he climbed down and gave one last blow into the large seashell - aimed in the direction of the gathered crowd - to complete the ritual.

Alex turned to Victor Martinez. "That's one way to start this party on a high note!"

Vic laughed.

"Seriously though, I am guessing that's to welcome the sunset, a traditional salute?"

"You got it, Alex," answered Vic, "You seem to know the customs here as well as I do then - but it is definitely customary for an occasion like this."

"Actually, I only said that because I've been to more than a few *luaus* that sometimes feature performers doing Tahitian and other countries' dances and songs...many of them do start with the conch ceremony, sometimes combined with a ritual unveiling of the meal, things like that. I thought it was Hawaiian in origin...but then, the Hawaiians are believed to have come originally from around these islands. So, it was an educated guess, I guess!" Alex smiled.

"The conch shell he used to blow the horn is called a 'pu,'" explained Rai, who had now returned with Meg from their "interview" as well as a couple other quick ones the American girl had done along the way with two of Rai's local cousins. "It's actually called many other names by people from other cultures who also blow into conch or similar shells to celebrate important get-togethers all around the world. And yes, the conch sunset salute, from our

Tahitian descendants, is an important part of our culture, and it was often sounded on other important occasions."

Pointing toward the corner of the gathering area, Rai continued. "Also important, actually a huge part of family life here on Moorea, is the food preparation. The many native dishes - you'll see some tonight - we have prepared in some cases for centuries, and still, almost the same way as they always have been. Remember how Hawaiians do kalua pig, buried in the imu, or underground oven?"

"Sure, we learned about that on our last trip," Keely responded.

"Well, in Tahiti, or Moorea, or other islands in French Polynesia, we do things a bit differently, though some of the dishes are similar in name and substance. What you'll find here is that my family members and I have prepared several dishes, some for hours, in a similar oven pit, lined with hot volcanic stones. It's called an *'ahima'a.'* Tonight, we are not serving pig, but we *are* cooking fresh local fish, chicken from my cousin's farm, and even our *uru*, or breadfruit, inside it. All these ingredients are wrapped in leaves to keep them tender and juicy. Wait until you try the *"pouletfafa"* - this is chicken marinated in coconut cream and spices. We also serve taro leaves in a variety of ways, one which is cooked in the oven and wrapped around larger pieces of fish and marinated shrimp." She pointed again, to where several men and women were carefully removing what looked like large, hot dishes from the oven, itself dug several feet into the ground just outside of the area containing the tables, chairs and stage.

Rai went on with her menu descriptions. "Then of course, we have our famous poisson cru, or what we call here in Tahiti '*iaota*', which you've tried, I'm sure?"

"We LOVE poisson cru!" said Jess, and Alex nodded his head vigorously in agreement.

"Plus," continued Rai, "we also will be serving several other vegetables and fish dishes, including marinated raw shrimp, or crayfish, accompanied by a curry sauce, and something called '*pahua taioro*,' which is clams marinated in coconut juice and seawater. And, of course we couldn't have a party like this without our famous breadfruit paste - which goes with everything else. It is called '*popoi*' and before you say it, no, it's not exactly like 'poi' in Hawaii, but there is a similar texture and maybe taste too. You'll have to try them all.

And maybe even the '*fafaru*' – in case you are really adventurous?"
She looked at her son.

"Eewww! That's that raw fish in seawater, yuk!" exclaimed Linc.

"Yeah," echoed his father, Vic, adding "I'd agree that's an
acquired taste, for sure!"

Rai resumed counting the dishes with the fingers of her hand.
"Oh, and I almost forgot we do have another sweet dish as well, called
'*poe*' which is starch and stewed fruit preserves, and we've used
mango and pineapple tonight. And I haven't even mentioned the
three desserts...but we can talk about them after the meal, when we
serve them with coffee during our special show!"

"Wow, Raiana...this is the most amazing party ever, and it's
barely started yet! I am sure we will love everything...even the poe!
Or the popoi, or you know, the stuff most people think they don't like
- until they combine it with other things. Thank you again for inviting
us." Alex blushed a bit while he spoke, admittedly a bit awkward in
trying to remember his manners, along with all the names for the
exotic dishes they were soon going to experience.

Jess beamed in agreement, and reached out to hug Rai, who
embraced her in return.

Rai continued, "But before we start, it is time for the welcome.
See over there?" she said pointing towards a table where several of
her female relatives stood. "Come with me..." As they all followed,
wondering what was next, they soon discovered the answer.

"These are called '*hei u po o*' and we have one for each of you, our
family's honored guests," Rai proclaimed, as she then placed round
chains, or crowns, of flowers, with a mix of various blossoms and
leaves on the each of thc Wcbstcr contingent's heads.

"Is that a plumeria?" Keely asked, seeing what looked like familiar
blossoms.

"Yes, except we call it '*tipanie*' and of course," turning to smile at
her daughter, "we have the *tiare* as well. The others you see are
pandanus leaves, which Tahitians call '*fara.*'"

Stepping back and smiling, Rai motioned for Alex's camera.

"Pictures!" she exclaimed, as Alex dutifully removed it from
around his shoulder.

Rai took the camera and snapped a couple of photos of the family,
posed with the sunset in the background. Then Alex and Jess asked

Rai and the rest of the Martinez family to join them, and one of Tiare's cousins was happy to do the honors for several more group pictures. As they finished up, Rai smiled at the Websters, looking at each and said "You are now part of our family too. Our '*utuafare*.'"

What had already been an incredible experience soon grew even more so, as Rai led the now-flower-crowned Websters to their table. It was topped with huge leaves of banana and coconut palms, and small wooden bowls were set at each place. There were cups that looked like they were made from bamboo – and some were simple hollowed-out coconut shells.

As they sat down, Vic asked "What would you all like to drink?"

"What's available?" Alex replied.

"Well, we have local beer, white or red wine, fruit punch, water...or for a bit stronger taste, we have..."

"I know, I bet you have *Mai Tai's*?" Jess piped up.

Vic laughed. "You are right, Jess, we do, and they are very 'maita'i' (good) too! Made with pineapple rum from right here on the island. Want one?"

"I do!" she answered enthusiastically. "But just one, and I'll nurse it...I am pretty sure this is going be a long evening!"

She gazed over to where Julian was talking with another member of the family. He caught her glance with a lingering smile and she grinned back.

Alex raised his thumb to their host. "I'll take a Mai Tai too, Vic, thank you. Kids?" He looked at Keely, Meg and Cal.

"I'll have some of the punch," answered Cal.

"Me too, Dad," said Meg.

"Water's fine for me right now," said Keely, looking over at Tiare. Then, when her dad and Jess turned away for a moment to take in the surroundings, she mouthed the words "*We have to talk!*" to her Moorean-Mexican-American friend.

Cal was in deep thought. He screwed up his courage and decided it was now or never if he was going to approach Tiare's mom for help with his school report on the Heiva festival. He stood up to walk over to where she was standing. Just as he had almost reached her, a man, dressed in regular clothes and not looking festive at all, stepped in front of him and said something to her, and he wasn't smiling. She gave him what Cal thought was a really angry look. *Kind of like she was disgusted*, he thought. They said a few words to each other, in Tahitian, probably, that he couldn't understand. Then she turned and walked away quickly, going over to where the food tables were being set up for the buffet.

Realizing it was probably not a good time to talk to her after all, Cal returned to the family's table.

"What's up, bud?" his dad asked him, seeing his son's look of disappointment mixed with a bit of embarrassment.

"Oh nothing...I'm just trying to get my project done, and I thought I could ask Mrs. Martinez to tell me a little about the *Heiva I Tahiti* festival. But she's busy."

"Well, you might try Julian," Jess suggested. "He's an expert dancer and has been doing it since he was younger than you are now. I'm sure he could tell you all about the festival."

Cal looked over to where he had previously seen Julian. He was now helping set up the rest of the stage. Cal walked up to him and told him about his class project. To his relief, Julian was thrilled and took a moment from his duties to sit down on a chair. Then he told the nearly ten-year-old some key details.

"Heiva is really important, a really big deal around here. There are hundreds of people competing, including groups from not just here in French Polynesia, but all over the world. Some come to participate and some just to watch. There are many divisions, by age and type of dance. Actually, they also do other competitions, like stone lifting and climbing trees as quickly as possible, like I did tonight for the conch ceremony."

"How do you decide what to do, and get ready to compete?" Cal asked.

"It is really hard to practice and prepare, but also lots of fun once you get there, including incredible dancing, great food that's served constantly during the festival, and even some time to play around and meet new people. Just an amazing experience. You might actually see something like that tonight."

"Really? You are going to dance like you do at the *Heiva I Tahiti* tonight?" Cal asked.

"We will do at least one routine like we do there, and who knows, we might be looking for some new recruits for the team!" Julian grinned, noting that the boy from America suddenly realized that the Tahitian was talking about *him*, or maybe his sisters?

Cal blushed, which was tougher to notice now, given the pink cast of his face from their long day in the sun and on the water. "No way, Julian! But thanks, my sisters are the musical theater people. I'm not good at dancing and singing. I play video games."

Julian laughed. "We'll see, Cal...but, listen, I hope my explanation helps. I gotta go get some things ready before dinner now, but we can talk more later. Maybe you can take some video of our performance tonight to share with your class as part of your report?"

"Sure, that's a great idea, Julian. Thanks for that and for all the really interesting info you gave me on the Heiva."

"*Aita pea pea*, Cal. Hey, it looks like it's time to eat!"

It was. With the sun down and darkness descending except on the horizon, the guests were lined up to fill their plates, which Alex noted were made of some sort of wood. *This all seems MUCH more authentic than any event I ever went to at a resort,* Alex thought.

As Jess and the girls led the way behind several smiling Tahitian family members, he was a bit confounded as to how to engage Rai's relatives. They'd all been introduced around to each table of different cousins and aunts and uncles, but Alex had already forgotten most of their names, and just smiled and nodded back.

Meg looked around the long tables. "Hey Dad, where are the forks and stuff? Or do they use chopsticks or something?"

"Nope!" said Tiare. "Tahitians eat only with their hands - at least traditionally."

"You mean I have to pick up mush and fish with my bare hands, and pudding and stuff too?" Meg asked with a fearful look.

"You can, or you can use leaves or bread to wrap it, or pick it up. But if you really want a fork or spoon, don't worry, we have a few here."

"No, I'm going to give it a try. I'm sure I can do it. *Aitapeapea, I Eat with No Fear-a*, right?"

Keely giggled at her sister's humor. "Good one, Meg."

Chapter 53

Bad blood flows, and Tiare pitches in

The food - and not just the hot dishes from the ahima'a oven - was (mostly) delicious to the tastes of the visitors from the US. Some of the flavors and textures, the Websters agreed, were, well, a bit different than they were used to. Maybe, in a couple of cases, not likely to be lasting favorites. But the experience, the atmosphere, and most of all, the setting, combined for an incredible evening.

"Totally," was preteen Keely's answer when asked if she liked the food. Even usually finicky Meg and Cal found some new favorites on the family-style menu for the feast. And of course, they'd made sure to jot down a few notes - as Meg had brought along one of their 'Food Review' worksheets to help document what they had sampled. Already full of interesting tidbits on the dishes they'd tried on the trip, the list would now be a lot fuller - just like the well-fed Websters - once they added in the ones they'd enjoyed at the Martinez-and-extended family tama'ara'a!

"This fish is really tasty, Dad. And I love the chicken...I've been mixing it with the popoi paste and that combo is really pretty good!"

"I'm proud of you, Cal, for having the courage to at least try most of these new things."

"Yeah, but no way am I trying that raw marinated fish, it stinks!" retorted the boy.

Jess chuckled. She too had found the dishes mostly appetizing, but as a semi-vegetarian, she had resolved to stick to the seafood and vegetables. Any sweets that came later were fair game, of course. The shrimp was really flavorful, whether cooked or marinated, and of course she had taken a healthy helping of the poisson cru and put it in its own bowl in front of her to munch on during the meal.

"What do you think of the food, Meg?"

"I like the clam and shrimp dish with coconut pieces. It's really kind of crunchy. What's it called again?"

Rai helped her out: "That's '*pahua taioro*' and I'm glad you like it. Keely, what do you think of the baked fish?"

"It's to die for, really. I love the spices on it, and I took some of the coconut sauce and put it on top, then I wrap it in one of these cooked taro leaves - they're kinda like spinach - and put a few pieces of ginger on it. Then 'BAM,' I launch it all right into my mouth. Delicious. Heavenly!"

"So glad you're enjoying the food...what about you, Alex? What's your favorite?" she asked the tall American.

"Well, Jess and I clearly both love the poisson cru, and this one you've all made tonight is a little fresher and spicier than what we've had at the hotel a few times since we've been here, and it has a bit better flavor overall too. But I also really like the moistness and combined spices on the fish from the oven, the ahima'a? And the chicken is great by itself, or as Cal said, combined with the shrimp, and popoi or even the stuff like poi combined with the curry sauce. Wow, what an amazing mix that is!'"

"Oh, so you've made the pouletfafa into a combo with the fish and the chevrettes, the curried shrimp? Great idea!" Rai exclaimed.

Taking a break from eating, Keely caught Tiare's eye, sitting directly across the table. She whispered, again as earlier, "*We have to talk!*"

Tiare stood up and came over. She whispered into Keely's ear: "I think we should tell our parents about the box."

Keely looked at her, raised her thumb up with a smile, then grasped her new friend's arm and answered, "Me too!"

To ensure all agreed, Keely and Tiare leaned sideways and explained their plans to Cal, Linc and Meg. The trio nodded, weary of keeping their exciting find a secret. The deception just wasn't fun anymore.

Keely was just about to tap her dad on the shoulder and start to tell him about the box, when she was interrupted by a commotion. Rai's cousin was walking briskly up to their table, where in a moment, the very tall man stood next to Rai's chair.

Alex recognized him as the same one who had been arguing with Rai when he'd passed by on the bike ride yesterday. He stood up, glancing at Rai and then back at the man. "What's up, Rai?"

The man rudely ignored Alex and began speaking directly – in hushed Tahitian - to Rai. She put up her hand, got out of her seat, and walked off to the side of the lawn with him. Jess could see the tension in Rai's face, as could everyone else at the party.

"I wonder what's going on, and where's Vic?" Alex asked, looking around for Rai's husband. Apparently, he was at the restroom or maybe, someone whispered, he had gone back to their hotel room? They all heard a few sharp words from Rai, then the man abruptly strode to the rear of the seating area, where he had apparently been sitting at a smaller table with two middle-aged women they didn't recognize.

Returning to her own seat across from the Websters and Jess, Rai was clearly upset. But, in this awkward moment, especially given they were 'honored guests' at the event, none of the Tacoma-based travelers, including the adults, really wanted to ask her any tough questions. However, Rai looked up, sighed, and began to explain anyway.

"I'm very sorry for all that. That was my cousin, well, distant cousin, Tanetoa. He is a property developer here, or actually, he's a 'wannabe' as we call it in the States. I grew up going to school with him here, but we never got along. Then he went to college in the UK, so speaks very good English, even though he chose not to when he just approached me. He thinks he's smarter than everyone here, but really, he couldn't 'make it' there in business, in fact he failed at several things and was forced to come back to Moorea with nothing but his inflated ego. So now he's here and has allied himself and this shady real estate company along with his side of the family - most of whom our side has never agreed with on just about anything for, let's see, four generations, maybe? Anyway, this time it's about a very important issue that may decide our family's legacy on this island forever. And once again he's leading a fight against my family, at least those who are left on my father's and mother's sides."

"So, what are they trying to do, Rai?" Jess asked.

"They are trying to take over operation of this hotel. And not just that, they want to change, dramatically, the plans we had worked so carefully on to renovate it. They want to tear down many of the buildings and also, most of the ancient marae over there...because they say it's in too valuable a location, so close to the sea. In fact, they want to put a parking lot and some other spa building in its place, because the resort they want to build will be three times bigger than it is now," she said, as she pointed across from their table to the marae. Apparently, she wasn't aware the kids, especially, already knew the historical site quite well.

"I also think they're planning to bring in an inexperienced hotel operator, because it's someone else in Tanetoa's partner's family who wants to be part of the deal. We think it's all a bad, bad idea that will lead to more disagreement and eventually failure, maybe as bad as what happened with Fun Club. Have you seen that property?"

"Yes, we walked around the site last weekend. It's completely destroyed, abandoned. Such a shame," Alex replied.

"Wow, Rai, can they really do all that? I mean, isn't the marae a historically protected monument or something?" Jess asked.

Rai shook her head in disbelief, and disgust. "You would think so, wouldn't you? But there are always exceptions...Tanetoa and the French company he is working with are very 'connected' in Papeete, they know lots of people in government there, and that's where all the rules that apply around here are usually made. And even though my close family members and I disagree with almost everything about their plans, we may end up losing to Tanetoa and his buddies in the end."

"I saw you arguing with Tanetoa the other day, and wondered what it was all about," Alex said, just as Vic returned to the group.

"What did I miss?" Vic asked, a bit bewildered by all the troubled faces around the table. *Sheesh! One quick trip to the restroom, and...*

"Dad, Cousin Tanetoa was just here again, and he got mom all upset, again," Linc answered, glancing with worry at his mom who looked very serious as she wiped a tear from her eye. Vic walked over and put his arm around his wife's shoulder, as Rai explained.

"I was just telling the Websters about the fight for the Moorea Ra'i and our family's land - and legacy," she said, squeezing her husband's hand with a half-hearted smile. "So, Tanetoa just had to come by, at our big family celebration, to argue with me about it, can you believe it? This is supposed to be a happy, peaceful time, and he wants to ruin it all!"

Jess walked over to Rai's side. Keely, in the chair next to her, decided it was a good time to stand. Jess sat down, whispering

"Thanks, Keel," then turned her face towards Rai. "So, what, exactly, was his news?"

"Well, you might have heard - I don't know what our kids may have told you - but we've had several family meetings on plans for our ancestral property since we arrived. It's one of the main reasons we came here on this trip...I was begged by my sister and close relatives to come and help them. You know - I think I mentioned it - that we sold off part of our family's land and properties many years ago, and some of it is now occupied by the Montcalm, where you guys are staying."

"Yes, and I had heard some more background on that from the management there," Alex answered.

Rai nodded. "Right, and they've done a very nice job with the Montcalm renovation; in fact, we'd like to emulate their approach and success in whatever we choose to do. But we are a family, and sometimes...," Rai looked at her family members, and then across at the Websters, "families disagree on things."

"Boy, do we know all about that!" said Meg, and her brother and sister rolled their eyes in agreement.

Jess smiled, in spite of the seriousness of the situation. Alex thought about Rai's statement. *Yep, reality is reality. And families can, for sure, sometimes get a bit...messy...*

"You are right, Rai," Alex said. "Families, no matter what anyone thinks, aren't easy to keep together, communications can get screwed up, mistakes made, and feelings hurt, sometimes seriously. Ours ain't perfect, that's for sure!"

"Thanks, Alex. Anyway, we've all agreed that it's time to do *something* with the property, but most of my family wants to plan a careful, tasteful renovation, not necessarily *slow*, but done over time, the right way. Tanetoa and his developer buddies want to go big and go fast. They have the money to do what they want, and they don't want to wait for anything. We were able to get a legal 'stay' to stop their plans, but only for a couple of weeks, pending review by a judge. That made Tanetoa and his side very angry. That's why you saw us arguing over by the marae. Now, he's gone back to the judge with a document that he claims shows the land doesn't really belong to our side of the family. We think it's bogus, possibly faked. But he says given that this property's ownership is in dispute, the only way to resolve it is by a majority vote. So, a pivotal, all-family meeting is scheduled next week, before we return to Denver. But many people on our side are losing heart, and getting ready to give in. They think it might be easier than fighting Tane and his cronies, plus, they'd all get healthy returns from what they'd get paid for their shares in the family's property. You know what they say...*money talks!*"

Rai paused for a moment. Vic reached out to grasp her hand. She looked at her watch and frowned. Then she continued her explanation. "Now...with this new document that the judge is considering, we may not have any say at all. We might lose the property anyway, and then our family will have no voice whatsoever in what happens to the Moorea Ra'i and all our ancient lands. This place has been in our family for at least five centuries! Even the marae..." Rai's voice trailed off, and tears streamed down her cheeks. "I just feel it is so important to preserve this land, this place we love, as much as we can. You know, to employ local people, share our local culture...even though...I'm no longer really a part...of the life here."

Abruptly, she straightened her shoulders, wiped her eyes with a handkerchief Vic handed her from his pocket, and said, "Hey, we're not going to talk about this anymore tonight, OK? We've got some dancing to do. This is a *Tama'ara'a* - this is a party, and we're here to have fun. We can deal with the sad and bad stuff another day, especially with such honored guests like all of you here to join us and our...family."

Just then, Rai's sister came up to the table. She saw there was a deep conversation going on, and seemed reluctant to interrupt.

"Tapa, what's going on?" Rai asked her, turning to explain to those seated at the table, "I think you met my sister, Tapairu? She lives in one of the nearby villages, and owns a small shop there. We've been borrowing her car? Anyway, we've been spending lots of fun times together while we've been back on Moorea, and she's one of my main dancing partners tonight."

Alex thought she looked familiar, but couldn't quite place her face...

Tapairu nodded and smiled, then said something in what sounded like Tahitian, in low tones, in Rai's ear. "Oh no! How are we going to do our main one? We need three girls, or it won't look or sound right!"

Rai glanced around the table full of family and new friends. "You know that expression, 'When it rains, it pours'? Well, it's pouring now. We had three dances planned for tonight, nothing too elaborate, but ones we know well and have performed many times together - even at Heiva," she said glancing fondly at Cal, who smiled back.

"Did you know I was doing a project on that festival?" he asked with wonder.

Rai smiled, answering with a twinkle in her dark eyes - and a wink at a blushing Meg across the table, who then grinned at her little brother. "A little bird told me. Anyway, our third dance team member is sick and can't come tonight. So, I guess we'll just do a quick version, sort of a duo-dance..."

"I can do it, Mom!" blurted out Tiare.

"But honey, you don't know the moves, the steps," Rai said, turning to her and smiling, slightly embarrassed by her daughter's outburst.

"Yes, I do," Tiare countered.

"How? You've never wanted to come to any of the dance practices at home, or certainly while we've been here on this trip. In fact, I didn't think you had much interest in *anything* here in Moorea, or in our local culture, at all!" Rai turned towards her daughter, who now stood to her side.

Tiare straightened, and bravely pressed her point. "I know. I've been kind of a brat, I've been complaining about the things we don't have here that we do at home, like decent internet, and malls, and fast-food places, or nachos. But...I've had some great times exploring and hanging out here with Keely and Meg and Cal - and even with Linc," she said with a quick grin at her brother.

The 11-year-old continued. "You didn't know it, but I've watched you dance, Mom, for years. I have seen the lessons, the videos, the pictures. You thought I stayed in the car when you went to the studio, but many times I snuck in and watched you practicing the moves, there, and more than a few times when we were at home. Plus, I saw you teaching everyone tonight's routine yesterday out at Auntie Tapa's. I have practiced the same moves many times myself too. I can do it!"

Rai stared at her daughter, remembering their too-frequent discord lately, yet realizing this might be a sort of 'opening' for the future. Tears began to well in her eyes, and in those of a few others at the table too, Jess, Vic, Keely, and even Alex, joining in. Her husband had to turn his head to hide his own.

Rai sighed loudly, this time in happiness and relief, and as Tiare leaned over to hug her, she said, softly, "OK, *of course*, you'll be great. Thank you, this makes me so happy, Tiarenui!"

"Me too, Mom!"

"Now," Rai pushed her chair back and stood up, "We've got to get dressed...it's *Ori Tahiti* time! That's what our dancing here is called. Write that down, Cal, and make sure you video us so we can explain the moves later, and about all the dance routines we've performed in the past during the Heiva in Papeete!"

Anyone who has ever been to a luau knows that they are often lavish, certainly always lively affairs. Usually, they include an emcee - often a singer him/herself - who leads or explains the performances of a troupe made up of a dozen or more members, male and female. Complex steps and movements accompany special songs, often with chanting routines from several Polynesian cultures. The ones featuring Tahitian dancing, *Ori Tahiti*, as Rai had explained, are often the highlights of such multi-cultural events. Why?

Because they rock, literally! The Websters and other guests were about to see up close just how much Tahitians love music. Now, the band, which had been strumming and singing nice, friendly melodic tunes before the meal, was transformed for the dance show.

The three male musicians they'd seen previously on stage had changed into outfits with pareo on the bottom, nothing on top, and elaborate crowns of feathers and leaves on their heads. And each had a different type of drum. Soon, they began beating them with an insistent tempo, and the Webster clan members almost unconsciously began to bob and weave with the rising rhythms. A voice from behind the stage called out "Maeva to our family, and our honored guests, the Websters from America, and from *Aotearoa - Land of the Long White Cloud*, New Zealand - too."

Jess put her hand to her mouth in shock, then smiled and clapped along with the others. The announcer continued. "We will be doing just a few brief dances for you tonight. Thank you for coming, and please enjoy our *Ori Tahiti!*"

Suddenly, the lights were all turned off. Cal squinted to see, as did the others, their eyes slowly adjusting as three figures quickly moved onto the stage. Then, just as suddenly, the spotlights came on, the drums started again, and on the stage were Rai, Tapairu, and Tiare. Dancing very fast, moving their hips to the pulsating rhythm of the drums in a circular and up and down motion, clothed in bright pareo, tall headdresses, and with faux-coconut shell cups across their chests.

"Wow, do they look fantastic!" said Jess, and Keely and Meg, hearing the loud yells of encouragement from audience members around them, joined in with whistles and calls of "Yeah, Tiare!" and "Go, Rai, Go!"

"What an entrance!" Alex exclaimed, looking at Vic and then Cal, who watched intently, mesmerized along with the rest of them.

As the female dance members completed a variety of steps and moves, Jess was keenly observing how they carefully kept their posture erect, while their hips and knees worked together to keep the rotations going, around and round, up and down, and back and forth, even as they moved their feet in almost perfect unison, traveling short distances across the stage and back.

Soon, three male dancers joined them, performing their own elaborate moves, bending down, pointing up at an angle towards the sky, uttering loud cries in Tahitian, perhaps calling to the gods as was the ancient and continuing custom of the local dance. All of it was punctuated by the continued pounding of the drums.

Jess was fixated on one of the dancers... Julian, of course. The way he was able to move his own hips and rotate so smoothly and effortlessly back and forth across the stage, well, that was a marvel in itself. She looked over at Alex, saw he was grinning at her and blushed. *I'm probably absolutely crimson-cheeked right now!* she thought. But she giggled and quickly turned her attention back to the stage, where this first dance routine ended a few moments later. Loud applause from the audience followed.

"Mauruuru roa... merci... thank you, thank you!" said Rai, holding one of the microphones in her hand. "For those of you who don't know, that was called '*Fa ara pu*' - or, in Spanish...let's see, maybe..." and she looked at her husband in the audience. "*Caderas que se balancean rápidamente?* OR, in English," she paused, then giggled and pointed at the Websters' table - "Super-fast swaying hips!"

"Boy, I'll say!" Alex exclaimed, noting the amazement and gleams of approval in the eyes of his kids, then looking across at Linc, Cal, the girls, and Vic, who nodded vigorously in agreement.

Rai spoke again into the mike. "Next, we will slow things down a bit, so you can see how we do these dances. This is called the '*Tumami.*'" She swept her arms first to the left, then to the right. "I'd like to introduce my sister, Tapairu, and my daughter, Tiarenui. Tapa and Tiare," she shouted, "show us how it's done!"

The drums began again, this time in a slower beat, and the dancers moved their hips, knees, arms, and hands in a more subdued fashion, with the hip rolls larger, more defined than the quicker *fa'ara'pu* movements had allowed.

Keely noticed that Tiare, her mom and her aunt all had actual tiare blossoms behind their ears, in addition to the many flowers and leaves woven into their headdresses. She vaguely remembered reading something about that, but quickly dismissed the thought as she continued watching in awe. Tiare was able keep up almost perfectly as Rai and her sister led their way through all the intricate steps and movements of the dance, consistently staying in rhythm with the powerful drumbeats.

Keely also observed that Julian was a great dancer and surprisingly flexible – for a guy - she thought. Once again, Jess was clearly embarrassed when she noticed Keely chuckling with Meg as they caught their nanny following her Tahitian friend's every move as he performed onstage with the members of his extended family.

Tiare smiled straight at Keely and Meg and they grinned back and waved. Then, when the song ended a few moments later, and Rai began explaining what was next, suddenly, Tiare bolted to their table.

She reached out her hand to Keely, then Meg, and motioned them to grab her hands. But she didn't stop there, she next moved to Cal, who turned away and pretended as strongly (and creatively) as he could that he was quite interested in something way, way out in the lagoon, resisting her insistent pulling at his arm. But then, as his sisters stood up, laughed, and began to follow Tiare to the stage, he relented, and accepted her outstretched hand, albeit very reluctantly. Right behind him on the way to the dance platform came Rai, Vic, and Linc, with Linc's Aunt Tapairu right behind him. She had a firm grip around Alex's arm also, and was tugging him along to the stage.

Jess wiped her brow, and was sort of relieved that she wouldn't be dancing. She picked up the camera that Alex had been using to record the event, and took a couple quick photos. Suddenly, as she reached for the video camera, she felt an arm on her back. Turning, she jumped in momentary shock, then laughed, as Julian said "*Iaorana*, Jess, won't you join me for this dance?"

Standing quickly, Jess answered, despite her initial trepidation, "Heck yeah! *Aitapea pea*, let's go!" Luckily, one of Rai's cousins came over and took over the videography duties in response to her rapid request. *They'd all surely want to watch this later...I think?*

With all of them now onstage, Rai issued quick instructions to her new "class" of dancers. "OK, so now we have all of our honored guests up here, and *maeva* to any of the rest of you who wish to join us. You all saw us do both the slow moves...*tumami*...and the fast ones...*fa ara pu*. Now, we're going to give you a quick lesson on how to do both, and we'll see how you all do."

"*Arriba!!!!*" yelled Vic, eliciting a huge laugh from the audience. Rai looked at him with a mock glare of disapproval, then grinned wisely and chose the Tahitian words for his cheer instead: "*Haere tatou!* Let's go!"

The drums started again, beating out a steady, slow rhythm. Each of the Websters, and Jess, followed the lead of the person across from them, Keely and Meg with Tiare, Cal and Linc with a cousin of Rai's who had jumped onstage and clearly knew what she was doing, Jess with Julian, the former getting lots of 'special' help, and Alex with Tapairu. Rai was trying to direct her husband, but it was clear that her Spanish language familiarity far exceeded Vic's grasp of essential hip movements, as he (and Alex) struggled mightily to overcome their lack of grace and awkwardly followed - with little success - the deft movements of their expert 'teachers.'

Then the band stopped, just for a moment, and suddenly restarted. This time the rhythm was faster. Now Keely and Meg, who had tried to draw on their ballet and musical theater backgrounds to help them keep up with Tiare's moves, began to swing and sway (and sweat) wildly - both decidedly out of coordination with their Tahitian friend. Hair was flying, knees were knocking, feet stepped on toes, and amazingly, nobody fell off the stage or got hit by a wayward arm, finger, or leg!

The drums pounded while lots of hot and happy people gyrated back and forth, round and around, again and again, though only for another couple of minutes. But throughout, everyone was smiling, trying gamely to not embarrass themselves (or just giving up) amid a continuous flow of encouraging and joking calls from the standing, clapping crowd.

When the final drumbeats sounded, followed by sudden silence and a brief dousing of the lights, they all burst out with laughter, applause, and *high-fives*. Then the lights came back on, and as Rai started a chain of joined hands among all on stage and flashes popped on cameras across the seating area, the whole group took a huge bow toward their 'audience' of family and friends, and then another, bringing even more applause.

Tiare motioned her arm up in salute to her mom, and the rest of the chain turned toward Rai and saluted their 'leader' and host as well. Rai pulled her daughter and son close, hugging both, while pointing straight at her daughter and urging the audience to also clap for Tiare. She was very, very proud of her near-pro performance - and into the microphone, in a loving mix of English, Spanish and Tahitian, she exclaimed, *"Mi tamahine!* That's my daughter!"

Chapter 54

Triumph, then a tough night's end for all

With Rai and Tiare's 'dancing duties' done, and the rest of them also hot and still perspiring from the exertion and lingering heat, everyone sat back down at the table. "Time for some cold drinks, or coffee if you like. Plus, we have dessert!"

Rai seemed much happier now. For that matter, they all were in brighter moods following the energizing and uplifting, if at times uproarious stage antics (especially Alex and Vic's gangly attempts at dance moves.) Now, as they fanned themselves with napkins and plates, they were all ready to cool off and relax a bit.

One of Tiare's cousins brought over a tray of various desserts and set it down in the center of the table, along with a few more small plates (and forks, too) to go around. That was a huge relief to Meg, who was worried she'd have to eat pie or pudding - or whatever was served - with her hands!

Vic got up to grab coffee for himself and punch for Tiare and Linc, while Alex took orders from the Webster clan and went to get drinks for all. Jess was already sipping on a large glass of ice water Julian had gotten for her before he started helping take down part of the stage and sound system. Two of the band members played acoustic, unamplified music onstage, just to keep the fun going for a bit longer.

Turning to the evening's host, Jess asked, "What's your secret? How do you manage to stay in such great shape to do those beautiful, and tough, dance moves, Rai? And you too, Tiare, what a surprise, we had no idea you could dance so well!"

Her daughter beaming, the tall Tahitian smiled and answered, "You know, it's really just regular aerobics, practice, and even some yoga and Pilates. Plus being raised as a dancer since I was a little girl, it's in my blood – and maybe Tiare's too, I guess."

Keely and Tiare glanced at each other, then at Meg, then at Cal and Linc. A moment later, Alex and Vic came back, carefully balancing trays of drinks for everyone. Keely looked down at the table in front of her, took a breath, and decided it was time.

"We have a secret to share."

Jess looked at her in puzzlement.

Tiare was next. "And we feel kinda bad for lying about it, or at least not telling you."

Alex looked pointedly, with a bit of worry, at his oldest daughter. "Wow, Keel, what's this about...and why would you do that?"

Rai, who had still been reveling in the euphoria of the dancing, shot a questioning look at Tiare. Jess mused to herself, with a bit of dread, *you can tell she's thinking 'No more bad news today, please!'*

Before any of the others could say anything, Meg piped up. "It's not just them. We were all involved."

That got Vic's attention even more. He looked first at Tiare, and then pointedly at his daughter, then son. "Is that true, Tiare, Lincoln?"

Linc stared down at his toes for a moment, then answered "Yes, Dad."

Now it was Cal's turn. *Time to answer MY dad's next question before it's asked.*

"Yep, we were all part of it. We thought it was treasure, and it took us a while to even get it out of the hole where we found it."

"What treasure? What are you *talking* about, all of you?!" Rai was now seriously confused. Alex and Vic's faces also showed consternation.

Keely saw her cue. "OK. Let me explain. We were exploring over at the marae one day, you know, just playing around, that day when it rained a lot. Remember?" She stole a guilty look at Jess, who suddenly realized that she had been truly in the dark on the kids' actual activities that day.

Tiare continued. "So, we poked around in this deep hole we found by accident in the side of the marae and..."

"You could have been hurt, Tiare!" interrupted her mom.

Tiare glanced at Rai, and continued. "I know Mom, but I wasn't, um we weren't in any danger, really. We were just looking at something. Anyway, well, so, inside this hole we found a box. But we couldn't reach it right away. We had to come back the next day. Then we hid it. And..."

She faltered under her parents' glares. The Webster kids were also looking down, sideways, anywhere but into their dad's and Jess's eyes.

Alex held up his hand. "What's in this box, and where is it now?"

Tiare answered. "It's in our room. And we don't know what's in it, yet."

Her mom looked shocked. "*Where* in our room?"

"In our closet, Mom, under some of my stuff."

"You are really pushing it here, Tiarenui, you know!?" said Rai. She turned to Vic, who was staring again at Linc, who looked like he was about to cry.

"Sorry, Mom. I'll go get it right now." Tiare said.

"I'll go with her!" volunteered Keely.

"Keel, I think it best that you just sit down and wait 'til she comes back, OK?" Jess said. "Sorry, Alex, didn't mean to jump in there, it's just..."

Alex shook his head. "Hey, Jess, no need to apologize to me, I totally get it. In fact, any further explanations might need to come from other people at this table, and three of them are sitting beside you and me."

Meg thought she just might die of embarrassment and regret from the look her dad fixed on her, on Keely, and on Cal.

Everyone sipped their drinks uncomfortably, not really tasting them though, while Jess kept thinking, *what's really been going on around here?*

Soon, Tiare came back, at a very fast trot considering the bulky box in her arms, taking only about five minutes to cover the whole distance to and from the Martinezes' room. She set it down on the table in front of her mom.

Rai looked closely at the decayed brass container, rusty or tarnished and dented in several places. She touched its sides and lightly pulled on its top. It didn't budge, and it looked VERY old to her. "Hmmm, interesting. I've never seen anything like it before."

Vic reached across her arm and asked, "Can I take a look?"

He leaned down and picked it up, slowly turning it over in his hands. He guessed it was about the size of a very large cigar box, if there was such a thing. Smaller than a box for fishing tackle. *Maybe like a larger jewelry box?*

Flipping it back upright, Vic set it down on the table and pulled out his pocketknife. "Would you like me to open it?" he asked, first checking with the other adults, then turning to face all the kids.

"Sure! Do you think you can?" Meg replied.

"Yeah, Dad, that would be great," added Linc, as Cal nodded vigorously in agreement.

Vic looked this time at Keely and Tiare as if to say, "Are you sure?" They answered together. "Yes!"

He pulled out his pocketknife, actually one of those 'multi-tools' with many blades and gadgets in one case. He was about to try to pry the box open, when Rai touched his arm. She and Alex exchanged glances. Rai spoke to her husband. "Do you think it's OK to open it, Vic? I mean, it might be some sort of historic relic, or..."

"Yes, but if we take it to any preservation experts, they'll have to open it to see what's inside. Don't worry, I'll be very careful."

Carefully inserting a thin, rectangular blade from his knife into the opening, Vic slowly poked and twisted it around for a few moments. As they all watched breathlessly, he suddenly stopped.

"Lots of old gunk or rust in the keyhole here. Just a minute..."

Vic stood up and carried the box over to the pathway out to the beach. He leaned down and dropped it flat onto the hard grass and dirt path, several times, being careful not to bend the box, or dent or scratch its lid or bottom. Then he shook it a bit, blew into the keyhole, shook it again, then brought it back and set it down on the table.

Once again, he inserted the knife into the keyhole first, then several places along and under the box's lid, then back into the keyhole. He turned his knife blade again, ever so gingerly, with only as much pressure as he dared. Sweat trickled down his face. Just when he thought he'd have to quit trying, or possibly break the blade or the box's lock, the "key" (his knife blade) slowly turned, just a bit. Then it stopped. Vic tightened his grip on the knife handle, then began trying to turn it a bit more. It moved a fraction, then kept moving, little by little in a circular motion until, Cal noted, it was turned almost half-way around from its original position.

Now is the moment of truth, Keely thought. *What's in there?* Around the table, all of the others had similar thoughts.

With the lock now turned to where it should be to enable the box to open, Vic decided to try the nail file part of his "all in one" knife and began to gently pry around the edges, also very sticky due to age, dirt, or rust. He worked the long, thin file blade along the rim of where the box top met its bottom. Suddenly, with a loud "POP," the whole thing sprang open and he lost his grip on it. Luckily, Alex was able to catch the box before it fell off the table onto the ground. He set it back down in front of Vic, who opened up the top again on what were very creaky hinges. They all leaned in eagerly toward his seat at the table to peer at what was inside.

Nothing. There was nothing in the box, nothing at all.

"Well, that's a big bummer," said Meg, the first to speak.

"Darn!" said Cal. I thought there'd be ancient coins or something!"

"Yeah, treasure!" added Linc.

"I was hoping it would contain some jewelry or art, maybe preserved on old leaves or fabric or something," said Keely.

Tiare frowned. "I didn't know what I was hoping would be in it, but it *is* a very interesting box. We can keep it, right Mom and Dad?"

Alex spoke next. "I was hoping you'd all say, 'I wish we would have told our parents - or Jess' just what we'd been doing. "

Rai and Vic nodded their agreement. Rai added, "Exactly, Alex!"

Keely was first to respond. "I know Dad, Mr. and Mrs. Martinez...Rai. And we are really, really sorry we didn't just tell you. And same to you too, Jess. We should have told you right away," she said, looking at the nanny with genuine regret.

Jess was a bit dismayed, and also embarrassed for what the kids had gotten up to on her 'watch' - when she was entrusted with caring for them. And then she thought about what she'd been like, as a kid growing up. She and her friends had gotten into more than a few scrapes and situations along the way.

Looking first at Alex, then Rai and Vic, she broke into a grin. "I know you might not approve, as parents of these guys but...even though they didn't tell me what they were really doing when they found and then hid the box, I don't think they meant any harm. And they DID find a treasure box, didn't they? Even if there's nothing in it...I know as kids we always dreamed of finding hidden treasure, buried by pirates or something."

Alex looked carefully at Jess, then at Vic, then Rai. "Well, that's very generous of you, Jess. And, um, Vic, Rai, this came from your family's land. What do you think about this, er, *revelation* from the kids?"

Vic turned his head toward the lagoon, but not before Keely glimpsed what seemed like a grin on his face. As for Rai, she tried to look serious for a moment, and then she started giggling, a bit nervously. "No way do I need any more drama in my life, or for that matter, on this particular trip. We've had such a great time tonight...mostly." She stopped momentarily to gaze over toward her cousin Tanetoa's table as she said the last part, noting he wasn't seated there anymore. "But anyway, I actually think it's kind of a cool discovery you guys made!

"However, now that the box is open," she continued, "we do need to decide what to do with it. It looks quite old, and it's an interesting relic, empty or not. And it doesn't belong to us. I think taking it to our local museum in Papeete is the most sensible idea."

Vic spoke up next. "But I don't know when we can take it, Rai. We're not planning to spend much time at all in Papeete before we go to the airport on our return to the states."

"We can take it to the museum." said Alex. "We'll have lots of downtime in the afternoon before our flight on Saturday. We'll make sure it gets there, and fill out any forms required, answer any questions that we can if they ask, and let them know your name and where you are staying if they need more info. Plus, where it was found is on your family's land."

Rai looked a bit pained at this last comment, remembering the ownership controversy they'd all heard about earlier that evening.

Alex continued. "Even though no real harm has been caused to the box or the site...I know it's important to document these things...so, maybe tomorrow, could one or all of you show us where you found it? We can take some pictures, then tell the museum those details too. They can determine what should be done next."

Rai nodded. "Thanks, Alex. Really appreciate your willingness to help. If nothing else, what the kids found, just playing around, shows that we need more time - and to take more care - to protect the marae and others like it from being bulldozed, and really, to protect all of our historical and cultural treasures, our artifacts. Even if it's an empty box, it's still a treasure that may have meant something special to our family, and to our Moorean people as well."

Just then, Rai turned, and saw her cousin Tanetoa was coming over - yet again. This time, she was ready. And so were Alex and Vic. They both pushed back their chairs and stood to face the large Tahitian.

"Hey, Tanetoa, it's been a fun evening. Maybe you should just leave whatever you want to say for another day, OK?" Vic called out, but he was ignored. The man kept walking closer. Alex moved to where he could step between the two other men, if necessary.

Rai was furious, and after the up-and-down day she'd had, was in no mood for more arguments. "Back for more? Why are you doing this, Tane? Especially tonight!"

"Because it means money and a better future for my family. You don't care, you went to America, you like it there, you're living it up with your rich family. We have to live *here*, make a living here, and we can only afford to do so, and live like you do in the U.S., *maybe*, if we develop this whole property like we should have done years ago."

Tanetoa turned and glared at the Webster kids, then pointed at Tiare, his own distant cousin.

"I was watching you carry that box tonight, and one of our relatives overheard what you said and told me. You kids were playing where you didn't belong, and you removed something from a sacred place. So clearly you don't really care about history or such things at all, contrary to what your mom says. And also, I don't really care either. There's business to do around here and we've waited too long to start doing it."

Turning to Rai, he snapped - with more than a little glee, "I called the judge, and told him about what you said earlier, before dinner. As long as we have more votes on my family's side than yours, we will make our case and win the right to continue the renovation project as we planned. The delays you started will stop - soon. And I'm going to see the judge in Papeete personally, soon, with our lawyers, to get the papers signed to get it done. We have the votes to beat you. And we will."

Then he walked off. They heard a car start up and leave the adjacent parking lot. The silence that remained around the table was deafening.

Chapter 55

Aftermath & lessons learned

*So that was **it***, thought Alex. What had been a great evening, a wonderful, amazing, utterly memorable experience for all of them, was now tainted. As for the surprise news of the secret from the Webster kids and their friends? Well, maybe, he decided, that was sort of like "no harm, no foul," or "kids will be kids" (and *what they found was pretty exciting*, he thought), even if their announcement about finding the box was a bit of a shocker. But the real downer was the situation faced by their new friends. He cringed at the sadness he saw in Rai and her whole family at the prospect of losing their family's legacy lands.

Meanwhile, Keely was thinking that it had really been a dumb idea to keep what they found a secret from their parents and Jess. Especially since there was probably nothing in the box anyway. *None of all our planning and scheming was worth it. And it almost spoiled what could have been one of the best nights of our lives, even if it ended up getting spoiled anyway.*

When the Websters got up to leave the party, Meg and Cal joined Keely, Tiare, and Linc in realizing in common - judging from the looks they gave each other before the Websters began to make their way back to their bungalow at the Montcalm - that they agreed with Keely. And they all felt really sad about Rai and her family's dilemma. It was a long return trek from the Moorea Ra'i, past the marae, across the beach, and up the path to their room.

As they reached the door, Alex, who had been huddled in conversation with Jess for a few moments, said "Family meeting inside." He and Jess had stayed mostly quiet the whole way back, walking ahead of the kids after they had quickly thanked Rai and Vic for the food and entertainment. They had again expressed their sympathy for what had transpired with their cousin and what it might mean for the family's long-held property. Now, Alex had had a little time to think about next steps.

Joining everyone in the main room, with Keely, Meg, and Cal side-by-side on the bed, Jess in a chair and himself standing, Alex addressed the situation.

"OK, so lots of stuff to talk about here. But I'm too tired to talk about it all tonight. I do want to ask one question of each of you, separately. What have you learned from this?"

Nobody said anything for a very long moment. Then Meg started.

"We screwed up. We weren't thinking straight. I don't know why...stuff just happened."

Keely looked embarrassed, but less so than how she felt inside.

"Yeah, we got so excited when Cal saw the box while he was climbing on the marae that..." She started to play back all the different ways they could have handled things. But even if none of the adults seemed that mad about the situation, she knew, and wished they'd been more forthright with Jess, especially.

"And Cal, just one question. What were you doing climbing around on the marae anyway?" Alex asked, staring at his son.

"I was just joining Linc. He had to stand on the other side of the rocks there so people couldn't watch...while he..."

"While he what?"

"You know, peed on his own foot after stepping on the sea urchin."

"Oh my gosh, that's right, I remember hearing about that, but are you kidding me? So, THAT'S why you were crawling around on the marae, because he was peeing on a puncture? And then, you found the box."

Alex had to laugh inside at the situation, and again at the 'folk remedy' that Linc had used. Luckily, his mom said she'd later cleaned the wound thoroughly, then disinfected and bandaged it, as he knew was actually the course of action recommended by medical professionals for such situations. But no need to mention that now.

It had been a long week. Alex was ready to just put it all behind them, and go to sleep. Clearly, everyone else was exhausted too.

"OK, I'm beat. Let's just go to bed. But hey... Keely, you're getting up in the morning and swimming your assigned distance, right? I'll be down there with you, hoping for no rain. But we're going, rain or shine. And as for you other two... Meg, I know you captured lots of video from people tonight, and Cal, you got started on your interviews too, right? How about you both focus tomorrow morning on completing your school assignments while we're down at the lagoon? If needed, right after breakfast."

"Hey Alex?" Jess cut in for a moment. "I almost forgot. Julian is stopping by, probably after lunch but before he has to work the late shift tomorrow - it's Friday, so a busy night for him and the restaurant. Maybe we can set up a quick follow-up interview with him for Cal? He went to the Heiva festival as a dancer and a stone-tosser - and a climber too - a couple times as a teenager and for a few years after that. He can help Cal get the details he needs to finish up his report. Or maybe even find somebody else to give him another perspective on it?"

"That's great, Jess. Thanks for your idea and for helping out. Appreciate your asking Julian when you see him tomorrow. You heard her Cal. Be ready, just in case. Also, Bernie Tetuanui - Jean-Paul's brother - is the IT guy I've been working with at the Montcalm. He's really cool and also immersed in the local culture here. He might have ideas for you too, not sure, I'll ask him when I get to the office."

Alex was past ready to wrap up the 'lesson' for the night, though he didn't really have any 'map' to guide him on how to proceed with his kids. This was a new situation for him, and it wasn't going to be easily 'tied up with a bow' with quick resolution.

"Anyway - you all have your tasks to complete. I'm still wondering why you thought you had to keep this all a secret, even lie about it to Jess and me, and Rai and Vic too? Though I will say I'm relieved that your escapades haven't resulted in any worse outcomes for the Martinezes and Rai's family. That cousin of hers is not a nice guy. And I don't think he even cares about what you found or that you were playing on the marae grounds... it's all about the money."

Alex sighed. "OK, some very useful lessons learned, by all of us. What a day! What a wonderful - and then maybe not so wonderful - trip to the motu, time at the party, and all that food and dancing too. That's kind of the way life can be sometimes. You want to live it to the most - have fun. And when stuff happens, or when things go wrong, you want to be able to honestly say you did your best to do right, or at least correct your mistakes after you make them. But today's already in the past, and it's time now for all of you (and me) to go to bed. Goodnight."

He sent a silent look of thanks to Jess, then hugged the kids, all at once, as Jess watched.

After their dad left, but before they split up for bedtime, Keely, Meg, and Cal converged on Jess with a vigorous group hug, and one last round of sincere *'I'm sorry'* messages from each. Soon after, the lights went out in the bungalow. And that was how Thursday - Day 7 in paradise for the Worldwide Websters - came to a close.

Chapter 56

One final plunge in the lagoon

December 2, Friday

When Alex awoke, he had almost forgotten the events of the night before, both good and not so good. He'd actually slept pretty well, and no roosters greeted him before the clock read 7 am. This, he acknowledged, was a very positive start to the Websters' final full day on the island of Moorea. They all needed to be reminded of positive things and move on, which would be both easy, and hard, to do amid all the tropical splendor. *They'd have some amazing memories of their trip - and most, for sure, would be good ones.*

After a quick trip to the bathroom, splashing water on his face to try to eliminate his lingering grogginess, he put on his swim suit and a t-shirt, grabbed a towel and his goggles, and knocked lightly on the door to the girls' room. Keely came right out, ready for her morning swim. They quietly opened the door and left the bungalow together.

"How did you sleep last night?" Alex asked his oldest daughter as they walked together down the path to the beach.

"OK, I mean, Meg and I talked for a while about everything, you know, what happened, and what you said last night. And we both feel kinda bad about how stuff turned out. I don't know why we thought we had to keep everything so secret. I did write about it in my journal...the one mom gave me. I wanted to make sure I wrote down my feelings...who knows, I may one day look back to learn from this situation - but hopefully not after doing something else dumb!"

"Hey, good thing I'VE never made a mistake or done something I regretted," Alex said wryly. "Or said things I wished later to take back...But it sounds like you're going in the right direction with your thinking. Speaking of which, for your workout today, how far are you going to swim out there this morning?"

Keely looked forward as they walked the path to the beach. "I'm ready to really clear my head, and the weather's nice too, so I'll swim crawl straight out from the beach, about 200 strokes, then maybe 10 or 11 times back and forth in front. I'll alternate with back and breaststroke too. I may even try to go faster, even sprint, on a few of the laps."

"How about I join you? Maybe not right next to you but nearby, and I might just swim out a bit further while you're doing your repeats. Should take us around 40-45 minutes, right?"

"Sure, Dad!" Now arriving at the beach, they dropped their towels, shirts, and sandals, adjusted their goggles, and entered the water for what might be their last early-morning swim on the island.

Keely took mental and visual aim at three points from where she entered the lagoon. Standing up with the gentle waves lapping the bottom of her racing suit, she looked left, right, and straight ahead several hundred meters in each direction, then decided to head out toward the reef first. Her dad was already on his way there, where she knew he liked to hang out and sometimes float, and think. She dunked her head under and started her workout.

So many fish here...definitely more than I remember in some other places, Keely thought. As she stroked steadily out towards her first point of reference directly opposite the shore and aiming towards the left center of the waves breaking out on the reef, her mind began to wander. At times like these, even with the added attraction of tropical fish of every color, shape, and size around her, Keely tended to 'play music' in her head. This time it was a favorite song, but sometimes it was a tune she didn't really like, one that had become an 'earworm' she just couldn't get out of her mind.

As she progressed steadily outward from the beach, she replayed the events of the prior evening, the music still on "auto-play," but now in the background of her active thoughts.

Well, Dad's probably right that despite failing to find any secret treasure from the marae - which ended up just being an empty old box, apparently - we didn't likely hurt anything. As far as the decision to sell the Moorea Ra'i - Rai's ancient family property, I wonder what's going to happen to the Martinez family and their cousins who live here? Tiare was so devastated last night, and so was her mom, even after the night started so happily, all that great food, the dancing, how Tiare stood up to help her mom right when she needed it, when she had just been confronted by her jerk cousin about the property. MOST of that was so cool.

But now...Sad times for Rai, Tiare, Linc, and Mr. Martinez too. It's too bad their family's hotel and land is being sold, but they'll still make money from selling it, right? Maybe they can use some of what they get for it to travel other places just as beautiful, or as interesting, as Moorea. Maybe they can come visit us in Washington! But...I doubt they'll be happy losing their land - the place of their ancestors.

Keely found herself wishing that she or the Webster family could do something to make the Martinezes feel better. *But maybe there's nothing to do, just be their friend, stay in touch, maybe connect somewhere else, sometime in the future? We can write each other emails, or letters. Or text messages even. But it won't be like hanging out here again, in magical Moorea...And what about Jess and Julian? Where's that going to go...hmmm.*

Just then, the other side of Keely's brain 'pinged' that she had reached 200 strokes and the physical world came to the fore of her mind. She stopped and surfaced, pulling down her now slightly-fogged goggles. Turning in all directions, she took a few moments to float and think. Then, focusing on a point almost the same distance diagonally toward her right and back toward shore, she started her next interval swim, still crawl stroke, but faster this time. This was the second of ten vigorous sets, with some backstroke, breaststroke, and maybe even some butterfly mixed in for her last big swim here in Moorea. She planned to mostly crisscross the lagoon from side to side, but maybe take one other diagonal route back toward the reef near where she now treaded in the warm lagoon waters.

She spit and rubbed her finger around the rims of her goggles then positioned them over her eyes. Round two of her last Polynesian paradise practice session. *Ha-ha, Dad would love how I put those three words together!*

Meanwhile, Alex had been daydreaming while swimming too. The water was very calm (*as usual for this place*, Alex thought) and he was enjoying combining exercise and exploration for what amounted to 'light' skin diving (no fins, mask, or snorkel, but with his goggles for clarity.)

After finishing several hundred strokes in each direction (except toward the shore) he meandered around the lagoon for about 20 minutes, all the while staring down in wonder at the abundant creatures and plants. He was coming up for air out near the reef line - after diving deep toward an interesting outcrop with some particularly brilliant sea anemones in shades of purple and pink and yellow - when he saw Keely standing in the shallows. A check of his watch showed 8 am. Time to wrap things up and head into shore. *But first, a quick dive down, one last look at the reef area.*

Alex made an extra effort to propel himself deeper this time, and while he was rewarded with a surprising glimpse of a sea turtle and also a pretty large Puffer fish - his very first sighting of the latter on this trip - what grabbed his attention most in the few moments he was down below the surface was a plaintive wail, almost like a human crying, a sound similar to many he had heard in the past.

Was that a whale? Alex knew from asking around, from Cal's initial research, then from conversations at the hotel and when they were out on the boat with Julian, that the Humpback whales that visited French Polynesia typically were gone from Moorean waters by early November, some years by late October. But it was definitely a familiar call...and he knew that even though each whale has a different song, there are some commonalities between them. Though he couldn't be sure of what exactly he had heard.

In Maui, he knew, more than 600 whales typically frequent the channel between that island and its neighbors Lanai and Kahoolawe each late fall into spring, when the waters between those islands (and those surrounding other nearby islands in the chain too) become sort of an extended 'bowl' in which the humpbacks roam and romp, with not much eating done at all for several months. Instead, according to marine biology experts, they're mostly wooing, mating, and calving - giving birth to baby whales - these activities being the main purpose for their lengthy trek from the cold, krill-rich feeding waters of Alaska to the warmth of the Hawaiian Islands. Apparently, Alex had heard, it was the same here, just flipped in terms of winter/summer routes, with the French Polynesian humpbacks heading south to Antarctica for their primary feeding season - at the same basic times of year as their seasonally opposite northern cousins - but just in a different direction.

His attention back on the lagoon in front of him, Alex surfaced, adjusted and defogged his goggles one last time, then began to swim vigorously toward shore, still aware of all the thousands of fish below him. He was intent on relieving some stress, clearing his thoughts, and getting to the beach as quickly as he could, pushing his arms and legs hard in one final, bracing fast interval for his last real 'power' swim in Moorea.

As he neared the shore more than one hundred strokes later, the sun began to brightly light the reefs and rocks around him. *Wow, what an astonishingly colorful, vibrant, unpredictable place this is. Just like its people!* He kept propelling his long frame toward the beach, and after around 30 additional crawl strokes his knees lightly scraped the soft sandy bottom.

He stood up, and slowly turned around to take one more look back toward the surf pounding the reef where he had been only a few moments before. Then, with a satisfied, somewhat weary smile, he joined his eldest daughter to dry off on the beach. Time for a quick shower and breakfast to get on the go for the Worldwide Websters' last full day on Moorea!

Chapter 57

Local flavors & bittersweet farewells

"OK, guys, let's get going! I've only got use of the jeep until 2:30 this afternoon. Just found out Montcalm has a special event later, a wedding, and they need all their spare vehicles. So, we gotta have lunch and do some sightseeing and shopping - then make sure to be back here in less than four hours. Besides, I figure everybody could use a final 'down' half-day to relax and enjoy the beach and the resort before we head for home tomorrow."

Alex stood outside the bungalow and watched as another van-full of guests was just arriving from the ferry dock...or maybe the airport? He'd already witnessed three similar arrivals while enjoying coffee outside the room on the patio. David the GM had told him the Montcalm was sold out for the next several days.

Alex thought back to when the Websters had arrived from the ferry landing one week prior. It seemed a long, long time ago...so much had happened, they'd experienced so many activities and adventures together, and yet, they still had only really seen a fraction of the island.

Now, he did a quick scan in his mind through their plans for the day. It was 9:30 am. They'd start with a leisurely drive back up to the Belvedere lookout, this time going counter-clockwise, and then onward to a couple of the nearby towns around Cook's and Opunohu Bays. They'd do some souvenir-shopping, and then take a few more photos from above the resorts near the airport. Finally, they would head back in early afternoon for beach time and packing. Later, in the evening, Alex was looking forward to a leisurely final meal at the Montcalm's restaurant. Despite how busy they expected to be with new arrivals, the Websters had already been assured a table with a great view outside on the patio, not far from the pool, with a reservation starting just before sundown. It had a sunset view, too - and all of this thanks to Julian's help. Alex chuckled to himself. *It pays to be friends with the restaurant management!*

Once Jess and the kids had clambered into the jeep and buckled up, this time with only one cooler and small backpacks to carry, Alex made a quick announcement as they pulled away from the resort. "Hey guys, there's one place - a surprise - that you haven't been that we'll visit on the way back, right before we stop by the Moorea Ra'i. Also, remember we've got to take a couple of photos of the hole where you found the box in the marae, right? And we have to pick up the box itself too, so we can take it with us to the museum in Papeete."

"Cool. But where are we going first, Dad?" Keely asked.

"The Belvedere. Remember that?"

"Oh yeah! The haunted marae and that incredible view from the movie!" Cal exclaimed.

"That's right," Alex answered with a grin. "A good chance for one last look from up high, at *Bali Hai*, then we'll head down to visit a couple of stores out by the airport, grab lunch and hang out in the park there for a bit. Then back here by way of the Martinezes' hotel."

The kids glanced at each other. "I hope we can see Tiare and Linc while we're there," Meg said.

"Yeah..." Keely added wistfully.

"I'm sure if they're around you can say goodbye," answered Alex. "But we'll be on a tight schedule. I called Rai and Vic to let them know we'd be by around 2 for a quick visit before we head back to the Montcalm."

Soon they had traversed the length of Opunohu Bay and were heading to the entrance of the verdant valley where the road snaked upwards into the mountains. "Wow, just wow. But, of course, we've all said THAT before," sighed Jess, as she leaned out the window to take a photo. She had a full view through the towering cliffs of Rotui and the other peaks, partially shrouded though they were in clouds.

As they climbed upward, the road seemed smoother than the week prior but Alex was glad they still had the jeep, especially as the other side of the loop was quite rough.

Passing by the Tetiaroa Marae, which they'd visited on their round-the-isle tour, Cal thought back to their escapades in the temple next to Linc and Tiare's hotel. *That was fun, even if we got in a little trouble for it. Oh well!* He hoped their new friends were OK, *but boy was Mrs. Martinez sad...*

Alex stopped the car when they reached the viewpoint. They all got out, cameras in hand. "I'm taking some different shots than last visit," he said, brandishing his video camera almost like a weapon.

As the family fanned out to various sides of the Belvedere parking area, Jess told herself to really look and feel everything this time. To smell the air, admire the vegetation, and listen closely to the sounds of the jungle around her. She was rewarded in the latter case with an answer of birdsong of maybe five or six different types.

Keely was consulting her new book on Moorea, and checking to see what types of trees and plants were around. The most interesting of all, she thought, right in front of the pyramid-like Mt. Rotui in her field of view, was the jasmine tree, fully ten times the size of any backyard-sized bush of this type she had ever seen, but as she neared it and captured its star-shaped white blooms with her camera, its sweet, spicy fragrance wafted past her nose.

"Hey guys, come here and smell this!" Keely said, and soon she and the others were enjoying the wonderful scents, and sights, as they also found tiny orchids nesting in air it seemed, growing right from the branches of several of the trees. Also present: tiare, or gardenias, plus tons of other lush, green plants, many the same or similar to those common in North American homes - except orders of magnitude larger owing to the extremely hospitable climate and growing conditions of Moorea. *I'll never look at our houseplants the same again!* Keely mused.

Meg positioned herself back at the railing, and looked down through her tiny binoculars, past what Keely explained were lots of pineapple fields, into the water, far away from their lookout perch. She watched two large outrigger canoes, each with what looked like five or six occupants, stroking their way smoothly and rapidly across the mouth of Opunohu Bay. She imagined for a moment what it must have been like 200, 300, or even 500 or more years before, when Tiare's mom's ancestors had traveled, fished, and fought battles using such watercraft for transportation. She closed her eyes, opened them, and had a brief, astonishingly clear vision of one of the ships of Bligh's expedition sailing into the bay. She laughed at herself for carrying the fantasy this far, and shook her head to clear it of this crazy image. She figured it was likely from her mind recalling the movie they'd watched the previous month at home.

The travelers from Tacoma spent only about 15 minutes at the lookout this time, capturing the highlights, drinking in the views, trying to etch them into their brains for recall during the windy and cold fall-to-winter weather they'd be returning to in Washington, and hopefully for many years thereafter. After a final family "*Ia Orana from Moorea!*" video clip and photo done using the timer and setting the camera in a notch next to a handy tree limb, the Webster gang clambered back in the jeep and retraced their route to the fork in the road. From there, they took the option towards the right and bounced their way - more slowly this time - down the narrow, winding, bumpy, and unpaved road to Paopao.

As they entered the town, they pulled into the small supermarket parking lot and went in, still seeking a few souvenirs. Jess and the kids found a fun refrigerator magnet while Alex grabbed a couple more bottles of sparkling water to replenish their supply for their final day on the island. Outside in front of the store, they decided they couldn't pass up one more lunch of chow mein sandwiches, so everybody got one 'to go.'

Continuing their trek, Alex drove around the east side of Cook's Bay past the collection of small hotels and houses aside the turquoise-blue waters, and soon after they rounded the corner into view of the lagoon, they reached Maharepa. With the small dress shop he had visited on his bike - and later with the kids - on their right, Alex recalled meeting Rai's sister the previous evening. Suddenly, he realized where he'd seen her before - it was there, at the store, during his bike ride, when he'd made the quick visit and glanced over their clothing and jewelry selection. "Tapa" - as Tapairu was nicknamed, hadn't been in the store on the second trip when they'd bought the earrings for Jess – probably why he hadn't made the connection when they were introduced at the tama'ara'a.

Because Jess was with them now, and they wanted her jewelry gift to remain a secret until later that afternoon, Alex kept his thoughts to himself and kept driving. Soon they were passing by a public beach, which looked very active with both tourists and apparent locals enjoying the grounds and water activities.

Speaking of Jess, she was thinking quietly too. *Friday's a happy day everywhere, I guess!* She pondered this while watching the lively scene off to the left side of the vehicle, and let her mind wander to images of the prior day in the boat with Julian, and of his dance performance at the show. *There's no way this thing could ever work,* she chided herself. *How many thousand miles away? School to finish, and we've nothing really in common with each other except - a love of beautiful places and people. He's a really nice guy. A great guy who's fun to be with. That's all fine, but surely, it's not enough basis for a relationship?*

The always-sensible New Zealander was snapped back to reality from reverie when Keely announced, "There's the airport, we're coming into Temae," as she consulted the driving map in her book. This was one town they hadn't really explored much, so Alex pulled into a small shopping village, sporting a sign that read *produits locaux* - or "local products" in English.

As they got out of the car, Alex suggested, "Maybe we'll find some nice presents for my team and our family/friends here. You know - fun, yet affordable gifts to bring back?"

It turned out to be a smart stop. They found a nice boxed collection of local vanilla in small bottles, just large enough to use occasionally but not difficult to transport. The vanilla definitely cost more than the types they could buy at home, but given some research Keely had done, they knew that Moorean vanilla was some of the most prized in the world. It would be great to give to their grandparents and Alex's work friends as presents from their trip.

They bought a few more trinkets and small carvings made mostly of wood, several postcards and then they all agreed that the locally made "*monoï*" coconut soap - it looked like what was supplied in the bathrooms at their hotel - would be nice as small gifts to everyone else. Counting up all the people they wanted to share with, Alex ended up buying a dozen of the small wrapped soap bars. Luckily the clerk gave him a discount on a convenient multi-pack box of them so they could lie flat and secure in his suitcase on the way home.

By this time, everybody was getting hungry, so they hit the road again, driving on past the airport entrance and toward another beach not far beyond it. In a few minutes, they saw a small parking lot, and Alex edged the jeep into a space near a picnic table, way off to the side of the beach. Savoring the breeze coming off the reef and ocean beyond, they settled down to enjoy their sandwiches and sodas.

The view of the sea here, through the lagoon hugging the shoreline, was due east. Now at the upper Northeast portion of the island, they could look straight across the nine-mile channel to Papeete, its buildings and boating activity faint in the distance.

"Hey Dad, aren't we pretty near the ferry landing?" asked Meg.

"Yep, it's just a little way down the road. I guess this is Temae Beach? I knew we wouldn't have time to stop here at this beach tomorrow, but I heard it was nice, and I figured it would be fun to come out for lunch."

"I agree," said Keely. "I like getting additional views on stuff. What about you, Jess?"

"Yeah, I've been thinking of lots of perspectives on things, for sure," she answered, with a mysterious look in her eyes.

This side of the island definitely had a more 'industrial' feel to it, in that there were businesses, steady traffic, and everything that you usually find near airports and ferry docks. People congregate near such places, and though the beach here was off the beaten path, and nice, albeit with a few more rocks than some on the island, it still didn't have quite the magic about it as the one fronting their hotel and others they had visited.

That, Jess thought, was kind of sad, in that in many tourist areas - not just in Moorea but almost everywhere she'd been - you often had to pay for a room at one of the resorts to gain quick, convenient access to the nicest beaches. But...she remembered from her conversation with Julian...apparently the locals on Moorea weren't too worried about access, as they all had their own favorite public beach or easily reachable swimming, snorkeling, surfing, and boating spots - some being family or friend-owned locations. And, Julian had told her with a wink, if they *really* wanted to visit a tourist resort for a day, there were ways to do so. Jess didn't ask how, figuring *that's a question for the next trip!*

Cal was savoring the final bites of his chicken chow mein sandwich. "Dad, we really have to try and make these at home. They are awesome!" Everyone else nodded in agreement with the youngest in their crew. Clearly, this was the consensus winner of the 'culinary discovery award' of their trip - if they decided to name one.

Finished with their lunch, it was time to start heading back toward the Montcalm. But first, they took a detour up to the overlook nearby, the one they'd visited on their trip around the island. They could see the buildings of one hotel below them, this one with overwater bungalows, a newer, more modern-design property than the hotel that had originated the concept in Cook's Bay in the 1960's. Now, gazing from a much higher angle towards Tahiti, they had a wider view, both above and through the scudding clouds, of the main island of French Polynesia.

As Alex took some snapshots and a few more minutes of 'last-day' video, Meg trained her binoculars toward the small Moorea airport, though no planes were taking off or landing just now. She craned her head to the right and past a few small villages including the larger one they'd just visited - and the beach park where they'd had lunch. Far in the distance, the ferry they'd taken from Tahiti to Papeete was speeding across the waters toward Moorea. "Is that the *Aremiti*, Dad?"

"Looks like it, and check it out, the *Moorea Express* is heading back the other way toward Tahiti." Alex pointed to the car-carrying ferry – now much closer to the Vai'are dock but traveling in the opposite direction.

Taking in the whole view of the island - the lagoon, the boats and ferries, mountains, tropical foliage, and gorgeous blue-green waters - Meg thought of her school project topic, how the colloquialism she had chosen to explain in class back home completely summed up the feeling you got hanging out and enjoying places like this. *Aita pea pea for sure. Problems just don't seem so important when you feel like you're in a...tropical paradise. No problem!*

Checking his watch, Alex saw it was almost 1 pm. "Time to head back, one last time, guys. But as I promised, we've got a fun stop left first before our quick photo/pickup at the Martinezes' hotel."

"Where are we going, Dad?" Cal asked.

Alex just smiled. "You'll see!"

They headed down the hill, then kept driving back the way they'd come a couple hours earlier. This time, they passed quickly through the towns of Temae and Maharepa, and in 15 minutes they wound back around the mountain side of Cook's Bay.

Just before reaching the lagoon, Alex turned off on a small road. In a couple of minutes, they pulled into the fruit juice factory he'd visited twice by bike and car earlier in the week.

"Surprise! Who wants to try some fresh local juice and sparklers?"

"Yay!" replied Keely and Meg, and Cal was quickly out of the car to get in line for the next tasting line-up. As a group of three tourists in front of them finished up their samples and paid for a small purchase to take with them, the Webster clan stood in a row for their samples.

"*Ia Orana! Maeva!*" said the host, the same man who'd been working the booth during Alex's prior visit. "Welcome back! You bring family! Want to try different kinds?"

Alex gave him a thumbs-up as he answered. "Sure, and actually, small samples for each of us are fine. We are leaving tomorrow, so, if possible, we just want to try what you have and take a couple cans or bottles with us back to our hotel for the beach - and maybe tomorrow morning."

Turning to the kids and Jess on either side of him, Alex said, "OK, the challenge is to try them all and then decide which is your favorite. Then we'll buy a couple of the top three choices to bring back with us to the resort."

"Hey Dad?" Keely asked Alex. "Can we buy two to bring to Tiare and Linc and their parents?"

"Yeah, Dad, can we?" echoed both Meg and Cal.

"I think that's a great idea! And you know what, I'll buy a bottle of the special liqueur they have here to give to Rai and Vic to thank them as well. Who knows, they might not have tried it yet, during this trip anyway, and maybe it will help them all feel a little better about the situation they're in."

Jess beamed, gratified that the kids showed such consideration for the feelings of others, especially given the tough night they'd all had with the explanations about the box and the property squabbles between Rai and her extended family.

Keely agreed with her dad. "Yeah, I think it will help, but I still wish there was more we could do..."

Jess turned to face her oldest 'charge,' who really was growing up fast.

"You know, Keel, sometimes you can't make everything work out. You just have to do your best and see what happens. But I'm really proud of you, and your brother and sister too, for trying."

"Well, one way we can really show we mean it is if Dad at least uses some of the money he already gave us to buy the gifts for the Martinezes." Keely replied. And with that, she handed her dad the 2000 CFP note, the largest one of French Polynesian currency she had and the only local bill other than a few coins she'd saved from their trip to the store earlier in the week. Meg reached into her wallet and handed over the CFP 1000 bill that she had left, and even Cal got into the spirit, handing his dad all the local change that had been jingling in his pocket.

Alex was absolutely blown away...he really hadn't expected this kind of response from the kids. It wasn't that he thought they didn't care or were unaware of people's feelings - or didn't understand the true cost of the things they might have taken for granted as part of the family's travels. Mostly, he was surprised just because he tended to 'take care' of almost everything, all the arrangements, all the expenses, on trips like this. Maybe he had underestimated his children. *Or maybe they were just turning out the way any parent would hope they would*...he mused, as he fought back the tears that he felt welling around his eyeballs. He looked away, then turned back and reached over and hugged each of the kids. "Thanks guys...this makes our gift to the Martinez family - and this trip too - more meaningful than you'll ever know."

They all focused back on the tasting exercise. When their relatively quick run-through of all the available juice flavors was complete, they each announced their favorite flavors, and the winners were "Mango!" "Passion fruit!" and "Pineapple-Guava sparkling soda!" Alex bought one of each variety. He made a special point to add the bills and coins from the children to the pile he handed over to the host, paying for two more tall bottles of the fruit juice and the one of liqueur for the Martinez family.

As their host packaged up their purchases, Meg said, in an exceptionally strong voice, "*Maururu!*" and he answered, just as forcefully, "*Aita pea pea!*", which drew a huge laugh from all of them. Meg then caught everyone by surprise as she grabbed her dad's video camera and looked pleadingly at the man in the booth.

"Could you say that again? I've got a special school project to present on important sayings, and my choice is *aita pea pea*..."

He looked like he only partially understood. Then suddenly, "SURE! *tamahine apî*," he answered as she switched on the camera.

"*Maururu roa*," said Meg, smiling, not knowing what he had just said in Tahitian, either.

"*Aita pea pea*...no problem, young lady!" Then turning to the rest of the Websters, he said "Thank you for visiting our factory, and *au revoir*. Please come back soon!"

"Got it!" Meg reached out, right across the bar, and gave the main a big hug. Then, with a chorus of '*Nanas*' from the two Websters (Meg and Keely) who remembered how to say "Goodbye" in Tahitian, they waved farewell and were on their way.

The brief stop at the Moorea Rai was last on their agenda for this final island excursion. Minutes after leaving the juice factory, Alex pulled the jeep into a parking space near the middle of the Martinezes' property, next to the path over to the marae.

"Right over here, Dad," said Cal, as he jumped from the jeep and led them all through the trees and bushes to the rock wall where he and Linc had found the ancient box. He pointed to the small hole, and reached his hand in to show where the box had fallen.

Alex took a few photos, first of the larger view of the marae, then a couple close-ups of the hole and one aiming downwards inside using the flash. Then, they all turned and headed back toward the hotel parking lot. Rai was just in the process of getting out of her car with Tiare and Linc.

"Hi, Rai!" said Alex.

She smiled back, a bit wistfully, as they walked toward her. "How are you guys doing? Enjoying your last day on Moorea?"

"Oh, we've had a fabulous time today," said Jess.

Alex asked, "Do you have the box for us to take to the museum tomorrow?"

"Oh, yeah. I'll go get it!" said Tiare, and she ran to their room to retrieve the relic.

While they waited for Tiare to return, Alex stepped over to the jeep and grabbed the bag of gifts from the juice factory. He pulled out the two bottles the kids had chosen and handed them to Keely and Meg. "The kids wanted to say 'thank you' for all you've done to make us feel welcome, Rai. And you, Linc, and Tiare too. They bought these with their own money." He finished speaking as Tiare came back, puffing a bit while carrying the heavy old brass box in her arms. She set it down as Keely pointed to the gifts in hers and her sister's hands.

"Oh, cool!" said Tiare, breathlessly.

"Thanks!" said Linc as the Webster girls handed each of them a large bottle of juice. "Yay! My favorite is passion fruit!" he exclaimed.

"And mine is mango," Tiare added. "We haven't even had these on this trip yet. Thank you, Cal, Meg and Keely!"

"Aita pea pea, Tiare!" answered Keely. Then, looking at Rai with some embarrassment, she said "Mrs. Martinez, er, Rai, we are all so sorry for any trouble we caused you with our secrets and not telling the truth about the box and stuff."

"Thank you for the apology, Keely," answered Rai, "and it is a cool old box. I'm actually really glad you found it."

Meg piped up, "Same from me, I'm so sorry Rai/Mrs. Martinez - and to Mr. Martinez too."

"Yeah, me too," said Cal.

Rai smiled and gave each kid a big hug, which they returned with no small sense of gratitude and relief.

"Hey, where is Vic, by the way?" Alex asked.

"Oh, he's in town, actually out by the airport, near Temae, talking with one of my cousins about some business matter. I don't think it's related to the problems we shared with you last night, but I don't know for certain. Frankly, I was just exhausted after everything that happened at the tama'ara'a. And just about everything going on with the property, period. Sorry, I don't mean to be so downbeat on the last day of your vacation..." She sighed and looked down at the ground.

"Hey, we were just out that way eating lunch. Sorry we missed him. Anyway, no need to explain at all, Rai. I totally get how you must feel, and I know we all do. It's not fun. In fact, it really..." - he stole a glance at the kids then looked back to her - "*sucks* to be in such a situation. I really, really hope there's some way your family can hold onto the property."

Alex pointed to his camera. "On that note, we did take a few shots of where the kids found the box. We'll share them with the museum when we deliver it. Also, we all wanted to thank you for your tremendous kindness, on so many levels, and to let you and Vic and

Tiare and Linc, and your whole family, know that we had a super time at the tamaaa er..., well, you know what I mean. What a blast, great food, amazing dancing, and..." - he paused to look Rai in the eye - "very, very nice people who we'd like to call our new Moorean-American best friends!"

He reached into the bag and pulled out the bottle of local liqueur.

"I'm guessing you've had this before, but we thought it might help a little to take your mind off the conflict here in paradise. Maybe you and Vic can share it one night before you return home, or take it with you on your flight back to Denver!"

"Oh, thanks, Alex, and all of you, very much! Believe it or not, we haven't tried this yet, and yes, we will definitely sip some at sunset, no matter what happens over our final days here. After all, this is my family home, and this," she said holding up the bottle, "is from that home, and my people. And you all are OUR best new American-Kiwi friends!" She hugged Alex, then Jess, and then everybody was embracing everyone else. Plus a few tears were shed too.

"OK, well, I hate to break up this 'hug-fest' but..."

"Wait!" Keely interrupted her dad and ran back to the jeep, reaching into their cooler in the back seat. "Sorry, Dad. We have one more gift for all of you...it's *Almond Roca*, from home. We brought a couple of extra boxes just to thank someone, for something, while we were here. My Dad gave a couple boxes to the hotel staff. He loves to share them with clients too, but this time, I'm going to take charge..."

The 12-year-old walked up to Tiare and handed her a small pink, red, and gold cellophane-wrapped box. "I kept it in our cooler in the car so it wouldn't melt. It's the most delicious blend of toffee and chocolate and almond pieces. Put in your fridge right away and enjoy it together sometime before you leave?" Keely asked their new friend.

Tiare's eyes grew wide as she accepted the box from Keely.

"Are you kidding? I love this candy! I had no idea it came from Tacoma! Thank you, Keely, Mr. Webster, Jess, Meg, Cal. All of you!"

Rai grinned and Linc nudged his sister to get a look at the box.

"If you've never had it, and you like chocolate and toffee, you'll love this, I promise you, Linc!" said Cal. The two high-fived to seal the deal.

Alex laughed. "OK, well, thanks to *Brown & Haley*, who made it, and to Keely for the thoughtful gesture, you'll have some awesome candy to add to the local Moorean liqueur and juice. Unfortunately, we have to go now to get the Montcalm's jeep back. Lots of wedding activities going on today and they need all the vehicles they can get!"

"Yes, lots going on over there," agreed Rai. "We're heading over soon, after we drop by my sister's, in fact. The kids are helping me demonstrate pareo-tying for the guests after the ceremony, at the reception. And I'm sure we'll sell a few pareo that we've already made this past week as well, especially since most of the wedding party and family just arrived. They'll need something to wear here for the next week...right?"

They all giggled at the image Rai suggested of a whole passel of tourists trying out various styles of pareo-wearing each day, and Alex said "You know, I forgot to tell you, I/we visited your sister's store and...anyway...I kinda wish I'd gotten one when I was there, but we were looking for...anyway, oh well, maybe at the airport..."

Alex's voice trailed off in embarrassment, due to his not wanting to divulge – yet - the surprise gift they'd purchased for Jess.

Rai, with her own secret, or at least, knowing of another gift that hadn't yet been shared, looked quickly, first at Jess, then at the kids. She turned to Alex, who didn't seem to notice her furtive glances at the others.

"Sure, Alex. Aita pea pea. No problem, you'll find a pareo you like a lot, before you leave the island. I'm sure of it! But, before you leave, let's get one last photo together, of all of us American tourists here in Moorea!"

Chapter 58

Presents, pareo & a memorable last Moorean meal

They got the jeep back to the Montcalm lot with only about five minutes to spare. After brief stops to use the bathroom and change into their swim suits, they headed down to the beach. Decidedly lighter in mood than they'd been that morning, and especially the previous night, the Webster adventurers were ready for some final afternoon fun. Their cooler was packed with juice, water, and a couple of beers for Jess and Alex, plus snacks and some scrumptious Australian-made cookies too.

"I figure this should tide us all over until dinnertime," Jess said, gaining a nod and a grin from Alex.

"It better, and we better save room for our final meal here. I can't wait to try something new before we leave."

"Me too, we'll be adding about the 35th or more items on our food lists!" said Meg, noting their huge roster of dishes tried during the trip.

"Can't wait to share my list with everybody at school, and listen to them try to pronounce all the dishes too!" Keely agreed.

"Can't wait to make those chow mein and French roll sandwiches at home either!" Cal's statement drew a chorus of hearty agreement.

Following a couple of hours of swimming, sunning, and some last-chance snorkeling, the Websters gathered together at their special spot under THEIR palm tree, though they realized they'd have to relinquish it to other guests of the Montcalm soon.

"Alex, this is such a wonderful place and it's been a fantastic trip - even with some of the 'adventures' I didn't expect to have!" Jess said, with a grin, a wink, and a mock look of fear on her face, all in succession. The kids chuckled, albeit a bit nervously, as they jointly recalled their parts in the last point their nanny had mentioned.

"Jess, we couldn't have made this trip without you. I'm so glad you could join us," Alex replied.

"Yeah. Yay, Jess!" added Cal, with a fist-pump, earning a squeeze of his shoulder from the New Zealander.

"Hey, we better get ready for dinner, that sun's starting to head down, Dad," Keely announced.

"Yep, you're right, Keel. It's almost 5:00, time to head back, shower and get dressed for our final meal...bwaaahaaaaahhaa!" He used his 'Dracula' or monster voice that even today tended to scare the kids a bit.

"Stop it, Dad!" cried Cal, proving it still worked.

"Sorry, bud. Race you back to the room!" And he was off, with the almost-ten-year-old close behind, the girls taking their time and bringing up the rear on the path to the bungalow.

About 30 minutes later everyone was clean and refreshed, and Alex had just returned from having a quick, 'farewell' beer with David Thomson and Bernie Tetuanui at the hotel bar. He overheard Jess talking with the girls about what they were wearing to dinner, then knocked on the already open door to Keely and Meg's room. Jess had already returned to her own room, and he beckoned to his two daughters.

"Let's get together and surprise Jess with her gifts!" he whispered.

"Yeah, Dad, great timing too!" agreed Meg.

Alex stepped back into his and Cal's room and retrieved the wrapped box from his closet, then called out. "Hey everybody, and Jess, that means you too, can we get together on the patio outside for a moment?"

She called out through the closed door to her room, "Sure, Alex, but I've got to get dressed first, can you wait a few minutes?"

He persisted. "Why don't you just put on a t-shirt and shorts, just for a second, OK? I have to show you all something. It won't take long."

Jess came out with a casual top over her shorts, noticing that the kids and Alex were already dressed, and looking a bit worried as they had to be at the restaurant in less than fifteen minutes. But she smiled anyway.

Alex felt a little bit bad about being pushy, and about the secret they all were keeping from Jess (and considering the recent history of his kids and secrets, they were hiding this one really well, by the way!) But he was pretty confident this was one surprise that would make her very happy. Keely, Meg and Cal were glowing with anticipation too.

"What?" Jess asked, seeking answers as she swiveled to read each of the Websters' faces, not sure why they were all grinning.

"The kids and I got together yesterday, and went to town..."

"Yeah, to Mrs. Martinez's, um, Rai's sister's shop," Meg volunteered.

"And we found something beautiful," Keely said.

"Just for you, Jess!" added Cal.

"Because we appreciate you so much, Jess, and to officially welcome you into the Worldwide Websters traveling family!" Alex smiled widely as he pulled a small wrapped box from behind his back with a flourish and handed it to her.

"What?! Oh my gosh...What?...you didn't need to do..."

"Open it, Jess - and we promise *this* box isn't old and rusty!" Keely urged her with a laugh.

Jess sat down on a chair and gently removed the ribbon and pretty floral wrapping paper. When she lifted the top off the box, and pulled the soft tissue within it to the sides, she gasped.

"This. Is..."

"Gorgeous, right?" prompted Keely.

"Do you like the present?" asked Cal.

"You can wear them tonight!" blurted out Megan.

Jess pulled the earrings out of the box. "Wow! These are stunning."

"They're made right here, and the pearls come from French Polynesian waters, according to Rai's sister," explained Alex.

"We thought they'd look great with one of your dresses, maybe, or maybe a pareo? Your first Tahitian pearls too, right Jess?" said Meg.

Jess couldn't hold back. She brushed away a couple tears from her cheeks and turned to look at Alex and the kids. "This is the nicest, and most surprising, gift I've ever received. Ever. Thank you all so much!!"

"Aita pea pea, Jess. You deserve it," said Alex, winking at Meg and the others. "Now try them on!"

"Let me finish getting dressed. Be right back!" Jess gathered up the box and paper and ran into her room and shut the door. Two minutes later, she returned, twirling to show off her new earrings, which perfectly complemented the pareo she'd created in Rai's class.

"WOW!" said Meg.

"Wow is right, Jess. You look stunning!" Keely beamed with joy at how great the pareo - and earrings - looked on her.

"Amazing, that's really a beautiful sarong... er, pareo," said Alex.

"Check out the earrings too – they DO match!" added Cal.

After the last-minute gift-giving surprise, the Websters were just in time for their dinner reservation...and walked happily over to the restaurant where they were seated promptly at what Alex realized was probably the best table on the patio. *No big surprise at who had assigned himself to their table as waiter,* Alex smiled to himself - *must be a busy night huh, for the Assistant Manager to personally take over for one of the wait staff?*

Jess stretched around Alex, seated next to her and blocking her view, to catch the eye of Julian as he came out the kitchen door.

"Hey Julian, *Ahiahi (Evening)!*" Jess wasn't sure if her greeting was correct, but she giggled as the Tahitian/Moorean, seeing her and what she was wearing, almost dropped the tray of drinks he was carrying to another table. He deposited them there, then returned to where the Websters were seated.

"I, I...um, you look, amazingly...er...nice pareo, Jess!" Then: "Hi everybody!" he mumbled to the rest of the Webster crew, looking a little bit flustered as he knelt down to kiss Jess lightly on the cheek.

"Thank you, or I should say *Maururu,* Julian, I created the pareo design myself, with the help of your Aunt Rai, right here at the Montcalm! And of course, the pearl earrings are from the islands too, an amazing gift from the Websters. You like them?"

"Oh, yes, I knew the pareo was crafted here right away. The moment I saw you. But I haven't seen that specific design before, nor a pareo look...so beautiful...on anyone before. And the pearl earrings. We have a word for it all. It doesn't sound as pretty as it should. *Nehenehe.* But it means *Beautiful.*"

Jess blushed and smiled about as wide as a smile could get without her face cracking. Keely and Meg glanced at each other and giggled. Alex just grinned, while Cal looked up from the menu.

"Hey Julian! Great dancing last night. Nice table you got us too. Now, what's good for dinner?"

The boy's matter of fact manner brought a huge laugh from all of them. And the night was officially on!

The Websters' last full Moorean dinner was a festive occasion - the drinks flowing and plates arriving one after the other. Just before the sun went down a few minutes after the Websters were seated, Cal quickly confirmed some details on his *Heiva* project with Julian. Then Alex, with help from Julian and one of the other waiters, was able to get some great final photos of the family, Jess, and the kids, and including Julian too - and of course one wonderful picture of Jess and Julian together, by themselves - silhouetted by the rays of the setting sun against the tropical trees and flowers behind them.

Now, after sampling two types of fish and some of their favorite poisson cru - along with a nice salad, octopus, oysters, mussels, and a thick coconut and vegetable soup and lots of French bread - they were all more than full. But of course, they'd saved room for dessert.

Jess was finishing her second Mai Tai and decided that while delicious, it would be her last for the night. She wanted to remember everything about this magical evening. Besides, there was still more fun to come...

Standing up, she tapped her glass with a spoon to capture the attention of everyone at the table and said she had an important announcement. Just then, Keely returned from a quick run to the bungalow, carrying two book-sized packages in her hands. One she gave to Jess, and the other she held while she looked over at her dad.

Beaming, Jess waved to Julian, now delivering dessert plates to another table. He nodded and exchanged a few words with the couple there, then walked briskly over. Jess held out the package to him.

"I know you probably have a lot of these, but not one like this, because I made it for you. *Maururu Roa*, Julian, for your kindness, your friendship, and for the wonderful trip you gave all of us on the *Mateata*!"

Julian was stunned, and as he started to unwrap the package, Keely and Meg took up the call.

"And Dad, we wanted to give you something special to thank you for bringing us all on this super cool trip..."

Meg, grabbed her sister's arm. "Well not really that cool, it's pretty hot and humid here, actually..." she drawled.

As everyone laughed, Keely continued. "Anyway, thanks to great teaching and direction from Mrs. Martinez - Rai - and to some good advice from Tiare and Jess too, we were able to make this for you. We hope you like it, and *we love you*, Dad!"

As Keely handed Alex the package, she looked around the table. So much joy and fun only one day after the mood had been so cloudy. *Now if only her dad really liked the present they'd made!*

Julian pulled out the pareo Jess had created, just as Alex ripped off the last of the paper enclosing the one the kids had designed for their dad. The two men looked at each other and without speaking a word between them, held their handmade presents up together for all to see.

"Very, very nice. I love the colors!" said Julian, pointing to Alex's garment.

"*Seahawks* colors, Dad!" yelled Cal to more laughs all around.

Julian and the others looked admiringly at his own pareo, with its intricate design. The Tahitian turned to Jess. "You made this? For me?"

Jess nodded. "Yes, with lots of guidance from Rai of course. Do you like the colors?"

"No, I don't *like* them. I *love* them, and nobody who ever sees this pareo will know that it was made by someone from New Zealand on her first try, and not a native Tahitian or Moorean who has made many. Thank you, Jess. It's beautiful, and a very, very precious gift."

She shined with pleasure - for once this trip, not embarrassed at all - by his attention. "Well, I guess that's two of us - or actually three, including Alex - who've received amazing gifts tonight!"

Meg yelled out, "Put them on guys!" and the others joined in the call, but Alex held up his hand in feigned protest.

"Hey, I'm all for trying this on, but how about tomorrow, OK? Julian has to work for a bit longer anyway, and we still need to have our dessert. I promise I'll wear it tomorrow, at least for a quick trip to the beach and back before we leave to catch the ferry to Tahiti!"

Dessert was another selection of delectable dishes shared around the table, with three kinds of tiny, shiny chocolates, some rich and chunky banana and mango pudding, and the most amazing cake with a pineapple and vanilla cream glaze. Alex ordered one special bottle of the best, dry sparkling pineapple wine from the island, for everyone, even the kids. With everyone's glass filled, more or less - based on their age - he raised his, gesturing with the other hand to Julian to come back over to the table for a moment, one more time.

"I'd like to say something about my family, and also about this wondrous place, Moorea. First, as a parent, you know you love your kids, and you know they love you too. At least most of the time!" Meg and Keely giggled, while Jess stifled a chuckle, and Cal laughed loudly.

Alex continued. "Now, even though we jokingly - yet lovingly of course - call ourselves the *Worldwide Websters*, there really is no time more challenging to keep that love going, that mutual respect, that kind behavior (*almost*) always present, and having each other's back - than when you're traveling. Even if you're on vacation, even if it gets you away from the cold of winter to a tropical paradise. Because, still, you're exploring a new place, with new experiences, new cultures, different food, unfamiliar surroundings, new sleep patterns. And here, all of that AND roosters screeching outside your room at 5 am!" More laughs.

"Now, to have those kids not just be fantastic, flexible, resilient, and kind, Jess too by the way - though sadly, I can't claim her as my kid (he mock sobbed to more chuckles around the table). But - to also see your kids really learn some valuable things, even 'life lessons' during a trip, ones they will never, never forget, like the memories of the lush landscape, the towering mountains, the mists of Bali Hai – even if it's not really the real one. The stories of Moorea, its marae, its *mana*, and its history. And the super nice and interesting people they've met. Well, I know for a fact, that they'll carry those visions and memories for the rest of their lives. As will I."

Jess wiped a tear from her eye as Alex continued. "And, before I get too poetic, I must say to Cal, Meg, Keely, Jess, and to this magnificent place, Moorea, and to our new Moorean friends, like you, Julian, and the others who aren't here tonight but are in our thoughts...*Manuia! Cheers!* and *Maururu*, for your beautiful island, for all you are, and for all you have given of yourselves to enrich our lucky lives."

They all raised their glasses to the toast, with echoes of "*Manuia!*" ringing around the table as they clinked them together. As diners all around the restaurant smiled and watched the festivities, Alex gently held up his hand for one last moment of quiet, turning to raise his own glass again to Jess, then to Julian, following a quick sip with a smile.

"And finally, I'd like to add my particular appreciation to Jess's, Julian, for that wonderful boat tour and especially the chance to learn about stingrays - and to experience them the right way. You honor us with your sensibility about nature, and your knowledge, and your care to do things right. I salute you for your consideration and stewardship of this place you love, and the planet we share. *Maururu roa*, Julian."

Alex whispered to Meg: "Did I get that last expression right?"

She nodded with a broad smile, and squeezed his arm.

Julian caught the eyes of Jess, then each of the Websters, last of all Meg, with a wink and a mischievous grin. Then in almost perfect English, he turned back to her father and replied: "You're very welcome, Alex. So happy to meet you and your family, and Jess, of course. And as for the boat trip...it was *no problem...no problem at all!*"

Chapter 59

Homeward bound: Papeete puzzles, new surprises

December 3, Saturday

After a late night, but a great night indeed, their last morning on Moorea came a bit too soon for the Websters. It had rained lightly while they slept, too, Alex saw, as he opened his eyes, and remembered hearing the pattering sound of drops on the roof sometime during the night. He was feeling the effects of all the food and drink, enjoyed to a bit of excess but oh, what a fun and festive evening it had been!

Rolling out of bed and into the bathroom, then out and into his swimsuit, Alex was determined to have one last 'bonus' dip in the lagoon, even if much shorter, time-wise, than the previous day's final, vigorous workout. Then he remembered his promise, to wear his new pareo down to the beach. *What are the chances the kids might forget that promise?* he thought. *Maybe they'll give their dad a break on his last day of the trip?*

Naaah. No such luck. He should have known.

Keely breezed into the room, ripe and ready to hold her father to his pledge. "Good morning, Dad! Do you need help putting your pareo on?"

Sheesh. No rest for the weary, can't they cut me some slack? Keeping his thoughts to himself, Alex grunted in confirmation.

"No, I can do it myself, just give me a few minutes. I have to get it to somehow fit over my swimsuit. Are you going to do a full workout today?"

"Yep, but we've got plenty of time, right? I mean, I packed all my stuff last night, so after we swim, we just need to come back, shower, have breakfast, then we get picked up to go to the ferry dock, right?"

"That's right, Keel. Is your sister coming down to swim too?"

"I don't know, she's still sleeping..."

Meg's voice rang out from the bathroom. "No, I'm up! I'll be there in a minute."

"What about Jess?" Alex asked his eldest daughter.

"I haven't seen her yet. I think she got home pretty late. She was planning to go out with Julian for a while after he finished his shift at the restaurant last night."

"Well, let's let her sleep in, 'cause she had to pack last night too."

They heard a groan from Cal, also just waking up. "Are you guys going swimming? If you are, wait for me. I just have to go to the bathroom first."

In a few more moments, all the Websters were assembled at the door, ready to head down the path. It looked a little damp, but the sun was starting to come up...and their walk to the beach was later than most other mornings since they'd arrived, almost 7:30 already. Breakfast was served by the hotel until 10 am on Saturdays, and their ride to the ferry landing wasn't scheduled until 11. So, they'd have plenty of time to swim, shower, eat, and get everything all packed up that wasn't already, then check out and begin the first leg of their trip home. Home from Moorea, and back to the chilly Northwest.

The island delivered one of their best swimming days yet. The lagoon's waters were surprisingly clear, though whipped up by a light wind and currents that also dispersed most of the runoff and silt from the rain. Alex did an abbreviated version of his usual stroke-counting out and back from shore then around the reef area, some eggbeater kicks, plus spent some blissful time just resting on his back and leisurely surveying all the gorgeous tropical scenery around him. He saw a few more fish, at least he thought so, than he had during swims earlier in the week. He also took time to count his blessings and knock on wood (virtually) that nobody had been hurt (except Linc, a bit), gotten sick, or had other bad things happen on the trip. Though he tried not to think about it, he started to run over the logistical details for the coming day and their long plane rides home. *That's what dads -or parents of any kind - do, I guess, even if sometimes they'd rather just lay in the surf, or on the beach for another day, or another week - or forever -* he mused with more than a little wistfulness.

When Keely had finished her workout, several new groups of people had come to the beach for their own early swims. She figured that given the wedding party and chock-full resort, some of them might be enjoying the Montcalm's beach and lagoon for the first time.

She glided along the water, not just slowly, but as leisurely as possible without stopping, toward the place where the shell-dappled sand came up to her stomach and prevented her moving any further. She didn't want to leave this warm, aquatic wonderland, full of strange fish and all sorts of other sea life. But she *was* a little hungry. Now at almost 8:30, the sun was starting to warm the sand, even underwater. *Just like it probably almost always does*, Keely thought. *What would it be like to live here all the time? Julian knows. I'm sure Rai knows. Or knew, once.*

Meg was sitting on a blanket pondering her project. She had done some quick in-camera editing of various video interviews over the past day, when she'd had a few spare moments. Now, she was 'writing' the 'script' for her presentation in her head, ready to put it on paper once she had her notebook and pad handy and a place to write.

She had also been sharing a few thoughts each day in the journal her mom had given her to take on the trip. She couldn't wait to tell her friends about their trip, and share her favorite Tahitian stories, and of course her favorite colloquialism and hopefully a bunch of spoken examples of it on video with her class.

Cal was using his mask and snorkel, no fins needed, to dart around the shallows, not more than 15 yards from the water's edge. He was fascinated by all the fish, even in this shallow depth, *especially those long silver ones with long noses, that flittered without really moving anywhere, right where the little waves broke onto shore. I wonder, are they eating something in those waves? They sure like hanging around the same place.* He also saw a turtle bobbing round a few yards offshore. But best of all was something he saw that he had NEVER seen in the wild before.

Jumping out of the water with glee, the almost-ten-year-old yelled to his dad and sisters, who were making their way back to their towels arrayed under "Webster Tree" at the western side of the beach.

"A seahorse! I saw a seahorse!" The delicate little animal looked just like those he had seen in aquariums, *and boy was it fast*. He had just glimpsed it swimming around the bottom near some rocks a few feet offshore, and then - in a flash - it was gone.

Oh well. He was still excited, but rather than attempt to chase it, he ducked underwater instead - a few times - to try and find it again, to maybe see it swimming, gracefully, beneath the surface of the tranquil tropical waters. So many thoughts went through his head as he slowly pulled himself above the rocks and coral of the lagoon. *What a cool island Moorea is,* he mused. *I can't wait to watch that movie, The Bounty, again and see some of the places we've been on the big screen. But, being here, with my family and all the cool people we've met, is really the best.*

Breakfast was great as usual, the menu shifting back to dishes from the previous Saturday of their trip. Lots of fruit, pastries, bread, and eggs. Each of them had some, and Jess joined them about 15 minutes into their meal, looking a bit bleary-eyed from the adventures of the night before.

She was happy and eager, like they were, to head back home, despite the wonderful times she'd had with the Websters and in the past few days, with Julian too. Where that relationship was going to go, she still didn't know. *But I sure like spending time with him,* she thought, with fond visions of their adventures together swirling through her mind.

Julian wasn't working the breakfast shift, but he had promised to come to the hotel to say goodbye to everyone before they left. Alex just had one last task - to settle the bill for all their 'extras' and food and equipment they'd used, rented, ordered, or eaten during the week. He planned to stop in to the office to deliver a quick thanks to the staff there, though the GM David Thomson wasn't yet in after a busy previous night with all the resort's special wedding-related group activities.

Back at their bungalow, it was now 10:15 am. They'd all packed everything up, the girls with their bags stuffed full - but not *too* heavy, and Alex had disassembled most of his camera accessories, then carefully inserted, braced, and wrapped them with clothes to protect them in his suitcase. He found a way to carefully cram in some of the presents he was bringing back for the LodgeSoft team in Seattle, glad he'd left room in his main suitcase *and* brought a second bag to check in the luggage compartment instead of carrying it all onboard the plane along with his backpack. *It will be a lot easier to make the baggage transfers across terminals in LA and then onward on the plane to Seattle-Tacoma tomorrow morning,* he thought. *At least we'll have part of Sunday to recuperate, once we get back home. But probably not enough...Monday will be here before we know it. Oh well,* Alex smiled to himself, *this trip was TOTALLY worth it!*

Soon, with the 'business' side of things finished, they had all said their goodbyes, waved to the servers at the restaurant, smiled and thanked the housekeepers who came by with a big bag of new linens and sang their beautiful Tahitian tunes as they began changing out the bungalow's bedding and towels. Keely and Meg had enjoyed one last sparkling water, paid for with French Polynesian notes from their dad, while working on their projects at the beach bar for a half hour or so. Before they departed one last time, they thanked the bartender and server there for their friendly service during their visit.

Julian pulled up in his truck right after they'd made their way to the driveway outside the lobby. He stepped out and walked over to where they stood, nodding and smiling to the kids. He and Jess moved off to one side, talking in low tones.

They looked sort of awkward, Keely thought, as in *"So, what do we do now?"* She wasn't sure if Jess really liked Julian a lot, but she thought she might. *I'll ask her about it later,* the pre-teen decided.

Just then, Alex came out of the hotel entrance with his file folder and a small box. "Guess what we got from Rai? More of those figure 8 pastries you guys had last week. I can't wait to try them. You know, '*firi firi*' donuts? She left us a whole box in the office, homemade and everything, to take home with us!"

"If they make it that far!" replied Meg, eagerly eyeing the parcel of goodies in her dad's hand.

Right then, the transport van they had requested arrived in the Montcalm parking lot, signaling it was time to load up and move out.

Julian shook Alex's hand, and Cal's too. He hugged Keely and Meg, and then he and Jess embraced. To Keely and Meg's special delight, they enjoyed a quick, passionate kiss together. Even Alex blushed and looked away, but he also thought to himself, *why not? You're young, you're in the tropics, and it's always a love-ly day in Moorea!*

A couple moments later, Jess picked up her bag and carried it to the van, and Julian got in his truck, took one last look - an especially long one - at Jess, waved to her and the Websters, and called, "Come back soon!" and in Tahitian, "*Araua'e, Jess!*" Then he drove slowly away.

Everyone was surprised and delighted that their driver to the ferry landing turned out to be Jean-Paul again - as he was fitting their 'taxi' trip in between two shorter-than-usual morning and afternoon tours he had scheduled for that day, before, as he explained, he would be working on the stage setup at the Ti'i Village for a wedding-related event during the evening. He was very happy to see the Websters too. "Have you enjoyed your visit to Moorea?" the tall Tahitian asked them.

"Oh YEAH, JP!" exclaimed Cal, to a hearty chuckle from the driver.

After they had piled in and begun to make their way through one last circuit around the sides of Cook's Bay, Cal and Meg and Alex shared in turn some of the adventures they'd had, even telling Jean-Paul about the box they had found at the marae, and how they were donating it to the museum on the Martinez family's behalf.

He agreed that the find was quite interesting, and marveled at their stories about their climb up to the waterfall, their Motu Tiahura excursion on Julian's boat, and how they'd gone swimming, gently, with the stingrays in the lagoon there.

JP grinned when Alex mentioned their reef shark encounters, and as Cal shared his surprise sighting of the seahorse, but his face fell when after asking them how they liked the *Tama'ara'a*, they told him the food, dancing and atmosphere was wonderful, but that the night had ended on kind of a sad note. Not wanting to gossip, Alex just said there was a family disagreement. But it was pretty clear JP already knew of the growing controversy over the Moorea Rai's ownership, as he frowned and shook his head in response to Alex's brief explanation.

Meg sat right behind and peppered their driver and tour guide with several questions along the way, and then asked him, just before they pulled into the ferry parking lot, for one last favor.

"JP, would you be willing to do a quick interview on the usage of the expression *Aita pea pea*? It's for a school project."

"I will be happy to!" he answered.

With the short recording finished about three minutes later, Meg produced from her bag a small pack of candy cane-flavored chocolate fortune cookies - brought along on ·the trip from the Emily's Chocolates factory in Fife, Washington, near their home in Tacoma. She gave him the box of candy, purchased right before they'd left and kept in her suitcase the whole trip up 'til now. Then she gave him a big hug. "*Maururu Roa*, Jean-Paul - but keep these cold until Christmas or whenever you eat them - or they'll melt!"

JP smiled broadly, hugged the almost-11-year-old, and placed the small square box of unique treats from the Pacific Northwest in a corner of the ice-filled cooler he kept next to his seat. Then, as he returned Meg's Tahitian *thank you* with, of course, "*aita pea pea, Ms. Meg!*" she captured that on video as well.

After the kids exited the van and their bags were unloaded, Keely counted to three and they joined in a loud joint farewell of "*Nānā, JP!*" Then, as part of their goodbye, Alex made a point to inform their guide that their tour with him had been one of the major highlights of *all* the family's trips together - anywhere in the world.

"You are a Worldwide Websters *legend*, JP!"

"*Maururu Roa*, Alex!" The Tahitian-Frenchman was clearly proud of the acknowledgment. He urged Alex to plan a return trip with the family soon. Just before they parted, he patted Cal on the head with a mock warning. "Stay away from those scary starfish!"

Cal gave him a hearty thumbs-up in return.

They all watched JP drive off, waving and smiling. With still about a half hour 'til the ferry arrived, Alex offered everyone a beverage, having emptied most of their fridge's leftovers that could be easily carried into their collapsible cooler along with a little ice from the hotel. The kids had some of the sparkling juice they'd bought from the factory, and Jess and Alex tipped a "Manuia!" to each other before opening and quickly quaffing their still ice-cold Hinano beers.

Jess spoke a bit wistfully of having to leave Moorea so soon. "I had no idea, really, what this place would be like. I mean, I read some brochures and articles, and saw some links online. But I never knew it would be THIS beautiful, this lush..."

"Or this HOT!" whined Keely, as she wiped her brow theatrically.

"Nope, we KNEW that part!" laughed Meg, and the rest of the Webster clan giggled right along with her. It was so true, there's only so much you can learn about a place, and its people, until you actually *go* there. Moorea was - more than many places - truly *one of a kind.*

The *Moorea Express* was soon nearing shore, the blast of its horn signaling to the Websters and other tourists and commuters that it was about to dock. Alex gathered the kids to await the boarding call. It came only two minutes late - which Jess felt was in line compared to the trend she'd seen on the island of punctuality not being all that important. "We call it *'Moorea Time'*" JP and Julian had both explained of the island's leisurely approach to just about everything. *And why be in a hurry anyway, in a place like this?*

Once onboard the ferry, the Webster kids - now "pros" on crossing the waters between Moorea and Tahiti - went straight up to the top deck, as far forward on the ship as they could get. Meg had Alex's video camera, determined to get a few more *"aita pea pea"* stories from unsuspecting (but hopefully willing) fellow travelers. Alex couldn't resist the chance to grab another beer from the onboard cafe, while Jess opted for a sparkling water for the crossing.

They'd made it about 2/3 of the way to Tahiti, with Alex taking some panoramic shots of the view back to Moorea, when Cal rushed to his side.

"Dad! You gotta come see this! Whales!"

Sure enough, even though it was a few weeks at least after typical whale migration season, there they were - two humpback whales enjoying what had to be their last days in French Polynesia before venturing south. As one breached - only a couple hundred yards away and in the same direction the boat was heading towards Tahiti - a large group of gathered passengers pointed, grabbed their cameras - too late of course - and yelled *"Ooooh"* and *"Aaaaah."* Alex had kept to himself that he thought he had heard whale song during his swim the day prior, but this sighting confirmed *he might have been right after all!*

Meg marveled at just how lucky - given the timing - it was that they actually got to see humpbacks in Moorea. That had been her absolute favorite part of visiting Hawaii during the winter and early springtime.

As they watched the whales, cruising along in the Moorea

Channel, Keely joked, "These guys are kinda slow, sorta laid back when it comes to rushing to get things done, just like the people on Moorea!"

The horn soon sounded to signal their imminent arrival to Tahiti, and everyone lined up for disembarkation. Soon they docked and the Websters followed the other passengers off the ferry to where several taxis and other vehicles were waiting. They found a small van that had enough space for the five of them and their luggage, then piled in. Alex communicated in broken French/Tahitian/English that they wanted to get to the baggage storage area at Faa'a airport.

"Why are we storing our bags, Dad?" Meg asked.

"It's a lot easier than lugging them around, plus we are bringing back a few things that might not handle the heat. This way, we can just take our backpacks with us to the museum and into town. Then when we come back for our flight tonight, we'll just pick up our bags here and check in."

It was an easy process, though it required dealing with a bit of a line and ten minutes or so of waiting. The cost wasn't cheap either, at around 5000 CFP or $50 US equivalent for all their bags, but they all agreed later it was the best and most comfortable option. This way, they could travel relatively lightly and simply for the rest of the afternoon preceding their flight - as they explored French Polynesia's capital and largest city.

Their driver had graciously agreed to wait for a small extra charge while the family checked their bags, and when they returned from the storage area, he drove them to the museum, which was in the opposite direction from Papeete, but not a long trip at all. They still had more than five hours until they'd have to be at the airport, so even though it was a little out of the way, Alex figured a visit was worth it, especially given the situation the Martinez family was in. *Who knows?* he thought, maybe donating the box as a cultural relic would add some weight to the case Rai and her sisters, brothers and cousins were trying to make to keep and protect the *Moorea Rai* and lands around it for their (side of the) family.

When they arrived at the museum, Alex paid the driver with some of the last hundred dollars or so worth of local currency remaining in his wallet. He resisted the urge to tip - a tough habit to break, but in

Tahiti and Moorea, tipping just wasn't expected. He overruled his hesitation, noting to the kindly 50-something-aged man that he hoped his family could visit the US someday - and perhaps feel American hospitality like they had received from their Tahitian hosts. He handed him 500CFP plus a crisp 10-dollar "Alexander Hamilton" bill and thanked him again for his courtesy and service to the family.

The museum, it turned out, did have a few paintings by famous artists of the region. They looked for Gaugin pieces, but couldn't immediately see any in their brief walk through the lobby. It was pretty quiet. The young woman at the reception desk greeted the five Websters with *"Maeva!"* and Alex explained that they had an appointment with the Assistant Director, Francois Poulet, at 1 pm.

As she went to get him from a nearby office, Alex turned to the others.

"Well guys, let's hope this box is worth something to the people on these islands. Maybe this gesture - donating it here - will make up for some of what Rai and her family are going through. Let's see, where is it again...?" He looked at his backpack.

Cal piped up. "It's right in this pocket, Dad. Let me get it!" And before Alex could tell his son that he would remove the relic, Cal had unzipped the backpack, reached in and grabbed the box, and while pulling it out - probably due to its unwieldy size and weight - he suddenly lost hold of it. With everyone watching in horror, it spun out of the boy's hands and crashed to the stone floor of the museum.

Just then, a man in a suit walked up to the stunned Websters, including a very embarrassed and worried Cal, who watched while Jess bent down to carefully pick up the box.

"Whew! It's not broken, nor is the floor. That's the good news...but wait, something's rattling inside." Jess shook the box. "That's weird, because it was empty when we opened it..."

Lifting its top to look within, Keely noticed something different about its insides. It looked uneven. As she reached down, feeling a loose edge near the box's bottom, she asked for help. "Does one of your staff have a nail file or, ummm, a screwdriver, a really thin one?"

"Well, so this is the box you spoke of on the phone yesterday, Mr. Webster?" said the museum's Mr. Poulet, introducing himself in heavily accented English. He then added, "We may have a screwdriver here at the desk, or - wait, we do have a letter opener.

Will that work?"

"I think it might," said Alex, handing the tool to Keely after the museum attendant passed it to Poulet – who passed it to him.

Keely carefully inserted the tip of the letter opener in the tiny slit - only a quarter-inch wide at the bottom of the box. Ever so carefully with her small, yet strong hands she pried the pieces of metal apart. Suddenly the gap became larger. She stopped and looked at her dad.

"Should I keep going...I don't think I'm damaging it but..."

Alex peered inside, and Meg too. "It's almost open, Keel, both where you have the letter opener as well as on the other side. See?" Meg pointed at where it appeared a layer of the box was separating from the lower part of the enclosure.

Keely jimmied the lower portion with the letter opener. After a few seconds, they all heard an audible 'pop' and peered inside. A dull, heavily tarnished object sat under the partially-removed false bottom.

"It's a ring!" Cal exclaimed. And that's what it looked like, indeed.

"Yes, and luckily no worse for wear it seems, even with the big drop to the ground!" Alex looked at Cal with a hint of exasperation. Cal, for his part, was now about as relieved as a kid could be since they'd confirmed he hadn't broken either the box or the floor due to his clumsiness.

"*Oui*. Let's take a look," said Mr. Poulet, holding the ring from the box's false bottom between his thumb and forefinger, peering closely at it while turning it around.

"I think it is very old. Silver, perhaps. Fairly large in diameter," he said, holding it up against his own finger to gauge its relative size.

Even though it was heavily tarnished, the ring didn't appear to be scratched too badly. Meg asked if she could see it and as Mr. Poulet handed it to her, she peered closely at the underside, which was its cleanest part. "There's something here, see?" She pointed to what appeared to be a tiny inscription. It was flowing script of some type. But it appeared to be only a few letters. Or maybe less?

Jess took a look. "You know, that might be French or something."

Poulet took a small magnifying glass from his pocket, and confirmed Jess's guess. "I'm not sure it's French, but I believe it is two letters, in old-style script. "Yes, I can read it now, I think. *FC*?"

"Hmmm...I wonder what that means?" Alex asked, as he

borrowed the museum director's magnifier to take a look for himself.

They all glanced quizzically at Mr. Poulet, and then at each other. Their host obviously didn't have any more of an idea than the Websters of the inscription's significance.

Alex made a suggestion. "Well, Mr. Poulet, it seems best to give this ring and box to you and your staff to examine further. Maybe you can determine what those letters mean, and who "*FC*" was or maybe it's short for something else, a name, a place, or who knows?"

He handed the box to Poulet, who carefully placed the ring they'd found back inside and closed it. "But at least it's now here where it belongs, in the Museum of French Polynesia, thanks to the family of Rai Martinez, or Raiana Temarai - as her family has been known on Moorea for many generations. We're just glad we can deliver it safely to you, and hope that it helps you in your historic and artistic studies here at the museum." The kids nodded.

"*Merci*, and *Mauru'uru roa*, Mr. Webster."

"Please, Mr. Poulet, I deserve no credit. The children here found the box in the marae, with their friends - Rai and her husband's kids. Maybe you can make note of their contribution if you decide to ever add it to your display of local antiquities here at the museum? Oh, and can we take a quick picture of it to share with the Martinez-Temarai family?"

"Of course!"

Turning to the children, the museum manager smiled broadly. "*Merci, Mauru'uru roa* to you children too! Thank you - each of you - for finding this box, and the treasure inside it! We will be very careful as we try to determine its origin." He waved his arms around the building. "Now, would you like to take a brief look through our 'local' wing and displays? We have some very beautiful and interesting ancient Polynesian art works, as well as pieces from a few famous people you just may have heard of back home!"

"Sure...we have time, don't we Dad?" Keely, who was already becoming a big art lover, implored of her father.

Checking his watch and seeing that it was still only about 1:30 pm, Alex nodded. "Yep, we've got a few minutes, lead the way Monsieur Poulet!"

What an unexpected adventure the next thirty minutes offered. The pottery, intricate woven baskets, and faded but resplendent designs of ancient tapa garments and blankets, still-gorgeous wooden outriggers and other boat exhibits and other priceless objects were all exquisite. And then they saw the *Gaugin* pieces...

"Oh yeah! I thought I had read about these!" Jess exclaimed. She and the Websters now stood before a large painting that was unmistakably a work of the Frenchman who had spent many years in the islands here.

"The museum has several pieces painted by Gaugin, and others from Europe who lived and visited here." As they walked around the gallery, Cal wandered over to a corner, transfixed by one picture in particular.

As Meg came over to join him, the youngest Webster called out to the others, "Hey, take a look at this picture." He pointed at the artwork, which was a portrait of three native Tahitian women. They were standing in front of a large wooden structure, perhaps some sort of temple, maybe? Palm trees ringed the building behind them, and they wore bright floral headdresses. Not an unusual setting around the islands, either then or even now, they all guessed. But suddenly, Meg noticed something else.

"Hey, look what's hanging around that woman in the middle's neck! That looks a lot like the ring we just found!"

By this time, Alex, Jess, Keely, and Mr. Poulet had joined the two youngest Websters gazing at the portrait on the wall.

"That DOES look like the ring...or at least a lot like it. But it's definitely shinier in the picture than it is now." Keely glanced at Mr. Poulet. "When was this painted?"

The museum official paused, then excused himself for a moment to walk quickly back to his office. In a few moments, he was back, holding a large binder. He had it open to a page near the middle.

Running his finger across the spine of the opened book, Mr. Poulet explained the painting's origins. "I believe this was completed before around 1820, certainly very early in the 19th century. But we don't know exactly who these women were, I'm sorry."

"But it's possible that the ring we found might actually be the same one as the one in the picture, right?" asked Cal.

"Yes, I guess it is possible, but we can't really know until we examine it more closely. Which I assure you we will. Our restoration team will be very, how do you say - "*eager*" - to work with this piece. I cannot thank you all enough, again, for finding and bringing the box here, but also for finding the ring."

"And's it all because of you, you clumsy squirt! If you hadn't dropped the box, we probably would have never found the ring in it!" Keely smiled admiringly at her little brother, who flushed with pride.

Meg was very quiet, deep in thought. Suddenly, her face brightened and she blurted out, "I've seen that picture before! I knew it! It got my attention, for some reason, when we first arrived at the airport last week!"

"Oh yes, we do have prints of some of our most popular local paintings displayed at the Faa'a airport," said Mr. Poulet.

"Wow, what a cool coincidence, Meg!" Keely said.

But Meg, for her part, was thinking again. *SO weird that I noticed that painting right when we got here, and even more weird that it might mean something related to the box we found on Moorea...hmmm...*

Her dad's announcement that it was time to leave the museum brought Meg's mind back to the present.

"Well, I think that's more excitement than we ever thought we'd experience at the end of an already amazing trip, right kids?" said Alex. He turned to the museum official.

"Please let Rai Martinez know what you find out about the ring and its connections. I'm sure she would love to know, so would we!"

"Of course, Mr. Webster. Leave me your contact information and hers. I'll send you both an email with our findings once they're complete."

As they headed back to the lobby, everyone shook hands with Mr. Poulet, who, with a big smile, presented them with one of the nice, large paperback books from the museum's gift shop, showcasing its artworks. As Alex thanked him (while he wondered a little how they'd add it to their growing pile of carry-on baggage) the museum director graciously offered to called them a taxi van for their trip into Papeete.

A few minutes later, in the cab, Keely let out a big sigh. "After all of that, I'm super hungry!" she said, and everyone agreed. Their first stop, after some brief trinket shopping at Papeete's sprawling street market stalls, was a restaurant nearby that Rai had recommended they visit if they had a chance to stop before leaving for the airport.

"I guess we can call this "linner," right?" Alex asked everyone, as they sat down and perused the menus. The place offered, for their combination lunch and dinner meal, a selection of French, Polynesian, and American food, likely catering to as many varieties of guests and appetites as they could. But Rai had assured Alex that all the dishes were of high quality and well prepared by a local restaurateur and her team.

Cal was thrilled to see familiar options. "I think I want a burger, Dad!"

With "Yeahs!" all around, they each proceeded to order burgers with various toppings, some decidedly different than typical American fare. Jess's was a veggie burger with shrimp. Keely and Meg had pineapple slices and brie cheese on theirs.

Alex and Cal stuck with simple burgers, with mayo, pickles, and cheese. The boy polished off half of his in about one minute, then felt nature calling. "Hey, Dad, I have to go to the bathroom. I'll be right back."

Cal had been gone about three minutes, tops, when he came back and stood in front of the seated Websters. He had a funny look on his face.

"Hey, there's another painting of one of those women we saw. I'm sure of it. But she's older, or at least I think so?"

"What??? Where?!!" came the chorus of replies from his siblings, his dad, and Jess.

"Follow me, I'll show you!" Cal said excitedly. Quickly, they un-squeezed themselves from the tiny booth where they'd been sitting. As they reached the hall leading to the restrooms, they all saw it right away. A large portrait was hung on the wall at its end. Sure enough, its subject bore a strong resemblance to one of the women, and in the same style of painting that they had just seen with the trio depicted in the museum. However, this was a single portrait, and the woman in the picture looked a bit older than the very young one, almost a girl, who had posed with others of a similar age in the museum work.

They were all admiring the picture, which appeared to be an original painting, when suddenly Meg cried out.

"Look!"

Following her pointed finger, their eyes were drawn to the lower left of the frame. Partially hidden by a palm frond that was apparently part of the portrait's background, they saw it. A ring around the woman's finger. And it looked a LOT like the same ring they had just been talking about at the museum. Maybe the same one that they'd found in the box when Cal had unwittingly dropped it and loosened its false bottom.

While the Websters stood there, wondering, and trying to contain their excitement, a sharp voice sounded behind them. "May I help you?"

As they turned to look, a very tall, slender Tahitian woman approached them from the hall. She followed their gaze and, turned to Alex. "Why are you and the children looking at this painting so closely?"

Cal could barely contain his enthusiasm, blurting out why. "Because we found a cool old box that we gave to a museum!"

Meg held up her hand, then explained her brother's outburst, pointing at the portrait. "We found a ring inside the box. And it looks just like the one that lady is wearing in the picture!"

The woman glanced back at the painting, then at Alex, Jess, and Keely. A strange look came into her eyes. "Where did you find this box, and...this ring?"

"Moorea," Keely answered. "We found it in a hole in a marae there. We weren't trying to disturb the marae, we really weren't, but my little brother and his friend found it there."

The woman paused, then apparently convinced of the children's sincerity, she spoke. "I am from Moorea," she said, "and that is a painting of my great-great-great grandmother. She was a leader of our family and women of the island in the early 1800's. Many women in my family have been leaders in the community there ever since."

Keely looked closely at the painting, then back at the woman. She noticed her hazel-colored eyes - though of a shape quite similar to those of the woman in the painting - who had green eyes.

"My name is Valerie Teamoutu, and I am the owner here, of this restaurant. But please call me Valerie," she said, extending her hand.

Alex quickly returned the gesture and introduced each member of the Webster clan. Then Valerie asked, "What did the ring look like, exactly?"

Alex thought for a second, then pulled out his camera from its small case at his waist, clicking through a bunch of photos they had taken on the streets of Papeete, before he came to the museum shots they'd captured. He found a few photos of the box, and then stopped to display on the camera's screen a close-up of the ring that he'd snapped right before giving it to Mr. Poulet, the museum director.

Alex pressed a knob to zoom in on the image and display it more clearly. After a few moments of deep scrutiny, Valerie beckoned them to follow her, further down the restaurant's corridor, toward her office.

Keely, Meg, Cal, and Alex looked at each other, curious what it all meant. Even Jess had goosebumps with the anticipation.

Alex checked his watch. It was almost 5 pm. "Hey, you guys, we have to leave in less than half an hour. Sorry, Ms. Teamoutu, er, Valerie, I hate to be rude - we must catch our flight back to the US this evening."

"*Aita pea pea*. No problem, this won't take too long. I just have *petit*, umm, only a few questions more."

Alex nodded. "Sure, we've still got a few minutes to spare."

Turning to the kids, the tall, almost regal restaurateur asked, "Was there anything else unusual about the ring - either...on it, or... in it?"

"Yes! Show her, Dad. It says '*FC*' on it," Meg answered. Alex flipped his camera to show Valerie the photo they had taken of the inscription inside the band.

"We can't figure out what *FC* means," explained Cal.

Valerie paused, considered the boy's comment for a moment, then it looked like she came to a decision – to share more of why she was so interested in the ring.

"Well," she replied, "that *is* interesting. You see, the legend in my family is that my great-great-great grandmother was born on Moorea, but her mother wouldn't talk about nor share any information about her father. Never. This strange fact – or lack of information, really - has been passed on in our family stories through time. Nobody ever knew who he was, or if they did know, they would not talk of it. However, she had green eyes and so it was pretty obvious that someone - not a native Tahitian - was likely her father. Her name was *Te'mahana'piti*."

"What an unusual name. Does it stand for anything? I mean, does the name mean anything in particular?" asked Keely.

"I know, or, sorry, I think I know!" said Meg, turning a bit red in her haste. She had just recalled something she had learned while doing her colloquialism project. "I met with one of Rai's cousins at the tama'ara'a, and we were talking about the days of the week, and how to say them in Tahitian. It means, um, 'Tuesday' in Tahitian, right?" She looked questioningly at Valerie.

"You attended a Tama'ara'a?" Valerie expressed surprise at this fact, and also that the young American knew her ancestor's name's meaning. "Yes, that is what it means. *Tuesday*, in English. It's remarkable that you remember!"

Suddenly, Alex thought of something else - from his own memory – research he'd conducted before their trip. He cleared his throat.

"You know, something funny, maybe...I read an article about the actual mutineers from *The Bounty*, who sailed from Tahiti to several islands. You know, then eventually they went on to Pitcairn Island...where everyone knows the mutineers settled after leaving port – from near here, of course, from somewhere on this island.

"Anyway, Fletcher Christian's children born of – I can't remember her name..." Mowat..."

"Yes, Mauatua," confirmed Valerie, as Alex struggled with the pronunciation.

"That's it! Mauatua. Christian and his Tahitian wife, evidently named their kids after the days in the week. But none - as far as I remember that is - were named *Tuesday*, or its Tahitian equivalent, and I didn't think he and the boat ever actually sailed to Moorea...But WAIT! Keely...you've got that book on Moorea...can you find that section you showed us on the history of marae on the island?"

Keely ran back to their booth, reached into her backpack and pulled out her book. Quickly thumbing through it, she located the passage she was looking for as she rejoined the group in the restaurant office.

"Here's the part that talks about the actual mutiny of HMS Bounty's crewmen, and officers if you include Christian, who was the main instigator." As the others waited, she looked down the page, then across to the next. "Here it is!" she exclaimed, looking at her father first, then she gazed back to the page and read aloud:

"According to **Maude** - (the author who researched and wrote about it, she explained, in 1958) and one of the women who was on the ship, Teehuteatuaonoa (Keely tried her best to pronounce the Tahitian name) - who was asked about the ship's mutiny and departure, in 1829, the *HMS Bounty* HAD stopped near Moorea (offshore), 23 September 1789."

Keely glanced up in wonder. "That's about 40 years earlier!" She kept reading. "On that day in 1789, it says, 'Six 'rather ancient' women were allowed to depart on an approaching canoe, after which the Bounty sailed westward.'" She read aloud the footnote to the original article. "(*Maude, 1958; Teehuteatuaonoa, 1829*)."

They all looked at each other in amazement.

Meg spoke first. "Could one of those "ancient" women be the woman in the painting here?"

"No, she'd be too old," answered Alex. "That woman was really young in the first photo, and older, but still pretty young in this painting up here, also," he said, pointing to the wall.

"But...what if one of the women who left the *Bounty* near Moorea was expecting a baby? Even if nobody knew it at the time?" asked Jess.

Alex looked, in puzzlement, toward the restaurant manager. "I know you told us your first name...is that your family's name too?"

"I go by Valerie at work, but actually prefer Vai. My real first name is Vahinetua – I was named for my great-great-great grandmother in that painting."

"I'm curious...what does your name mean in Tahitian?" Keely asked, a bit tentatively.

"It means, 'daughter of the open sea.' Interesting that you should ask, by the way. Because, in our family stories, there was a legend that one of our women had, umm, an 'encounter' with a member of a ship's crew."

Meg covered Cal's ears, stifling a giggle as she did so.

"Hey!" her little brother complained, as he pushed her hands away from his head.

Vai/Vahinetua/Valerie looked a bit embarrassed, but continued. "Yes, the story was she became very close with a foreign visitor...but I never heard more, nor did anyone tell me or my recent ancestors just who that man might have been. Besides, there was great shame for a long time that the French eventually took control of our islands from our people, so it was a particularly delicate subject – one almost never brought up in our family at all. But now...perhaps things are starting to make more sense?"

They all pondered what Vai had said for a moment. Meg was the first to speak. "Oh my gosh," she said, "Vahinetua - that's a really cool name. We met someone named "Raiana" here – also from Moorea!"

"REALLY?" exclaimed Vai, loudly. "I wonder - could that be my niece, Rai? She's actually also named Vahinetua, Raiana is her middle name, after me - and before that our ancestors on the female side of the family. All carried the same names, either at the front or middle of their full given names. Our family owned a large section of land on Moorea for hundreds of years, in between Cook's Bay and Opunohu Bay. We have even operated two vacation resorts there up until a few years ago, with only one left now...but we're probably selling the last of them. I had heard Vai and her husband and children were here visiting, but I haven't been able to meet with them yet on this trip." She paused. "We in the family are all a bit sad about the whole affair. I am worried it may be my niece and her family's last trip home here, to Moorea..."

Alex couldn't believe his ears, Neither could Jess and the kids.

"What an amazing coincidence...again! We were just staying at one of the resorts your family once owned. And we've also spent lots of time with Raiana. As you know, her last name now is Martinez, but I think..." He looked at Jess. "How was her last name pronounced again?"

"*Temarai*. Rai's family name before she got married," Jess recalled.

"Right! I am sorry I already forgot it even after we talked about it at the museum." Alex continued, "In fact, the Montcalm – the resort property I mentioned, is where I was working on a software implementation. It's the main reason we came here to French Polynesia." He looked at the others. "But it won't be the only reason we come back!"

Vai nodded, then frowned in agreement. "I don't wish to be too harsh, but the Moorea Rai, our family's remaining resort, well it's been a bit...how do you say it - 'difficult', or, declining, in the past years. There are structural problems...and, some issues with the management there, and rising costs to maintain it as well."

"Well, that's it then, there's no doubt. Of course, we are definitely talking about the same woman. And the same resort. Same family too." Alex smiled at Vai. "So glad to meet you, and it seems we may just have found some clues to our "*FC*" mystery, and the box the ring was found in, too. Right, kids?" He looked at Cal, Meg, and Keely.

"At least part of it, but..." answered the oldest of the Webster siblings.

"I guess we'll have to leave the rest of that mystery for the experts to solve, right Keely?" Alex replied.

Grinning, Keely looked up at her dad, Jess, and Vai, and then glanced at her sister. Together, they answered, with a determined tone in their voices, "Not if WE can help it!"

"Research time!" Molly added, with a grin.

"Yeah, but it's only about ten minutes 'til we have to leave for the airport. So that research will have to wait, unfortunately." Alex glanced at his watch. He looked regretfully in Vai's direction, conveying with his eyes and words: their time in Papeete was unfortunately nearing its end.

"Of course!" she quickly replied. "I completely understand. Please, enjoy the rest of your meals. I will call you a taxi to take you to the airport when you are finished."

Vai returned to the front of the restaurant and the Websters quickly sat down to finish the last bites of their delicious 'linner' dishes. A few moments later, Alex, Jess, and the kids rose to say their goodbyes to their latest new friend.

What a small world...and very mysterious too! Keely's mind was positively *racing* with the possibilities. She looked at Meg, who nodded, clearly thinking similar thoughts.

Alex asked for the bill, and Valerie waved her hand in protest, instead insisting on making their meal her treat as restaurant owner.

"No need to pay, Alex. It is my honor to meet, and to serve, all of you. The gift you and your amazing children have given my family and me is priceless. It just may help us solve a more than 200-year-old family mystery, and help preserve centuries of heritage." She exchanged warm hugs with each of the traveling party.

Alex, paused on his walk to the door, pondering Vai's words.

"A ring with the initials "*FC*" doesn't guarantee it, and I'm not sure if there is a way to actually prove it, but there might indeed be a connection with your and Raiana Temarai Martinez's ancestors from the late 1700's/early 1800's. Only those ancestors – and those of an Englishman named Fletcher Christian, wayward first mate of the *HMS Bounty* – may truly know the answer."

He then smiled directly at Vai, and shared an old expression, something he'd been thinking might have gained a new meaning for him after he glanced at the portrait in the hallway one last time.

"*The eyes have it.*"

Alex wasn't certain, nor did he or the others really understand what it might actually mean, if indeed there was such a link between this modern Moorean family and the most infamous of the HMS Bounty's mutineers. *But it sure was fascinating to think about!*

A few minutes later, they tumbled into the taxi van that Valerie had graciously ordered for their final airport trip. They were touched by the Tahitian restaurant manager's parting message - just before Alex closed his front passenger door.

"*Maururu Roa*, Webster family. Thank you again for the creative 'detective work' during your visit. Won't you come back soon? We need more thoughtful tourists like you to be part of our family, our *utuafare* here. Until we meet again, *Nānā!* Please stay in touch, and tell your friends that there is more, much more, to Moorea and French Polynesia than even *you* have yet discovered!"

"Oh, we will stay in touch. For sure!" Meg answered, as Keely and Cal waved from the back and called out their agreement. Jess nodded and waved too.

Alex spoke last. "Yes, we'll be back Valerie...you'll be seeing the Worldwide Websters again. Meanwhile, we're all eager to find out how your family's *Moorea Mystery* turns out, and maybe that'll be one more very good reason to come back, someday soon, to this beautiful place!"

Epilogue

The adventure continues...

Christmas Day, December 25, 2005
3:30 pm Tacoma

The applause may not have been 'deafening', but it sure was loud,
Alex thought to himself.

He was at home, in the Websters' living room, watching the video
clip, again, of Meg's school presentation on her *colloquialism* project,
part of a DVD compilation of the best of her fellow students'
recordings of their individual findings. Each participating student
had received a copy.

Meg's offering - like the rest, each just under five minutes'
running time - stood out from most of the other fifth graders' efforts,
he thought. Not just because of the lush and varied places around
Moorea where she had recorded video interviews on the Tahitian
term, *"Aita pea pea."* It was also because of the generous spirit and
especially the smiling - and occasionally laughing - answers from her
diverse selection of heavily accented interviewees. The audience at
her school especially loved JP - their driver and guide Jean-Paul from
the Websters' round-the-island tour and ferry drop-off trips – and
his various and clever responses to Meg's prompts in either English
or unintentionally mangled Tahitian. In one, he rippled the tattoos
on his arm while he spoke, drawing huge laughs from the crowd.

Cal's presentation on the *Heiva a Tahiti* festival was also a hit as
part of his class's *"Holiday Celebrations Around the Globe"* project.
Like Meg's, her younger brother's report was shared with parents at
the final family event of the year at Armour Elementary School, which
took place two days prior to the students' dismissals for the
Christmas and winter holidays.

Cal's report to his teacher and fellow fourth graders wasn't
required to include any audiovisual elements. But they clapped

loudly after watching the video montage of his informative interviews on their festival experiences with Julian and Mrs. Martinez. Cal's presentation – the most admired in his class for sure - also included event photos and a few video clips from the *Tama'ara'a' a* dinner/dance the family attended at the invitation of their new Tahitian/Mexican/American friends.

It helped that Cal's video contained a link to parts of an excellent **YouTube** recording from a recent *Heiva* festival, courtesy of Mrs. Martinez's aunt Valerie "Vai" Teamoutu, from the restaurant where they made the discovery of the possible connection between her ancestors and the ring hidden in the false bottom of the centuries-old box they'd found. The museum and family were actively researching the ring's relationship to the women in the paintings they'd seen - seeking answers to a long-unsolved mystery dating back to the time of the *HMS Bounty*'s visit.

As for Keely, her Madison Middle School French teacher and her eighth-grade classmates were thrilled with her ten-page special report – plus additional pictures and video - on the challenges of protecting the culture and environment - as well as the many natural wonders and historic structures - of French Polynesia.

Along with that photo and video montage of some of Moorea's most beautiful scenes and sites, Keely's presentation highlighted several of the most pressing issues facing the local economy and the residents of Moorea as well as its neighboring Society Islands. It noted the relatively high cost of living in a remote South Seas nation with only a few material resources to call its own.

Her report also explored some of the difficult choices posed by the ongoing modernization of Moorea, including efforts to improve its infrastructure - like roads, buildings, housing, and tourism resources. It emphasized how preserving historical and cultural assets like the ancient marae temples, local agriculture, Tahitian language, traditional dancing, singing, worship, and pareo-making - among other endeavors - wasn't easy to do in the modern world.

To wrap up her presentation, Keely shared a bonus appendix - a list of all the delectable dishes - with a few choice photos included - that the Websters had tasted, many with French or Tahitian names. She explained how the Websters' "*French Polynesian Food Review*" was a 'side project' she and her siblings had undertaken, and how it had all started on that first rainy day on Moorea - the "island of the yellow lizard."

(As a side note, some of Keely's presentation was included in a story Jess wrote for the University of the Cascades *Ascent* newspaper on concerns about the coral reef conditions in French Polynesian islands. Jess and her editor even gave the eighth-grader credit as a "Contributing Editor" for her part in producing the published article!)

Keely's teacher, Mr. Borgan, was so impressed with the quality of her work that he shared it with the school principal and other teachers at Madison. Not only did nearly everyone say that they wanted to travel to Moorea themselves one day, they also became aware through the information and photos Keely shared of the increased impacts of human activity on the island's native plants and animals. Her presentation explained about coral reef damage brought on by sunscreen chemicals and other toxic substances (like fuel, pesticides, fertilizers, and sewage) leaching into the water, and the danger to sea life of being struck by inattentive boats or snorkelers. Keely gave particular mention to unique threats from specific predators - like the deadly *Crown of Thorns* starfish they had seen and photographed on their initial tour around the island.

Finally, Keely outlined some of the other most harmful practices undertaken by tourists. She included the cautions from Julian about feeding the sting rays during the daytime, and disturbing the migrating humpback whales by getting too close to them with jet skis and other motorized craft.

The oldest Webster sibling had ended her presentation with recommendations for everyone to be more careful and considerate of local resources, culture, and customs when traveling. She urged her audience to be ambassadors of their own countries who would gladly be invited back by their hosts. And most important, she said, when visiting other places, make sure to meet and talk to local people, try the language – no matter how difficult, and taste the local food, wherever they went. Keely said doing so created "the best (and most delicious!) memories of all" from the Websters' visit to Moorea.

Back in the present, as Alex turned off the TV, he glanced into the kitchen where Keely and Meg were busy cooking the Christmas dinner. They were "on their own" along with their brother for this meal. Alex decided to let them get creative with the preparations, and stayed out of the way. Meanwhile, Jess had left a few days prior to travel home to New Zealand to visit her parents for the long post-semester holiday period.

It's a pretty big mess in there, Alex thought, but he wasn't really worried about it. The two sisters had just finished up their chicken and vegetable chow mein preparations - simmering in separate bowls on the stove - and were now toasting the French rolls in the oven and gathering the lettuce and condiments from the fridge to add to each "*Strange and Marvelous Chinese and Moorean Sandwich*" aka "SAMCAM Sandwich" (A name and initials the three Webster siblings had come up with together.) They all agreed with Alex that it perfectly described the surprisingly delicious concoction they were hoping to duplicate from their post-Thanksgiving week trip to the French Polynesian island.

Cal, sitting next to Alex in the living room and enjoying a new video game, looked up to follow his dad's gaze. He would soon have his part to play in the festivities, by carefully loading up each person's SAMCAM rolls with the delectable mixture and serving them on special plates. It was sure to be one of the family's most unique holiday meals ever!

Indeed, all was well in the world for this day...and Alex was glad to be resting at home with the family – away from the office and work concerns - for the rest of the calendar year. So much had happened since that fateful last afternoon in Papeete...

The Websters had slept through most of their long flight back from Tahiti's Faa'a airport. Keely and Meg said later that they barely remembered arriving in Los Angeles, super early on that Sunday after their discoveries at the restaurant and museum in Papeete the day prior, though the trip through U.S. Customs and Immigration there hadn't taken too long, surprisingly, Jess and Alex agreed at the time.

After they'd eaten a small breakfast meal at LAX, their next flight home to SeaTac airport was so much quicker, and also uneventful. That was a good thing - because despite catching a few more 'zzzs' on the plane they were all exhausted, especially Cal. He had fallen right back asleep when they finally loaded their bags from the airport parking shuttle into their car and Alex drove the 35 minutes home to Tacoma. The kids' grandparents were waiting there to warmly greet the groggy Websters and Jess upon their return that afternoon, which was *more than three weeks ago now,* recalled Alex. He was amazed at how quickly time had passed since they'd departed the tropics.

And what about that *other* exciting news connected to their *Moorea Mystery*?

While he was working in Seattle at the end of the week following their return, wrapping up details on the Montcalm project and finishing reviews of other software implementations and sales activities before LodgeSoft's year-end, Alex had received an email from Rai (Temarai) Martinez. It contained a short message, including links to an exciting (and very gratifying) news story - all of which he'd shared, to huge cheers, with the kids and Jess when he got home later that evening. What he hadn't anticipated was the surprise package that arrived at their door in Tacoma the very next day, all the way from Tahiti.

Inside the huge, thin box, they were thrilled to find a full-sized print of the painting they had seen at the restaurant. Enclosed with the nicely mounted and protected artwork was a photo of Rai in a beautiful pareo, with the actual ring they had found in the box slipped onto her third finger. In the picture, apparently taken at the museum before their friends had left Tahiti to return to Colorado, Rai stood next to her Aunt Valerie (Vahinetua/Vai) Teamoutu, with Tiare(nui) on one side and Lincoln on the other. The Websters and Jess guessed that Rai's husband Vic had been the one to take the photo.

All wore big smiles as they stood in front of the original painting of their ancestor, the woman who'd originally been depicted with the "*FC*"-inscribed ring on her own finger, early in the 1800's. Enclosed in an envelope within the box sent from French Polynesia by express delivery was a special clipping from a local Papeete newspaper. Next to its headline in French, Rai had taped a simple strip of paper to translate it: "*Resort plans scrapped, Moorea locals win fight to keep marae from desecration.*"

In a separate letter that arrived from Denver just before Christmas, Rai explained that she and most of her family members had ended up voting almost unanimously, only a few days after the

Websters left for home, to veto her cousin Tanetoa's and his cronies' radical construction plans for a drastically enlarged new Moorea Rai resort. They had decided after all of the excitement surrounding the box the kids had found - with the ancient ring secretly hidden inside and given its subsequent link to their ancestors in the paintings - to partner together to sensibly renovate their family's resort, while protecting the marae from development or destruction forever.

Rai went on to share some further news. After speaking with the local authorities on Moorea and in Tahiti, her family's designated construction management committee had agreed to take a very environmentally sustainable approach to their resort's modernization, with plans to use three of Moorea's natural assets to help with this. They would incorporate solar panels into the resort's design to produce a significant portion of its electricity, and they'd also be installing several large rain catchment tanks to aid in irrigation for the surrounding shrubs, trees and flowers. They even had plans to fill the swimming pool through a special filter using salt water as part of a more natural disinfectant process. Alex had explained to the kids that such measures were part of a growing movement in the construction field called '*green-building*' design.

The final big news their Tahitian-American friend shared surrounded her own family. Though Vic, Rai, Tiare, and Linc had returned to their home, school, and work lives in Denver after the momentous family vote, they were now actively planning to move to Moorea - at least for a few years, once the school term was over the following June.

Given his extensive real estate background, Vic had been selected to run the family's soon-to-be-renovated resort as General Manager, assisted by Rai. They were also excited to set up a mentoring relationship with David Thomson, General Manager of the Montcalm. He and his team had pledged to help with the Moorea Rai's renovation project and the transition and reopening of the resort to guests once it was complete.

Rai explained that not just her family on Moorea, but the entire local community had been extremely supportive when they heard of the resort's planned rebirth.

Finally, in *extra* happy news for Alex's firm, Rai noted that one part of the Moorea Rai remodeling project would involve modernization of the guest services infrastructure. Thus, they had expressed strong interest - with David Thomson's advice and endorsement - in purchasing and implementing LodgeSoft's hotel management software to improve their operations and service standards.

After Rai had closed her letter with warm wishes for the holiday season and once again thanked the Websters and Jess for all they had done to help her family preserve their land and culture during their Moorea visit, she added a postscript to Alex: "Let's set up a time to talk about your trip back here to handle our software implementation - soon!"

Alex and the kids had shared a chuckle when he read the last part of the letter aloud to them. That's because Jess, blushing crimson at the side of the table when they'd opened it, already had scheduled her own return trip to the island in a few months (to visit a few more special sites they'd missed on their first trip - and, she admitted - a *special friend* there too) during her final spring break from grad school. So, Alex likely wouldn't be the first member of the extended Webster family to venture back from the Pacific Northwest to their new favorite Polynesian paradise!

Now, on a chilly December afternoon, with light declining as one of the shortest days of the year headed towards evening, Alex walked around the family's brightly lit Christmas tree, bedecked with about 50 ornaments of various shapes, sizes and colors. He laughed to himself at all the remnants of wrapping paper and boxes scattered around its perimeter in the living room. Most held already-opened presents for the kids and himself. It had been an especially fun and creative Christmas morning, and soon his parents would stop by for the family's unique holiday meal, with even more gifts still to be exchanged. Then the kids would go to their mom's house tomorrow to spend the second week of the two they had for vacation from school until just after New Year's Day.

The aromas wafting from the kitchen right now were even more enticing than he had hoped, Alex thought. He felt extremely fortunate, grateful for all he and the Websters enjoyed in their lives. *It wasn't about the presents at all*, he thought, but it *was* all about the adventures they'd shared on their trip to the South Pacific, and the things they'd learned, the foods they'd enjoyed, the friends they'd made. And, of course, the incredible mystery that the kids just may have helped solve - *and to think it all started when one of Cal's buddies decided to use a 'local remedy' to disinfect his sea urchin sting!*

Speaking of Cal, the almost-ten-year-old put down his video game controller and surveyed the living room. Viewing the 'carnage' of opened gifts below their eight-foot blue-green Fraser Fir, he declared, "Well, it looks like there aren't any more presents to open. Let's eat!"

"Hold on, cowboy! We gotta wait for your grandparents. And before they arrive, there's one more present under that tree...take a look again," answered his father.

As their brother began to search around the base of the tree, Keely and Meg, having heard their dad's challenge, dropped their attention from preparing the sandwich elements, and loped quickly from the kitchen into the room.

Meg saw her sister look to one side of the tree, then extended her arm and fingers as far as she - though shorter than Keely - could reach to grab an envelope nestled securely in its upper branches.

Motioning to Keely and Cal to join her, and with their dad looking on from the couch, Meg opened the envelope. Inside, there was a single, small slip. It was cut out of a roughly folded piece of wrapping paper. She pulled it out, unfolded it, and together, they read its very messily scribbled message (their dad had TERRIBLE penmanship!) aloud:

"*Riddle: What's the best time of year to pass through the Sun Gate?*"

Just as they had finished reading the puzzling question, they looked and exclaimed in unison to their father.

"Daaaaaad!!!"

Alex grinned broadly, and responded, with his hands up in mock surrender: "We're all going to find out, because this summer we'll be doing it together."

Their curiosity now *fully* engaged; the three Webster kids ran straight to the computer on the table in the corner of the room. Keely sat down and quickly typed a few words into its search engine. When she saw the text and pictures come up on the screen in response, all she could say was "Oh my gosh!" She gazed in amazement at her siblings.

"Wow!" added Meg.

Cal didn't quite understand, yet. "Where?" he asked, leaning forward to see the computer screen's images and text more clearly.

His sisters giggled, because they had already found the answer, or at least a clue...about their upcoming destination, once school was finished in June.

The Worldwide Websters would be on their way together, to another exciting adventure, in another really cool and historic place - and soon!

Acknowledgments

You can't write about a place like Moorea that makes you want to visit - to live, laugh, love, and engage with its people, language, culture, and history - without people who inspire you to do so. Especially when it takes decades for an initial idea - to recreate the excitement and wonder, marvel and mystery of treasured family adventure stories - to finally result in a finished novel.

To my wonderful and unceasingly encouraging wife, Sharon Hamilton, and all our children, relatives, friends, and colleagues, thanks for your constant encouragement, honesty, and for putting up with what may have been one of the longest writing and editing projects in human history. (Ok, that's a bit of an exaggeration, but...)

You can't write a book about family dynamics, especially if they're somewhat non-traditional like the *WW Websters*, without input and insights from your own family. For those loved ones who accompanied me on our first trek to Moorea and French Polynesia, what a fun, magical, somewhat sad, certainly thought-provoking, and life-instructive trip that was, all at the same time. Glad you could join me again as we embark on this new journey there together, even if a few years down the road.

Some of you were inspirations for my Worldwide Websters characters, having lived many of their adventures or others described in the book along with me. Whether real memories or "combos" between truth and fiction captured in my imagination, you're the best. You represent the collective compass I always keep in my heart - to guide me to aim high, keep it real, and keep going to get it right.

On a technical level, I'm grateful to my daughters, Lindsay and Molly Hamilton, who were instrumental in developmental editing, design, and providing sensible recommendations for the story's structure, characters, content, and continuity. They and Sharon also provided honest and fair feedback and coherent suggestions through many additional rounds of editing. Lindsay also proved through her copy-editing expertise why it is so important, despite or especially because of the rise of artificial intelligence in our educational system, to get that sensibility - not to mention sentences, paragraphs, and punctuation - right, every time, for human readers.

Finally, I was so fortunate, also, to enlist the skills and insights of my multi-talented niece Cecelia Morriss, who designed the book's evocative cover and illustrations, and provided some sage stylistic advice along the way. Then Molly added the final technical touches to bring all the elements into line at publishing time!

Though I'll try my best at my website (thanks again, Molly!), I'll never be able to properly credit all of the individuals - authors, writing instructors, bloggers, experts on historical and language matters, online cataloguers, and cartographers who provided information, insights, and in so many cases, critically valuable details to help me create this story. When one sets a tale in a multicultural, multilingual place that has changed much since undertaking initial, primary research - and then has evolved even more since the time period of the story's setting - it's not at all easy to be accurate. This book is certainly not correct about everything, though I gave it everything I had to make sure I checked and double-checked even the smallest facts along the way. Thus, any errors of any kind – even within the timeline of the story's particular era - are my responsibility alone.

I welcome your thoughts, ideas, and reflections!

M. Scott Hamilton
www.theworldwidewebsters.com

About the author

M. Scott Hamilton conceived The Worldwide Websters series to relive the family adventure stories of his youth. These tales combine his loves for immersive travel, language, and creative writing to share the excitement, connection, and joy of discovery with his readers.

A single parent for most of his kids' lives, Scott visualized writing this series for more than two decades. He has made it a priority – since each of his own three children were very young – to try to consistently introduce them and himself to new places, people, and ideas.

Thankful for a career that provided opportunities to travel, he's occasionally been able to combine business and personal trips into family adventures. In every domestic or overseas itinerary, family members have sought and experienced firsthand a bit more than the average tourist about local history, culture, cuisine, and community - always actively exploring beyond the obvious attractions.

A former competitive swimmer, water polo player, and college newspaper editor, Scott has volunteered at his children's schools and in higher education, community development, global sustainability, and sensible business initiatives while living in Washington State, New York, and Connecticut. He was a contributor and editor for 2022's **The Carbon Almanac**, part of a worldwide, virtual, all-volunteer team that produced the book under Seth Godin's guidance.

Scott and his wife Sharon can often be found exploring a new spot on the map, enjoying live music, hanging out and sharing stories and discoveries with friends and family, and/or biking, swimming, hiking, or camping along the way. They live in the beautiful Pacific Northwest – never far away from their next exciting adventure!

THEWORLDWIDEWEBSTERS.COM